BEYOND THE RIFT

MICHAEL CICCARELLI-WALSH

Beyond the Rift

Book Three in The Zoboros Series

Cover designed by Momir Borocki

Table of Contents

For Chris, Troy, Zach, and Alexander,

the knights of the round writing table.

Prologue

The shuttle sliced through the atmosphere. Nothing shook as it ascended – not the handful of passengers, not the aquarium along the wall, not even the champagne flutes stacked behind the bar. It was by far the smoothest launch Yui had ever experienced.

And also the most dangerous.

Two Lusitani trailed her like twin shadows as she approached the window. She felt their eyes beneath their skull-shaped masks, intent on her every move. *Like I have anywhere else to go.* The sea of red sand dunes shrank in the viewport, and soon the whole planet shrank from view too, replaced by an endless cosmos. Never in a million cycles did she think she'd miss that awful desert. Yet here she was, wishing to go back.

A Lusitani flexed its wrist. Prickles ran up Yui's arms as she eyed the device wrapped around that wrist. To the uninitiated, it was just a thick metal bracelet, easily mistaken for a large communicator. But Yui had seen what those devices could do to her people, and she knew this one had been programmed specifically for her.

If only I could give them an excuse to use it. Lights twinkled on the dampener that cocooned her hands. It was no larger than a bowling ball, yet it held all the power in the galaxy. At least, all *her* power. She felt weak, weaker than when she'd been stranded and starved in the desert. It was a different kind of weakness, though. An emptiness. A reminder of what she'd given up in exchange for this ride off Mogaddu.

But she'd get her freedom back, no matter the price.

The Morabani sauntered over and stared out the viewport. They made quite the pair: her a petite Nurrano with argyle skin of blue-black, him a lanky Morabani whose coal-black scales were cracked with blue scars. In all their time stranded together, she'd never asked how he'd gotten them, nor had he asked much about her past. One tried not to get close, in this line of work.

"We're almost there," he said, his crooked smile flaunting a line of sharp teeth.

Close to what? They'd just left the atmosphere. The only thing out here was the blackness of—

Yui took a step back. It wasn't space she'd been staring at, but an object. A *ship*. Black as night, it became a blot across the stars – one that grew as they approached. She could just make out the spikes that jutted from its hull, ready to savage any vessel in its path. She knew only one species that built ships like that.

The shuttle trembled. Tractor beam. The force of the catch sent Yui stumbling forward, and Kazan blocked her with his own dampener before she struck glass.

"I didn't know he was working with Poterians," she said,

adjusting herself as if nothing had happened.

Kazan said nothing.

The cosmos disappeared as the Poterian ship swallowed theirs, leaving Yui in darkness to match her own thoughts. *What does he still want with us? And who else does he have working for him?*

A blast shield opened within the Poterian ship. Light burst out, enough to blind Yui as their shuttle glided inside. She blinked away the spots, and in their place she found hundreds of ships lined across a wide hangar floor. Small fighters, troop transports, frigates, all various sizes and equally various stages of completion. Workers scurried between the wiry frames of future ships. They looked like ants from up here, but as their shuttle lowered toward them, Yui realized something.

There are no Poterians here.

Kazan noticed her widening eyes and smiled. "Danadas has been busy," he said.

"Or he's about to be." They may have failed in their quest to acquire Project Vortex for the old Orlov, but that didn't seem to have stalled his plans for…whatever it was he intended to conquer.

Yui shuddered. It was no secret that Danadas had a prejudice against non-Humans. She drew herself up to her full height. It wasn't much, even by Nurrano standards, but everyone knew that what a Nurrano lacked in size they more than made up for in strength—powers or not. In her reflection, she practiced her cold, piercing stare; the one she'd used to shatter many an opponent in the fight rings. It was still on point.

A third Lusitani joined them at the viewport. This one had a red bandana, a style choice that puzzled Yui. Why would a warrior trained to fight in the shadows wear the loudest possible accessory? Was it inviting a head-on fight? The scimitar sheathed at its side certainly suggested so.

The Lusitani ushered them to the exit. Not aggressively, that was not their nature. They were a subtle bunch, which made each of their movements more significant, more threatening, so that even the slightest tilt of the head carried life and death with it. It was a power she had once thought only Taranis could wield.

But Taranis is gone. He'd still been battling Carmichael's team when she abandoned the *Dormarch*, but at that point it was a hopeless effort. Their side had lost, and to stay aboard would have meant becoming a prisoner of the IDF. Or worse. She had watched from her escape pod as the *Dormarch* crumbled from the inside, pulling thousands of lives with it into oblivion. Only one power could have caused that – the power they had sought. The power she wanted nothing to do with anymore.

But Danadas did.

She almost jumped out of her skin as the ship touched down. Kazan shot her a quick look but said nothing; he just smiled in his twisted sort of way.

The liftgate opened and the Lusitani led them into the fray of bustling workers. Despite the chaos, no one dared to step in their path. Yui did catch a few uneasy glances cast their way – nothing she wasn't used to as a Zoboros – but whether they were directed at her or the Lusitani escort was unclear.

A small crowd of workers waited for an elevator at the back of the hangar, but when Yui's little posse arrived, it dispersed.

A familiar uneasiness came over Yui, the same feeling she'd gotten when Taranis had recruited her into this world of secrets.

The Lusitani with the red bandana stepped up to a panel beside the elevator, removed its glove, and placed its bare hand on the scanner. *At least I know it's a Human*, she thought. How much humanity remained beneath the skull mask, however, remained to be seen.

They rode the elevator in silence. When the doors parted, the bridge of the great Poterian ship opened before them, its high ceilings wrapped over a massive viewport where stars twinkled by the thousands. Dozens of control monitors flashed around the room, yet no one was there to operate them except the man in the command chair.

"Thank goodness you're both safe," said Danadas, rising with the aid of his cane. It was an ornate creation of expert woodwork, but Yui's eyes darted to the jewel which crowned it. Larger than its owner's wrinkled fist...large enough to set her up for the rest of her life. *And then I'll never have to suck up to this bag of bones again.*

"All thanks to your timely rescue," she lied, bowing her head. It was as easy as breathing.

"Timely indeed..." trailed Danadas as he hobbled toward them, the tap of his cane echoing through the wide chamber. The effort seemed to absorb his concentration, but Yui knew not to be fooled. The old man was far stronger than he let on. And far more dangerous.

"You got an offer for us or what?" asked Kazan.

Yui winced. The Morabani was used to rich people giving into his demands because, well, he made them lots of money in the fight rings. But Danadas was a different breed. Money was merely a tool for him to build greater things. A tool that could be easily replaced.

Just like they could be.

But the old man simply flashed his enchanting smile. "Revenge," he said. That got a smile out of Kazan, though his was far less enchanting, while Yui paled. There was only one group that they could possibly want revenge on. And if Carmichael's team survived the *Dormarch*, that meant the woman who destroyed it survived too.

Danadas cast his sharp gaze upon her, his crows' feet riddled with a sinister wisdom. "Your concerns regarding Project Vortex are warranted," he said. "But I ask you: how long before that power falls into the wrong hands? How long before its destructive force finds whichever planet you next take refuge on?"

Who's to say your hands are the right ones? Yui wanted to ask, but instead she said, "We failed to bring it to you once. Why ask us to do it again?"

"Because rumor has it there is someone else trapped with Carmichael's team." His gaze shifted toward Kazan. "Someone you'd be eager to find."

Kazan's slow mind got to the answer well after Yui did, but he was the one to blurt it out. "Taranis?!"

Danadas nodded, and Kazan beamed. Somehow, the Morabani looked even more terrifying when he was happy.

"A change is upon us," Danadas continued, pacing the floor in front of them while his cane tapped along. "Plans are in motion which require him once more."

"What plans?" asked Yui.

Danadas turned toward the viewport, toward the vast sea of stars at his fingertips. "Plans much older than I. Suffice it to say the galaxy will look much different when this is over. And you'll want to be on the right side when that happens."

Kazan stepped forward. "Well I know where to place my bets."

Yui, however, was not so easily swayed, especially about things older and more sinister than Danadas. "Carmichael has a sizable team, and there are only two of us."

"Three," came a familiar voice. Yui tensed. Mila appeared out of thin air beside them, looking arrogant as ever with her black nails drumming along her folded arms. "Did you miss me?"

Yui ignored Danadas's precious granddaughter. "That still leaves us heavily outnumbered."

"I would not be so sure," replied Danadas. "They are up against the entire known galaxy. The IDF, the Taipa Kanani gang, the surviving members of my family: *everyone* is hunting Carmichael and his band of Zoboros, and my media channels have ensured there's not a rock they can crawl under where they won't be recognized." He stopped beside her, his breath upon her neck. "You'll find you have more allies than you think."

Yui moved away from him, shuddering. "It's not my fight. It never was."

"Really? Then was it fear which kept you alive in the desert?" Yui felt those all-seeing eyes fall upon her. "Why go months in the scorching desert with nothing but your ice powers to keep you hanging on by a thread? What kept you going through starvation? Through isolation? Was it merely a desire to live? Or was it a desire for something more?"

Yui knew the answer. It *was* revenge, but not against Carmichael's team. It was against everyone who'd ever used her. Who'd ever used people like her for their profit and entertainment. Her eyes fell once again on the jewel atop the old man's cane. A jewel she knew had been bought with blood.

"What happens once we find them?" she asked.

Danadas smiled, and it chilled Yui to the bone.

Chapter 1

Get in and Get Out

Kano surveyed the street. Still quiet. Just the same few vagrants huddled around a smoldering firepit. He hoped they got it burning soon; the temperature plummeted once the twin suns fell behind the shanty buildings. But for now, the city still felt plenty hot and balmy. That, or he was just nervous.

Where the hell is Makoto?

Shouts echoed from beneath Kano's perch. He hiked up his binoculars, but it was just the vagrants chasing off another rat before it stole what little food they had. That got under his skin. All the power in the galaxy, but he couldn't even protect these people from the rats. He'd seen poverty in every city they'd visited these past few months, but never had it been more pronounced than here on Darraden, where the homeless pitched tents along the canals and cast makeshift lines into the polluted waters. Kano shuddered thinking of what diseases might come with their fish.

A chill wind caught him from behind, cutting through the thin nylon of his flight suit. *Here comes the cold.* The twin suns cast twisted shadows over the street, and still the firepit below showed few signs of life. He wanted to bring down some of his team's extra coats to replace the scraps on the vagrants' backs, but he knew he couldn't risk giving away his position.

Focus. He scanned again, but still nothing. There was hardly even a sound except for the gentle thrum of his speeder as it idled beside him. Kano drummed his fingers on the binoculars. The mission was supposed to be simple: get in and get out. But the "get out" part should have happened half an hour ago. He scanned the building Makoto had entered for the hundredth time, but the windows were still shuttered, the doors still closed, and the smog around it so thick that the binoculars were rendered almost useless anyway.

Another chill wind, this one wafting up the stench of rotten seafood. Kano grabbed a scarf from his speeder and wrapped it around his nose and mouth, savoring the lemon scent that Cera had so astutely infused into it. *Famora never smelled like this*, he thought. In all fairness, though, Famora didn't have a harbor. That city floated hundreds of feet in the air. A city like no other. That's what the Famorans always said, and the more cities Kano saw, the more he agreed with them. There had been poverty – his adopted family had certainly not lived in the best of places – but it was paradise compared to the streets of Darraden, even after Taranis bombed it all to hell.

Now Famora floated just across the way. In fact, it would soon be visible in the night sky if not for all the smog. Kano wondered how things were going back there: the reconstruction, Nobara and her tavern, and Yuchi.

Guilt stabbed at him. Yuchi, the woman who had raised him and Makoto, had never even gotten a goodbye before he left. Carmichael had whisked him off Famora too quickly for that.

She deserved so much more. And how did he repay her? By sending her only biological son into a gangster's den, alone.

He was the best choice, Kano reminded himself. Makoto was the fastest runner. The best escape artist. And he wasn't as recognizable as most others on the team. *Because he doesn't have any powers to defend himself.* Kano shook the thought away. Danadas clearly didn't see Makoto as enough of a threat to plaster his face everywhere, but Kano knew better. He knew his brother just needed a chance to prove himself.

And this was it.

A security bot floated down the street. Kano ducked as its single red eye turned toward the rooftop. *Can't provide a homeless shelter, but the IDF can still invest in security bots.* The bots weren't even for the people's protection – Darraden remained a cesspool of gangs and fugitives. The Interplanetary Defense Force had dropped these bots solely to find the evil Zoboros who had destroyed their prized flagship. Typical. Kano couldn't believe he'd once thought of them as the good guys. My, how his opinions had changed. *A lot has changed these last few months*, he thought, scratching his beard.

"Any sign of him?" asked Li through his earpiece.

He jumped. He hadn't expected her soft voice in his ear; usually Jaden made the check-ins. *That means she's worried.*

"Negative," he said, raising his communicator to his mouth. He held it there, feeling like he should say more. The two of them hardly talked anymore. He just didn't know where to start.

The silence dragged out painfully until Li finally said, "Ok."

"Wait—" Kano heard the click of her communicator switching off and knew he'd once again missed his chance.

Stupid, stupid. He leaned against the railing, as if the effort would somehow summon his brother faster. As if it would somehow rid him of the guilt. *They all did this for me.* Makoto, Li, Jaden…even the mysterious Akio had joined this team to protect him. And now they were fugitives.

He switched to the main channel on his communicator. "No sign of the runner, captain. Permission to send in backup?"

"Ready to infiltrate," added Junior over the comms, ever eager for action.

"Let's wait until we know what we're dealing with," came Carmichael's charismatic voice. Even when he was saying no, the captain still managed to make it sound charming. *At least for most of us*, thought Kano as Junior's comms clicked off. He knew the former cadet was fuming from his position behind the adjacent building. Junior had always been hot-headed, but his temper had grown steadily worse since their mission on the *Dormarch*. Especially toward Carmichael. The others had learned to leave him alone or else risk his wrath. Most of them were confused by the mood change; Junior should've been happy to be reunited with his long-lost mother, but Kano knew the truth behind it. He could still hear Carmichael's infamous words echoing through his communicator.

"You and Akio have a new objective: terminate the asset." And Kano could have done it. He could have terminated Project Vortex. He could have killed Junior's mother. But he had chosen to spare her while keeping her out of Taranis's hands, just as the captain had intended. His mistake, however, had been thinking that his actions would have been the end of it. It didn't take long for Junior to figure out that Carmichael had given the kill order, and though Kano had denied it, it only

served to raise Junior's suspicions. *And his hostility.*

"Activity!" T8's tin-can voice shouted through the comms. Kano hiked up his binoculars. The building looked unchanged. But the bot often saw things that he couldn't.

The front door burst open. A one-armed Tenu raced through, its red face checking over its shoulder, its gloved hands shoving vagrants out of the way.

"Clemens is on the move!" Kano announced into his communicator.

"Backup team moving to intercept," said Junior, a touch of '*I told you so*' in his voice.

Makoto burst out the same door a few moments after Clemens, his red and black argyle face a blur as he sprinted in pursuit.

"Catch him, Makoto," said Kano to himself as he hopped on his speeder, watching as the security bot followed his brother. "And catch him fast."

Fire flickered in his palm as the Tenu approached his position.

"This is for all the Zoboros you enslaved." Junior leaped from the fire escape and plummeted toward the asphalt. Wind howled in his ears but did nothing to raise his blood pressure. Jets of flame erupted from his hands and struck the ground, slowing his momentum. Better yet, the blast sent Clemens stumbling into a heap of trash bags on the curb.

"Right where you belong," said Junior as he touched down, though he felt prison bars would be more appropriate.

But that wasn't their mission today.

He sparked a small flame in his palm as he approached. Clemens stared at the flame, sharing in the knowledge that it could become an inferno at any moment—an inferno that Junior was fighting hard to suppress. And how could he help it? Just staring at the snake tattoo running down Clemens's face infuriated him. It represented a gang that enslaved Zoboros, a gang that made him fight Kazan almost to the death and left him with a scar burnt into his back that ached to this day.

"You know what we want, Clemens. Don't make this difficult for yourself."

"*Difficult?*" spat Clemens, wiping the trash off his silk suit. "You don't know the meanin' of the word, Hendricks Junior. You're the son of a war hero. Grew up in a mansion, and with powers to boot! You neva knew what life was like for the rest of us." He motioned toward the garbage at his feet.

The flame grew brighter in Junior's hand. "Don't talk to me about an easy life. Not after what you did."

"What *I* did?" Clemens gawked. "You was fixin' bikes for a conman when I found ya. I made you a legend! And what did you do? You went and ruined everything for both of us."

"You deserve much worse than that," said Junior, stepping forward, flames engulfing his arms, tickling at the flame-resistant material of his combat suit.

Clemens laughed. "What do you have to threaten me with, Hellfire? I got nothin'! You wanna burn me? Go ahead. It'll be better than waiting for the IDF to drag us away."

"Wanna bet?" Junior grabbed him by the suit jacket with flaming hands. He expected the fabric to catch, but it didn't.

"What material is this?"

Clemens looked away. "Polyester."

"How the mighty have fallen."

"Junior!" Makoto arrived, hardly needing to catch his breath despite sprinting over. "Let's just calm down for a second. You can put the Tenu down."

Here he goes, acting like I need to be kept on a leash. Something Makoto picked up from his brother.

"I'd listen to the kid, Hellfire," said Clemens with a sly smile. "Wouldn't want you to get hurt."

"Don't threaten me," said Junior, his flaming hands eating into the suit. "You've been excommunicated by the Taipa. You have no backup. No protection. Nothing."

"Be careful, Junior. He—"

"You can talk when you quit screwing up your missions!" barked Junior. His gaze shifted to Makoto, watching as his words cut like a knife, but his eyes should have been on Clemens. Or at least on his fingers, which had melted clean through the cloth. The gangster slipped from his grip and ran, the tatters of his suit jacket flapping in the breeze. Junior readied a fireball when T8 shouted into his earpiece.

"Incoming!"

Junior saw them before Makoto did: a swarm of bots descending toward them, hoverpads buzzing. "Look out!" he cried, but he was too late. The bots snatched Makoto in their wiry arms.

"Hey! Let me go!"

By the time Junior had a fireball ready, the bots had already hoisted Makoto too high in the air. Even if Junior hit his target without burning Makoto, the fall would break the Nurrano's skinny legs. Not that Makoto seemed concerned about that. He flailed and fought in the air, desperate to prove he could handle himself. And he would have to. Their target was already halfway down the street, where security bots were lowering a speeder for him.

"The bots are working for Clemens!" Junior called into his communicator. "And someone needs to get Makoto down!"

"On it," replied Kano over the comms, revving his speeder.

"Negative, Kano. I need your speeder to catch Clemens." Already the gangster was launching down the street, the distance between them growing ever wider.

"He's my brother!" Kano fired back, wind muffling his voice as he accelerated.

"Clemens is getting away!"

"Cera and Akio will handle Makoto," came Carmichael's voice, calm but firm. "Kano and Junior, focus on the target."

There was a pause on the line. "Yes sir," came Kano's voice.

Junior heard the hum of its approach. He reached out and snagged onto the speeder as it passed, then vaulted onto the seat behind an unhappy Kano. Clemens was ahead, banking around a corner at a steeper angle than Kano could manage.

"You'll never catch him driving like that," said Junior, reaching over with his big arm and leaning the handlebar tighter into the turn.

"I've got it!" said Kano, but the cautious way he leaned into the next turn didn't do much to reinforce the point.

"Scoot over, Grandma." Junior grabbed Kano by his combat nylons and slid him back across the seat. Kano protested the whole way while Junior climbed over him, but Junior could tell the effort was half-hearted. They both knew who the better driver was. And even if Kano disagreed, there wasn't much he could do against Junior's superior size, short of using his powers.

Junior jammed the throttle while working the gear shift, the resulting burst of speed forcing his now passenger to cling onto him for dear life.

Clemens's speeder came back into view on the next turn, the distance closing fast. The Tenu's red face glanced back at them and sneered before giving his speeder another burst of speed. Junior smiled. The chase was on.

He placed his thumb over a big button at the edge of the handlebar.

"Please don't," said Kano, grip tightening against Junior's back. Junior pretended not to hear him over the roar of the wind. He wasn't going to miss his chance to use this, the crown jewel of upgrades that Sterling had made to the speeder.

"Junior, I'm warning you!"

Click.

Blue flame ignited in the thrusters. Junior felt the air forced from his lungs as the acceleration smacked him like an invisible wall. Wind whipped at his face, water leaked from his eyes, and all the while Kano's grip dug into his skin.

"You're...coming...in...too...hot!" huffed Kano.

That means it's working. The distance was closing. Just an arm's length away—

A bot slammed into the side of their speeder. The concrete walls along the narrow street came up fast; Junior swerved the opposite direction, then swung back to avoid the buildings on the other side. Back and forth he went, zigzagging so their momentum didn't pulverize them.

"I told you!" shouted Kano.

"Shut up and give us some cover!" More bots swarmed in behind them. Junior heard the crack of Kano's shockwaves while he focused on Clemens, the distance growing as the extra boost from the thrusters fizzled. He needed a different strategy. He needed to cut Clemens off somewhere, but where was the gangster going?

Clemens jammed on the brakes, causing them to sweep past him, then he veered down a side street. Junior jammed on the forward thrusters, the force slamming him against the handlebars as they decelerated. Kano sandwiched in behind him, depriving Junior of any oxygen until they finally came to a stop.

"Jaden…" Junior gasped into his communicator. "Jaden…where's he headed?"

"Looks like he's got a shuttle on the Southside," replied Jaden through the comms. A holographic map of the city appeared between the handlebars — another addition of Sterling's — and two red dots appeared, a stationary one on the complete opposite side of the city, the other zigzagging wildly toward it through the streets.

"We'll never catch him before he reaches it," said Kano.

"No shit," said Junior. "Li, can you intercept?"

"Not alone," she replied. "The whole place is surrounded by bots. And these ones are armed."

Junior punched the handlebar, causing the map to fizzle for a moment. They'd placed Li on the Southside to keep her away from the action, then call her in if anyone needed healing. But now the action was coming to her.

And she had no backup.

If only Carmichael would put Warp in the damn field. She

was mostly recovered from her knife wound on the *Dormarch*, yet the captain still hesitated to use her despite how game-changingly helpful her ability to teleport could be. Just another of the captain's decisions that baffled him.

"We'll need to drop someone in," came Carmichael's voice. "Any volunteers?"

Crickets. Everyone waited for someone to cave. Junior was tempted to pick up the hopeless pursuit just to compensate for lost time.

"I'll do it," said Chenji.

Junior gulped. Now they were really in trouble.

Chapter 2

The Streets of Busu

"Are you sure you're ready, kid?" asked T8, the red dot on its mechanical visor pinging back and forth. Chenji had a feeling the bot was detecting the fear inside him.

"The team needs me." Chenji gripped the handrails tight, his insides shaking as he stared at the liftgate. Lightning flashed through his mind. *Tune it out*, he told himself, but that just made him think about it more: the convulsions on the floor, the electricity shooting through his muscles, the masked face staring down at him aboard that fateful train on the *Dormarch*.

Of all the powers for Taranis to have, why did it have to be lightning? The injury had dredged up an old pain, a pain he'd thought was far behind him. And now, months later, he still didn't know what his body would do once that liftgate opened.

T8 hummed to itself as it fixed the parachute to Chenji's back. It was one of Ristin's songs, Chenji realized. He sometimes wondered whether the bot felt a connection to the team…if it could feel any emotion at all. *Will it feel anything if I end up splattered on the pavement?*

"Pull the cord when Carmichael gives the signal," said T8.

Chenji put on his flight goggles and drew a deep breath. The bot's pinging stare lingered on him a moment longer, then it pressed a panel on the wall and the liftgate released with a blast of compressed air. Wind roared into the cargo hold, whipping Chenji's shaggy hair back as he inched toward the opening, hands clenched on the rails to either side of him.

"As easy as teleporting, right?!" called T8.

If only. Chenji wasn't about to pull Warp into action if she wasn't ready for it, though the white clouds whirring beneath his feet certainly tempted him.

Focus. Somewhere below those clouds, his friends needed him.

"Jump!" ordered Carmichael through his earpiece.

Lightning flashed through his mind again. He froze up, hands glued to the rails, feet planted on the floor at the edge of the liftgate.

"You're missing your window, kid!" called T8. "Do it now!"

His body wouldn't move. All he could do was stare at the rush of clouds.

"Chenji," came Li's voice softly. "We need you."

Something sparked. Chenji set his foot firmly and thrust himself into the cold rush. Time stood still. Adrenaline spiked. A sensation of weightlessness, and then a sharp plummet toward the surface.

He kept his arms flat at his sides like he'd been taught, resisting every urge to clutch onto the pull cord. If he triggered the parachute too soon, he'd never reach the surface in time.

"I'm loading the path into your flight goggles," came Jaden's voice through his earpiece, barely audible over the wind. Pixels scattered across Chenji's field of vision and formed together into a red line leading straight through the clouds. The ETA displayed above it – just over two minutes.

"I've been spotted!" came Li's voice. Gunfire rang in the background.

Chenji's chest tightened. Suddenly two minutes seemed like a lifetime. He angled himself lower, veered slightly off the marked path, his speed increasing. The timer rolled back. One minute fifty-eight seconds, one minute fifty-six...not fast enough. His heart raced. *Stay in control*, he told himself. *But she's in danger!* screamed another voice. An instinctual voice. An animal voice.

He convulsed. His back arched, ruining his momentum. The ETA shot up, but that became a passing concern. Fur sprouted from Chenji's arms, claws from his fingertips. And lightning flashed through his mind.

"We're losing him!" cried a voice in his ear. It sounded familiar.

"Don't transform yet, Chenji! You're not ready!"

Who's Chenji? The cool air filled his nostrils. He wanted to hunt.

"Chenji, *focus!*" came another voice, this one stern. He knew that voice.

Li...the mission! Chenji pulled the cord. The parachute exploded from his back and yanked him from his free fall. He floated there, claws retreating, body returning to normal, only now to realize his error.

"You pulled too soon!" said Jaden.

"I know, I know!" Chenji barked back, a little animal left in his voice. It was in his brain too, scrambling his thoughts, making him lean toward instinct rather than intuition.

More deep breaths. *This didn't used to happen.* His mind had once been his own, no matter what form he took, but ever since his fight with Taranis the line had blurred.

"Snap it and use the reserve chute!" ordered Carmichael.

Reserve chute. Right! But the ETA in his goggles now registered eight minutes to landing. His timing had been ruined, even if he switched chutes.

"Hurry!" cried Li, the roar of blaster fire much louder than before.

Guess I'll have to fly the old-fashioned way.

Talons sprouted from his hand and he slashed the lines on his chute. Gravity yanked him toward the surface. He allowed it to, angling his body like a missile. The clouds parted and Darraden's port city of Busu appeared before him, a labyrinth of concrete buildings interwoven with narrow streets and canals, the stench of low tide rising off the murky water where ships spat plumes of thick smoke.

Whatever you do, don't turn into a fish, he told himself.

The landing zone appeared in his goggles, but he almost didn't need it with all the blaster fire flashing from It.

"Pull the chute," ordered Carmichael.

He kept on the path, arms locked at his side.

"Chenji, pull it!" shouted Jaden.

Chenji the Changeling doesn't need a parachute. He tuned out the noise: the voices, the wind; everything fell away until there was nothing but himself and the target. He passed between towering rooftops. Wings burst out his back, tearing the straps of his parachute pack and sending it tumbling toward the ground. He swooped, his body sprouting feathers, his nose morphing into a beak. The goggles adjusted to his new facial structure, a nice upgrade of Sterling's. That was the last familiar thought he had before the animal took over.

Now there was only the bird and its prey.

He spotted them: puny bots spraying fire from their sticks of death. Vines whipped at them from behind a barrier. The vines of a friend; he knew that much. They snagged the bots two at a time and smashed them against the earth, but never fast enough to stop the pack from pressing forward. He spread his wings, caught the wind and grazed over the bots, his talons slicing through their wiring like paper.

Only a fraction of the bots remained when he made another pass, but now their fire came his direction. He dipped out of the way, fire chasing him along his arc. The friend emerged from behind the barrier, beautiful and angry, hands aglow as she commanded the vines to snatch up the bots one by one and smash their gears against each other.

Soon the field was clear. He landed beside her on his two webbed feet.

"It's good to have you back," she said, stroking his feathers with her argyle hand of gray and gold.

He bowed his head. She climbed onto his back and weaved her vines gently around his beak as reins.

"Let's fly, Chenji," she said.

Chenji, the bird thought. *Yes, that's my name. Chenji the Changeling.*

◁◆▷

"Well this is typical," said Makoto to himself as his legs

swung over a fifty-story drop. Two bots carried him, one on either arm, their metal fingers digging into his argyle skin as they hoisted him higher.

"Almost there," said Cera through his earpiece. "Just hang tight."

Hang tight?! He'd already messed up the mission enough, just like Junior said. He wasn't about to wait around for the adults to come save his sorry ass. Not when he could fix this.

The dual stun batons at his sides were out of reach, but the bots would be easy to take down without them. It was the fall he was worried about. The rooftops were too far away to leap to, and each moment took him farther away from solid ground. He scanned his surroundings when, as if by some miracle, the bots led him over the canal. Perfect. Well, not *perfect*…. For all his strengths, Makoto didn't consider himself the strongest swimmer: one didn't have many opportunities to practice, growing up in a city that floated in the air. That, and he could smell the sewage from way up here.

Whelp, here's to a long shower tonight.

He swung his arms together, smashing the bots into each other. Their hoverpads spluttered and Makoto felt the sharp tug of gravity. He dove feet first past the towering buildings and plunged into the murky depths. *Not so bad*. He opened his eyes, and then it got very bad. They burned in the rancid water, the pollution so thick that he couldn't tell up from down. It was all one brown abyss. He flailed in one direction, pushing with all his Nurrano strength, praying with every stroke that he'd picked the right one.

His vision started to blur. *Gotta get out!* He pressed harder, strength sapping from his arms, his muscles clenching up like a machine with not enough oil. He'd never known this feeling, to be without oxygen. He'd never realized how much of it his two beating hearts needed. And now his tunnel of vision was narrowing to a fine point. He saw a light at the end of it. *This is it. I'm dying.* Strange that no one ever told him the light at the end would be green…

Something yanked him by the waist. Water rushed past his face and suddenly he was in the sweet open air again, gasping as much of it as he could. His rescuer set him down at her feet – a tall, gorgeous woman, her blonde hair flowing in the breeze.

"I couldn't…find…the surface," gasped Makoto between gags of nauseating water.

"It's ok," said Cera. She knelt beside him and placed a hand on his back. "Blow bubbles next time. Those should lead you to the surface."

"Bubbles…genius!" Makoto flopped onto his back, still gasping like a fish as a much more fishlike being padded up beside him. It glared down at him with bulbous eyes, its blue scales shimmering beneath the last shreds of sunlight, its long arms crossed over its disproportionately short body. It was odd looking up rather than down at the Jakari. Makoto found master assassin much more intimidating from this angle.

"We told you to hang tight, errand boy," hissed Akio. He sheathed a knife beneath his gray poncho – the same gray poncho he'd been wearing since Makoto had met him months ago in a Famoran interrogation room.

"Didn't want to waste your time," said Makoto. "And I'm not your errand boy."

Yet something in Akio's gaze told Makoto that he very much

was. He felt disappointment in Cera's stare too. He'd really messed this one up, and he wasn't about to let Clemens get away because of it.

"Which way?" he asked.

Cera smiled. "Follow me."

"I see it!" shouted Kano, pointing to the blaster fire radiating from the heart of the city. Spotting was about all he was good for with Junior driving. At least until they encountered more killer bots, of course.

"Hang on."

Kano clutched Junior's combat suit tight as they rocketed through the city. *Thank goodness I didn't eat lunch before*. The G-force alone had practically inverted his stomach with every sharp turn that Junior took. And there were many.

The dizziness was bad enough, but Kano knew there was a greater cost to all this wild driving. He checked over Junior's shoulder, saw the fuel gauge teetering on empty. Junior seemed unfazed, focused on reaching the action. And Kano hoped they did. Putting Li and Chenji in the middle of gunfire was never part of the plan.

"Guys, we have a problem," came Li's voice.

Before Kano could enquire further, a flash of light emanated from between two buildings, far brighter than the blaster fire happening nearby. A rumble shook the city streets: the rumble of a prelaunch sequence.

"You guys got about two minutes to make something happen," announced Jaden over the comms.

Junior jammed the throttle as far as it would go. Kano clenched tighter to him as the city whirred by, his eyes constantly flicking back to the fuel gauge, the speeder shaking under the enormous pressure.

"Li, Chenji, can you two slow it down?" asked Kano into his communicator.

"Negative. Too many bots," replied Li, the roar of the rocket's engine almost enough to drown out the overwhelming boom of gunfire around her.

Junior glanced back at Kano. Not a word was spoken. They both knew what they had to do.

The shuttle came into view as they rounded sharply out of a side street. It looked like a giant goldfish rolling down the main road, with three fins in the back and a large, oval face in the front. Though instead of gold, it was a rusty reddish brown, something the Taipa had clearly been saving for a rainy day long before Clemens arrived in Busu.

They angled toward the shuttle as it picked up speed along its launch path. Bots swarmed around the path like flies, but their bullets were still concentrated on Chenji as he flew between the nearby rooftops. The perfect distraction.

Junior swept in alongside the shuttle. Kano threw out his hands. Twin shockwaves clapped against the cloud of bots, launching them into the abandoned street like bullets, their parts spraying out in mechanical gore. Those that impacted the shuttle, though, pinged right off. If they'd left a scratch, it wasn't noticeable against the shuttle's dilapidated exterior.

"We're gonna need some firepower to breach that hull," said Kano. Junior was readying a fireball when their engine sputtered. Their momentum slowed and the shuttle pulled ahead. Junior swore as his fireball missed it. Clemens glanced back at them through the viewport and gave a long, toothy grin.

"Shoulda stayed in the desert!" the gangster jeered through the shuttle's loudspeakers. Kano felt Junior tensing in front of him, the former cadet's face turning a bright red.

"Stay calm," said Kano, despite knowing it was a futile effort.

Junior punched the red button. Blue flame sparked behind the speeder in a last adrenaline shot of life. It rocketed forward, threatening to fling Kano off as Junior steered them over the top of the shuttle.

"Jump!" shouted Junior.

"What about you?!"

"*Just jump!*" Junior tugged at his combat suit. Kano's fingers slipped from it and he fell backward, off the speeder and across the top of the shuttle. He caught onto one of the fins, his head in a whirl as wind whipped his face and the engines roared at a deafening pitch in his ears.

Asshole! He searched the sky, but the dying speeder was no longer above him. He glanced back in time to catch it plowing into the asphalt.

"NO!" Power came screaming into his fist. He slammed it against the fin and a shockwave exploded out. When he retracted his hand, he found a dent in its place. He punched again and again, leaving dent after dent, but still the shuttle barreled ahead, the wheels beginning to lift off the street.

"Break, dammit!" he shouted, power exploding with each savage strike. "Clemens has to *pay!*" The last word boomed as power shot up his throat and screamed out his mouth in a shockwave that tore the fin clean in half.

Kano froze. *Did I just...?* The shuttle tipped sideways, grinding along the building beside it. Kano tumbled forward, shielding his face from the chunks of concrete raining down, finding no purchase between him and the edge of the shuttle.

"Gotcha!" A burly arm caught his own. *It can't be.* He looked up and saw those familiar orange eyes staring down at him.

"The speeder...how'd you do that?" asked Kano.

"I was about to ask you the same thing," said Junior, nodding toward the severed fin as he hoisted Kano back on top of the shuttle. Kano had no answer. His powers had never channeled from anywhere besides his hands. But before he could question it, a hatch opened, and an angry red face emerged from it.

"I've *had it* with you damn Zoboros!" cried Clemens. He drew a pistol with his only hand. Kano flinched. They had nowhere to go, no cover with the fin broken apart. As he braced for the bullets, a vine snapped around Clemens's hand and slammed it against the shuttle's surface. The gangster cried out, lost his balance, and tumbled back down the hatch and into the belly of the shuttle.

"Great timing," said Kano, smiling as Li and her trusty steed landed beside them.

Li dodged his eyes. "What are the chances this thing makes it into the atmosphere?"

The shuttle groaned as Clemens pulled up on the throttle below them. The wheels started to lift, then crashed right back down, sending Li sailing off Chenji's back and into Kano's arms.

"I gotcha," he said, a warm rush rising through him.

Li's eyes widened as they stared into his. *My moment.* A

moment he'd been waiting months for. He was about to seize upon it when Chenji cawed. Kano snapped out of his trance, realizing she'd been looking not at him but over his shoulder the whole time – over at a bridge that stood in their path, packed with spectators eager to catch the show that their team was putting on around town. The bridge arched high enough for them to pass underneath, but as the wheels lifted off the ground again, collision became imminent.

"You cats better do something or you're going right through the nosebleeds," came Jaden's voice over the comms. "Carmichael's—"

The signal cut out. Kano tapped his communicator desperately. "Jaden? Carmichael? Someone come in!"

Li and Junior tapped their earpieces and shook their heads. They were on their own. Kano took a deep breath and assessed the situation. *What would Carmichael do?*

"I'll take care of Clemens," said Junior, marching toward the hatch.

"Wait!" said Kano. To his surprise, Junior stopped. "Li and I can take him. Junior, I need you to keep this shuttle grounded. Chenji, can you clear the bridge just in case?"

Chenji cawed and swooped off the shuttle. Junior glanced back at the hatch, eager for blood. Kano held his breath, unsure what to do if Junior defied him. The pyro simply marched to the front of the shuttle, placed one hand on it and aimed the other high. He let out a jet of flame that pressed the shuttle lower.

"GO!" shouted Junior, straining as he fought to keep the engines from lifting them any higher. Up ahead, the changeling swept onto the bridge, his feathers retreating into his skin, replaced by a thick, furry pelt. Hooves replaced his feet, massive paws replaced his hands, and tusks rose from his newly formed snout, the snout of a great and terrifying Kimikan hog. Kano had seen that form on the *Dormarch,* and it had frightened him then too. Chenji let out a roar so fierce that it was quickly drowned out by the terrified screams of the crowd as they poured out either side of the bridge.

Well done, Chenji. Kano turned to Li, and together they approached the hatch.

Bullets pinged out of it in Li's direction. *Clemens!* Power surged into Kano's fists, overcome with an instinct to protect. He threw all his might down the hatch, the resulting thunderclap blasting out the windshield below in a shower of glass. He froze. *Did I just kill Clemens?* The gangster could easily have been ejected by his shockwave and thrown underneath the shuttle. Kano had never taken a life. The idea of it made him sick, even if it was a life as tainted as Clemens's.

He slid down the ladder. Anything that hadn't been bolted down within the cramped space was either overturned or ejected onto the street. It seemed he'd really done it this time.

Then he heard a groan.

"Clemens?!" he spun around, relief sweeping over him as he found the gangster lying underneath a fallen chair that had previously been bolted down. He lifted the seat and Clemens scrambled back, all the color draining from his red face.

"Stay away!" he cried. "Please!"

"We have questions for you," said Kano, scooping him up by the collar.

"No…no questions…" trailed Clemens, his eyes rolling around. That's when Kano noticed the blood trickling down from a fresh gash in the Tenu's scalp. *He's dazed.* "C-can't answer questions. Can't sever the head."

"Sever what head?" asked Li, climbing down the ladder.

Clemens licked his viper tattoo and gave a wicked smile. "He's coming for you."

"Who?" demanded Kano, pulling the gangster closer.

"Be careful, Kano," said Li, her glowing white hands sensing Clemens's injuries. "He's concussed. He's not in his right state of mind."

"Y-yes I am," hissed Clemens. "I-I'm the V-Viper of Mogaddu. I can't die!" He pulled free from Kano and jammed the throttle all the way down.

"NO!" The bridge came up on them fast. It clipped the bottom of the shuttle and sent Kano, Clemens, and Li sailing out the missing windshield and through the foul air. Li snatched him and Clemens each in a vine and pulled them together and away from the dead ship as it plunged into the murky waters. They too splashed down, the sudden intake burning Kano's eyes and throat. He kicked himself up to the surface, flailing against the wild surf the shuttle had created.

"HELP!" he cried out, sinking under. Despite all their travels, he'd still never learned to swim. *A little late to figure It out now.* He grabbed the vine still latched around his waist and tugged at it. He felt a pull from the other side, and soon Li had him back at the surface, a broken shuttle fin under her arms.

"Grab on!" she said. "He's getting away!"

Kano caught his breath as he pulled himself onto the fin. Li started to kick the water and he did too, pursuing Clemens's splashes as he swam for the nearest dock. The vine tying them all together kept Clemens from getting too far away, but he was still the first one there. He pulled himself up with whatever strength he had left and drew a knife from his soaking suit jacket.

"Adios, Zoboros." He cut the vine and cackled with delight, but when he turned, he found himself staring down the barrel of a shotgun.

"I wouldn't be so sure about that," said Carmichael, pumping a cartridge into the chamber. Akio was perched on his shoulder, Cera and Makoto stood either side of him, and an angry giant hog loomed just behind. Junior floated down next to them on twin jets of flame that snuffed out upon landing.

Now the real work begins, thought Kano.

Chapter 3

Interrogation

Ragar wiped the oil off his hands and onto his shirt. *Finished.* He smiled as he guided the speeder into the lineup with its brothers and sisters, newly tricked out with a better engine, state-of-the-art suspension systems, the works. After *months* of searching and scrapping, he could say he had a fully stocked shop.

Almost. His wandering middle eye caught the empty slot in the lineup and his smile faded. *They better bring it back in one piece.* It was inevitable that he'd be found by that ragtag team. They seemed to pop up wherever he went. And they always brought trouble.

He checked out the window for the fiftieth time since they'd left on their anonymous "business". He hoped whatever they were doing was quick and quiet. Somehow, he knew it wouldn't be.

His first instinct had been to kick them off his doorstep the moment they'd arrived, but they had made an...intriguing offer. *Damn my curiosity.* But when he really thought about it, how many other shopkeepers in Busu could boast Poterian tech in their speeders?

The door burst open. Ragar almost jumped out of his shell as the whole entourage poured in. Eight of the galaxy's most wanted fugitives, some of them soaking wet, plus a newcomer that they were dragging between them, face concealed by a garbage bag.

It was shaping up to be an interesting Tuesday.

The hostage cursed beneath the bag as they threw him into a chair, rancid water dripping off his suit. Ragar had to admit the guy had a sense of style, even if he smelled like a fish that'd been left in the twin suns all day.

"Who's this guy stinking up my place?" he demanded.

"Bolt the door, Ragar," ordered the team's captain.

Ragar folded his four arms. Did this IDF turncoat really think he could boss him around the way he did the children on his team? That was all they were to Ragar: children. And not just because he was a 300-cycle-old Bolani. He'd watched many of them grow up on Famora, and he believed they should still be there, safe and happy. Not on Darraden. Not on the run.

"Answer my question," said Ragar, standing firmly upon his four crab legs. "I've been patient as a Taloan with you for three days now. I can ignore the fact that you didn't bring my speeder back. I can even look past the fact that you're a damn Carmichael. But this is *my* shop and I have a right to know what you bring into it."

The hostage cackled beneath the garbage bag. "You people been waitin' three days just to talk ta me? I'm flattered."

Ragar froze. *That voice.* Throbbing pain shot up his once-broken leg. It had mostly healed in the months since he'd left

Mogaddu, but there was always that tingle of remembrance from where a gangster had savaged it with a hammer.

"Wait, don't—" started Carmichael, but Ragar was already ripping the bag off the hostage to find the sinister smile hidden underneath.

"Do I know you from somewheres?" asked Clemens.

"I'll tell you where you know me from!" It took three team members, including his old apprentice Junior, to restrain Ragar from an unnatural fury. Bolanis were not a violent people. Scheming and clever, sure, but the idea of using his hard shell against someone's flesh felt foreign to him. Yet right now the thought gave him immense pleasure.

"Get him out of here," said the blonde woman.

"No," said the captain. "He might be useful."

"Useful?!" Ragar spat back. "You think you all get to decide whether I stay in my own shop? If anyone should leave, it should be the Viper. Preferably with the police!"

"I *own* the police," said Clemens, the snake tattoo slithering on his face as he laughed.

"Shut up!" said the Nurrano girl, the one whose grandmother worked near the Famoran Dockyards. Ragar liked her attitude, at least.

The captain grabbed the gangster by the chin and turned his tattooed face toward Ragar. "You're going to tell us what we want to know," he said. "And every time you lie, I'll set the Bolani on you."

"Is that all you got, Carmichael?" said Clemens. "You're a far cry from your old man. *He* knew how to get answers from people. But this?" He gave Ragar a once-over. "This is just pathetic."

"You're one to talk," said Ragar, pushing forward while the young Famorans held him back.

"Go ahead! Show me, then."

"Don't do it, Ragar," said Kano.

Ragar felt his spark of anger falter, and not just because he didn't want Kano to see him lash out like a lunatic. Truth be told, he could have overpowered those holding him back if he'd really tried, but Clemens was right. He didn't have it in him.

"That's what I thought," said the Viper. "Bolanis are predictable. Just like you people."

"Predictable how?" asked Kano. "We caught you."

"Yeah, just like you came for Snipes, Ray, Domovoi…everyone in the quadrant with a fight ring. It's funny, people think you're actually noble for doing it."

"Ending the fight rings *is* noble," snapped the blonde woman. Ragar caught Carmichael giving her a warning look, and he knew the Viper caught it too.

"Never too late to get back on the roster, Blockade." Clemens's smile stretched from ear to ear as the blonde woman turned bright red. "You're better off there than with these—"

A large hand of green energy reached out of the woman's own hand and caught Clemens by the neck. "I'll be better off with you hanged from the docks!" she shouted.

"If you're gonna kill him, do it outside!" said Ragar.

"Go ahead…kill me," choked the Viper. "I'm dead anyway."

"Not until you tell us what we want to know," said Carmichael, doing nothing to stop his subordinate from strangling their hostage.

What do *they want to know?* Ragar wondered. He hoped

they got the information soon. All this shouting was sure to draw attention from outside.

"Nobody…tells me…nothin'…" the Viper managed, his face turning purple as the fingers of energy tightened around his throat.

"Then who do they tell?" demanded the blonde woman.

Shouts echoed from outside. From the distance came a rolling thunder, steady and unyielding. The Nurrano boy from Famora checked out the window. "IDF," he said. "Lots of ships."

The woman's grip loosened. Clemens gasped, and his furious gaze turned toward Carmichael. "You better hope they catch you first," he said, "cuz my people ain't so forgivin'."

Something snapped in the captain. He grabbed the Viper by the collar and hoisted him into the air. "They catch us, they catch you. And I'll bet they'd love to make you sing, Clemens."

The gangster laughed again, only this time it sounded half-hearted. "You wouldn't let yourself get caught," he said.

"Then we better make this quick," Carmichael whispered, a devilish smile on his face. The smile of a desperate man. Clemens tried to put on a tough face, but Ragar had seen enough crooks in his day to recognize the lump in his throat. The Viper was scared. Hell, even Ragar was scared.

"Tell us what we want to know," continued Carmichael.

"What the hell *do* you people want to know?!" exclaimed Ragar.

"They want access to the other side!" shouted Clemens, eyes boring into Carmichael's. "They want access to Poteria."

Ragar almost laughed. "Do you think I'm stupid? No one in their right mind would want to go…" He paused. Every tired face in that room looked dead serious.

"Desperate times," said Clemens, his smile returning. "They'll need the help of the Taipa to get there."

"The Taipa may control the only entry point to the other side," said Junior, "but *we* control how many Taipa get tied up and left for the IDF to deal with."

Clemens's red face turned even redder, somehow. "Didn't you hear me before. Hellfire? I'm excommunicated thanks to you. I don't know nothin' no more."

"Excommunicated people don't get access to the city's security bots," said Junior, fire flaring in his palm. He held the fire close to Clemens's face, and the gangster jerked his head back as far as he could. "Tell us how to get across the Rift without the Taipa blowing us to kingdom come, and you get to tell your boss that you were the one who got us to—"

"Only he knows!" blurted Clemens. "Only Mon Chogorath himself grants access to the—"

An IDF trooper burst into the room, clad in shiny blue armor, face concealed by a standard-issue helmet.

"Officer, I can explain!" cried Ragar, raising his hands in the air while the others assumed defensive positions. That was when Ragar realized the officer was unarmed.

That won't stop these Zoboros from tearing up my shop, though. He approached the officer slowly, the clatter of his crab legs now the only noise in the room. "Sir, listen to me: you're outnumbered. If you walk away, this will never have happened. I'll be long gone, and you won't have to fight—"

What happened next, Ragar wasn't sure. One moment the officer was still, the next it had him by the arm. Ragar heard a *snap* and a searing pain shot all the way to his fingertips. He collapsed, his exposed arm muscle lying useless amid a broken shell, shock overtaking him as the officer marched across his shop.

◁◆▷

Lusitani. Junior had seen a similar fighting style from the other Zoboros-hunting assassins. It would explain how the "trooper" had dispatched a 400-pound Bolani with such ease.

But the rest of them wouldn't go down so easily.

He heaved a fireball. The attacker leaped over it *and* Junior, landing a solid ten paces past him. *Impossible*. Lusitani were known to be nimble, but to jump that high with that much armor on? Junior didn't see any of the usual tech upgrades the Lusitani sported. He made to throw another fireball, but his opponent was too close to the others to get a clear shot. No matter. The others were about to make their move.

Kano struck first, driving a shockwave-infused punch right for the trooper's armored chest. The trooper dropped beneath the attack, its back contorting at a sharp angle. *Too* sharp of an angle. The shockwave released above his folded body and threw Li and Chenji to the ground. The attacker then swept Kano's legs and charged forward.

Right for their hostage.

"It's with the Taipa!" Junior shouted. "Don't let it near Clemens!"

Makoto leaped into the attacker's path, twin stun batons drawn. He let each one pulse at the tip with electricity before unleashing a flurry of attacks. The trooper dodged each one in an intricate dance, so quick that by the time Junior caught up

49

with its movements, the trooper had stolen the batons and stunned Makoto with them.

Cera kept her distance, two green arms of energy surging toward the trooper, who heaved one of the batons between them and caught her in the chest with a pulse of electricity. The trooper was past her before she even hit the ground.

Akio and Carmichael came at the trooper from either side. The trooper stunned Carmichael with one hand and caught Akio in the other, then flung the cursing Jakari across the room.

Who the hell is this? Junior had fought some tough Lusitani before, but never one this efficient. Never one this *powerful*. He was tempted to throw a fireball, despite Li and Chenji being so close to the attacker, figuring they would probably be down before the fire reached them anyway. In her defense, Li did make a good move with her vine to catch the attacker's arm in mid-swing, but the attacker switched the remaining baton into its other hand and took her down with it before she had another chance to strike. Chenji readied to pounce in his tiger form, but all the attacker had to do was pulse the electricity at him to make him whimper.

How does it know about Chenji's phobia? Not even Chenji had told them where it came from.

Junior drew a fireball back to throw when the trooper dove behind Clemens and held the prisoner up as a shield.

"Hey now, I'm no good to anyone injured," said Clemens, holding up his one hand in surrender.

"How about dead?" hissed the trooper. It wrapped its arm around Clemens's neck and twisted. There was a crack, and the Tenu fell limp to the floor.

A gasp rippled through the team as they struggled back onto

their feet. Even Junior froze as he stared at the body of his former slave master, but only for a moment. He sprayed a jet of flame at the assassin, who once again vaulted over it.

But this time, Junior expected that.

With his other hand, he launched a second jet straight into the air. The assassin cried out, clutching its arm, and crashed through the door in a plume of smoke. It laid upon the asphalt outside, armor glowing from the heat, but the fire had failed to penetrate.

Yet.

"Junior, stop!" cried Carmichael, but Junior was already racing out the door, not caring that the IDF was out there, not caring who saw him, not even caring that the assassin had murdered Clemens. All he cared about was finding out who had just dispatched an entire team of Zoboros.

The assassin scrambled up the fire escape and Junior followed, launching fireball after fireball. His target kept dipping away from them, always a flight of stairs ahead. The game continued until the assassin finally came to a dead end on the rooftop.

"There's nowhere left to run," said Junior, catching his breath. The assassin just stood there, staring at Junior from beneath its helmet. Too tall to be a Nurrano, too short to be a Gorv, and too flexible to be Human. If there was a species as strong and nimble as this, he'd not encountered it yet.

The assassin, seeming to read Junior's thoughts, removed its helmet. *He is Human*. The face was so plain, yet the smile so sadistic it gave the late Clemens a run for his money. Junior stepped forward, fire ready in his palms. There was only one way a Human could accomplish what this one just had in

Ragar's shop.

Zoboros.

"Who are you?"

"I'm whoever I want to be." The assassin watched Junior inquisitively with his yellow eyes, like the pyro was a specimen in a lab. "But who are you, Hendricks Junior?"

"Don't play games with me."

"You're certainly not your father," continued the assassin, taking a step back toward the edge of the rooftop. "So dull, that one. You do look like him though. Just missing one key feature." The assassin drew a line down his cheek with his finger, the same path as Junior's father's scar, a scar Junior had seen enough times growing up to know that this assassin drew it a little too perfectly.

IDF ships thundered from the distance. Out the corner of his eye, Junior saw troop transports swarming into the city.

"There's no sense in running," said Junior, his flames dimming. "Turn yourself over. You'd be safer with us than with the IDF."

"You and I both know that's a lie. Your team dances on a knife's edge as it is."

Engines roared from the other side of the building. *Escape vehicle!* Junior charged, reaching out with a flaming hand as the assassin tipped over the edge. His hand missed, but the flames licked at the assassin's face, just close enough to make it...split? Junior wasn't sure, but he swore he saw green scales appear beneath the skin.

The assassin fell beneath his grasp, landed on a speeder, and jetted away. Junior stood there as rain began to patter down, watching the assassin go, his mind spinning as the mysterious pieces dredged up an old memory from Famora.

Green scales. Yellow eyes. My father's scar. His eyes widened and he bolted down the stairs.

Chapter 4

Escape

"Everyone to the shed!" ordered Carmichael. The team began scrambling out the door. Kano lingered, making sure everyone got out. But Junior had still not returned from his chase, and Li was still tending to Ragar's arm.

"I'll live," said the old mechanic. "You need to get out of here."

"Almost done," she said, running her glowing hands over the swollen muscle beneath the broken bits of shell.

Kano placed a hand on her shoulder. "Li, we need to—"

"I said I'm almost done." She didn't look up. Kano retracted his hand, started backward toward the door. He wanted to tell her not to be too long but decided against it; he'd incurred enough of her temper already.

Rain pelted him as he stepped out the door. What had started as a drizzle a few moments ago had quickly transformed into a monsoon. He could barely see the shed on the other side of the street. Perhaps that was for the best – less chance that the IDF would spot them, though Kano knew the captain wouldn't be taking any chances now that Junior had run into the open.

He reached the shed just as Chenji and Makoto had finished pulling the wooden doors open. The *Shirlena* sat inside – Sterling's pride and joy, on display in all her hideous glory. Long and narrow, she stared at Kano with headlights that looked like bug eyes, and that was hardly her best feature. Her viewport angled out awkwardly to give the appearance of an enlarged forehead, and she sported antenna-like thrusters along either side of her hull for extra maneuverability. No two thrusters were the same color, but he supposed that was part of the charm.

"Let's move, people!" Carmichael led them up the ramp and through the ship's liftgate, where Jaden was waiting for them.

"I'm taking bets now whether Carmichael will kill Junior," said Jaden, his long blond hair swaying as he followed Kano through the narrow hallway. The IDF had made Jaden cut it while aboard the *Dormarch*, and he'd since dedicated himself to growing it all back.

"That's not Carmichael's style," said Kano as they approached the ladder to the main deck. "Besides, he has to deal with the Poterian first."

T8 joined them at the ladder, its wiry arms and legs clanking as it climbed. "The boss says we're not taking off in this weather."

"Tell that to Carmichael," muttered Jaden, breath heavy as he climbed. Physical tasks were never his strong suit.

"He already has."

When they entered the bridge, Carmichael was squared off against Sterling, who loomed a full head and shoulders higher than the stocky captain, the tusks along either side of his red chin in danger of poking Carmichael's eyes out if he leaned any lower.

"You're overreacting," said Sterling. The gears in his bionic fist clinked as he clenched it.

"If they saw him on that rooftop, then this is our only window to escape."

"They're not going to see anything through this." Sterling pointed out the viewport at the deluge outside. "And neither will we if we try to fly through it."

"I'm—"

"Don't give me an order." There was a hiss of hydraulics as Sterling took a step forward on his bionic leg. "Not on my ship."

Kano noticed his brother keeping back as he entered the room. Makoto's people were not particularly fond of Poterians, after they had ravaged the Nurrano homeworld, and Sterling was certainly not one to help bridge the racial divide.

Carmichael held his ground against the lumbering pilot when Cera stepped up beside him. "It wouldn't hurt to run the prelaunch sequence," she said. "Just in case."

"It would hurt! Their scanners will—" Sterling paused as Junior burst in, drenched and exasperated.

"We need to get out of here," he said, hurrying toward their Poterian pilot. "He's coming for us."

"Who?" demanded Carmichael, but Junior kept his gaze focused on Sterling.

"The Jaculus," he said.

Kano didn't presume to know Sterling particularly well, but he could safely say he'd never seen so much fear on the Poterian's face before. "Are you sure?" Sterling whispered.

"I saw the green scales beneath skin that wasn't his."

Sterling dove into the command chair and ignited the prelaunch sequence. "T8!" he bellowed. "Calculate us a launch vector, now!"

"Wait, wait, wait. Who's this 'Jaculus?'" asked Makoto.

"An assassin," said Junior. "From the Poterian Empire."

That got a rise out of the team. A hundred questions flooded his way, but he waved them off.

"I met a man on Famora, someone who used to work for my father," he explained quickly as the engines roared to life. "He said his parents had been killed by an assassin sent by the Poterians, and that my father had gone after this creature and…failed." He instinctively rubbed the part of his cheek where his father's scar had been. Kano could put two and two together from there.

"What could the Poterians want with us?" asked Kano.

"It may not be the Poterians," said Sterling from the command chair. "The Jaculus goes where he wills and serves whatever cause fits his twisted mind."

"You think he works for the Taipa, then?" asked Ristin, emerging timidly from the hallway. An odd sight: their newest member, who had once performed for huge crowds on Vasilia, shrank in front of their small band of rebels — though that was probably because some members had still not warmed up to him.

"He's covering their tracks, isn't he?" said Junior dismissively.

Ristin was about to retreat to his cubby when Kano caught him by the arm. "Stay," said Kano. "We should all be here for this."

Ristin nodded, a small smile crossing his face. He still wasn't allowed on many of their missions or meetings for fear he might relay that information to a certain someone aboard their ship. But Kano believed Ristin had put that old alliance far behind him. Besides, Kano knew someone else was about to fall into Junior's crosshairs. Someone the former cadet hated much more.

"Whoever he is, it doesn't change the fact that you disobeyed orders," said the captain.

"What are you gonna do, send me to my room?" asked Junior.

Carmichael frowned. "Do you want me to call that bluff?"

"I *want* you to stop pretending like you own me! Like you own any of us. You're not a captain anymore. This ship isn't even yours. We're all fugitives, one and the same, thanks to you."

Carmichael drew a deep breath while Kano and the others waited nervously for his response. "We are a team, thanks to me as much as everyone else in this room. Everyone except you. You know strategy, you know how to fight, but you don't know how to work with a team. Your selfishness endangered everyone today. Think on that."

Junior scowled, his orange eyes boring into the captain's. Kano felt the tension hovering over the room so tightly it was liable to choke someone. It was an act of mercy when Junior turned and walked away.

"The ship wouldn't be taking off if it wasn't for me," said Junior as he marched out the door toward his cubby. "Think on that."

Carmichael sighed. The others exchanged looks but said

nothing. Just another lovely day with Junior, as far as they were concerned. But Kano was very concerned.

"It's gonna be a bumpy ride, folks," announced Sterling, reminding everyone that they were still, in fact, about to run a blockade. "But I'm sure you're all used to that by now." He guided the ship out the shed and onto the street, rain drumming against the roof as he set them on T8's launch vector.

Kano glanced around the room. The others were getting seated in a viewing area just behind the viewport, though there wasn't much to view through the rain. It only took a quick head count for him to realize something.

"Li! We've left her—"

"I'm here!" she exclaimed, wringing out her shirt as she entered the bridge. "I reduced most of Ragar's swelling. I would've done more, but I heard the engines starting."

Carmichael nodded. "A kind gesture, but next time I ask for everyone to leave, we leave. Understood?"

Kano could tell by that defiant look in Li's eyes that she wanted to argue the point: to say that Ragar had done so much for them that they owed him a healing and then some for all the trouble they'd caused, but she only nodded and took her seat. She knew better than to cause a scene when they had more pressing matters to attend to, unlike some people...

Junior rounded a corner to find a pale face staring at him from beneath a hoodie.

"Not now, Warp." He marched past her. She reappeared in

front of him through a puff of smoke, arms crossed.

He sighed. "Well at least *you* won't lecture me."

She raised an eyebrow.

"Don't give me that look. Carmichael had it coming, thinking he can order me around like that."

She signed to him.

"I would leave if he hadn't made me a fugitive." He leaned against the wall as the ship lumbered its way through the atmosphere. "I was right to get away from him on Famora. I should've done the same on Mogaddu, but I thought I was helping him to stop some evil weapon at the time. Instead, I helped him try to murder my mother."

Warp frowned and shook her head.

"Deny it all you want but it's true. And if our ship gets compromised, don't think he'll hesitate to pull the trigger himself. You saw how eager he was to leave Busu. He won't risk losing his prize to anyone if he can help it."

She signed again.

"I'm not so sure my mom could fall into worse hands than his. He's up to something. He has been for a while now." Junior hesitated before asking the next part. "Did he tell you why he took you off the mission?"

Warp shook her head, though not as confidently as before.

"But you do know something, don't you?"

She started to back away.

"Come on, tell me. What's he planning?"

Warp signed, but half her signs were unfamiliar to him.

"I'm still a little new to this."

She rolled her eyes and pointed toward the ladder at the end of the hall. The one that led to the lower decks. To the monster on board.

"What does Carmichael have planned for him?"

She shrugged.

Junior rolled his eyes. "Well maybe while you're sitting around here during our missions you could make yourself useful and find out."

Warp huffed. A puff of smoke, and she was gone. Junior sighed, guilt sinking in.

"I take it your father never taught you how to talk to women." His mother emerged from her cubby, dark hair coming down in curls, hands voluntarily bound in those stupid anti-Zoboros cuffs.

"I'm not here to make friends. I'm here to survive. And to do that, I need to beat Carmichael at his own game."

Angeline rubbed his shoulders, her orange eyes checking him over for injuries. A maternal instinct, he supposed. "Regardless of what he did or did not do, you have enough people out there to 'beat': you don't need to be adding one of the few who actually wants to help you." Junior started to protest, and she raised her hand. Somehow, all these cycles later, it still silenced him instantly. "You feel alone, Junior, but that is a self-inflicted wound. The people here care about you deeply. That is a rare thing to find."

"So are the number of enemies we have," muttered Junior.

"And yet the bond here still holds."

But for how long? Junior wondered. He thought about the assassin, about the peeling face. How real it had looked. What technology did the Jaculus have at his disposal? Or worse, what abilities? Someone that powerful could do more than break the bond of this team. He could smash it to pieces and burn what remained.

"What did Dad tell you about the Jaculus?"

Angeline tensed. "That he was a monster."

Junior glanced back at the bridge. Maybe Sterling knew more. But Junior would have to brave all the people he'd just miffed in order to ask.

"I do know that the assassin answered only to the Poterian Emperor," added Angeline quietly. "Emperor Palorex was as secretive as he was distrustful. I doubt anyone else was allowed to interact with the Jaculus...besides his victims, of course."

That's comforting. Palorex's name was synonymous with evil. Junior wondered just how many victims the Jaculus had racked up on the Poterian Emperor's orders, and if any had been as lucky as his father, walking away with nothing worse than a scar.

The sword! A memory came flooding back, a horrible one that he often tried to suppress, but here it was necessary. The moment when Taranis stabbed his father. He'd claimed it was the same sword that had scarred his father's face.

The same sword the Jaculus once had.

"Is something wrong?" his mother asked.

"No. Not at all," he said, staring down the ladder to the monster's lair.

Chapter 5

Rough Night

Sleep eluded Kano. Again.

He kept thinking about Darraden. According to a file he'd once stolen on Famora, Darraden had been his secret birthplace. Secret, because his parents wanted to hide the paper trail to their Zoboros child, and perhaps to themselves too. Kano had hoped the mission might give him an opportunity to learn something about them, about their whereabouts, but it proved to be just another frenzied sprint from their enemies. He felt foolish for even getting his hopes up. Foolish and sore.

And now apparently an intergalactic assassin was on their scent. Was his team really that cursed? The Rift was already an impenetrable space storm, shouldn't that be enough? But no, the Taipa had to control the one entry point and kill off anyone with any information on how to find it.

But did the Jaculus even work for the Taipa? If he did, why not kill the team when he had the chance? From what Sterling had said, this assassin didn't play by normal rules. He could be working for anyone…even Poteria itself.

Feet pattered outside. Kano rose. *Another night owl.* He opened his door but found the hallway empty. Goosebumps crawled up his neck. "Is someone there?" he whispered. Silence. Power thrummed instinctively into his hands.

Could the assassin be *here*? Kano crept along, inch by inch, checking his corners.

A figure crossed the hallway, face hidden under a hood and cloak dragging across the floor, sweeping straight into Makoto's room and shutting the door behind it.

But the figure was too tall to be Makoto.

Kano ran over and pulled the door open. Water gushed out, blasting him back against the wall. *What the hell?!* Behind the door wasn't a room or even a part of the ship, but the outside world. A sandy shore, to be precise, with a great stone door at the back of it. The Gate to Iramwerta. That's when it clicked: the cloaked figure wasn't an intruder on the ship. It was an intruder in his dreams.

But those dreams had stopped after the *Dormarch*.

He shut the door and another opened across the way. He approached it, expecting to find the usual vision: jagged black mountains in the pouring rain. But the cloaked man had brought him something new, something horrible: the floating city burning, crumbling, whole hoverpads filled with buildings sinking like ships into the cloudy abyss. He'd endured a simulation like this months ago, only then it had been a fiction conjured by Carmichael and his superior. This felt different. Perhaps it was the screams. Or perhaps it was the Poterian warships raining fire and death upon Famora.

Yuchi! Nobara! All the people he knew there, all the places too: Downtown, the new Dockyards, even places he hated, like the Sphere, were in ruins. He turned away and the man stood there, an old man beneath a blood-red cloak, face hidden and body frail, veiny hand outstretched. Kano knew he was supposed to take it, but he ran away, realizing too late that he'd gone through the door and was falling through clouds.

He snapped up, forehead damp and chest heaving. *Not these again*. He climbed out of his sweat-soaked bed feeling as parched as he was bewildered. He passed door after door, each closed, the friends inside hopefully enjoying the sleep that he could not. *Why am I the one getting these stupid visions?*

A lot of strange things had happened to him since these visions began. Namely, he'd been able to find the lost city of Iramwerta using nothing more than a magic Orlov spear. Danadas claimed it was because Kano was an Orlov too, though that didn't explain why Kano's connection to the spear was so much stronger than that of the patriarch of the Orlov family, especially if the connection was supposed to weaken between generations. Nor did it explain why he, Junior, and Taranis were able to open the Gate to Iramwerta, something which, to his knowledge, had only happened in legend. In The Three Kings of Mogaddu, to be precise; the story of the very first Zoboros. Kano desperately wanted to understand his connection to all these things. And he believed the cloaked man could explain to him...if the cloaked man ever spoke.

Footsteps padded behind him. He groaned, hoping it wasn't another nightmare. The first had been bad enough, but a dream within a dream just sounded nutty.

He turned. At first, he thought no one was there, but when he looked down, Akio was standing in front of him, chewing an energy bar with his needlelike teeth.

"You need psychologist." The Jakari waddled back toward his room.

"Wait," hissed Kano, catching up. "You served with Poteria before."

"Unfortunately." He crunched into his bar again.

Kano knelt to Akio's height. "Do you think they would ever invade again?"

"War is their culture. It is why they destroyed mine." Akio's big eyes turned away. "They lost greatly in last war, but I would not underestimate their boldness."

"Is the Jaculus a sign of them coming? Did you know him over there?"

"I did not have the pleasure," sneered Akio, hocking a wad of green spit. "But Jaculus serves his own purposes. He could work with anyone, any time, for any reason. He is faithless."

"What do you think he wants, then?"

Akio shrugged. "There is only one constant with Jaculus. When he arrives, so does great change."

Something clanked down the hall. The Jakari gave a wide smile across his stretchy face.

"You are not the only one asking questions this night, boy of thunder."

What did he mean? Kano followed the sounds. Someone was climbing down the ladder. But there was only one thing to find down there. And Kano knew exactly who was going for it.

Junior stared at the figure for a long time. The figure who

murdered his father, tried to kidnap his mother, and burned his face on television…the figure who had haunted him since Famora, only now it had a face. The face of an outcast, a monster: half-Human and half-Poterian. Unwanted by everyone, but most of all by Junior.

"Why is he coming for us?"

"You'll have to be more specific," said Taranis. He stood behind bars of pure calladium – the most powerful metal in the known galaxy – which T8 had assembled just for their prisoner. The room itself was once a custodial closet; now all it stored were a handful of blankets at Taranis's feet for when the cold of space crept in. Taranis's hands were cocooned in a power dampener, yet somehow the months of solitary confinement had done little to whither the muscles that lined his tall, hybrid body. For all that strength, though, he failed to look Junior in the eye.

"Don't play dumb, Taranis. I know you like to eavesdrop."

"How would you know that? You never visit."

Fire flickered in his palms. "Tell me who the Jaculus is. Tell me what he wants."

Taranis glanced at the flames and rolled his eyes. "You know you can't melt calladium. If anything, you'd only risk damaging these cuffs, and that wouldn't bode well for—"

Junior tossed a fireball between the bars, setting Taranis's blankets ablaze.

"That wasn't very nice."

"Being nice never got me anything."

"Shocking." Taranis stamped out the flames while Junior summoned the smoke to his hand to keep the alarms from triggering. "You're more like your father than you realize,

Junior. Willing to go to any lengths for what you want."

"You don't get to speak about him. Not to me." Junior stopped himself when he noticed the small smile creeping across his enemy's face. *He wants a rise out of me.* Junior drew a deep breath, enough to quiet the storm inside him. "I know you carried the Jaculus's sword."

"As did you, once," replied Taranis. "How did it feel to wield all that power?"

Junior ignored the bait. "How did you find him?"

"He found me," said Taranis, eyes narrowing, but still failing to meet Junior's. "As I understand it, he finds whatever he's searching for."

"Quit trying to scare me and answer my question: what does he want?"

Taranis was quiet for a while. "You remain aboard this ship filled with fugitives whom you don't even like while your escapes get narrower and narrower." The room shook as if to reinforce the point. "I see no reason for you to stay. So tell me: what are *you* looking for, Aaron Hendricks Junior?"

The nerve of this guy. Junior had plenty of aspirations before Taranis came along. To go to the Hyb Military Academy, to become an officer, to protect people less fortunate. But now he was just scraping by to protect himself.

"I want to get us to our destination in one piece."

"*Carmichael* wants to get to Poteria. Come on, Aaron. Where do you want to go?"

"It doesn't matter what I want if the Jaculus stabs me in the throat."

"If he'd wanted to, he'd have done it already. The only thing standing in your way is yourself."

"And you!" blurted Junior. Fire flared. He took another breath. "You took everything from me. My life. My dreams. My freedom."

"That's a lie." Taranis's eyes met his for the first time. "I *gave* you freedom."

"You gave me a dead father."

"That's the same thing." Taranis stepped closer to the bars. "First him, then Clemens, and now Carmichael. I'm not the one who sought to control you. I *invited* you to join me, but you always had a choice."

"The other option was death," said Junior flatly.

"Only when you stood in my way. But when my work is done, when these…pretenders fall, then we will know true freedom. Then we will not need to hide, or fight, or serve their whims anymore." He leaned through the bars. "Then we will know peace."

Junior stewed on those words longer than he'd have liked. He had been in the service of liars and frauds just to get this far, and he honestly had no idea what he would do when he was ever free of them — if he was ever free of them. All he knew was the creature standing across from him was no better than the rest.

"I'm just trying to survive," he said.

"Then quit this team and improve your chances."

"It's not that simple."

"Isn't it? Their luck will soon run out. Where does that leave you when it does? Or your mother?"

Junior marched up to the bars. "I don't want to hear another word about my parents."

"But they were such an interesting couple. Sworn enemies

turned lovers. A story to warm the heart." Taranis spoke the last word as if fighting back a surge of nausea. "Your father was tasked with killing her but failed. As I understand it, your teammates were too."

Junior ground his teeth.

"As you said, I like to eavesdrop."

The ship pivoted hard. The floor slipped beneath Junior's feet and he collided with the bars. Taranis slid back, accepting the fall, and landed on his feet against the tilted wall.

Showoff. Junior clutched his shoulder as pain shot through it. That shoulder had partly healed from his fight with Kazan on Mogaddu, but he still found it tender.

"Has your healer not fixed it yet?" asked Taranis as the room leveled back out.

"What does the Jaculus want?!" Junior shouted through gritted teeth, knowing it was only a matter of time before he was summoned for whatever emergency had just befallen the ship.

Taranis shrugged. "He's a force of nature. Who am I to say what nature wills?"

Useless. Junior marched for the door. He had so many more things he wanted to ask: was the Jaculus a Zoboros? How did he replicate faces? He had a theory, but it was clear he'd never get far enough with Taranis to confirm it.

"Do you want to know why he gave your father that scar?"

Junior stopped, his hand on the knob. "Because he didn't like my father's face enough to steal it."

Taranis chuckled. Junior wasn't sure if he'd ever heard Taranis laugh before, but it sounded unnatural, like he was learning how to do it while he tried.

"Because your father didn't play his game."

"He's a shapeshifter, not a child."

"One that has lived for centuries, perhaps longer. We are but passing things to him, only as valuable as the entertainment we bring him."

Junior smiled. Taranis hadn't denied his shapeshifter theory. "How did you beat him?" he asked. "How did you get the sword?"

"By playing along," answered Taranis.

Alarms sounded, and the ship flooded with red light.

Chapter 6

Seeds of Doubt

Team members rushed onto the bridge: Li in her nightgown, Ristin in an oversized concert T-shirt, Makoto in nothing but his boxers (the Nurrano tended to run hot). Some had yet to emerge, like Jaden, who was probably sleeping through the blaring alarms. Chenji envied him for that. The changeling couldn't sleep even on a normal night.

"What's going on?!" asked Kano as he burst into the room. He was frantic but also...alert. Not yawning and groveling like the others. Had he been wide awake before the alarms sounded too? Chenji had heard whispers that Kano struggled with nightmares while aboard the *Dormarch*, but he hadn't noticed anything unusual during their time on the *Shirlena*.

"Tractor beam," answered Sterling, punching the controls with his bionic fist. "How did we not see this coming?!"

Everyone turned to the bot.

"Advanced cloaking," said T8, shaking its wide head. "*Very* advanced cloaking."

Chenji scanned the viewport but saw only the void of space.

Advanced cloaking indeed. "How close are they?" he asked.

The bot hesitated. "I don't know."

"What do you mean you don't know?" said Li. "I thought a ship had to be right next to us to catch us in a tractor beam."

"So did I," muttered T8.

"We're up against something new," said Carmichael. "To stations!"

The others scrambled for their combat gear, but Chenji kept staring out the viewport. Was the enemy ship too far away to see, or was it invisible? Either option meant technology beyond his comprehension.

Poterian technology.

Sterling remained silent at the controls, but the way he tapped his big fingers told Chenji that even the Poterian prince was nervous.

"Have you tried flushing the cannons?" asked Junior. The team stopped in their panicked tracks as the pyro entered, also looking far too alert to have just been roused. "If the radar isn't picking them up, we can spot them the old-fashioned way."

"We're too close to Republic-controlled space, fleshling," said T8. "The IDF would pick up the firefight on their scanners."

"Then we agree it's not the IDF who caught us," said Junior. "So whoever it is will have to engage the IDF too. That could give us the chance to slip away."

"Or get blasted in the crossfire," said Carmichael. "If they wanted us dead, they'd have fired on us by now. Let's wait and see how this plays out."

"I'll tell you how it plays out," snapped Junior. "They storm the ship, take my mother, and kill the rest of us."

Chenji made himself scarce, as did the others. This was

Carmichael's fight.

"They will attack if we shoot first," said Carmichael. "But no one in their right mind wants to storm a ship filled with Zoboros, so we bluff as best we can. Angeline, stay here on the bridge where we can best defend you." She nodded.

Defend against who, though? Chenji morphed his eyes into yellow cat's eyes, but still saw nothing outside.

"Chenji."

He turned, surprised to find the angry pyro behind him. Junior rarely spoke to him (or anyone for that matter). It made him uneasy.

"Can you shapeshift into anything intelligent?" he asked.

"Intelligent?"

"Like people. Humans. Nurranos."

"I mean, I can barely turn into a bird anymore without having some trouble." Chenji chuckled awkwardly at his own joke, but Junior's stare snuffed out any trace of humor. "I can't. Not to say my animals are dumb, I just...I can't turn into anything that you could have a deep conversation with. Why?"

"Never mind." Junior turned away.

"Wait!" Chenji caught him by the shoulder. For most team members that would require some reach, but he and Junior were of a similar size. "What would you have me turn into?"

"Nothing. Just curious."

Curious my ass. His cat instincts sensed fear. "What are you up to?"

Junior looked around. Everyone was too busy putting on their gear or discussing game plans to notice them, so he lowered his voice. "The Jaculus is a shapeshifter."

"What?!" Junior shushed him. "You think he's here?" Chenji

whispered.

"How do you think they found us? This ship uses cloaking tech too, and the chances of anyone catching us while using it are microscopic. Unless, of course, someone on board was giving away our position."

Chenji felt a knot form in his stomach. "Then he could be anybody...how do I know it's not you?"

Junior let a small flame spark in his palm. "This shapeshifter may mimic faces, but I doubt he can mimic powers. Your new eyeballs tell me you're still a changeling, but just in case." He held the fire close to Chenji's face.

Chenji flinched from its sting. "What are you—?"

"Heat made the fake skin peel."

"We should tell Carmichael. He—"

"No!" Junior blocked Chenji before he could take a step. "If the Jaculus is here, we can't risk him knowing that we're onto him."

"The Jaculus is here?" said Jaden. Chenji and Junior snapped around to find him standing there. Jaden shrugged. "Looked like you guys were having an interesting conversation."

Junior held his burning hand to Jaden's face.

"Hey, what the hell?"

"He's clear," said Junior. "Just annoying."

"Manners..."

"We need a more discrete way to find the assassin," said Chenji. "Something that doesn't risk burning everyone's faces."

"Why are we burning faces?" asked Kano. The three of them shushed him and pulled him into their circle.

"Use your powers," said Chenji.

"What?"

"Just do it," hissed Junior.

Energy thrummed in Kano's hand. Chenji and Junior proceeded to fill him and Jaden in on the situation.

"So your plan is to burn everyone's faces?" said Kano.

"We're workshopping it," mumbled Junior.

Chenji shook his shaggy head. "We should be more strategic. The Jaculus would have to corner someone to take their place." He paused. The thought of one of their teammates being left behind (or worse) upset him. The same concern was written on Kano and Jaden's faces. "Junior, you were the only one alone with him that we know of, but I'm banking on the theory that the Jaculus can't mimic powers."

"A theory which Junior came up with..." added Jaden.

"Before we go down that rabbit hole, was anyone else alone from the time Junior fought the Jaculus to the time we boarded the ship?"

Kano paled. "Li..." he whispered.

Chenji's heart almost sank into his gut. She had stayed behind to help Ragar. Alone. Now "she" was in her combat gear, loading seedling pods into slots beneath her wrists. "I doubt the Jaculus would know how to use her gear," he said.

"He's a master assassin," said Junior. "The Poterian Emperor trusted him. We can't take any chances."

Chenji wanted to ask where Junior was getting all this information, but he was too consumed by the thought that his closest friend on the ship could be gone.

"How do we...rule her out?" asked Kano, avoiding eye contact with the group.

"Watch and learn," said Jaden, marching toward her. If Chenji'd had a bad feeling about this before, he had an even worse one now.

"What do you want, Jaden?" asked Li. She didn't look up as she laced her boots.

"I've got this cramp in my leg."

"You're a big boy. Stretch it out." She jammed a seedling pod into her boot.

"It's really gonna slow me down on this mission. Could you just...you know..."

Cera hustled over. "Li, we need you to run a check on Warp's vitals. If anything happens, we may need her in the field."

"Coming." Li hurried past Jaden. "Get your gear on, Jaden. And comb your hair."

Jaden frowned, too busy adjusting his hair to pursue.

Junior rolled his eyes and started after Li.

"Wait—" said Chenji, but Junior was already well ahead, fire flickering in his palm. He held the flame to Li's arm, subtle enough so that no one else would have noticed, Chenji had to give him that, but Li immediately felt the heat.

"Junior, what the hell are you doing?"

"Sorry. Didn't notice I was doing it."

Li's stare shifted toward Chenji and Kano, both of whom were pretending to check the ship's scanners, but it was no use.

"What are you boys up to?" she asked, marching over.

"Just searching for the hidden ship," said Chenji. He pretended to peek out the viewport, but he was really looking at the reflection, where he saw Li's crosshairs shift toward Kano, who was guiltily rubbing his trembling hands together.

"Why did he just try to burn me?" she demanded.

"He wasn't trying to burn you," said Kano, eyes unable to meet hers.

"Stop talking…" muttered Chenji under his breath.

"Why did Jaden ask me to heal him?"

Kano turned a bright red. *Oh here we go.* "He wanted to check that you still had your powers."

Chenji cut in before she could cross-examine, figuring they might as well come clean before Kano dug a deeper hole. "We think the assassin is a shapeshifter!" Everyone stopped what they were doing. He hadn't meant to say that so loud.

"You thought…" Li paused, rage swelling in her face. "Well, I guess that rules out the four of you, because you're still idiots." She stormed past Jaden. "And I told you to put your gear on!"

Chenji had never seen Jaden move so fast. Nor had he ever felt more like an idiot than he did now. Not only had he hurt Li's feelings, but now he'd given away their strategy to the whole team.

"The assassin guy is here?" asked Makoto.

"He must have given away our position!" exclaimed Ristin.

Panic ensued. People started pointing fingers, loudly declaiming their innocence while loading their weapons in case anyone challenged it. Worst of all was Junior, who just stared at Chenji and Kano in cold, disappointed silence.

"*That's enough!*" barked Carmichael, stunning the room into silence. He rarely raised his voice like that. "We're almost there."

Chenji turned to the viewport. Blackness had consumed it. The only remaining stars sat along the edges of the glass, disappearing behind something. *A ship.* The hairs on Chenji's neck rose, and he let out an involuntary growl. He didn't know much about ships, but he recognized the spikes coming off the dark vessel. Anyone who grew up hearing stories about the war knew those spikes.

"Poterians," he muttered.

"Worse," said Carmichael, loading his shotgun.

"The *Derelict*," said Kano, looking even paler than when Li had yelled at him. "Palorex's old ship. The one Taranis used to escape Famora."

"Which means the Jaculus is working with Danadas," said Junior.

"Not necessarily," said Carmichael. "But he's certainly found a way to track us. Angeline, away from the windows and doors. Everyone else form a perimeter."

"That won't work," said Junior. "Not when the Jaculus could be among us."

"I know my team," said Carmichael. "The Jaculus is not on this bridge."

But he could be on this ship. It fit Junior's theory. Someone as skilled as the Jaculus could surely slip past T8's security systems.

An idea dawned on Chenji. Junior and Carmichael continued to argue about the plan, but he tuned them out and focused on the transformation. Lightning flashed in his mind. *Shut it out. The team needs me*. He took a deep breath, let the scales run up his arms and legs. He fell on all fours, lizard tail stretching out behind him, vision disappearing as his eyes were replaced by scales. Chenji the Changeling didn't need eyes.

He let out a pulse, felt it reverberate through the ship. Felt the footsteps padding across the bridge, all familiar. There was a pair of footsteps in the lower decks too, behind metal bars. A prisoner. *A monster.* Lightning flashed. What was all this noise? He hissed at the strangers around him, recoiled.

"Chenji, what's wrong?" a voice asked.

Chenji, that's my name. He shook his lizard head, refocused on the pulses. The monster still sat, heart rate calm and even. Wait...there was another pulse down there. A few doors from the prisoner, so faint he could barely sense it.

But it was there.

He morphed back into his Human form, his stretchy pajamas adjusting around him. He could see again, and he saw that all eyes were on him now.

"I found our assassin."

Chapter 7

Familiar Faces

The air grew colder as they followed Chenji's lizard tail down the ladder and into darkness. Kano gripped the rungs tight. Never had he been so afraid of their own ship. Even with Chenji knowing their enemy's exact location, Kano still felt they had a disadvantage. The Jaculus had taken down the entire ground team last time; what were three of them against the master assassin?

Makoto slipped on a rung just below him, then cursed as he corrected himself.

"Easy," said Kano. "This time, we're the ones with the element of surprise."

"I hope so."

They crowded into the dim, narrow hallway at the bottom of the ladder. Chenji took the lead, slithering along, while Makoto and Kano padded behind, checking each door in case the Jaculus had somehow tricked the changeling's senses. The rest of the team remained on the bridge; it didn't make sense to risk sending anyone else into such tight quarters, especially when they awaited an imminent confrontation with Orlovs.

Many, many Orlovs.

Chenji stopped at one of the sealed utility doors and hissed.

Kano cleared his throat. "We know you're in there!" he shouted in the deepest voice he could muster. "Come out, *now*!"

Nothing happened.

"Feels like a trap," said Makoto.

Power rushed to Kano's fists in agreement. "Open the door," he told Makoto, "but let me throw the first punch."

Makoto placed his hand on the button and braced. The utility closets were notoriously small – their target wouldn't have anywhere to go but forward.

"Ready?" asked Kano.

Two heads nodded, one Nurrano, one scaly.

Makoto punched the button and dove out of the way. Kano drove his fist forward but then froze with surprise.

"What are you waiting for?" asked Makoto, picking himself back up.

Kano shushed him. Inside the closet was not a master assassin, but a woman barely older than himself, with dark bangs and red nails that he'd seen before in a closet much like this one.

"Mila," muttered Makoto.

Kano was surprised that she hadn't turned invisible yet. But then he realized her eyes were closed. Her body was wrapped in a metallic stealth suit, her back against the wall and arms folded over her chest like she'd been laid to rest.

"Is she…dead?" asked Makoto.

"No," said Chenji, returning to his Human form. "I think she's—"

"Look out!" Makoto drove his baton forward. Kano saw why: steel glinted beneath Mila's hand, though she was too asleep to use it. He held his brother back, but the baton came close enough to zap the intruder. Her eyes shot open. She gasped and drove her knife at them.

Chenji morphed into a snake and lunged, coiling round and round until Mila's hands were forced to her sides and her knife rendered useless.

"She was sedated," said Kano.

"Not anymore," she said, struggling within Chenji's grip.

"Oops," said Makoto, rubbing the back of his bald head.

Kano turned to Mila. "How did you get here?"

"We heard rumors you were on Darraden," she said, the shock subsiding, replaced by her coy smile. "It didn't take long to figure out you were holing up with the Famoran mechanic. From there, finding your ship was easy."

"What rumors?" pressed Kano.

Mila shrugged. "I don't know where Grandpa gets his information." The ship shuddered. They had landed inside the *Derelict*. "But maybe you can ask him yourself."

Makoto sparked his baton. "Come out into the hallway," he said. "Slowly."

She rolled her eyes at the baton. "You got lucky last time. Don't push it."

"Luck had nothing to do with it," said Kano. That got a smile from his brother, who had subdued Mila with that same baton on the *Dormarch*. The smile faded, though, as Makoto's gaze shifted to the door at the end of the hall. The door to danger.

T8 claimed the prisoner's cuffs were still active, that he hadn't moved an inch, but Kano felt uneasy knowing he and Mila had been down here alone. She could have slipped him something, tampered with something, planned something in case of her capture.

"I'll check on him," said Kano, slapping the knife out of Mila's pinned hand. "You two get her upstairs."

Makoto frowned as he stared up the long ladder. "One of us is getting the better part of this deal." He hoisted Mila over his shoulder, Chenji still wrapped around her, and began to climb, grunting with every step. Kano waited until they were a good way up before approaching the infamous door. Power rushed into one hand. With the other, he struck the button. The door whooshed open and Taranis sat inside, still behind bars, still cuffed, and still meditating.

"You should be thanking me," the prisoner said, eyes closed.

"Why?"

"If I had ratted out your stowaway, you wouldn't have your rematch with Danadas."

"I don't want a rematch," he said, though his powers said otherwise. They churned within his hands at the thought of the evil old man who had betrayed him. The man who had sent him and his friends on the run. "And I don't need to fight. We have his granddaughter hostage."

"You watched that man slaughter half his family and you think *one* granddaughter will stop him from storming this ship?" Kano gulped. He knew it was true. "There is only one way you come out of this alive."

"What's in it for you?" he asked. Danadas had once been

Taranis's employer, though Kano knew there was little love between them. "This is your opportunity to be free of this prison cell. You'd waste it helping us?"

"After a while, all prisons start to look the same."

Kano was about to lash out, to tell Taranis that he was the reason they were trapped here in the first place, but then he realized Taranis was referring to more than just the Orlovs or the bars of pure calladium. He was referring to the time he'd spent as a child in an IDF prison, where Kano's parents had run experiments on him.

Kano sighed. "How do we beat Danadas?"

"He is powerful, but he has a weakness." Taranis stepped closer to the bars. "His vision. He wants the Orlov family restored to its former glory, something not achieved since they were banished from Mogaddu in the War of Three Kings. It blinds him. That is why, when he looks at Angeline Hendricks, he sees only a weapon."

"And you don't?"

"You miss the point. If you present Project Vortex to him, he will be blind to the knife at his back."

The ship shook. The lights flickered, casting dim shadows over everything, including Taranis.

"You should return to your team," he said.

For once, Kano agreed with him. He hurried out the door and up the ladder, his mind buzzing. Did Taranis really believe they could distract Danadas, or was he setting them up for failure? Using Angeline as bait seemed an easy way to lose whatever small advantage they still had, and Taranis could then take the credit for their downfall. There had to be another way out.

When he reached the bridge, though, escape looked downright impossible. Thousands of soldiers stood outside the viewport, every breastplate, boot, and blaster sporting the Orlov family's signature crimson. It made the *Derelict's* hangar look like it was bathed in blood. *And all we have is one measly prisoner.* Kano hated to admit it, but he could see Taranis's point. Nothing could stop the tidal wave that was about to crash down upon them.

Nothing except Project Vortex.

Kano joined the others. Everyone was gathered around Carmichael's command chair; everyone but Cera, who was holding Mila a good distance away with a rope of green energy. A quick head count told Kano that someone was missing.

"Where's Chenji?" he asked.

"Channel twelve," said Jaden, tapping his earpiece.

Kano adjusted his communicator. A buzzing noise came out. "Is he an insect?"

"It was the only thing small enough to slip past the Orlovs' sensors," said Carmichael. "We need him to reach the *Derelict's* mainframe and disable the tractor beam."

"How long until Chenji reaches the mainframe?" asked Kano.

"Too long," muttered Sterling. Outside, the sea of crimson was parting down the middle, and out of the newly formed passageway hobbled Danadas Orlov, his wrinkled hand balled around the massive jewel that topped his cane. *A cane he barely needs.* Kano clenched his fists as he watched the old trickster approach.

"Let's see how much time our new prisoner buys us," said Carmichael. He nodded to Cera, who led Mila toward the glass.

"Wait!" said Kano. He hurried over and blocked Cera and Mila from reaching the main viewing area. "This is the man who killed half his family in front of us. Mila won't stop him from storming the ship." The words tasted bitter coming out of his mouth, but that didn't make Taranis's point any less true.

"I told them the same thing," grumbled Junior.

"It's the best play we have right now," said Carmichael.

"Not exactly." Kano turned to Angeline, who stood there as firm and dignified as ever. Slowly, heads started turning her way. She stiffened but looked no less resolute.

Carmichael's eyes narrowed. "What are you proposing?"

"We take her off the ship and dangle her in front of Danadas. That'll get him talking with whoever we send out to negotiate while Chenji disables the tractor beam."

"That gives up our only real advantage," said Cera. "He'll just mow over us with his forces and take her."

"Not if we take those cuffs off her."

Protests erupted from the team. Li told him he was reckless; Ristin said he was suicidal. And all the while, not a trace of emotion betrayed Angeline's face. Kano wondered what she was thinking. Did it bother her to be offered up as bait? Or had she just gotten so used to people deciding things on her behalf?

"If her powers go off while we're still stuck under the tractor beam, we'll be destroyed too," said Cera.

"Then we better get that tractor beam turned off," said Kano.

Carmichael smiled. "And who would you put on the negotiating team?" he asked.

Kano blinked. He hadn't expected the captain to go along

with his idea so easily. "Myself for starters. Danadas and I have history, not to mention the same powers. It'll be easy for me to get him monologuing."

"Wait, you're not actually considering this, are you?" said Junior, marching up to the captain.

"Weren't you the one who hated the old plan?" asked Jaden.

"Doesn't mean I have to like the new one. That's my mother we're using as bait."

The sound of static erupted from outside. They all looked out the viewport. Danadas had finally reached the front of his army, and now was tapping a microphone against his hand.

"Carmichael and company," the old man's voice boomed through the hangar, "you have sixty seconds to deliver Project Vortex to me. Do so, and I will release you."

"That is shit of the bull," muttered Akio.

"It's the best offer you'll get," said Mila, stiffening as Cera tightened the rope.

Light flared outside, making the Orlovs' armor glisten. Kazan descended to Danadas's side upon twin jets of blue flame. His bare, coal-black feet touched down ever so softly, his twisted smile letting everyone know that nothing else he was about to do would be quite so gentle.

Kano turned to Junior, who now had his full attention set upon the viewport. Kazan was the maniac who had burned Junior's back and nearly killed him in the fight ring. That certainly didn't bode well for Kano's negotiation plans. And it made him wonder how many others from Taranis's old crew had survived the destruction of the *Dormarch*. As if to answer his question, Yui emerged from the crowd and took her place opposite Kazan. Kano noticed a smile spreading across Mila's face.

Arguments exploded across the bridge, half the room agreeing with Junior to keep his mother here, the other half demanding to send her out. Kano was dumbstruck; he hadn't realized his plan would be *this* controversial. *Goes to show where Taranis's ideas get you.* But with the Orlov army looming, tensions were certainly high.

"I'll go!" announced Angeline. The room went silent. Junior stared daggers at her, but she ignored him, her gaze fixed on Mila. "If it holds off any unnecessary violence, then it is worth a try. Even if it is a 'bluff' as you say, captain."

Carmichael nodded. "It usually is."

"I'm coming too," said Junior, stepping forward.

"This isn't a party," said Cera. "We can't risk more of us getting captured or killed."

"If we lose my mother, we lose everything anyway. This stupid risk only works if we go all-in on it."

Carmichael studied Junior as he prepared his final judgment. "I put this team together to do the impossible," he began. "But I can't approve of sending you and Kano out there alone against an army."

"Thank you," said Cera and Li in unison.

"That's why I'm going too."

A new wave of protests descended upon the bridge, but Carmichael ignored them. "Sterling, lower the ramp at my signal," he ordered. "The rest of you: keep Mila secured. Once we take Angeline out there, Mila will be the only thing stopping Danadas from blasting the ship to oblivion." The others just stared at him, dumbfounded.

Is he insane? wondered Kano as he followed Carmichael to the exit, Junior and Angeline following behind.

Maybe we all are.

90

Chapter 8

Archenemies

They marched down the ramp, Carmichael at the front, Angeline at the back, Junior and Kano flanking either side of the formation. Junior checked on his mother, who nodded to him, a reminder to keep his cool. Not an easy task when facing down thousands of blasters.

Or the Morabani who tried to burn me alive.

Danadas opened his arms wide. "Finally, we meet again!" He hobbled toward them, his soldiers exchanging concerned looks, but the old man didn't seem the least bit worried for his safety. "Not since the days of Niscelles could anyone say they were in the presence of *two* Zoboros who opened Iramwerta's gate." He nodded toward Kano and Junior, the latter of whom rolled his eyes. He recognized Danadas's subtle threat. The story he referenced, Three Kings of Mogaddu, ended with the kings being consumed and destroyed by their newfound powers. In his father's circles, "Going the way of Niscelles" was code for a Zoboros who was a danger to themselves.

The real treat, though, came when Danadas stopped in

front of Angeline and bowed. "Madam Hendricks, it is a pleasure to meet you."

"I'm sure it is."

Junior couldn't help but smile at that. It fizzled, though, when he met Kazan's deranged stare.

"How's the back?" the Morabani asked him.

"How's servitude?" said Junior.

"Now, now, let's keep it civil," said Danadas, his eyes on Angeline's unrestrained hands. "Madam Hendricks, would you kindly step forward?"

A Lusitani emerged from the crowd of soldiers, a fresh power dampener in its hands. Carmichael waved to Angeline to stay put.

"The cuffs stay off until we are safely away from this ship," said Carmichael. "Any attempt to harm us, and things will not end well for you."

"You are in no position to negotiate," said Danadas. "I am extending you this courtesy to avoid unnecessary bloodshed."

"So am I." Carmichael waved to the viewport. Cera led Mila into view. Akio sat upon the prisoner's shoulder, knife in hand.

Danadas's once-cordial face darkened. "Release her."

"We will drop her off at the nearest habitable system for you to pick up." Carmichael paused. "That is, unless you leave us with no ship or crew to fly her there."

Junior noticed Kazan's smile widening.

"I did not want to do this," said Danadas. He snapped his finger. The soldiers parted and another Lusitani emerged. It had a leash in hand. Junior panicked. If Chenji was at the end of that leash, their plan was ruined.

But when the Lusitani tugged, it was Li who stumbled out of

the crowd, her green eyes puffy, an electric collar clamped around her neck.

"You bastard!" Kano started forward but Angeline held him back. Yui assumed a defensive stance, icy mist hissing from her hands while blasters aimed.

We were right *about the Jaculus*, Junior realized. Kano seemed hellbent on freeing Li, but Junior was more worried about the inside of the *Shirlena*. He glanced back. Ristin, Makoto, and Akio had already surrounded the "Li" inside the bridge. But they would need a hell of a lot more backup to subdue the imposter.

"It does not have to be this way," Danadas boomed, even without his microphone, his own power hurling his voice across the length of the hangar. "Zoboros blood is sacred. I would not have it spilled on my ship if I can help it. Bring my granddaughter to me and I will return your friend."

"Kano, Junior, I'm sorry!" cried Li. Tears streaked down her cheeks. "Someone hit me while I was healing Ragar in the shed. When I woke up, I was here."

"It's not your fault," said Kano, power thrumming into his fists.

Yes it was, thought Junior, though he kept that to himself. Li shouldn't have stuck around by herself in the...shop...

Why did she say 'shed'? She had been inside the shop where Ragar was injured. Everyone else was focused on their opponents, but Junior zeroed in on Li. Their eyes met. She winked, and in her iris flashed a bit of yellow.

"Kano," Junior whispered. "That's not—"

The ground shook. Soldiers tripped and bumped into each other, cursing in confusion.

"What's going on?!" demanded Danadas.

"One of our stabilizers blew out!" answered a soldier as the floor began to tilt.

Danadas spun left and right, baffled and furious, but when he noticed his prisoner's eyes were now fully yellow, he paled.

"You shouldn't have let me on your ship," hissed Li in a voice that was not her own. Her Lusitani guard reached for her when the lights went out across the hangar. Confused shouts erupted from the Orlov army in the total darkness. Junior heard many of them tumble down the floor as it continued to tilt. Emergency lights flickered on, and in their dimness, Junior saw the body of the Lusitani guard lying with the leash twisted around its neck.

Metal scraped against metal. Ships slid down the sloping floors, their anchors slashed, while soldiers ran from them or else were crushed in their paths.

"We need to get back to the ship!" shouted Kano. He sent a shockwave barreling toward Danadas. The old man dropped his cane and, reaching out his hand, did something Junior couldn't explain. He...*caught* the shockwave, absorbed it, the power thrumming in his wrinkled palm until it came rushing back at Kano. Junior expected Kano to dive out of the way, but instead Kano aimed his palms at it.

"Don't try it!" exclaimed Junior, but it was too late. The shockwave collided with Kano's powers as he attempted to redirect it, and the resounding crack launched Kano back toward the *Shirlena*.

Carmichael ran after Kano while Junior held his ground against Danadas, expecting another shockwave, but a squad of Orlov guards swept in between them instead and surrounded the patriarch, spears drawn. They escorted the old man deeper into the chaos of their ranks and away from the Zoboros intruders.

Or away from the Jaculus. Junior made to pursue Danadas when a familiar voice shouted behind him.

"I've been waiting a long time for this!" Kazan marched toward him, fire blazing in each hand, bare feet struggling to gain traction as the floor kept angling upward. Junior saw his opening. He sent a jet of flame high toward Kazan's head. The Morabani leaned back out of the way, and Junior used his other hand to lash Kazan's feet with a whip of flame. It was all he needed to send Kazan tumbling down with the rest of the blubbering Orlov troops.

Moron.

"Look out!" his mother cried.

Junior felt the chill against his neck. Just an inch from it loomed a blade of ice.

"Kazan didn't get the chance to tell you," began Yui, "but you bastards are the reason we got stranded in the desert, so forgive me if this feels a little personal."

"You got stranded because you took up with Taranis," said Junior, careful not to move with the jagged blade so close, though it was getting harder to avoid as the tilting floor leaned his weight toward it.

"It's better than what Clemens had for me," she said, edging the blade along his neck. Junior felt blood trickle out, only to freeze against his skin.

"But is it what you wanted?" asked Angeline, holding her ground. "Is killing him really going to bring you what you seek?"

Yui sneered, but her hand trembled. Junior saw the battle

raging beneath her dark stare. Then he saw the butt of Carmichael's shotgun strike the back of her head.

"Keep moving!" ordered Carmichael as Yui's unconscious body slid down the hangar floor. Junior paused, unsure how to feel about being saved by Carmichael. The captain kept marching toward their ship, blasting away any Orlov guards in his path while the engines hummed to life.

"Everyone get your asses inside!" shouted Sterling over the *Shirlena*'s loudspeakers.

Junior grabbed his mother and together they ran up the ramp, Carmichael beside them. They found Kano sitting inside the cargo hold with Li (the real one) running her glowing hands over his head, which had a considerable lump protruding from it.

"I can't believe you thought *that* was me," she said.

"I know, I know. I deserve this..."

Junior lurched as the forward thrusters engaged, pushing their ship backwards toward the edge of the hangar. The tractor beam was down! Junior felt a moment of relief as the liftgate sealed and his view of the fumbling Orlov army was cut off. Chenji had done it. He'd—

"Chenji's still back there!" cried Junior.

Carmichael spun around and pounded on the door control but the liftgate wouldn't open. The ground leveled beneath their feet, and they knew then they were too late. They had escaped the *Derelict*.

"Don't worry, captain, I've got Chenji all taken care of," hissed a voice from across the cargo hold.

Chapter 9

The Deal

Jaden had never run so fast in his life. *This can't be happening. This can't be happening.* He knew the others were thinking it too – Makoto, Ristin, and even little Akio had sprinted well ahead of him, their bodies much more conditioned for field work.

But field work wasn't supposed to happen *inside* their ship.

By the time he reached the cargo hold, the others were already positioned with their weapons drawn: Carmichael with his shotgun, Makoto with his batons, Akio with his knife, and the Zoboros (Li, Kano, Ristin, and Junior) with their palms raised; all focused on a single enemy.

An enemy who was still wearing Li's face.

"The galaxy's finest heroes," hissed the assassin. "I'm humbled."

"Shut up," said Chenji. He stood between the assassin and the team, the electric collar that the Jaculus had once worn now clamped around his neck. The Jaculus stayed close behind his tall body, using him as a shield while its finger hovered over the shock button on the leash.

"What are your demands?" said Carmichael.

"A conversation."

"Well you've got it."

The Jaculus smiled in a way that Jaden had never seen Li smile before. It made him shudder.

"I'm sorry, is my face bothering you?" asked the Jaculus, his yellow eyes zeroing in on Jaden.

"Yes!" exclaimed Li before he could reply.

The Jaculus grabbed his false face and ripped it off. Beneath it was a thinner face of green scales, but Jaden was more focused on the face he'd just tossed on the floor. The face of a friend. He caught Li staring at it too, her gray-gold complexion draining from her real face.

"Now that's better," said the Jaculus. He tugged away the rest like he was pulling off the hood of his jacket. Long, dark hair spilled out, casting shadows around his face, until all Jaden could see clearly were his rotten, crooked teeth.

Warp appeared in a puff of smoke along with Cera and Mila, the latter still bound in a rope of green energy. Their prisoner gave the Jaculus a look of pure disgust.

"I think we can all assume that you don't work for the Orlovs," said Jaden to the assassin. "So who do you work for?"

"I asked for a conversation, not an interrogation." The Jaculus teased the shock button with his thumb.

Jaden clammed up. He saw the frustration and defeat on Chenji's face. Under normal circumstances, the changeling could shrink to a smaller size and slip out of the collar, but the presence of electricity drove a nail in that. Fear made Chenji's powers unstable, unpredictable – he could turn into something too large and break his neck. Jaden didn't know where the phobia came from, nor did he know how the Jaculus had learned about it.

"What would you like to discuss?" asked Carmichael.

"An alliance."

Confused looks shot across the cargo hold. "A what?!" Jaden spat back.

"You want to go to Poteria. I can get you there."

That doesn't make any sense. A dozen questions and accusations erupted from the team, but Jaden's was loudest. "If you wanted to help us, why did you attack us on Darraden and kill our only lead?!"

"Clemens was a fool. Follow him and you would have been as dead as he is." Another unsettling smile spread across his face. "Besides, I wanted to see if you were worth my time."

Junior took an angry step forward, but Carmichael waved him back. "And what made us worth your time?" asked the captain.

Those yellow eyes flicked to the back of the room where Angeline stood. "Why, Project Vortex of course."

Figures. All roads led to her. Yet Jaden hadn't even realized she was standing in the room. Strange that the most powerful Zoboros he'd ever met could have such a subtle presence.

"She has a name," said Chenji, in response to which the Jaculus gave the leash a sharp tug. It made Jaden want to strangle their new passenger.

"Do not mistake me for an agent of the IDF," said the Jaculus. "Or worse, an Orlov." Mila seethed in the corner. "I'm not on some crusade to destroy people and armies with Angeline's powers. Quite the opposite. I want to remove her from the reach of those who would use her for ill."

"How noble of you," said Cera. She had generated a hand of green energy poised to reach out and snatch the Jaculus should she find an opening.

"Cera, is it?" asked the Jaculus. "Your face is familiar. You've had to do things to survive that you are not proud of, yes?" Cera stiffened but gave no reply. "I've seen your face over many lifetimes. The face of compromise. I've made compromises too. And they are always for the betterment of the galaxy."

He can't be serious. Did this creature just claim to be both ancient *and* a hero? If any of that was true, then why in Jaden's vast study of history had he never stumbled on the Jaculus (or any species remotely like him)? Surely Palorex's top assassin would have gotten a mention somewhere in the books. Either the Jaculus was full of shit, or he was really good at his job.

"Why not have this conversation on Darraden?" asked Carmichael. "Why make us go through all this trouble before offering any help?"

The Jaculus returned his stare to Mila. "Because I can smell an Orlov trap a mile away. They were going to snatch you outside of Darraden. By posing as your healer, I got a chance to cripple their ship and give you a small window to escape. I suggest we take it before they regroup."

More uneasy glances shifted around the room. No one was convinced.

"You were an assassin for Poteria," said Jaden. "If you really can get us through the Rift, who's to say you wouldn't sell us out and hand Angeline right to them?"

"I served the former emperor only. You can ask your

deposed prince upstairs."

"I can vouch for that," Sterling's voice came suddenly over the intercom. He and T8 had remained upstairs to guide the ship away from the Orlovs. "But I wouldn't trust another word out of his mouth."

Chenji shifted uncomfortably beneath the collar.

"My, my, Chenji," hissed the Jaculus. "You've been such a good little doggie. Maybe I'll take you for a walk later."

"I'll tear your face off," said Chenji through gritted teeth.

"Beat you to it." The Jaculus scooped Li's "face" off the floor with his foot and flung it at Chenji. The changeling squirmed, and many members of the team, including Jaden, took an angry step forward.

"The ship to Poteria leaves in two days," said the Jaculus quickly, twiddling his thumb over the shock button. "And *your* ship is already heading in the wrong direction, Captain. You'll need to decide soon if you want that ride through the Rift."

Gazes shifted toward Carmichael, who was deep in thought, shotgun still aimed.

"You can't seriously be considering this!" exclaimed Junior. *Here we go.* "He's a liar by trade. He's going to sell us out, either to the Poterians or someone else. And when he does, they'll take my mother and kill the rest of us."

The Jaculus's smile widened. "So dramatic, I love it!"

"Shut your damn mouth!"

"That's *enough*, Junior," said the captain, finality in his voice. "From what I've gathered, the Jaculus is too prideful to serve any one person or group."

The Jaculus gave a small bow. "Guilty."

"So what *are* you interested in?" asked Carmichael.

"Time, Captain Carmichael, time," said the Jaculus, yellow eyes glazing over all the people poised to strike him. "Time kills everything: people, nations, causes...but time allows it all to grow back too. Something threatens that balance. Something so powerful it could erase existence as we know it." Jaden glanced back at Angeline, who still managed to hold herself high despite what this murderous maniac was implying. "The IDF created some quiet with their containment strategy, but now the cat's out of the bag, and everyone who's anyone is coming for the prize."

"And you think Poteria would be *better*?" asked Li. "They're the most ruthless people in history." She glanced nervously at the intercom, knowing Sterling had heard every word.

"You'll find that Poterian politics have gotten interesting of late," said the Jaculus. He exchanged a look with Angeline; it was quick, but Jaden caught it. "Frankly, they might be too busy squabbling to even notice your presence. And the place I plan to bring you is far removed from their silly games anyway."

"And if that should change?" asked Jaden cautiously. "If the Poterians prove to be as brutal as we know them to be, then what?"

The assassin smiled, his hand brushing over the knife in his belt. "Then you can rest easy knowing I'll be around."

Silence fell as the team grappled with his proposition. It was insane, Jaden knew that much. And filled with lies – or at the very least half-truths. Yet if the Jaculus had wanted to hand them to their enemies, he could easily have done so by now. So what did he stand to gain by getting them across the Rift? Was it to get them in the hands of Poteria? It didn't sound like he had much love for the Poterians either.

The Jaculus cleared his throat. "Time moves fast, Captain. Tick tock. Once that ship leaves, you're back where you started, running from soldiers and Orlovs and whatever else the galaxy should like to throw at you. I know you are all tired. Tired of worrying that the clock will run out."

Carmichael drew a deep breath as he sized up the Jaculus. "Once I've got the coordinates for this ship from you, what's to stop me from ejecting you into space?"

"That ship will not leave without my say-so. Besides, what kind of friend would I be if I didn't see you off?"

"Who are we meeting there?" Cera cut in.

"I'll provide you the names of all the smugglers on the way. I'm sure T8 will do its due diligence on background checks, though the findings might be extensive."

Great. As if Jaden didn't have a bad enough feeling already. His family had used smugglers to conduct much of their business, and it was always messy. *How could it not be, when you hire people who play for the highest bidder?* Carmichael likely had similar concerns as he stepped closer to the Jaculus.

"I prefer to run from the enemy I know rather than take up with the enemy I don't," he said.

"But it's not them you're running from, is it?" whispered the Jaculus, so faint Jaden had to strain to listen. "It's her. The thing that destroyed your father and everything he could muster. You run because you don't want to see that happen again. Not anywhere. Not to anyone."

"Says the one who claims to preserve life," said Carmichael.

"We want the same thing." The Jaculus released the leash. Chenji scrambled toward the others, where Li and Makoto were quick to snap the collar off him. "Let me help you before it is too late."

Carmichael stewed on those words. Jaden didn't envy his position. He hated everything about the Jaculus's proposition, but he also hated this lifestyle: running and hiding, never knowing when luck would run out. They were in the desert, and even the rancid water looked tempting.

"We'll change course toward your coordinates," said the captain. "And while we travel, I'll want everything on these smugglers, right down to the size of their shoes. I want to know everything you know about the Rift, about the place you plan to take us, and every single creature we might happen to see in the window on the way. Is that clear?"

"Crystal," said the Jaculus. He turned toward Jaden and smiled. "Though I feel confident these smugglers won't be too much trouble."

Carmichael rolled his eyes. "Why?"

Jaden got a bad feeling in the pit of his stomach as the Jaculus continued, his stare never faltering. "Because their employers would not wish you harm."

It can't be. Jaden's heart began to pound. There was no way the galaxy could be *that* small.

"In fact, their employers paid a great deal of money to send you to Famora, Jaden," said the Jaculus. "Why not pay a little more to send you farther?"

Chapter 10

New Purpose

Famora burned. It was a bright star on the horizon, impossible to reach from the mountaintop. Kano could only listen to the distant screams and the thunder of rockets raining from Poterian ships.

"Why are you showing me this?!" he cried out. His voice echoed off the shiny black rocks of the surrounding mountains – mountains that didn't belong on his home planet – without anyone there to answer. No one ever answered him in these visions.

"*HELP!*" screamed Li. Kano turned, but she wasn't there. Her voice had carried all the way from the burning city, yet it rang much louder than any of the others.

"*KANO!*" cried Makoto. Explosions drowned out his voice.

"This is evil," Kano said to himself, heart racing.

"This is war."

He jumped. He hadn't realized the man was standing beside him, hidden beneath a blood-red cloak.

"You can speak?"

No answer came. But the questions poured out of Kano. "Is this the future? Why is this happening?"

"You can stop it," said the man, holding out his hand. Kano knew what it meant. He knew the power that frail, veiny hand held within it. He'd experienced it once in a dream like this: the thrill, the ecstasy, the overwhelming feeling that nothing could stop him. *Not even a Poterian fleet.*

"*Kano, help us!*" screamed Li in the distance. Explosions plumed across Famora. Whole structures crumbled in clouds of their own debris. Screams were silenced.

Kano grabbed the man's hand. Power surged right through to his brain. He felt awake. Alive. Like whole planet had shrunk into the palm of his hand. The whole galaxy. Power orbited around his fists in angelic wisps of white. It whispered to him.

"*Find us.*"

Find who? It didn't matter. Nothing mattered when he had this much power, not even the distance between him and the city. He looked to the man, a silent request for permission to use this. *Like I need permission.* Kano reached toward the city and let the power explode out. The shockwave erupted from his hand, a tsunami of energy rippling through the air, shaking the rocks on which he stood even when it was miles and miles away. It struck the Poterian fleet with a *crack*. Ships were crushed and shattered, their remains raining onto the city.

The wisps returned to his hand. *So much power*. Enough to destroy Danadas, and Taranis, and the entire army of—

What am I saying? Kano wasn't a killer. A destroyer. He rubbed his head, heard voices inside it that weren't his own. "*Find us, find us, find us!*" He looked at the wisps and saw something terrifying. Something that didn't belong. Something evil.

The man frowned. He waved his hand and the wisps came undone. Kano felt the energy collapsing inside him. It wanted to be free.

"Stop!" he cried, but speaking caused the shockwave to explode out his mouth and blast the mountain before him with a great, thunderous crack. It kept coming, all that power, tearing at his throat as it crumbled the rocks beneath his feet and sent him falling into the depths of the earth.

Kano jumped out of bed, a fresh puddle of sweat squishing beneath him. He was back in the infirmary, which was really just a corner of the cargo hold where they'd set up some beds, the rest of them thankfully empty. His heart began to settle while the monitor blipped beside him, running occasional brain scans to ensure that Danadas's blast hadn't caused any serious injury. Kano tapped the bump on the back of his head and winced. It was less swollen, but no less sensitive. A reminder of his defeat.

But could they be heading toward an even greater defeat? Had that dream been a warning? Could he prevent it? The man's power seemed like the answer, but he knew how the old stories went. How Zoboros went mad with power and destroyed everything. It could all be propaganda against Zoboros, but Kano saw the Three Kings at least as more of a cautionary tale. Whatever the case, he wished the man had offered an explanation, considering they were just hours from meeting their ride to Poteria.

Kano got the feeling that he should check on Jaden – maybe because he knew Jaden was about to face the demons of his past, maybe because Kano wanted a little company after that nightmare. Whatever the reason, he found himself tiptoeing down the hall to the hacker's door. Jaden was probably awake, tinkering with something like usual. When he gave a knock, though, there was no answer.

"You awake?" he whispered. Still nothing. He was about to go back to his bed when something told him to check anyway. Just in case. He tapped the panel and the door whooshed open. Jaden sat beside his bed as expected, only he had nothing to tinker with. He just stared at the wall.

"You didn't have to get all gussied up for me," said Jaden, unblinking.

Kano looked down and realized he was in nothing but a medical gown. *No wonder the walk here was so breezy.* "Promise I won't flash you."

"If I should be so lucky…"

Kano laughed, but his laughter died against Jaden's cold silence. It was unnerving. Jaden was supposed to be the idea guy, the one who was always inspired to do something, to try something, to say something out of pocket and not care about the consequences. But this rendezvous with his family's contacts had really done a number on him.

"You never told me about your family," said Kano. With anyone else, he would have used a gentler approach, but he knew with Jaden it was best to get right to the point. Still, the hacker was silent. "Do you know the smugglers we're about to meet?"

"Probably."

The door whooshed open, just in time to save Kano from fumbling through more questions.

"I checked the infirmary but Kano's—" Makoto stopped,

finally noticing his brother. "Well, a note would've been nice."

"Didn't realize I was so popular." Kano kicked back on the bed and set his bruised head tenderly on the pillow, quietly pleased to know he was being checked on. There was something comforting about having the original trio back together. They didn't often get time to themselves aboard the crowded ship, especially given how they were constantly trying to escape certain death.

Makoto angled his hand to block Kano from his vision. "Ok *Chenji*, there's no need for that."

Kano looked around, expecting to see their friend disguised as some insect or rodent, only to realize that Makoto was referring to *him* and, more specifically, to everything he'd just revealed by lying down in nothing but a medical gown.

"Don't act like you're not impressed," he said.

Jaden cracked a smile.

There he is. Kano knew this was his chance to get Jaden talking, though he would be more cautious this time.

"Random question: do you guys ever miss the *Dormarch*?" he asked.

"I don't miss the Sim," said Makoto, folding his arms. "Or everyone on board trying to kill us."

"The tanning room was nice though," said Jaden, looking sadly at his pasty arms. "Wish we could've brought that with us."

"Instead we got a stupid sword and spear," said Makoto.

Kano stirred. Carmichael had hidden those ancient weapons somewhere on their ship; weapons that were incredibly dangerous in the hands of a Zoboros. Just another reason for everyone to want to capture them.

"What's this?" asked Makoto, peeking under the bed. He drew out a bottle of Scorcher. "You steal this from Sterling?"

Jaden shrugged. "Well, we are hardened criminals now, aren't we?" He reached under his bed and pulled out three shot glasses – likely stolen too.

Makoto beamed as he poured out the drinks. They raised their glasses.

"To the most illegal thing we've ever done," said Jaden with a wink.

"To the tanning room," said Makoto.

"To the tanning room!" they cheered.

The night sped on as they laughed and reminisced over their adventures. Kano didn't realize how late it was until he noticed the bottle was almost empty.

"Wha-what do we cheers now?" asked Makoto, his head tipping forward.

"Famooora," said Jaden.

Kano hiccupped. "To Famora!"

They drank. Kano lay there in a daze, recalling memories of home while the room spun around him. When he turned to his brother, the Nurrano was passed out on the bed with the bottle cradled in his skinny arms.

"Hehe…Famora," giggled Jaden.

Kano blinked. He had questions to ask Jaden. Important questions, he was sure of it. He just couldn't remember what they were right now.

Wait, he had one. "Why'd you come to Famora?"

"Because it's a premium tourist destination," said Jaden, smiling as he raised his glass. It was only after he put it to his lips that he realized it was empty.

"Family ever visit?"

"They had an assistant to check on me." Jaden giggled to himself. "'You'll inherit the family business one day,' they said. 'At least *ten* percent of it is legal.' Boy, that was a generous figure. Hard to look legitimate when you smuggle everything imaginable, even…" he trailed, his face turning bright red.

"Smuggle what?" asked Kano. Jaden dodged his stare. Kano leaped off the bed, suddenly sobered. "Smuggle what, Jaden?"

His friend sighed. "Sounds like you already figured it out, buddy."

Kano stepped back in disbelief. He'd known Hendricks had smuggled Zoboros, but not Jaden's parents. And by the sound of it, they may not have been doing it for the Zoboros' protection like Hendricks had.

"How do you know for sure?"

"My parents thought teaching me the family business would be a good thing. They run a 'tech' company, and I learned the tech much faster than they expected. Soon I was tapping into places I shouldn't have been, and by the time they realized it, I had already dug up more than enough juicy details to blackmail them with."

Kano gulped. He disliked Jaden using blackmail against his own family almost as much as he disliked the idea of smuggling Zoboros for profit. "But were they part of Hendricks's plan?" Kano pressed. His hands trembled. Everything he thought he knew about his friend hinged on this one question.

"I don't know. I never saw anything tying them to Hendricks or Famora…not that I knew to look for that back then. They sent Zoboros all over, along with plenty of…other things. Things that would make any decent person question their morals."

Kano put his head in his hands. "Why didn't you tell me?" he asked.

"Because I wanted it far behind me. I still do. At least I can be proud of this." Jaden gestured at his little cubby: with barely enough room for his twin-sized bed, it was a far cry from his studio apartment in Famora. "At least I can be part of something good." Jaden's head slumped forward.

"You are," said Kano. He patted his friend on the shoulder, only to get a snore in reply. *Figures.* Kano hoisted his sleepy friend into bed. Jaden looked different lying there, like there was a new layer on him. A layer that separated them.

Kano lifted his brother, who was still clinging to the bottle, out of Jaden's bed and hauled him back to his room. *I need some water.* He tucked his brother in, the room spinning, then turned toward the door, where the man in the cloak was waiting for him.

"AH!"

"What?!" Makoto leaped out of bed, brandishing the bottle like one of his batons.

Kano looked again, but the man was gone. "Nothing. It's late. I'm just seeing things."

"Probably that bump on the head," said Makoto, tucking himself back in. "Not many can take a hit from Danadas and live to tell the tale."

"I wish I could've been the one dealing the hit..."

"Hey now!" Makoto was fully upright now, still waving the bottle. "That geezer has been training with his powers since way before you were even born. Plus, he had an army behind him. You can't beat yourself up for not doing the impossible."

"But if I had been stronger, if I had beaten him, I could've stopped the Jaculus from capturing Chenji. And then none of this would've happened."

"Who said none of this should've happened?" shrugged Makoto. "Maybe this is how it's meant to be."

"Not for me," said Kano.

"What's that supposed to mean?"

"It's…" Kano threw his hands up. "I can't explain it. I just get these…I see these…signs that tell me I'm supposed to be more powerful than I am. That I have so much more to unlock, but I don't know how to do it."

Makoto's eye twitched. Kano knew that was the tell that his brother was angry. "But you're one of the most powerful members on the team. Now you're gonna tell *me* of all people that you're not strong enough?"

"That's not what I meant." Kano felt a little hot under the ears.

"And what did you mean? Huh? Do you feel like you have extra weight to pull? Are mortals like me weighing you down?"

"Hey, I never said—"

"*Everybody* said!" shouted Makoto. "Everybody."

Kano sighed. He knew Makoto's lack of powers had been a touchy spot for some time. He didn't know when it started, but it seemed to get worse with each mistake Makoto made. Kano sat down beside him. "You'll get your chance to prove yourself to the team. I promise."

"You don't get it, do you? If this works, and the Jaculus somehow gets us across the Rift, then there won't *be* a chance to prove myself. Because there won't be a team anymore. We'll be finished. No more enemies chasing us – unless we manage to piss off some Poterians – and no more Zoboros to rescue. Our whole cause will be half a galaxy away, and we'll be in the half where Zoboros are accepted. We have no fight there, no purpose." He lowered his voice. "And no place for a normal guy like me."

There was a long silence. Kano had been so focused on just getting to Poteria, just surviving the day-to-day chaos they'd become so accustomed to, that he hadn't stopped to consider what would happen after they reached their destination.

"Whatever happens, Makoto, I'll always need you by my side." He patted his brother's shoulder. "You'll always have purpose to me."

That managed to get a smile out of Makoto, however small.

The door opened. Cera stood there. Kano wondered how much she might have heard through the door. Judging by the sleep she was rubbing from her eyes, he assumed not much, if anything at all.

"Good, you're both awake," she said. "We're approaching the planet now."

Chapter 11

Cloraxia

Rain pattered against Jaden's cloak. He minded his step as he followed the Jaculus down the slippery ramp and into the warm, dank air of Cloraxia.

"Perfect habitat for a snake," muttered Carmichael, his blue eyes fixed on the Jaculus's every move. Jaden was thankful the captain had taken on that responsibility. He didn't think his aching head could manage it.

How did we down the entire bottle? he wondered. At least, he assumed they'd finished the bottle. He wouldn't be surprised if Makoto had snuck the leftovers into his room. What *was* surprising, however, was what he might have told Kano last night. His memory was fuzzy, but if it was what he thought, then it would explain Kano's coldness on the ship. His friend had kept to himself in the hours leading up to the rendezvous time, and when Carmichael had chosen Jaden to accompany him in the field, Kano had been the only one *not* to volunteer to take his place. Jaden didn't blame him: profiting off slavery could certainly put a dampener on a relationship.

His shoes sank into mud as he stepped off the ramp. The whole blackened field in front of them was covered in it. *Why did he have to pick me?* He glanced back at the viewport, hoping to see his friends watching him through the glass, but they had already disappeared beneath the ship's cloaking device, the rainwater streaming off its invisible framework. Despite their protests about being left behind, Carmichael believed the greater threat here wasn't an ambush at the rendezvous, but an ambush on the ship, so he'd ordered them all to stay.

Jaden wasn't too fond of that decision. Would *one* Zoboros really have been too much to ask for? Especially considering who their guide was. Even the way the assassin walked made him uneasy. Soft, tender footfalls that sprang from one to the other, creating the illusion that the Jaculus was floating over the mud. Meanwhile, Jaden and Carmichael looked like silly tourists squishing into the rotted earth with their boots, each step dredging an odor that he guessed came from dead things buried beneath the muck. It made his head throb even more.

The captain smiled. "Long night?" he asked.

"Something like that."

"*Patrol,*" hissed the Jaculus. He dove onto his belly, his black cloak blending into the earth. Carmichael did the same, but Jaden hesitated as he stared at the bubbling mud beneath him. It made his stomach turn.

I hate field work.

He covered his nose and knelt. His knees sank in, but he refused to lay flat on his chest, hoping his cloak would still camouflage him at this height.

A ship rumbled overhead. Its engines sounded labored.

Jaden chanced a glance once it was far enough away: a freighter, only it had five separate wings all at odd angles, and all having originated from different ships. Typical Del Clorans: always function over form.

Jaden felt a tug on his shoulder and suddenly he was up on his feet, shocked at the strength of the Jaculus as he stared into its yellow eyes.

"You'll not survive here for long, pretty boy, if you're afraid of a little mud." The Jaculus shoved past him. Jaden looked to Carmichael, hoping for some backup, but the captain only patted his shoulder.

"Do as he says. And stay alert. Del Clorans aren't the only danger on this rock."

Don't need to tell me twice. The only thing that could make him feel worse beneath this bleak gray sky was the thought of who they might be meeting. *Please let it not be him*. Jaden knew who his parents might have hired for a smuggling job like this, and if his suspicions were correct, the Jaculus would be the least of their worries.

Great towers rose in the distance, their long shadows eclipsing the three travelers with every flash of lightning. The towers looked unstable, like each floor had been piled haphazardly upon the other. As they drew closer, Jaden realized the towers had been molded by clumps of hardpacked earth. Strange. The Del Clorans were famous for turning others' trash into shelter and machines. Why would they build with mud?

"Bioscans on those towers are negative," came T8's tin-can voice through their earpieces. "The Del Clorans abandoned these nests a long time ago."

Abandoned or not, Jaden prayed they didn't have to enter any of them. Not when the eyewatering odor seemed to be concentrated among them.

"Stay vigilant," said Carmichael, shifting his gaze from one tower to the next. "Anyone with a decent cloaking device could be hiding in them."

Oh, he'll have a more than decent cloaking device, thought Jaden, hand hovering over the pistol on his belt. Up close, the towers looked soft and spongy, almost like clay. He prodded it with his finger and it molded to his touch.

"Do the Del Clorans even use cloaking devices?" he asked.

"I wouldn't expect that level of technology from a species that lives in its own dung," muttered the Jaculus.

Jaden jumped back and wiped his finger furiously against his combat suit. "I hate this planet!" It took everything he had to keep his breakfast down. It didn't make him feel any better when the Jaculus approached the entrance to one of the towers.

He took a deep breath. Somehow, it seemed fitting that his family would crawl back into his life in the form of a giant pile of dung.

"Klio niet!" cried a nasally voice.

Jaden and Carmichael raised their pistols and stood back-to-back as a dozen armed Del Clorans emerged from the tower. The Jaculus waved for the two of them to stand down, but they ignored him. Del Clorans were a tricky bunch. Jaden wasn't even sure what they looked like; each of their faces was concealed beneath an intricate breathing apparatus, and each body covered in a pressurized suit. The only feature partially exposed were their large, compound eyes, but even those were protected by a pair of goggles. Jaden almost pitied them – their sensitive bodies couldn't even handle the atmosphere of their homeworld.

Or could they? It seemed strange they wouldn't move to a different planet with better conditions, especially considering how migratory they were. And why had the Jaculus assumed they weren't using a cloaking device when they most certainly were? He tried listening to the signals that the Del Clorans gave each other for a clue, but they communicated in clicks that he couldn't decipher.

"What are they saying, T8?" he whispered into his communicator.

"Nothing matches my databases," said the bot.

"A native dialect, maybe?" suggested Carmichael.

"Even that would register at least a partial match," said T8. "This just looks like gibberish."

Because it is, Jaden realized. The suits, the language, the cloaking device...they'd given themselves away so easily.

"Captain," Jaden whispered behind him. "I think we've found our smugglers."

The captain nodded.

"You can drop the theatrics now," announced Carmichael. "We come here as...customers."

The "Del Clorans" held their ground. *Why doesn't the Jaculus say anything?* They had brought his slippery ass all the way here to make the introduction, yet he just stood there smiling his creepy smile. It wasn't until one of the smugglers got a good look at Jaden that they finally broke character.

"Ruddy hell, it's lil' Upton!" exclaimed a gruff voice that Jaden knew all too well. *Dammit.* The smuggler ripped off his apparatus. The Human face underneath was half-burned, the flesh on the burnt side rippled and tender, the ear tattered as though carrion birds had pecked at it.

"Nice to see you too, Hauser," said Jaden. The other smugglers began removing their apparatuses as well, including the compound eyes, which had been glued onto their helmets. Each face was either Human or Nurrano, and none of them familiar.

Then again, Hauser's crews never did last long.

"Family friend of yours?" asked Carmichael, lowering his pistol.

Hauser laughed, a deep laugh that shook his round belly. "Taught this kid everything he knows, I did! Not them fancy computers, though. Just the essentials. Like how to survive."

"More like how to hotwire hovercars and cheat a lie detector," said Jaden.

"Same thing." Hauser turned to the Jaculus and the smile vanished from his mutilated face. "Back from the dead, I see?"

The Jaculus bowed his head. "I like to show up when things get interesting."

Another engine rumbled in the distance, headlights knifing through the rain.

"Patrol's back. Everyone inside!" ordered Hauser. His crew hustled into the tower. Jaden hesitated as Carmichael started toward it.

"Captain, there could be a trap in there."

Carmichael shrugged. "If they wanted to take us prisoner, they'd have done it out here. They seem willing to talk. We should focus on making sure that goes well, and it starts with you taking your hand off that pistol."

Jaden hadn't realized he was still holding it. He holstered it and then rubbed his temples. It did little to alleviate the throbbing.

They hurried into the hive's narrow entrance. The walls rubbed up against Jaden's shoulders, their soft "material" molding around him as he pressed through. *Disgusting, disgusting, disgusting.* The stench didn't make it any better. In fact, it made the sewers on Darraden smell like roses by comparison. He stifled a gag.

Darkness consumed them along the path. Soon Jaden couldn't even see the captain right in front of him. He could only follow the squelching sound of the walls as Carmichael pushed between them. Claustrophobia set in. Jaden felt the dark cramped walls closing in around him. His heart quickened, matching the pulsing in his head.

"I hope you're proud of yourself."

Dad? Jaden turned. There was nothing. Just darkness. Even Carmichael's footsteps had ventured past his hearing.

"I won't ask you to understand what we've done," his mother's voice echoed off the walls. *"Maybe someday you'll understand how hard this galaxy is. And the only way to do that is by facing it on your own."*

"You need to relax."

Jaden jumped. He hadn't heard the Jaculus coming up behind him. Now he could feel the creature's breath against his neck. It was *cold*.

"Is this amusing for you?" asked Jaden.

"Not as amusing as what comes next."

Jaden pressed on and, to his relief, found the passage opened into a much wider room. He heard the patter of the smugglers' feet in the darkness.

"That's the last one," one of them said.

"Seal the door," said Hauser. A thud echoed from behind Jaden. "Lights."

The sudden burst of fluorescents stung Jaden's eyes. He blinked away the spots and discovered what he assumed had been a supply room. Depressions on the floor told him crates had once sat here, and mounts on the wall suggested rifles and munitions had hung on display. But now not even a bullet remained.

"You caught us jus' in time," said Hauser, leveling a suspicious glance at the Jaculus. "We were packin' up shop for the season. Got a call we might have some stowaways. Seems someone ignored my advice, lil' Upton."

"You once told me to trust my instincts," said Jaden, glancing around the room of hardened strangers. "And right now, my instincts tell me that you're moving some serious cargo."

Hauser grinned, and Jaden spotted a few new golden teeth glittering there. "Never misses a beat, this one." His face went all-business again as he addressed the Jaculus. "I run a big risk takin' them with my shipment. If I get searched by the Taipa—"

"The Taipa will not be a concern," said the Jaculus. "For the right price."

Hauser rolled his eyes. "Name it."

"Not from you." The Jaculus turned to Carmichael. "I'll take a ship. The one called the *Shirlena*."

"Like hell he will!" boomed Sterling's voice through Jaden's earpiece. Jaden saw Carmichael rip his earpiece out and so he did the same, cutting the barrage of expletives short.

"What purpose does our ship serve you?" asked Carmichael.

"I would ask you the same thing." The Jaculus slithered toward Carmichael in his strange, loose-step manner. "Once you depart with Mr. Hauser, your ship will remain. And I'll need transportation. Believe it or not, the weather here doesn't agree with me."

The captain's eyes narrowed. The Jaculus's request was certainly suspicious, but Jaden couldn't see why anyone in their right mind would want to fly the most wanted ship in the galaxy.

That's just it. The Jaculus isn't *in his right mind. That, or he's just desperate for some excitement.*

"What guarantee do I have that you won't sell us out once we leave with Hauser and his crew?" asked Carmichael.

"Does it matter what I say?" said the Jaculus. "You won't trust me anyway, good captain. But you can trust that I would have sold you out a long time ago if I'd wanted to. Instead, I have brought you here, and true to my word, you are safe."

He's not wrong. Jaden's head ached even more as he tried to puzzle out what the Jaculus was after. If not Project Vortex or the bounty on their heads, then what?

"I still haven't agreed to shit," said Hauser. "What protections do I have against a group of Zobies on my ship? How do I know I'm not settin' myself up for mutiny?"

"You have me," said Jaden. "If you deliver us safely, no harm will come to you or your crew. You have my word, if I can have yours."

Hauser rubbed his chin, a glow of pride in his eyes. The

smuggler had taught Jaden that there was only one currency in the galaxy better than pure calladium, and that was honor. *Honor among thieves, maybe.* "But it's not just your lot, is it?" he said. "There's another you been stowin' away, or so I hear."

Jaden and Carmichael exchanged a look, one that pivoted quickly toward the Jaculus, the only one who could have leaked that information to Hauser.

The assassin shook his head. "Your cargo is not as secret as you think," he said. "Among certain circles."

Carmichael turned to Hauser. "Taranis is carefully secured. Believe me, if he ever got loose, he'd come for my team first. It's in our best interests to keep him under control, as we've been doing for months already."

"But why bring him in the first place?" asked Hauser. "You ain't comin' back. And he's got no information that would be helpful to you once you cross to the other side. Best thing for all of us would be to leave him here to the Del Clorans. I heard he's killed a fair few of them in his travels. Sure they'd be happy to roll out the welcome wagon."

Jaden raised an eyebrow. In all his worry about confronting his past, he'd not considered Taranis. Why did Carmichael still need him? It was a question he'd asked more and more as the months wore on. For a while, he'd assumed Taranis would be a bargaining chip with the Orlovs should they ever have the team cornered, but the exchange on the *Derelict* made it clear that wasn't the case. And Jaden doubted that Taranis, despite being half-Poterian, had any useful information about the Poterian Empire to offer. He was just a deadweight. A dangerous deadweight.

"He comes with us or there's no deal," said Carmichael. "As

I understand it, if the Jaculus can facilitate your journey through the Rift, he could probably also make it much harder." The Jaculus nodded, another twisted smile forming on his face. "He wants to see us across the Rift. I'd suggest you oblige him."

Hauser folded his arms, his look of disappointment falling on Jaden. "Some instincts you got, boy." He nodded to his crew and they dispersed, each gathering what few belongings remained in the room. "Leave it to you to find a crew as crafty as you are, Jaden. But I got rules on my ship, and should anyone tickle me the wrong way, they'll learn just how quick the Rift can swallow em up."

"I'm sure that won't be a problem," said Carmichael. They shook hands.

Jaden gulped. Knowing their luck, that was about the biggest lie Carmichael could have told him.

Chapter 12

What Comes Next

"You think you can just hand my ship over to that *thing*?!"

Carmichael's talk with Sterling was going about as well as expected. It didn't help that the Jaculus had already seated himself in Sterling's chair. Most of the others had started packing just to make themselves scarce, but Kano couldn't focus on anything but the argument.

"We're not coming back, Sterling," said the captain. "The ship serves no—"

"It serves a purpose to him!" Sterling aimed a bionic finger at the assassin. "He would use it while he paraded around in our skins. He'd make us even more hated than we already are."

"Since when do you care what people think about you?" Junior cut in, more focused on a flame he'd sparked on his finger than on the conversation. He'd been resigned ever since they'd let the Jaculus onboard. Kano assumed Junior had given up fighting Carmichael's questionable decisions.

Sterling gave the pyro a harsh stare. "I care about my peace and solitude. Something you robbed me of, *boy*, when you found me on Mogaddu. If we let this snake loose, he'll give the IDF a reason to chase us across the Rift. Then nowhere will be safe."

Kano saw the delight on the Jaculus's scaly face. The assassin was basking in the drama; he wanted a rise, so Kano stepped between Junior and the angry Poterian to settle things. "Your ship served us well, Sterling. If the Jaculus does use it to impersonate us, at least he'll keep up the illusion we're still here."

Sterling frowned. "Well while you run and hide, boy, this psychopath will undo everything you've fought for. Or does that not matter to you? Out of sight, out of mind, is it? Humans..." Sterling stormed off the bridge before Kano could refute him, his footsteps echoing long after he'd left.

The Jaculus yawned. "If I was going to cause such a stir, do you think I'd want the galaxy seeing me in this rust bucket?"

"You got what you wanted," said the captain. "Let's part ways on that note."

The Jaculus smiled. "Don't miss me too much." He swiveled around in his new chair, the conversation over.

But Kano still lingered on Sterling's words. Were they really giving up by doing this? Crossing the Rift was supposed to be *the* victory, the thing they'd been chasing since they became fugitives. It wasn't until Makoto said they would cease to be a team that Kano started having second thoughts. And now it seemed everything the team stood for could be lost too. All the progress they'd made to bring Zoboros back into society, gone. When people thought of their team, they'd think of cowards and villains. Not heroes.

Hauser entered and, sensing the awkwardness in the room,

cleared his throat. "We have your 'prisoner' loaded on my ship. You better be right about them cuffs. I'm runnin' a big risk bringin' him with my cargo."

"Our people will handle Taranis," Carmichael assured him. "As long as your people handle the Rift."

Hauser gave a gold-toothed grin. "That I can guarantee. Ten minutes till takeoff."

Kano began packing his gear as the smuggler departed. As if he didn't have enough reasons to dread this journey already; now they had to trust smugglers to get them to Poteria.

He sidled over to Makoto, who looked like he wanted to crawl his hungover self into his luggage rather than pack it. "Did you learn anything about Jaden's meeting with the smugglers?" he asked. "Do you know where they're taking us once we cross?"

"Ask him yourself," said Makoto, rubbing his aching head.

Jaden stood off on his own, meticulously filing into his satchel every adapter and accessory for his datapad. They'd not spoken since Kano had learned the truth about the Upton family enterprise, and now he wasn't sure how to approach without acknowledging the Kimikan hog in the room. He shuffled over slowly to give himself time to come up with a conversation starter. But nothing came. Just when he thought it was a lost cause, Jaden turned to him.

"Okeanos," he said.

"What?"

"That's the name of the planet we're going to." Jaden nodded toward Makoto. "You guys aren't as quiet as you think."

Kano felt a little hot under the ears. "Does that name ring

any bells for you, Mr. History?"

"Sort of. T8's databases didn't have anything on it, but the name is interesting. Okeanos was a river spirit to an ancient civilization. But an ancient civilization on *our* side of the Rift."

That was interesting. And it brought Kano's train of thought naturally to the one myth involving a river that he was familiar with. "Any connection to Iramwerta?"

Jaden shrugged as he closed his satchel. "There's only one person here who could answer that." He nodded to the command chair, its back facing toward them.

Kano gulped, suddenly aware that the others were clearing out of the room with their belongings.

"Good luck," said Jaden, heading toward the door.

Kano watched him go, wanting to ask him to stay but afraid, with their friendship in such an awkward place, to do so.

"Jaden!" he finally called.

Jaden turned. For some reason, he still looked different in Kano's eyes. Like Kano wasn't looking at his best friend anymore.

"Thanks."

"Sure." Jaden left.

Kano stood there for a while. This should have been a happy moment: they were finally escaping all the enemies they'd amassed since their journey began. They'd gotten what they wanted. And yet Kano felt as empty as the bridge.

"Sentimental, are we?"

The Jaculus swiveled around, yellow eyes watching him from beneath locks of black hair.

"Not sure that's what I would call it." Kano took a nervous step toward the exit.

"This ship has been the site of many of your adventures, no?" The Jaculus waved at the surrounding bridge, at its familiar consoles where they'd coordinated their missions, at the viewport where they'd stared into the farthest reaches of space, at the seats where they'd gathered to talk about their plans and ideas and, if they ran out of topics, Famora. "It is natural to grieve the loss of a thing, even when that thing was a source of hardship."

"Are you looking for a position as team counselor?"

"From what I heard, that position wouldn't last very long."

Kano froze. Had the Jaculus been listening to his conversation with Makoto last night? Or did the assassin just see the writing on the wall?

The Jaculus sighed. "When you've lived as long as I have, you see patterns in things, in people. Necessity binds you all. It has from the beginning. But when it's gone, what will there be to keep you together?"

"I'm sure we'll still need each other," said Kano quickly. "Knowing our luck."

"Not everyone is out to get you, Kano. There are ones who would...reach out a hand and offer you something."

Kano's eyes narrowed. *Impossible.* The Jaculus couldn't know about his visions. It was just a coincidental choice of words. Though somehow Kano didn't think there were any coincidences when it came to the Jaculus.

The assassin smiled. "Like I said, I see patterns in people. I know the ones who have trouble sleeping."

"And what happens to those people?" asked Kano.

"Fate is a fickle thing. Who am I to say what is decided by the gods?"

"Is that what this is then? Gods and myths and river spirits?"

The Jaculus rose from his chair and marched toward Kano. For every step he took forward, Kano took one back. "You are venturing beyond everything you think you know. I would keep an open mind on this journey." Kano found himself backed into a corner. The Jaculus leaned closer and whispered in his ear, his breath cold. "A little parting advice: stop trying to look at things as good or evil. As light or dark. Anyone can pick between two options given to them. Only legends make up a third."

"And is that what you are?" asked Kano. "A legend?"

"I certainly thrive in the gray." Engines rumbled to life outside. "Best hurry along, Kano. I'm sure our paths will cross again."

I should hope not. Yet of everything the Jaculus had just told him, he somehow found that the easiest to believe. He hurried out the door, eager to put some distance between himself and the snake. It wasn't until he was halfway down the exit ramp outside the ship that he thought to take a last look back. The *Shirlena* sure was ugly, but she'd been a good home given the circumstances.

Hauser's ship loomed just across muddied terrain under the cover of night. Kano had to activate his infrareds just to see it: a ship shaped like a torpedo, long and narrow, its color unknown in the dark. What he did know was that they could easily fit at least five *Shirlenas* inside it. Suddenly, a new home didn't sound so bad.

He climbed the ramp and found the entrance hall empty. Everyone else was probably getting settled into their bunks. At least he hoped. Knowing his friends, they were probably already snooping around for Hauser's mysterious cargo. *A quick way to get ourselves kicked off.* But the more Kano walked around, the more he realized the smugglers weren't keeping any sort of watch on them. Did the smugglers trust them already, or did they just not care? Kano was drawn to the latter conclusion. Though if Hauser's crew wasn't one to take precautions, what did that say about their ability to navigate the most dangerous space in the galaxy?

Chatter echoed from down the hall. Familiar voices, Chenji and Jaden's among them. A warmth came over Kano, a sense of home in an otherwise foreign place. He followed the sound when something else caught his ear: the clank of metal on metal.

Of cuffs against bars.

Kano turned. There was a short corridor to his right with a single door at the end of it: an airlock chamber. And he knew exactly who it was inside.

"You shouldn't let him inside your head."

Kano jumped. Li emerged from the opposite way. "Were you waiting here just to lecture me?" he asked. It seemed a logical reason for her to break her silent treatment.

"I'm on watch duty," she said, folding her arms. "We're all taking turns. But don't worry, I didn't want to waste your time, so I had you taken off the rotation list." She gave a smile, one that told him everything: she'd made sure he wouldn't talk to Taranis.

"I visited him one time. And that was none of your business."

"It is my business if it affects our team." She stepped closer, uncomfortably closer, enough to stir more than just Kano's anger. "Don't think I don't know where you got that hare-brained idea to bring Angeline in front of Danadas." She flicked the bump on Kano's head and a needle of pain shot through his skull. "Everyone here looks to you, for leadership. If Taranis starts talking through you, it could be dangerous."

"I wouldn't let that happen." There was plenty more Kano wanted to say, but he left it at that.

Li sighed. "Taranis is smarter than you think. I don't want him using his leverage over you."

"What leverage?"

"Oh, give me a break." She turned away.

"What leverage?!" he demanded.

"Your *parents*, Kano!" She glanced at the airlock door, then hushed her voice. "He's the one person on this ship who knew them. The one person who can make you feel any connection to them. I know because if I had a window into my family, I would look through it every chance I got. It makes you more vulnerable than you think."

Kano stared at the airlock door. He'd known what Taranis could offer him, had known it for a while. But he'd kept away for the very reasons Li had just described. He knew she was right, and he didn't understand why it made him angry.

She stepped closer. "You're hurting, Kano, and you don't even know it. Once we head through the Rift, we give up on our old lives. Our old plans. Our old dreams. Like finding your parents. You don't realize it, but right now you're—"

"Grieving," finished Kano. "I've heard that one before."

Li started to slink back, but he grabbed her hand.

"How do you...pick up on these things?" he asked.

She shrugged. "When you've healed enough people, you

learn that only so much of it can be done with powers." She stepped closer.

"And did you...have any other healing techniques in mind?"

"Maybe you'll find out on the other side of the Rift." She broke away and headed down the hall. Kano smiled. Suddenly, a fresh start on the other side of the galaxy didn't seem like such a bad thing.

The engines grew louder. Kano hurried along, not wanting to miss the launch from the bridge. But where was the bridge? He listened for his friends' voices, but they had all disappeared. "Li?" He rounded corner after corner but saw no sign of anyone. He raised his communicator when a voice leaked through a nearby door.

"I warned you about the dangers." It was Angeline. Kano stepped closer and listened.

"Your son's in more danger here than in Poteria," said Carmichael.

"You don't know Poteria like I do," said Angeline. "What they would do if they knew he was within their grasp."

What does she know about Poteria? And why would they want Junior? Kano recalled hearing a similar conversation between Angeline and Sterling shortly after the battle on the *Dormarch*, where she'd admitted to keeping a secret about her son.

"Well thank goodness the Jaculus is sending us somewhere safe."

"That's not funny."

"Evil as he may be, he understands the importance of what we're trying to do."

"What *you're* trying to do, Carmichael! I'll have no part in this game." Hearing her heels clicking in his direction, Kano rushed around the corner and out of sight.

Games, games, always games with these people. But what part did Junior play in all of it? And what did Carmichael really have planned for them beyond the Rift?

Chapter 13

The Eye of the Storm

Junior stared at the airlock door. For three days, they'd been on this stupid rotation, and for three days Taranis had proven exactly what Hauser told them from the beginning: the airlock couldn't be opened from the inside. Yet for the next four hours Junior would be here, forced to think of worse ways to waste his time.

A shiny red button blinked beside the door – the airlock release. One push and Taranis would never trouble them again. So simple. Junior would take heat from Carmichael, of course, but that was almost a reward within itself. Besides, once they passed through the Rift, it wasn't likely they'd need a captain much longer anyway.

Clank, clank, clank. Taranis rapped on the other side of the door with his cuffs. Junior ignored it. The murderer just wanted to get inside his head again. Junior was still grappling with the question Taranis had left him with in their last conversation.

What do I want?

Clank, clank, clank.

Junior checked up and down the hall. No one was coming, and likely wouldn't for four more hours.

Clank, clank, clank.

Was he going to have to listen to this the whole damn time?

Clank, clank—

Junior jammed on the control panel. The vaulted door lifted, and behind it was a secondary door of glass, the half-Poterian looming on the other side of it.

"I'm hungry," said Taranis.

"Cera will bring you dinner on the next shift." She had to handfeed Taranis to avoid removing the power dampener (she took the added precaution of feeding him with energy hands rather than her real ones). Regardless of technique, Junior found it disquieting to see his sworn enemy fed like an infant. He often had to remind himself what Taranis was capable of.

He reached for the door control and Taranis responded by slamming his cuffs against the wall.

"You'll eat when I say you can eat!" Junior shouted.

Taranis stood there, silent. Not stunned but...amused. Junior sensed a wildness in him, something borne out of the isolation.

"Authority comes naturally to you, Aaron. I'm surprised the others don't look to you for leadership."

"Take it up with Carmichael," said Junior, reaching for the door control again.

"I would if he'd visit. But he hasn't spoken to me in months." Junior paused. *Months?*

"Ah, did you think he was interrogating me?" asked Taranis. "He tucked me in his little deck months ago and has been waiting to put me in play ever since."

"Waiting for what, Taranis?" Junior was annoyed at himself for taking the bait.

"You tell me. You're the one with access to the captain…assuming he's trusted you with anything. Otherwise, you're as much a pawn as me."

Don't let him in. "Once we land, we'll be free to make our own choices."

Taranis smiled. "Carmichael told you that?"

He hadn't. Footsteps echoed down the hall. Junior reached for the door control.

"Always a pleasure, Aaron."

Can't say the same. Junior hit the button. The vaulted door fell, and Junior suppressed the many questions plaguing his mind as Kano rounded the corner.

"Did you, um, have a second?" asked Kano.

"I have four hours."

There was an awkward pause. Kano obviously needed something. *But why would he come to me of all people?* Worse, why had Kano come during the one time when Junior could be caught alone?

"I don't think we're going to find safety on Okeanos," Kano finally said. "In fact, I think Carmichael's up to something big."

Junior glanced back at the airlock door. "Who are you getting this from?" he asked.

"I overheard the captain." Kano paused again. "And your mother. She was worried about something on Poteria. Something involving you."

"What?!"

"I'm not sure. Maybe you could ask her about—"

"Kano." Junior held up a hand. He didn't have the patience

to bounce around the ship looking for answers. "Whatever you heard is good enough to start with."

"Right...she's afraid the Poterians will find out that you're inside their empire. There's something secret about you that they know about. That they want."

"What is it? Why?"

"That's all I know. I swear."

Junior sighed. "I believe you." Everyone else was keeping secrets from him, why not his mother? Could it be related to his father's work with the Zoboros? Or maybe Junior's own powers, like how Taranis had once come for Kano's...though they'd learned later that Taranis just wanted a hostage to draw Kano's parents out of hiding. Frankly, Junior didn't see himself as much more than that: a hostage to unlock Project Vortex's power.

"Who else knows about this?" he asked.

"Sterling knows something, I'm sure, and T8 by proxy," said Kano. "Possibly Cera. I doubt any of the others. I haven't told them anything yet. And Carmichael mentioned something about the Jaculus being somehow aware of his plans."

"Brilliant." All Junior's favorite people in one basket. All they were missing was the maniac in the airlock. *A maniac who already knew Carmichael was plotting something.* Was Taranis in on it, or was the captain just that predictable? "This might sound crazy, Kano, but we could try asking—"

"Asking who?" Carmichael emerged with Li in tow.

"If someone else would mind covering my shift," said Junior, frowning. "Kano just reminded me of something that I needed to check on."

Kano nodded, thankfully not saying a word. Junior always

found him to be a terrible liar.

Carmichael's gaze shifted between the two of them. "Well, it can wait. We need everyone up on the bridge. Now." He turned to Li. "Go ahead and secure our guest."

Li approached the airlock, vines emerging from beneath her wrists.

"Is it time?" asked Kano.

Carmichael nodded. Even Junior tensed. Only one thing could require all these precautions.

They had arrived at the Rift.

Junior nodded to Kano. They would continue this conversation later, when the captain's suspicions had hopefully died down. Kano waited with Li while Junior followed Carmichael to the elevator (a major upgrade from the *Shirlena*'s creaky ladder). They rode it in silence for a while, the tension dragging out each uncomfortable second.

Carmichael leaned over. "You know I put the kill order on your mother, don't you?"

"Yes." Heat swam toward Junior's palms.

"Do you know why?"

"You didn't want to risk her falling into the wrong hands."

"I didn't want to risk my father's mistake being repeated," said Carmichael. Junior blinked. He wouldn't have considered destroying the Poterian fleet a "mistake", even if it had killed everyone on both sides of the battle. "It's hard living in your father's shadow, isn't it? Living with his...choices?"

Junior said nothing.

"The more we try to correct their mistakes, the more mistakes we make ourselves," said Carmichael. "We can only hope that when everything's said and done, those mistakes amounted to something good.”

The elevator opened, and Carmichael offered Junior to take the first step out.

“And what’s your solution?” asked Junior, refusing to move. “Did you plan to bluff your way to a happy ending?”

“Sooner or later, you’ll realize everything is just a big bluff,” shrugged Carmichael, stepping off. “One day I’ll teach you how to do it, too.”

Can’t wait. Junior veered the opposite direction that Carmichael was headed, passing between the smuggler crew as they rushed from station to station, checking readouts and adjusting settings. It wasn’t hard to keep out of their way – the bridge proved far more spacious than the one aboard the *Shirlena* – but otherwise it all looked the same to him. A prison was a prison, no matter how big.

He stepped down from the raised control platform and into the seating area in front of the viewport. Most of the team members were already strapped in, mesmerized by the blue-yellow swirl of hyperspace. He chose a spot near Sterling and, therefore, far away from the others.

“On my mark,” announced Hauser, holding his hand steady as his crew awaited the signal. “Now!”

The smugglers pulled their final levers. The swirl of hyperspace vanished from the viewport. Everyone gasped. Even Junior’s jaw dropped. Straight ahead, stretching as far as the eye could see in every direction, was a glowing mass of what he could only describe as clouds. Yet they didn’t move like clouds. They wove and spun in an intricate dance, folding into one another, then exploding out in incredible patterns of light and color. It was like the cosmos had come to life before their eyes.

"Ladies and gents, welcome to the Rift!" announced Hauser.

Junior craned his neck to see the top of the Rift through the viewport, to see where the clouds ended and the blackness of space resumed, but there was no end in sight. The clouds just kept climbing.

Lightning flashed within the Rift like artillery in the night, each bolt far thicker and redder than any lightning Junior had ever seen. He wasn't even sure the scale of what he was seeing. For all he knew, each bolt could be the size of a moon. A planet. Maybe even a star. Certainly enough to incinerate their ship on contact. He took the liberty of strapping on his restraints for whatever good that might do him.

"Never thought I'd come back to this shit," muttered Sterling.

"Well hopefully everything goes according to plan," said Junior. That garnered a side-eye from the Poterian, but nothing more. *He knows something.* That had to be the case for Sterling to even consider returning across the Rift. He was already unwelcome in Poterian culture, both because half his limbs were missing and because whoever currently held the throne probably wouldn't like knowing the rightful heir was mulling around. *But what does bringing me along have to do with any of it? Why would the empire care if I'm there when the prince is sitting right next to me?*

The radar pinged just behind Junior.

"Two warbirds incoming," said the crewmember closest to him.

Warbirds? That wasn't a direct class of ship so much as a

general term for any ship built to fight, particularly of the Poterian persuasion. Junior scanned the viewport but struggled to see anything beyond the Rift's powerful glow. He squinted, the bright colors fading together, and noticed two silhouettes approaching, mere specks against the mighty Rift.

"Hail them," ordered Hauser.

Static filled the loudspeakers. It was audio from one of the frigates. Hauser cleared his throat and brought his mouth to a microphone hooked to his control chair.

"Warbirds, this is the *Ontstappen*. Requestin' an invitation to the picnic."

Only static followed. Junior shifted in his seat as the two warbirds neared. He spotted the signature spiked hulls of Poterian battleships. Old models from the war era, so unless the Poterians hadn't upgraded in twenty cycles, these were probably abandoned vessels that had been commandeered by the Taipa. Despite their age, though, they still retained enough cannons to blast Hauser's ship to oblivion in a fraction of a second.

"*Ontstappen*," a woman's voice finally shrieked through the loudspeakers, loud enough to make everyone jump in their seats. "Our scans indicate you have double your usual crew. This was *not* agreed upon."

"Contact your employers," said Hauser. "Mine have already made the necessary arrangements."

Junior glanced at Jaden, who opted to keep his eyes on the floor. Tired eyes that were lost in thought. No doubt Jaden's parents had been the ones making those arrangements, or else one of their subordinates. Pity they didn't make the same effort to stop this voyage before their son abandoned them forever.

"Captain," the crewmember behind Junior whispered to Hauser. "What if the Taipa board us? We can't—"

Hauser smacked the man upside the head before he could finish. "Keep your ruddy mouth shut if you know what's good for ya."

Junior tightened his grip on his armrests. So their smuggler escort had secrets too. Go figure. But Junior had a good idea where that crewmember's thoughts were going. The higher-level Taipa might have approved a few anonymous passengers, but if these thugs decided to board the ship, they would see those passengers had a considerable bounty on their heads and might just decide to cash in on it.

More static came from the other line, and it was getting stronger the closer they drifted toward the Rift. Junior started to worry how their instruments would fare inside that monstrosity, but first they had to make it there.

"You have the all-clear," the woman finally said over the loudspeakers, her voice laced with both static and disappointment. "Expect your tax to double on the next trip."

"Roger that," said Hauser dismissively. Something told Junior he'd pay that tax over his dead body. "In we go."

Levers pushed forward, engines hummed, and the Rift grew brighter in the viewport. Junior found the flashes of lightning were starting to hurt his eyes. One of the smugglers got up and began handing out glasses. A pair landed in Junior's lap with a surprising amount of weight. Its lenses were thick and black, and when he put them on, he found only darkness, plus a lot of pressure on the bridge of his nose. Then, slowly, the Rift materialized before him, its flashes of light diluted, yet the picture...crisper, as if he could see the individual particles making up the cloud-like formations.

"How is it doing that?" asked Chenji.

"It's reading our surroundings and feeding everything back to us on a three-dimensional plane," answered Jaden. "Come on, it's not nearly as wild as what's happening out there in space."

The ship began to shake. Softly at first, just nudging them in their seats, then harder and harder until Junior felt like he was made of gelatin.

Lightning shot across his entire field of vision, so intense that the pixels marking it remained singed on his glasses well after it had dissolved in space.

"How long are we going to be inside this?!" Junior called over his shoulder. The rumbling of the ship was getting too loud for casual chatter.

"Brace for entry," was all Hauser said.

Junior lurched against his restraints as a great force slammed into the ship. Then he was whipped back and forth, everything a blur, everyone around him screaming, panicking as they were shaken violently.

Another flash. Junior's glasses could no longer process the swath of clouds as the Rift swallowed them. Everything became a blistering web of static. The clouds danced around like demon hands coming to sweep them into eternal darkness, rocking the ship so hard it felt liable to snap in two.

Or twelve.

Or a hundred.

"Holy shit!" screamed Jaden. Ristin vomited all over his own seat.

"Up the shields!" ordered Hauser. His crew did their jobs quickly, but not quick enough to calm anyone's nerves.

"We're all gonna die, we're all gonna die…" Makoto repeated.

Junior's knuckles turned white against the armrests, his grip tearing into the fabric. He figured now was as good a time as any to ask Sterling a question while they were all preoccupied with certain death.

"If we survive this, Sterling, what happens to me?"

Sterling's red face had turned a shade of green. "You'll get a fucking drink on me, that's what."

And just like that, the shaking stopped. The ship settled. All was quiet.

Was that it? Junior heard the snap of restraints. Hauser's crew was already back on their feet, removing their special glasses and checking readouts.

"Pass complete," said Hauser with a gold-toothed smile. "Not too shabby this time."

I beg to differ. Junior undid his restraints and took off his glasses. The intense brightness in the viewport had faded. Now they floated in a tunnel, the Rift swirling around them in a wide arc of blue and white, wide enough to fit far more than just their ship.

Wide enough to fit a whole Poterian fleet.

"We've entered the Tani Pass," announced Hauser. A dozen confused stares came his way, so he explained. "Think of the Rift like a storm. One that never ends. This is its eye, its center. Legend has it some bugger named Tani once ferried a band of misfits safely to the other side. Pray we do the same."

"So it's a straight shot to the end?" asked Makoto.

Some of the smugglers chuckled. Hauser waved them back to their tasks. "Not quite. The ruddy thing zigzags for many lightyears, so we're gonna pull a series of well-timed jumps. You can lose those restraints now, though. Shouldn't be any turbulence from here on out."

"But what if you mistime a jump?" asked Li. "What happens if the ship touches the Rift?"

"If we miss a jump, dearie — which we won't — then those restraints won't make a damn bit o' difference," said Hauser. "But if it makes you feel at ease, be my guest. Just don't complain to me when we're eight hours in and you need to use the pisser."

Slowly, the team began undoing their restraints and moving about the bridge. Junior noticed his mother approaching him; his first instinct was to give her the cold shoulder, but a fiery venom sprang at the thought of her and Carmichael plotting in secret.

"I've been talking to Carmichael and—"

"Of course you have," Junior cut in. "Why not make plans with the one person here who's most likely to kill you?"

"This isn't about my safety, Aaron. It's about yours."

"Really? So you want to parent me now? Well you should've thought about that cycles ago."

He expected his mother's wrath in return, but instead her face retreated to its calm, emotionless form. Beneath the façade, Junior could tell something had shattered. It was written in her pained orange eyes.

Angeline turned with all the dignity and restraint she could muster and marched out of the bridge. Plenty of people stared, but no one dared say anything. Junior turned away from them.

He preferred to be alone at the viewport, to lose himself in the view and forget the hurt he'd inflicted, the hurt he felt. The sheer size of what faced him made for an easy distraction. He'd journeyed the cosmos and approached many a planet before, but never had he felt quite so small. A mere speck against the great powers of the universe.

That's when he realized they weren't the only specks in the Rift.

"There's something out there!" he shouted, pointing at the distant objects. At least he assumed they were far away – it was hard to judge distance out here.

"No signs of life," said one of the smugglers after a quick check on the scanner.

"Like I said, no need for restraints." Hauser steered them straight on, keeping as close to the center of the pass as possible. The specks grew in the viewport. Ships, Junior could tell that much, large ships like what the Taipa had commandeered, but ripped and slashed like they had been savaged by a giant animal, left to float in clouds of their own debris.

Loose parts bumped against their slow-moving vessel. "No jumps until we clear it," announced Hauser. A smart move – that debris could turn to bullets at a faster speed – yet something still didn't sit right with Junior.

"How do we know they weren't attacked?" he asked. "Seems easy enough to avoid the edges of the Rift out here."

"Probably took damage and lost control on entry," said Hauser. "Occupational hazard, I'm afraid. It's either that or—"

The radar pinged like it had when the warbirds arrived, only now it pinged much faster. Junior climbed over and saw dozens of dots swarming toward them on the screen.

"The hell are those?" he asked. All around him, the smugglers were paling.

"That'd be the other thing," said Hauser, activating the cannons.

Chapter 14

The Marauders

The team scrambled around the bridge like headless aivins. Each of them was trying to be useful, but Kano had a feeling they were only making Hauser's job harder.

"In your seats!" barked the smuggler as cannon fire lit up the viewport.

The ship rocked. Kano clutched a control console for support while some of his friends tumbled across the floor.

What was happening? Who was attacking? Where had they come from? Many of his friends were vocalizing these same questions, albeit with more colorful language. The only thing Kano knew for sure was that an attack this coordinated was no coincidence. Someone had known they were coming.

He started toward the viewport, minding his step as the floor teetered this way and that, ignoring the pandemonium around him. *Where are they?* He'd expected the enemy to have come from the front, but all he saw outside were tracers shooting past them and down the tunnel of the Tani Pass. Impossible. The enemy wouldn't have had time to sneak up behind them. They would have had to enter the pass at almost the exact same time. So where were they coming from?

"Only legends come up with a third option," the Jaculus echoed in his mind. Kano craned his neck, found ships descending through the Rift's mysterious aura. An aura that should have destroyed those ships on contact, at least according to Hauser, yet here they were. And one of them, a Poterian freighter, was closing in over top of their ship, its purpose given away by the harpoons on its sides.

"Boarding party!" shouted Kano over his shoulder.

"Get us a damn vector out of here!" Hauser barked at his crew.

"Aye!" answered a crewmember. "Hyperspace sequence initiated."

"Ready on the guns," said Hauser, plopping into the command chair. "Launch!"

Kano sailed backward as the sudden jump sent them surging into the swirl of hyperspace. He collided with Junior, which was the equivalent of hitting a brick wall. Only the brick wall was off-balance enough from the jump to topple as well, and strike its head on the arm of a chair.

"Junior!" Kano shouted.

"Everyone in your seats!" bellowed Hauser.

"You're the one who said we didn't 'ruddy' need them!" shouted Li as she hurried over to check the lump expanding from the back of Junior's head.

"I'm fine," said Junior, shoving her and Kano off. He tried to stand, and immediately started to teeter.

"You need to sit," said Li.

Junior glared down at her in challenge. Kano felt something

flare inside himself, a fierce instinct to protect. He and Li stood their ground until the big guy grunted and settled his dizzied self into a chair.

Li turned to Kano. "How did you know to look up?" she asked, indicating the incoming ships above with a lift of her chin.

"I...realized there might be another way in," he said, omitting how the Jaculus had inspired him to think outside the box.

Jaden hustled over, pointing an accusatory finger at his former mentor. "You said we couldn't fly through the Rift, but I just watched them come out on top of us!"

"*We* can't," said Hauser, "but marauders have sailed this space longer than anyone. If you'd prefer them as your pilots, you can take an escape pod over to their side. That is, if you don't mind being skinned alive." Seeing he'd sufficiently shut Jaden up, he turned to his crew. "Ready the forward cannons."

Forward cannons? Kano figured they should be readying the overhead ones for their pursuers. He strapped himself in and channeled his power into his fists, just in case that boarding party should find any success.

"Approaching jump point," announced one of the crew.

"Steady," said Hauser, raising a hand in the air. "NOW!"

They started firing before the *Onstappen* had fully emerged from hyperspace. A marauder freighter materialized in front of them as the swirl vanished. Their cannons had already ripped it apart. It never stood a chance.

The marauders knew exactly where to wait. Kano realized why they called this a "jump point" – the Pass curved to the left, forcing any incoming ship to change vectors or else plow head-on into the Rift at maximum speed. The marauders clearly knew that too. As the ship in front of them careened off in a cloud of debris, other freighters converged on them from every direction.

"No life forms detected on that ship, captain," said one of the smugglers, pointing to the one they'd just shredded. "Can't say the same for the others."

"A dummy ship," said Jaden to himself. Kano perked up. He hadn't realized his friend had taken the seat beside him. He found it comforting amid the chaos, watching Jaden absorb their enemy's strategy with his eyes.

"What do you see?" asked Kano.

"A debris field they forced us to create." Jaden pointed at the cloud of the ship's remains as it spread out across their path. "We'll lose precious time maneuvering around it while they close in. You and Makoto better get ready."

Kano saw that his brother already had his stun batons unlatched on either side of his belt. Makoto had refused to set them aside since joining the smugglers, and luckily no one had made a stink about it. Kano supposed that with a ship full of Zoboros, stun batons were the least of the crew's worries. And seeing the oncoming swarm of marauders, he figured the Zoboros were low on that list too.

"*Turn, turn, turn!*" ordered Hauser. The ship pivoted forty-five degrees to match the curve in the Pass. The radar pinged out of control. Kano knew just from the sound that their previous pursuers had arrived out of hyperspace to box them in.

"Persistent but predictable," said Hauser. "Engage portside thrusters!"

The force of the thrusters threw Kano sideways in his chair. Debris clunked against the right side of their ship as Hauser steered them away from the marauders' choke point.

"Almost clear!" announced one of the crew.

Tracer fire thudded against the ceiling.

"Just ruddy do it!" blurted Hauser.

The swirl of hyperspace resumed, throwing them back in their seats. Kano let out the breath he hadn't realized he'd been holding. They'd made it...at least until the next jump point. But something was off. The swirl of hyperspace seemed slower, more labored, like it hadn't fully rendered.

"We've got a ride along!" said the smuggler at the radar.

"Put a cannon on them!" ordered Hauser.

"Negative," said another at the gunnery position. "They hooked in too close underneath us. A blast could throw us hard off-vector."

Hauser swore under his breath and turned to Carmichael. "They're gonna breach the lower levels and float the cargo out. Once they've had their fill, they'll blast us to oblivion. We need someone to hold em off."

Kano and Makoto were the first on their feet. Junior wasn't far behind, though he could barely stand up straight, given his injury.

"You stay seated," ordered Carmichael, though Junior stood until an energy hand shoved him back in his seat. The captain gave Kano and Makoto each a once-over. "My usual suspects. Get some space suits on for when they breach. I'll get a few others suited as backup, including Warp. If you run into too much trouble, say the word and I'll send her to retrieve you." Carmichael tapped on his earpiece.

He's desperate if he's putting Warp in danger. Kano kept his thought to himself, though it made him wonder if she also factored into the captain's secret plans.

"We're coming too," said Chenji, Ristin right behind him.

Carmichael shook his head. "Two should be sufficient in tight quarters. But in the event of a second breach, you'll be top of my list, Chenji." He paused and turned to Ristin. "You too, newbie."

A small smile broke across Ristin's otherwise frightened face. The two of them retreated while some of Hauser's crew began fitting Kano and Makoto into spacesuits. Kano felt a nervous excitement as they pulled the baggy material over him. He'd experienced all sorts of strange gravity on Famora, but never *zero* gravity. Not beyond the weightless gravity bubbles that Ristin created, which didn't require any of these safety precautions. The suit was surprisingly light in most places, except for a weighted square on his chest that controlled the life support system. The smuggler placed a fishbowl helmet over his head and locked it in place. The air thinned quickly and his breath condensed against the glass. Once the smuggler activated the life support, the condensation rushed away, replaced by warm air that soothed his body and inflated the loose-hanging material.

"It's a little hot," he said as he tested his range of motion — a test that proved he could no longer fully bend his knees or elbows.

"You'll be thankful for the insulation when you're in a vacuum," said Carmichael through his earpiece. Kano jumped. He hadn't realized that all the sound beyond the fishbowl had been muffled. It was now feeding in from a microphone somewhere on his suit, which helped him to hear the great thud that echoed through the ship.

"They've breached!" announced one of the smugglers.

"That's your cue," said Hauser.

Kano found all his friends' turning toward him and Makoto, each looking at them as if for the last time. Strange, considering how many dangerous missions they'd gone on together. Then it hit him: the spacesuit changed everything. *Space* changed everything. One wrong move (which was easy given his limited mobility) could depressurize the suit or send him spinning away into the Rift. And that would be it.

"Be careful guys," said Jaden. He started toward them awkwardly, but once he pulled them in for a hug, he squeezed them tighter than ever before.

"Don't do anything stupid," added Li, managing to squeeze them even tighter than Jaden had.

"It's like you don't know us at all," said Makoto. At that point, everyone was taking turns for their hug: Cera, Ristin, Chenji (who had taken the form of a cuddly bear for the occasion), Warp, even T8 gave them a pat on the back with its wiry hand. Sterling offered a nod and a grunt from across the room, which was far more than Kano had expected.

Akio stood at Kano's knees, glaring up sharply with his big eyes. "They do not have a suit my size. But I will be watching, boy of thunder."

"I'm counting on it," said Kano, patting his protector's little head. Akio grimaced but didn't resist. The team marveled at his restraint.

The only one not to acknowledge their departure was Junior. He stared out the viewport darkly (and perhaps deliriously). Kano tried not to linger on it. They had marauders to fight, something Hauser was quick to remind them of.

"This has all been good and touching, but it's time to move your skinny arses."

Carmichael gripped each of his suited heroes by a shoulder and gave them a shake for good luck. And that was that. Kano and Makoto were off, through passageways that seemed far less spacious within the spacesuits. And hotter. By the time they reached the elevator, Kano was dripping with sweat. A part of him hoped they reached the depressurized zone sooner rather than later. Makoto, however, seemed unfazed, his species being more adaptable to hotter temperatures.

Neither of them spoke. They didn't need to. They had been doing this for months, throwing themselves into danger and working in tandem whenever possible. But the irony wasn't lost on Kano: the whole point of those missions was to reach the Rift and never have to run from their enemies again. The fact that they had immediately run into danger seemed somehow fitting given their track record.

"What do you think these marauders look like?" asked Makoto, breaking the silence.

Kano shrugged as the elevator doors opened. "Poterians, maybe?"

"I'd love to take on a few of those."

You don't need to prove yourself. Kano led them through the eerily quiet hallways of the lower levels. "Let's focus on containment," he said. "That way—"

"Boys, I have an update," came Carmichael through their earpieces. They stopped. "Your targets repressurized the infiltration zone."

"Then how are they going to get the cargo out?" asked Kano.

"They're not heading for the cargo. They're in a corridor parallel to yours, heading toward the exit ramp."

Kano froze. He and his brother looked at each other. There was only one thing over there that the marauders could be searching for.

The airlock.

They ran as fast as their suits allowed them, around the corner and into the next corridor where the vaulted door had been lifted. Taranis stood behind the second door, banging his fist against its glass while a tall creature in a shiny black spacesuit approached him. But the creature was not reaching for the release button…it was reaching for the shiny red eject button.

Kano hurled a shockwave that sent the creature clattering down the hallway. The noise drew two more marauders out of an adjacent corridor. Kano hadn't gotten a good look at the first, but these he saw clear as day: humanoid figures with helmets that stretched wider than the breadth of their bulking bodies. The only trace of what hid beneath those helmets were four long slits that glowed red from the eyes beneath, giving each one an insect-like appearance.

"Not Poterians?" asked Makoto, disappointed.

"Not Poterians." The moment the marauders raised their guns was the moment Kano blasted them back with a shockwave.

"You've got about a dozen more coming from either side," warned Carmichael.

"Probably pissed," said Makoto, smiling, but Kano barely

registered what he said. All he could think about was that eject button. A lot could happen with a dozen enemies crowding the hallway. It would be easy for someone to eject Taranis into oblivion.

"We need to get him out of there."

"What?!" Makoto caught him by the arm before he could reach for the door control. "Are you crazy?!"

"They tried to kill him."

Makoto glanced from Taranis to Kano. "Better him than us," he muttered.

He wasn't wrong. But it still didn't feel right. He couldn't let Taranis's life hang upon the push of a button.

"Let me help you," came Taranis's voice through the glass. "I heard more of them passing through here. You are outnumbered."

"And you're in cuffs," said Makoto, nodding toward the blinking lights on it that absorbed his powers.

"That hasn't stopped me before. You need my help."

"Do not release him," ordered Carmichael through their earpieces. "I'm sending backup. I repeat, do not—"

Kano switched off his comms. Blaster fire erupted from either end of the hallway. He and his brother pressed against the glass door. The space between the airlock and the hallway was narrow, and the blaster bolts hissed just inches from their chests.

"We need more space, and we need *him*!" Kano punched the release button before Makoto could protest. The glass door whooshed open and Kano stumbled backward into the airlock.

"Thank you," said Taranis. He vaulted over Kano and swung the cuffs into the helmet of the first marauder to emerge from around the corner. Makoto jabbed the next with a baton. Taranis swept the legs out from under another, and Kano sent a shockwave rocketing down the opposite way, eliminating two more.

"Over here!" hollered Taranis. He hit the deck as more marauders charged toward him. Makoto followed his lead, leaving an opening. Kano launched a shockwave over their heads that sent the incoming marauders sailing back.

"Not too shabby," said Makoto, standing up to observe the battered marauders lying across the hallway. "And here I thought Taranis would—"

The half-Poterian drove his bare foot into Kano's chest, knocking the wind out of him as he slammed against the back of the airlock. He gasped, his back throbbing as Taranis struck the door control, sealing the glass door between them.

"NO!" Kano struggled to his feet and pressed up against the glass. His brother stood on the other side of it, alone in the hallway against their oldest enemy, batons ready to strike.

"Makoto, don't! It's what he wants!" But Makoto didn't listen. He drove his baton forward. Taranis raised his power dampener and the baton struck it. Electricity exploded out, popping the little lights on the dampener. Makoto stared in horror, realizing his error as the cuffs clunked on the floor.

Taranis raised his liberated hand. Electricity leaped from finger to finger. "Ah. That's more like it." He launched bolts from his fingertips into Makoto's chest. Kano could only watch as his brother slammed against the glass between them.

"STOP!!!" Kano threw a shockwave at the glass, but it reverberated and threw him against the back of the airlock once more. Pain shot through the bruise on the back of his head as he watched his brother convulse.

The electricity ceased. Makoto sagged. Kano crawled to the glass. *No, no, please no.* Tears filled his eyes. Smoke rose from his brother's body; he looked for a sign, anything that resembled movement, and noticed his brother's breath condensing against the fishbowl helmet.

He's alive! Kano shook with relief.

"You spared me on the *Dormarch*, so I will spare him," said Taranis. "But neither of you will get in my way this time." He sent lightning bolt into the door control. Sparks exploded from it, and then Taranis was gone.

Kano sat there, frozen in disbelief. *He's loose. He hurt Makoto and now he's* – his senses returned to him. He switched on his comms. "Taranis is loose. He has his powers back." The message got a jolt out of Makoto, who sprang back into consciousness, wide-eyed and chest heaving as if the bolts of lightning were still coming for him.

"How long was I out?!" he blurted. He got back to his feet, then winced and looked at his chest. His spacesuit was in tatters, and beneath it harsh burns gleamed bright red upon his exposed skin.

"Not long. But I think Taranis…" Kano paused as Makoto struck the door control. Nothing happened. "Fried the controls," he concluded.

"Can you break down the door?"

"Already tried," said Kano, rubbing his bruised head. His mind raced for a solution. Who on the team could get him out? And why weren't they responding to his message? He figured Taranis getting loose would be *something* of a big deal. "Team, do you read?" Silence followed. "Carmichael?!"

Makoto tried contacting them too, then shook his head. "Something's blocking our signal."

The ship shook again. *Another breach?* Kano searched the airlock, but there was nothing he could use to escape. Nothing except…

"Makoto!" Kano opened a hatch in the wall and found a safety tether reeled there. "On my signal, you're going to hit the red button."

His brother ripped off his now-useless fishbowl helmet and brought his communicator closer to his mouth. *"Are you crazy?!"*

Kano latched the safety tether to his suit. "Yes, but that's not important right now. They're breaching us from an area that the cannons can't hit. But I can."

"You'll be killed!"

"We'll all be killed if I stay stuck in here."

Makoto looked from his brother to the red button. He gulped.

Chapter 15

The Breaking

"They've breached again!"

"Both of you, get down there!"

"They're coming from all sides!"

Junior rubbed his aching head as the bridge spiraled further into chaos. The bruise on his head pulsed like it had its own heartbeat, only each beat hurt like hell. And every shout and curse set it pounding all the harder.

I need to do something. But what? Thinking only made him dizzier. Meanwhile, everyone else seemed to have a task: the smugglers jammed on every button and lever imaginable; Jaden and Li tried to get a signal to Kano downstairs; Chenji and Ristin sprinted toward the elevator on Carmichael's orders; Sterling and T8 overturned tables to use as defensive positions should the marauders reach the bridge. And all he could do was sit there.

"Taranis—"

Junior sprang up. That had been Makoto's voice. He pressed on his earpiece, but now heard only static.

"I told you to sit down!" barked Li.

Junior brushed past her and searched for a spot with a better signal.

"...Repeat..." Makoto's voice pushed through the static. "...Taranis loose..."

That was all Junior needed to hear. He bolted out the door and down the hall. The floor wobbled beneath him, whether from turbulence or his own dizziness he wasn't sure. He crashed from wall to wall in a pitiful volley, but that didn't stop him. Nothing could stop him from saving her.

The elevator would be too slow. He found a spiraling stairwell nearby; it blurred in his hazy vision, stretching farther and then shrinking closer. He threw caution to the wind and took his first step – an immediate miss that sent him tumbling the rest of the way down. Pain sprang from every limb and joint as he sprawled out at the bottom, but still he got back up, stumbling forward until he reached her door.

"Junior!" his mother cried as he burst through, but it was too late. A hand snatched him from behind. Electricity pulsed through his body, and then everything went black.

The final lever was pulled. The *Onstappen*, overheated from the drag the marauder ship was inflicting on it, came out of hyperspace. The Rift still swirled around them, and soon a swarm of marauder ships did too.

So many, thought Jaden. He ran a quick headcount on the bridge. Little by little, the team had disappeared; first Angeline in anger, then Kano and Makoto in spacesuits, then Chenji and

Ristin as backup, and now Junior for seemingly no damn reason.

More harpoons pierced the side of the ship. They were being strung up like a wildebeest in a hunt. He awaited Hauser's next order, but the usually cocky smuggler stood frozen beside him.

"You've never seen this many marauders before, have you?" asked Jaden.

Hauser shook his head, sweat dripping from his half-burned face. He'd been racing around the bridge giving orders, trying to find a way out, but at a certain point there just weren't any more orders to give. None that Hauser could think of, at least.

Carmichael approached, keeping his voice low. "I believe it's time we use that cargo of yours."

Jaden's ears perked at the mention of the mysterious cargo.

"Over my dead body," replied Hauser.

More harpoons thudded against the hull.

"That might be the way things are heading," said Jaden.

Carmichael nodded. "It won't be long before your load of levithium takes a hit and sets off a chain reaction. The difference here is that *we* get to decide how it's used."

Levithium. Now Jaden understood Hauser's fears. That was the substance that kept Famora afloat; a substance so unstable that tampering with it could have destroyed the city in a hundred different ways. In fact, Kano and Junior *had* tampered with it once, and they had barely made it out with their lives. Jaden shuddered, knowing a bomb like that had been right under his nose the whole time. Only it wasn't a bomb in the traditional sense – setting it off didn't cause an explosion; it caused distortions in gravity. Distortions that could be exceptionally dangerous within the Rift…

"I've got it!" he exclaimed. Both captains turned to him, eyebrows raised. "Is the cargo hold still pressurized?"

"Aye, but there's twenty marauders between us and—"

"Warp!" Jaden spotted her standing awkwardly in the spacesuit Carmichael had made her wear. He hailed her over. "Hauser, do you have any electric charges?"

Hauser casually opened a drawer beside the navigation console. A bunch of little explosive orbs rolled around inside it, drawing horrified stares from everyone around him. "What? We had to keep em as far from the cargo as possible."

"We'll worry about your filing system later," said Jaden, placing several charges carefully into his satchel. "The levithium reacts to electricity. Warp, can you get us onto those ships?" He pointed at the spiked monstrosities reeling toward them through the viewport. She tensed, too frightened to offer an answer.

What would Kano do? Jaden asked himself. The answer was obvious, so obvious he blurted it out before he had time to think about it.

"I'll go with you!"

The shocked looks everyone gave him could only be matched by his own. He wasn't one for field work, but it was too late to rescind his offer, especially since it was having the desired effect. Warp began to ease.

"We need to get to the cargo hold first," he explained. It felt strange giving the orders, but Carmichael and Hauser seemed to be going along with it, so he took Warp's hand and nodded to her.

She nodded back. A puff of smoke surrounded them. All the

noise and confusion fell away, replaced by a cold silence. They stood among row after row of wooden crates that ran down the full length of their torpedo-shaped ship.

The floor rumbled, a reminder that time was not on their side. "Give me a hand," he said as he tried to pry open one of the crates. It was no use; the tops had been bolted down, and he had no tools besides the pistol on his belt and the charges in his bag, neither of which he desired to use near levithium.

"We have to go back and—"

Warp reached for the crate. Her hand disappeared in another puff of smoke while the rest of her remained beside Jaden. He jumped back, shocked at the sight of her handless arm, only for the hand to reappear with a clump of vials clutched in it, each filled with pulsing green ooze.

"You've been practicing," he said.

She shrugged, blushing. Jaden wasn't sure what amazed him more, Warp's new trick or the ultra-rare levithium glowing in her hand. He found himself instinctively taking a step back from it. There was something about the way it pulsed that seemed aggressive, like it wanted to break out of the glass.

"Be careful," he said. "I don't know how powerful the reaction will be if we break one."

Warp shuffled in place, Jaden's words making her tremble. He realized he needed to reel back the pressure a bit.

"We do this together." He placed a hand on her shoulder.

She nodded. A puff of smoke and they were back on the bridge. Hauser and his crew gasped and stumbled back at the sight of the vials, but Jaden ignored them. He was too focused on their first target: a freighter hovering uncomfortably close to the viewport, obscuring much of their view. He pointed to it.

"Make sure you—" Hauser began, but they never heard the rest. The puff of smoke had already consumed them. Now they stood in a hallway as black as the enemy ship's exterior. The marauders were somewhere ahead, shouting at each other in a language he'd never heard before.

"Pour one out," he whispered. "Carefully."

She uncorked the vial, her hand trembling as she tilted it sideways. Even Jaden flinched as the first drops hit the floor. He expected some kind of effects, like weightlessness or an imbalance in the ship, but the levithium just puddled out like any other liquid.

Jaden drew a charge from his pack and set the timer. Eight seconds. Plenty. He placed it beside the puddle and a moment later they were watching the freighter from within the *Onstappen's* bridge.

"How much did you—?" Hauser stopped, spotting the empty vial in Warp's hand. "Ah shite."

The freighter plummeted out of sight in the blink of an eye. Its harpoons tore from the *Onstappen* and whipped a nearby shuttle, shattering its viewport and launching its marauders out its depressurized bridge.

Carmichael cleared his throat. "Let's not count on luck next time, shall we?"

Jaden and Warp could only nod their heads dumbly at the shock of their near disaster. They clasped hands and reappeared in a new marauder vessel.

"Just a few drops from now on, got it?" he said. Warp nodded, and the cycle began: drip, set the timer; drip, set the timer. Sometimes marauder crews spotted them, sometimes not. It didn't matter. They zipped around too quickly to be caught. Drip, set the timer. Drip, set the timer.

By the time they returned to the *Onstappen*, Jaden had counted at least fourteen marauder ships that they had graced with their presence. Some were already feeling the effects of their handiwork: crew members floated in the viewports, whole ships veered in random directions. But even as more and more of them destabilized, they were outnumbered by the new ones coming in to take their places.

Warp was bent over catching her breath. Jaden couldn't relate to the fatigue of using her powers, but he knew he couldn't ask her to keep jumping between so many more ships.

A calloused hand clasped against his shoulder. Jaden found himself looking up into Hauser's burned face. "A damn good try, Jay."

Jay. He couldn't remember the last time anyone had called him that.

"*Hauser!*" Everyone turned as a smuggler came bursting into the bridge, clutching her bleeding arm. "They're coming through the—"

Two blaster bolts struck her in the back, punctuating the sentence for her.

The crew drew weapons and lit up the first marauder to come barreling through the door.

"Bring me Ol' Debby!" shouted Hauser.

Jaden had no idea who or what "Ol' Debby" was and didn't much care as he hit the deck, pistol in hand. Cries of battle and shrieks of pain filled the bridge. He crawled toward Carmichael as blaster bolts peppered the surrounding consoles, filling his nostrils with smoke.

"What do we do, Captain?!"

"Stay alive!" said Carmichael. "And if you can manage it, be more like Akio." He pointed to a marauder who was tumbling over the consoles, clutching a knife wound in its neck, its attacker already leaping onto the next victim.

Jaden tried to make himself useful, tried to fire a shot, but he couldn't get himself to stand up against all the blaster fire. A smuggler not ten paces from him tried it and hit the ground almost as quickly as he'd stood up. Jaden shuddered. He didn't belong in a shootout. He belonged behind a screen with a bird's eye view of the battlefield. He tried using the reflections in the viewport to get a sense of what was happening, but all he saw were the dozens of marauder ships pushing past the ones he and Warp had disabled.

We got farther than anyone thought we would. Jaden took some pride in that.

"Who's that out there?!" exclaimed Li. She pointed to the nose of the ship just outside the viewport. There *was* someone out there. Someone in a spacesuit, and though Jaden couldn't see their face, he had a feeling he already knew who it was.

Shockwaves erupted from the spaceman's palms. Their signature sound was lost in space, but the effect was more potent than ever with nothing to resist them. Hulls caved inwards, ships smashed against each other, explosions erupted to be immediately snuffed by space. And the waves kept emanating from Kano's hands.

Something came over Jaden. Seeing his friend out there clearing the field against the impossible made him feel...powerful. Like *he* could do the impossible, too. He leaped to his feet and fired at the oncoming marauders like a madman.

"Oy, that's the spirit!" shouted Hauser. A smuggler tossed Hauser a gun unlike any Jaden had ever seen, mainly because the gun's barrel was taller than he was.

And there were twelve of them.

The roar of bullets that erupted from those twelve rotating barrels drowned out every other sound in the room. Hauser marched forward, tearing down each marauder in his path. Jaden followed, firing his pistol at the attackers, though he doubted he was making any real contributions amid Ol' Debby's barrage.

Others joined them. Li disarmed marauders with her vines; Cera shielded any allies she could; T8 fired a rifle in its wiry arms; Sterling's bionic arm had morphed into a cannon that took out whole crowds of marauders with its buckshot. It wasn't long before the marauders (what was left of them) began to retreat.

"We got em on the run!" cheered Hauser. Ol' Debby rumbled to a halt, freeing Jaden's eardrums from the all-out assault. The smugglers cheered – though Jaden realized there were far fewer of them – when a voice came through Jaden's earpiece.

"Does...any...read...me?" came Makoto's voice through a web of static.

"I read you," said Jaden. "Be careful down there, the marauders are—"

The ship shook hard, far harder than anything the marauders had managed to inflict on them.

"Captain, someone's jettisoned an escape pod," said one of the crew.

Hauser dropped Ol' Debby and ran toward the console. That

was when Li screamed.

Jaden swung around. Kano was floating away, flailing his arms as he tried to swim back toward the *Onstappen*, but Jaden knew it was no use without something for him to push against.

"Why is he floating?" Li spoke so fast Jaden could barely understand her. "Why isn't he on the ship? What's happening?"

"The escape pod," said Hauser, assuming the controls. "The launch probably shook him off." He tried steering toward Kano but the ship barely budged. Hauser cursed under his breath. "Too much ruddy weight on us!"

Jaden scanned the battlefield. Most of the marauder ships had veered off, but others weren't so lucky. They floated lifelessly, still towing the *Onstappen* with their harpoon cables. But Kano had floated too far away to use them for leverage. Instead, Jaden saw him aiming his palms in the opposite direction of Hauser's ship.

Genius! He's going to use his powers to redirect himself. He's going – Jaden recalled the destructive force those powers had unleashed with nothing in space to restrain them – *to get himself killed.*

"Kano, don't!" he screamed into his communicator. There was no response, no signal. He banged against the glass over and over, knowing it was a futile effort in the vacuum of space, but he couldn't sit by and do nothing.

The force of the shockwave threw Kano sideways into a debris field. His helmet bounced off a broken wing and he floated off, head slumped, toward the swirling ceiling of the Rift.

"What's wrong?!" came Makoto's voice through his

earpiece. "What happened to Kano?!"

"He's unconscious..." answered Jaden, shock overtaking him. "He's floating away and we can't get the ship to him."

Carmichael was the first to run for the exit. "Where are your escape pods?!" he demanded.

"Three levels down, with a host of marauders heading toward them," said Hauser, not budging from his post. "You'll never get there in time."

The captain stopped. Everyone stared in disbelief. They were dead in the water, with no way to save Kano.

"I'm three levels down," came Makoto's voice. "I'll get him."

"Makoto, stop!" cried Jaden. "Makoto! Come in!" He kept shouting, but no answer came. His friends all stared at him, pain and pity in their eyes. "Makoto, you don't know how to fly!"

Jaden sprinted out the door, pistol in hand, a dozen voices shouting for him to come back, but he kept running, running before he lost both his best friends in a single stroke. He ran down three flights of stairs where wide faces beneath black masks fired at him. He put two of them down with shots to the chest before he dove for cover. He'd never taken a life before, and the realization had little effect on him in the moment's maelstrom of adrenaline.

Blaster bolts whizzed by. All he had for cover was an indent in the wall where a window stood, his back pressed against the glass.

"Get back here, Jay!" bellowed Hauser from the base of the stairs. Of all the people to come for him...

The ship shook again. *No!* He spotted the flare of the escape pod's engine in the window as it arced toward the speck that was Kano.

"NO!" screamed Jaden, pounding his fist against the glass. The pod kept soaring higher, engines blazing brighter, but it wasn't fast enough. Kano disappeared behind the veil of the Rift, and then the pod barreled through after him. Gone.

No. Jaden rounded on the marauders in the hallway, firing shot after shot at them. Hauser dove in, firing too, scaring the marauders further down the hall. With a burly hand, the smuggler grabbed Jaden by the collar and tugged him back toward the stairs. But Jaden kept firing.

And firing.

He fired even when there was nothing left to fire at.

Chapter 16

The Children

The pod shook. Junior stirred. Drool dribbled from his mouth and onto his seat. A dull pain pulsed at the back of his sagging head. Everything slowly came into focus, starting with the power dampener cocooning his hands.

Taranis! Junior surged forward only to have the seat restraints tug him back into place. There was a release button on them, but the cuffs proved too bulky to press it.

"Save your strength."

He froze at the sound of that icy voice. Its source sat two seats ahead in their cramped little pod, its half-Poterian face reflected in the viewport. Beyond that reflection floated a planet surrounded by starry blackness.

We're out of the Rift? How? There's no way Taranis could navigate—

He found the answer lying on the floor beside him: a marauder in a pool of its own pinkish blood. He winced, as much from the sight as from the sharp smell of iron filling what little air they had to share. Taranis's knife still protruded from the creature's neck, as much a warning to Junior as it was a tease: he couldn't pick up the weapon even if he could reach it.

He turned to his mother. She sat in the seat between Junior and Taranis, poised like she was the guest of some foreign dignitary instead of the prisoner of an intergalactic terrorist. It was the same annoying way she'd carried herself when he found her as a prisoner on the *Dormarch*. It screamed of submission.

"How's your head?" she whispered.

"We have bigger things to worry about than my head, Mom." He waved his cuffs at her.

"An opportunity will present itself. Until then, patience."

"Patience?" Junior couldn't believe what he was hearing. "Patience had you wasting away in an IDF prison. Patience had me going along with Carmichael when he let our greatest enemy stay on our ship. And look how that turned out for us."

"Are you quite finished?" She said it with such weight that Junior suddenly felt like he was six cycles old complaining over a broken toy. It was eerie, enough to stifle his anger for a bit. Seeing that he was subdued, she resumed. "This pod is bleeding fuel. Better to rendezvous with Taranis's people than steal it and strand ourselves in space. Once we reach our destination, we can determine the best course of action."

"Or have the best course of action determined for us," muttered Junior. He knew "Taranis's people" meant the Orlovs. Given the choice between them and starving in space, he wasn't sure which he preferred.

"You'd be surprised how much influence you can have from a cell," said Angeline. "Our pilot is evidence of that."

"He's evidence of Kano and Makoto's stupidity," said Junior. That warranted a tilt of Taranis's head, but nothing more. "You of all people should know what I'd be giving up to live in a cell. How many cycles do you think I'll lose to Danadas Orlov?"

There was a short pause. "It's not Danadas," she whispered, her voice strained.

What? The ship shook harder as it pressed into the atmosphere. The planet before them began to take shape, the blackened patches of land looking all too familiar.

"You're taking us *back* to the Del Clorans?!" blurted Junior.

"It's the nearest system," said Taranis.

Junior tightened his fists beneath the dampener. "I'm not sure if you recall, Taranis, but neither of us are very popular with the Del Clorans." That was the understatement of the cycle. After he and Taranis had sparked the Zoboros uprising on Mogaddu, the Zoboros ravaged the Del Cloran-controlled territory there.

"Leave the insects to me," said Taranis, accelerating. Dead earth filled the viewport, blacker than night, making Junior wonder if the Del Clorans would have done the same damage to Mogaddu if they had stayed. Just like he wondered what damage they would do to him and his mother.

Taranis steered them toward a collection of towers – hives – that jutted from the flattened earth. Unlike the abandoned ones they'd seen on their last visit, these had scavenger ships swarming around them like giant flies. Junior tensed. He expected some of them to divert from their seemingly random courses into an attack vector, but none paid their little pod any mind as they sailed into an opening in the tallest tower.

There was no light inside. Their pod's headlights panned

across glistening red sacks that covered the curved walls. Hundreds of them, each pumping with their own heartbeat.

Eggs. This was a nest. Though he knew little about Del Clorans, he knew enough about insects to know that they didn't simply let people walk into the nest without getting stung. So why did the creatures who had plagued Mogaddu with violence decide to let them in the front door?

Taranis lowered the pod. Junior kept expecting touchdown, but they just kept sinking deeper, passing more and more Del Cloran eggs. It reminded him of Sterling's tower in the abandoned castle on Mogaddu − a hollow casing that continued deep into the earth. *Maybe that tower had once been a nest too.* It would explain why Sterling had a similarly unpopular reputation among Del Clorans.

One of the sacks shook violently. A small arm punched through it, sticky with fluid. A creature skittered toward it along the curved wall on six spindly legs. Those legs ended at a wide abdomen, upon which sat a tiny head that was mostly just two large, compound eyes. The creature had two pincers as well, which it used to prod through the slimy sack and scoop out the crying newborn. It scurried away with the child before Junior could get a good look.

"That was a female," said Angeline. "They don't need the extra breathing equipment. The baby was probably a male. She has only minutes to get it on a breathing machine before it suffocates."

"How do you know all this?" asked Junior.

"I had plenty of time to surf the IDF's databases while I was 'wasting away', as you put it. Del Cloran culture may not sound the most enticing subject, but they have a large presence in the galaxy. Studying them was prudent, should I ever encounter one."

Or a few thousand. Another female scurried past the headlights, this one even larger and more intimidating, enough to squash any of the male Del Clorans he'd ever seen. "Did those databases mention why the males do all the fighting and exploring when the females are clearly stronger?"

"They suffer an overwhelming instinct to protect their young," she said as the pod touched down. "To separate them would be to carve out their own hearts."

Junior turned away. *Don't get sentimental on me now.*

Taranis opened the hatch and let out the stale, stagnant air within the pod. Junior had a moment of relief before the stench of the Cloraxian hive flooded in. His eyes watered at what he could best describe as a mixture of sewage and diesel. He'd have gagged if he'd had anything in his stomach.

"Keep it together," said Taranis. He hit the release button on Junior's restraints.

Junior immediately tried to jerk away from his captor, but Taranis's grip on his arm was both swift and firm. His mother shot him a sharp look. *Patience.* He took a deep breath and allowed Taranis to escort him out the pod and onto the sticky floor of the hive. His shoes stuck and tore, every step a grating rip that reminded him what the hive was made of.

Two Del Clorans waited beside the pod. Each had their weapons holstered, neither seeming in any rush to use them. In fact, they looked relaxed. Far too relaxed in the face of their enemies. Junior instinctively tried summoning his powers to his fingertips, only for the dampener to snuff them out.

Taranis retrieved Angeline from the pod along

with…something else. It was hard to see in the shadows, but when Taranis stepped down into the headlights, Junior caught the glint of its blade.

That bastard found it. Not even Junior had figured out where Carmichael had hidden the ancient sword. How had Taranis been able to retrieve it in mere minutes, and during a marauder attack no less? Then he remembered the link Taranis shared with it. He remembered holding the sword once to fight off Taranis, but when Taranis reached for it, the sword flew from his hand and into his enemy's. One of several things he'd seen it do that he couldn't explain.

The Del Clorans clicked to one another, then led the trio down a set of stairs.

"I don't suppose you learned how to speak Cloraxian in prison, too?" he whispered to his mother.

"No, but I did learn the sound for 'queen.' If I had to guess, I believe we're about to meet her."

Junior flexed his hands within the dampener. A Cloraxian queen? Of all the suitors to come after his mother's powers, this was easily the most ridiculous.

"Any advice for negotiating with their queen?"

"Yes. Straighten your back."

Junior blinked, suddenly aware of all his inadequacies: his slouch, his heavy footfalls, his rounded shoulders. Not like his mother. Even in this sticky, filthy hive she managed to walk like she was floating on a cloud. He wondered where she'd learned to do that; what life she had lived before the IDF's prison.

Their Del Cloran escort led them through a door at the bottom of the stairs and into a large cavern. The chatter of thousands echoed off the wide, curved walls. Light twinkled from red crystals wedged in the rocky ceiling, illuminating the crowd of Del Clorans amassed at the cavern's center, all clicking in frenzied excitement.

Junior tensed. The crowd reminded him of the Zoboros arena on Mogaddu: so many packed in without a care for personal space, all enchanted by whatever was happening in the center of the room. Only instead of a fight, the Del Clorans had congregated around a long pillar that rose through a hole in the ceiling. A pillar that was moving, pulsing, as something pushed through it.

It's not a pillar, he realized. *It's her.*

Their escorts waved their antennae. The crowd began to part before them. Junior followed the path as it opened, feeling claustrophobic as they ventured deeper into the Del Cloran masses. All males, Junior noted. And all laden with armor and breathing equipment. Their clicking got louder the deeper he delved into the crowd, overwhelming his ears until it was just one continuous layer of noise. Then, the compound eyes of those they had passed began to fix upon Angeline. Antennae waved, and the crowd went silent.

Junior braced as the final few Del Clorans parted, the rip and tear of their shoes against the floor being the only sound as they came face to face with the Cloraxian queen – if he could call it a face. There were no eyes or ears, just a round mouth at the end of her long, wormlike body, surrounded by pincers and seeping puss.

"You come seeking an audience with Her Majesty," announced a familiar voice from the crowd.

No. Junior wished now more than ever that he could summon his powers. The crowd across from them parted and the Jaculus emerged, a coy smile beneath his demonic yellow eyes.

"You're back sooner than expected," said the snake.

"What are you doing here?!" demanded Junior. As he took a step forward, all the Del Clorans reached for their weapons, so synchronized that their movements came out as a single sound. He held his ground, his mother's stare warning him to keep his cool.

"I am the new envoy to the queen," said the Jaculus. He tickled her just beneath her slobbering mouth and she gurgled at his touch. Junior found it even more nauseating than the smell. "Taranis contacted us requesting an audience, so I arranged it. You may state your case to me and I will decide if it is worthy of her royal ears."

Junior looked, but still didn't see any ears on her. What he also didn't see was why the Jaculus had chosen to stay on Cloraxia when he could have taken the *Shirlena* literally anywhere else.

"We've come with a proposition," said Taranis. "One that will see your lands on Mogaddu returned to you, if you are willing to fight alongside us."

Junior turned to his mother. "Proposition?" he hissed, knowing she was somehow a part of the bargain. She didn't answer, simply standing there like a royal puppet. *What the hell did I miss while I was unconscious?*

The Jaculus clicked something to the queen. Whatever he said caused her to writhe. She opened her mouth, and the shriek that came out nearly split Junior's eardrums. He fell to his knees, ears throbbing, wishing more than anything to cast off the power dampener so he could cover them.

He felt a warm touch, a sudden relief from the pain. The queen still shrieked, but his mother had covered his ears with her elbows while she endured the brunt of the noise. Sweat glistened on her forehead, her lips drew tight, but she showed no other sign of discomfort. Not in front of Her Majesty. *Or me, for that matter.*

Junior caught the Jaculus smiling down at him, somehow unperturbed by the noise, while the Del Clorans bowed their heads for her royal decree. When she finished, the Jaculus cleared his throat. "Her Majesty says that too much of her children's blood has been spilled on Mogaddu, much of it by you two who carry demon spirits of fire and lightning."

"Should I tell her you carry a 'demon spirit' too?" Junior whispered to his mother, who shushed him.

"Our spirit is tainted not by our power, but by the sin of hurting the children," said Taranis. "For this, we wish to atone." He raised his voice for the crowd. "Let our power overwhelm those who oppose you. Let us take back the lands which are rightfully yours while they are still contested."

Junior paled while the Jaculus translated for the queen. Not only was he being offered up in servitude to the Del Clorans, but he was being offered to help them fight Zoboros.

When the Jaculus finished, Junior braced for the queen's reply, but when she opened her mouth all that came out was a series of low moans.

"Her Majesty says those lands are worthless. There are other stars to cultivate."

"Respectfully, Her Majesty is mistaken," said Taranis, bowing his head. "What you sought on Mogaddu *is* there. I have seen it. And I intend to lead you to it." He drew his sword, its inscriptions gleaming in the red light.

The Del Clorans screamed.

"That blade is marred with the blood of the children!" shouted the Jaculus as the queen recoiled behind his thin body. "Many children."

"Then you understand its power," said Taranis. "With it at your side, even the Gate of Iramwerta would crumble before you."

So that's what this is about. Iramwerta might have been the only thing in the galaxy with more mystique than his mother's powers. He watched carefully as the assassin whispered to the queen. The assassin who had once been the owner of the very sword he claimed had killed Del Clorans. Hell, Junior wouldn't be surprised if the Jaculus had been the one to do the killing. At least until Taranis took it from him. As Junior looked from one to the other, from master to apprentice, it all made sense: why the Jaculus had stayed, why Taranis had chosen to land here. This was all a performance to woo the queen. One the Jaculus and Taranis had planned over the comms in the escape pod while Junior was unconscious, or perhaps even while they were both prisoners aboard the *Shirlena* (he wouldn't be surprised if they'd masterminded some secret mode of communication during that time). And by wooing the queen, they could carve themselves a path to Iramwerta.

"Did you know about this?" he whispered to his mother.

She shook her head. "But I am not surprised. Del Clorans are attracted to the mystic. Dangle Iramwerta in front of them and they will listen."

"But it's a sham. I've been there. Iramwerta is nothing but a tomb."

"Not everything is as it seems," she replied.

The "royal envoy" ceased his whispering before Junior could question his mother. The queen turned toward them. Though she had no eyes, Junior could tell her focus was fixed upon Angeline. The queen slithered toward her, puss dripping from her mouth, and Junior instinctively stepped between them.

"It's alright," said Angeline, nudging him out of the way. The queen wrapped her slimy neck around Angeline, each rotation making it harder and harder for Junior to resist his protective instincts. The only thing holding him back was the resolve in his mother's face. If she was frightened or disgusted, she showed no sign. Not in front of royalty.

The queen raised her eyeless face high above Angeline and looked ready to swallow her whole with that giant mouth, but instead she let out a low moan that ended in a high note.

"Her Majesty wonders if you are the key?" translated the Jaculus.

"I am," said Angeline.

"Key to what?" whispered Junior.

The queen's face twisted toward him. She hissed, and the Jaculus grinned.

"She asked what use this one is?" Junior stepped back as Her Majesty unraveled herself from Angeline and slithered toward him. "He bears no key, no sword," continued the Jaculus. "He is worthless to the children."

The joints of the queen's jaw unhinged, and row after row of razor-sharp teeth emerged.

"I can fight for you!" blurted Junior. "Sword or not, I can help!" The queen kept coming, hungry for her evening meal.

Angeline stepped between the queen and her prey. "You

will not harm him."

The queen hissed.

"Her Majesty does not take orders from a mortal like yourself," said the Jaculus.

"If she knows that I am the key, then she knows I can wipe out her children with a wave of my hand." Junior saw the lights on her dampener flicker. She was trying to summon her powers…and having some success. Junior was shocked, so much so he almost forgot how horrifying it would be if her powers were unleashed within this confined space.

Junior looked to the Jaculus and found the translator's grin had grown wider. The queen hissed again, apparently not needing the Jaculus's translation to understand a threat when she saw one. She slithered carefully around Angeline and toward Junior, her jaw rehinging, teeth receding, and began coiling around him, each rotation brushing her cold, wet exoskeleton against his skin. Junior fought down the urge to struggle, shivered as her slime leaked through his combat nylons and down his back. His mother watched, cuffs still flickering.

Her Majesty's face hovered over Junior. Her mouth opened and mucus spewed out, hot and thick and yellow. It caked over him, dripping off his shivering body in globs, the fatty smell alone making him even more nauseous than before. He dared not show his discomfort though, nor his anger or humiliation. Instead, he met what he assumed was her gaze with fists clenched beneath his cuffs.

"Welcome to the children," said the Jaculus.

Chapter 17

Picking Up the Pieces

"Stay with me!"

The smuggler convulsed. Li's glowing hands glistened with his blood as she held them over the exit wound in his chest.

Legs thrashed against the table. The smuggler's back arched. Li didn't even know his name, but she knew he would go into hypovolemic shock if she didn't stop the bleeding soon. *Why won't it heal?!* She pressed harder, arms shaking, every ounce of her power pouring out, yet the tissue refused to come together and stop the red river cascading from his chest.

"What do you need?" asked Hauser. He was the only one she'd allowed to stay in the room with her, mainly because it was his crew member on the table.

"More circulation. Lift his legs." Hauser obeyed. Li could tell by his subdued nature that, in his mind, he'd already said his goodbyes.

The bleeding smuggler stared at her, eyes wide and face pale. His thrashing stopped. Shock took over.

Li felt a lump in her throat. "I'm gonna get you home," she

whispered, as much for herself as for her patient.

A smile crept across the man's face. He was thinking of home, wherever that was. Li hoped it was somewhere far from this awful Rift.

"Li," said Hauser.

She looked down. The tissue…it was weaving back together. The wound was sealing! She pressed harder, stifling the flow of blood once and for—

"Li."

She realized Hauser was pointing at the man's leg. Blood pooled there, leaking from a wound she hadn't noticed. And then the leak stopped. The smuggler lay still, the smile frozen on his colorless face. She laid her head on the table beside his body, wanting to cry but finding no tears left to shed. Not after everything they had just been through.

Hauser bowed his head. That made seven dead — more than half his crew. Li pounded her fist on the table. *I couldn't even save half.*

She found the other injured smugglers waiting inside the breakroom, which they'd converted into a makeshift infirmary. Five faces turned to her expectantly, each battered and bruised, yet clinging to a shred of hope. But one look at her tired eyes ended that. Two of them entered the operating room to collect the body.

Chenji approached, icepack pressed against his head. Apparently, he'd had a messy transformation when he faced the marauders below deck, one that made him too tall for the low ceiling. The marauders had been too busy escaping to put up much of a fight though, so the bump on the head was thankfully the extent of his injuries. He didn't say anything; he just wrapped Li in a hug, not seeming to mind the wet bloodstains that checkered her shirt. She stood there, frozen, unable to hug back, unable to feel anything but the cold death lingering in the other room.

"How are the others?" she asked.

"Physically, nothing serious." He offered her a glass of water and she chugged. He waited until she drained it before continuing. "Morale-wise...I think we're in the worst shape we've ever been."

Li could only nod. Why did Kano have to step out there in that stupid spacesuit? Why did he always have to be the hero? She'd asked herself that a thousand times since the battle. And now all she could do was sit and hope that he and Makoto found their way back.

"Any sign of them?"

Chenji shook his head. "From what the smugglers told me..." he paused, his voice choking up, "...no one survives exposure to the Rift for that long."

"The marauders can. What if they got him?"

Chenji hesitated. "No one survives the marauders that long, either."

"Kano can."

"Sure. Kano can."

They walked to the bridge in silence. There they found about as much warmth as Li had expected. Aside from Carmichael and Cera, who were having a quiet discussion in the corner, everyone else had spread out into their own somber bubbles. Ristin and Warp skulked about collecting debris from the shootout. T8 called up damage reports on the control consoles and pinged them to Sterling, who was doing repair work somewhere within the ship. And Akio just sharpened his knife in a shadowy corner.

Then there was Jaden. He sat alone in one of the viewing chairs while the Rift swirled slowly by – the smugglers wouldn't make the jump to hyperspace until they knew the extent of the ship's damage – and seemed wholly uninterested in the view. Or anything for that matter. Even his datapad lay untouched in his lap.

Li felt the familiar impulse to help and fought against it. This was *Jaden* after all; the rude, pestering, narcissistic little insect that she'd been avoiding ever since he'd arrived on Famora. Or at least since he'd become Kano's friend and tried to force himself into her circle. But something had changed in him since they'd connected with the smugglers. He was vulnerable, and it didn't take her powers to sense that. Somewhere inside herself, she found a sliver of sympathy for him.

Miracles did happen.

She sat beside him against her better judgment, ready to bolt if he made a pass at her. But he didn't even acknowledge her arrival. They sat in silence for a while, watching the Rift rotate by.

"We will find them, Jaden. I know it."

He nodded. "It's us I'm worried about."

Silence again. Jaden didn't need to list his concerns; Li had surely run through them, and countless more, many times since the attack: a damaged ship, marauders in the Rift, the Poterian Empire on the horizon, and their team at a fraction of its former strength. And that was without mentioning all the things that waited for them should they turn back the way they came.

"I won't say it's the *worst* situation we've been in, but it comes pretty damn close," added Jaden, his gaze shifting toward Carmichael and Cera. "And the current leadership doesn't make it any better."

"They're doing their best, Jaden."

"For us or for them?" He lowered his voice. "They still haven't said a damn thing about what happens to us on the other side of the Rift."

"Maybe they're not sure either."

"Yeah, not sure what to do with *us*. Let's face it: Kano and Junior were their prizes, not to mention Angeline. They don't have much use for the rest of us."

"You sound like Junior." Just saying his name made her sad. No one knew for sure, but it was assumed that Taranis had taken Junior and Angeline in an escape pod back to their side of the Rift. "We should be turning around. The whole point was to bring Angeline to Poteria. If he's dragging her the wrong way, it's up to us to stop him."

"You should tell Carmichael that," huffed Jaden, busying himself with his datapad. "See if it fits into *his* plans."

Li crossed her arms. "As a matter of fact, I will!" She rose and started toward the captain and his first lieutenant.

"Wait. Li, I was kidding. Don't—" Jaden trailed as Li reached her targets, both of whom stopped their conversation and acknowledged her.

"We need to stop Taranis," she said simply.

Carmichael and Cera glanced at each other. "We agree," they said in unison.

"Then why aren't we turning around? We can't just sit here. We're losing valuable time."

"Pursuit isn't our best option," said Cera. "Not with Angeline's powers turned against us."

"She would never!"

Carmichael held up his hand. "She would never harm us under normal circumstances. But Taranis has her son, and a mother can be quite a different beast when it comes to her child's safety."

"Angeline's not one to break easily," said Cera, "but we have to assume that in a head-on fight, Taranis will have the upper hand."

"Then we get a message to the IDF. Let General Mezo know that Project Vortex is on the move and needs to be stopped. Better Mezo than Taranis."

Carmichael shook his head. "The Orlovs are too well embedded within the IDF. We'd only be helping them find Taranis."

"Assuming Taranis hasn't gone running back to the Orlovs already," added Cera.

"Well, we can't just sit here and do nothing!" exclaimed Li. Warp and Ristin stopped collecting debris to listen. Even T8 had paused its scans, its red eye focusing on them. "It's our job to save them and everyone they might endanger. That was the mission you gave *us*, Captain: to stop the threats that no one else can. Or did you forget?"

"I haven't." Carmichael turned to Cera, as if asking for permission for something. She nodded to him.

"What's going on?" asked Li. "What are you up to?"

Carmichael sighed. He waved to his team and they slowly gathered around him. "What I'm about to tell you all cannot be discovered by our smuggler escorts. Is that understood?"

Everyone nodded.

"Our mission was never to hide in Poteria. It was to make an ally of Poteria."

"What?!" blurted Jaden amid the team's gasps. Cera shushed him and he whispered. "This whole time, you planned to walk us right to their doorstep. Did you think they were just going to break out the champagne when we arrived?"

"No, but they might for the heir to the throne," came T8's tin-can voice. All eyes turned to its wiry frame. "The boss may not be the most well-liked over there, but his presence at least gets us an audience with the royals."

"And whether we survive that audience remains to be seen," said Sterling. He marched into the bridge with arms covered in grease. "My family doesn't like surprises, especially ones that can challenge their claim to the throne. When I agreed to go, I thought we'd have Angeline with us to balance the scales. We'll need a new plan."

"Already ahead of you," said the captain, gazing upon his team with a certain fatherly doting. "But our backup plan is much riskier, and I doubt Hauser will like it."

"He won't," hissed Akio.

Li jumped. The Jakari stood right beside her. How long he'd been there, she couldn't say. "And having smugglers here makes plan even more dangerous."

"What is this 'plan' we keep talking about?" demanded Jaden. "I thought Hauser was supposed to drop us far from Poterian-controlled territory."

"He is. Our plan will get us a new ride to Poteria and win royal favor in a single move," said Carmichael. "But it requires us to get our hands dirty."

When doesn't it? thought Li. And the more Carmichael told her of his plan, the more she wished Kano were here.

Chapter 18

A New Path

The bridge had no end in sight. Nor did Kano expect it to. Not when it was surrounded by cosmos.

Stars shimmered beneath the bridge's semitransparent surface. What was it made of? Light? Energy? It supported him yet had no weight to it, like standing on a cloud. He reached down, his body no longer constrained by a spacesuit, and his hand phased through it…yet his feet remained planted on it. It didn't make sense. But then again, these dreams never did.

"Your path lies ahead," said a voice that came from everywhere and nowhere at the same time.

Kano searched the cosmos. The distant stars reformed above him into the shape of a face half-hidden beneath a hood.

"Are we going to actually have a conversation this time, or are you just gonna float there and stare at me?"

The stars shifted so that the face could nod. "Our connection is stronger within the void. It is a part of me, as it is a part of you."

Kano blinked and suddenly they were surrounded by the

slow swirl of the Rift, its blue clouds reflecting off the bridge. "What is the void?"

The stars shifted, reforming closer to him as that same half-hidden face, its chin looking sharp enough to poke Kano through the eye. Far sharper than a normal Human chin. "It is made from the power that connects all our people. Those unworthy of it are doomed in the void. But for those like us, a new path opens."

Kano stared down the length of the bridge and saw the faded outline of a distant mountain. He started toward it when he noticed something floating above. A body.

"Who's that?"

"Someone unworthy," the man answered.

The body rotated toward him.

Makoto! Kano ran across the bridge. His brother's eyes were closed, body unprotected without a spacesuit. Vapor puffed out Makoto's mouth and into the cold of space with each weak breath.

"He's dying," said Kano.

"Such is his fate," said the man.

Kano looked again to the mountain looming at the end of the bridge, felt its power reaching for him, calling to him. All he had to do was keep walking. But when he looked over his head, Makoto was drifting away toward the edge of the Rift. Kano tried jumping, felt gravity loosen its hold as his feet parted from the bridge. He missed his brother by a good margin and drifted back down.

"It is useless," said the man. "Your path lies ahead."

It lies wherever I damn well please. Kano set himself a good distance from Makoto, then charged and leaped with all his strength. The higher he rose, the more gravity loosened. He kicked out his legs and began to swim through space, severed from the bridge's hold.

"You are making a mistake," said the man, his starry face reforming between Kano and his brother.

"I find that very subjective." Kano swam through the starry visage and was struck by a blinding flash of light.

Kano opened his eyes and gasped, his breath condensing against the glass of his spacesuit. He floated alone inside the churning clouds of the Rift. For once, he'd woken up to something more frightening than his nightmares. A pinging echoed through his helmet, and a readout displayed on the glass:

OXYGEN LEVELS LOW.

Just his luck. He searched the clouds for somebody. Anybody. He knew someone must have come to his rescue, so where were they? Where was Makoto? There had to be a reason his brother was in that vision, though he feared what that reason might be. He swam forward, the clouds making it impossible to see more than a few feet ahead. The alarm rang louder, his movements making the oxygen meter drop faster. It didn't help that he had no technique to his swimming. In fact, he probably would have drowned by now if this were water. He needed to find refuge, and fast.

But where could one find refuge in the abyss?

Stranger still was the fact that the Rift hadn't torn him apart yet. Was he too small for it to do him any harm? That didn't make much sense. A violent current was a violent current. Yet it brushed over him so gently that he wondered what had caused all the turbulence when they'd first entered it.

If it's so gentle, maybe I can push it out of the way. He reached out his hand and, praying he didn't throw himself horribly off-course again, channeled his power there. But before he sent out the blast, something strange happened. The clouds nearby began to drift toward his hand and swirl around it. Kano could feel it connecting with his power, enhancing it. There was a pulse to it, slow and uneven. But where was it coming from? He let the feeling guide him, swimming wherever the pulse was strongest while the alarm rang louder and louder in his ears.

The pulse reached a fever pitch as he swam into a clearing in the clouds. An escape pod floated within it, surrounded by tentacles made from the same material as the clouds. They swung against the pod's hull, each strike soundless in space, yet matching with the Rift's pulses so that Kano felt the ferocity of each impact.

"Those unworthy of it are doomed in the void."

Kano swam to the pod, adrenaline fueling each clumsy stroke. The ringing became deafening as his oxygen tank teetered on empty. His head grew lighter, his lungs tighter. He pressed on. His brother sat behind the pod's viewport, eyes bugging out of his skull at the sight of Kano. Makoto pointed toward the back of the pod, then scrambled to get his tattered spacesuit on.

Kano hurried toward the back of the pod with what little strength he had left, knowing his brother would die if he tried going out in that spacesuit. He found an airlock door at the center of his tunneling vision. It was small – fit for only one person should they need to eject from the pod in an emergency – and had a release lever on the exterior. The lever was meant for rescue teams, a luxury he wished he had right now.

Just as he grabbed the lever, a tentacle struck the pod and sent it spinning through space, and Kano with it. He refused to let go, sapping his remaining strength while the momentum threatened to pop his arm out of its socket.

More tentacles emerged as the pod slowed. "Stop, please…" he whispered, his breath heavy yet his head light as a feather. He raised a hand toward the oncoming tentacles and launched a shockwave at them, the force of it sending him and the pod spinning the other direction. His fingers began to slip. His vision shrank, becoming a dizzied sea of red spots. He tugged at the lever, but his fingers might as well have been made of noodles. He tried and tried, each attempt weaker, his ears barely registering the alarm blaring inside his helmet.

A tentacle slithered past his hand. *No…* He tried batting it away, but his limp hand just rubbed up against it. The tentacle wrapped around the lever and pulled. The airlock door opened and Kano felt a force shove him inside. The door sealed behind him and the room repressurized. His feet hit the floor. The next door opened and he collapsed into his brother's arms.

Makoto ripped off the helmet and Kano gasped in as much sweet, oxygen-filled air as he could. His chest heaved and his vision slowly returned to him.

"The…tentacle…" he gasped, strength flowing back into his limbs.

"I don't get it either," said Makoto, sitting beside Kano. "One minute they were attacking, the next they…cooled off. They actually *helped*."

Because I'm "worthy", thought Kano. He rose on shaking legs, needing to crouch beneath the low ceiling, and made his way to the viewport. The entire walk was only a few steps – the pod was just three seats arranged one after the other – but by the end he felt like he'd run a mile. Outside, the tentacles began expanding back into clouds, obscuring their view. Kano placed his hand against the glass and let his power collect in his palm. He felt a pulse again, this time softer, slower. Like a heartbeat.

"You sense something?" asked Makoto.

"A signal. I think it's coming from the Rift."

"You mean like it's trying to communicate with us?"

"Or someone else." Kano checked the gauges on the control console. "How much juice does this thing have left?"

"Just enough for life support," said Makoto, rubbing the back of his bald head. "I burned most of it trying to push through the Rift…and the Rift didn't like that."

That's not what it didn't like. Kano was surprised by his own thoughts. Why was he treating this force, this place, like a person? Like it had *feelings*. Like it could hate someone for not having powers. Yet everything so far seemed to prove his theory. He couldn't help but think of his other friends floating somewhere in its grip, several of them not Zoboros themselves. They could still be under attack by marauders for all he knew. Makoto unfortunately had little information to offer on the subject, having jettisoned shortly after Kano had floated away from Hauser's ship). For all either of them knew, the marauders could have captured everyone by now. Or worse.

Unless I'd stopped them. Kano recalled the intensity at which his powers had traveled through space, so much stronger than he'd ever experienced before, almost like he'd been tapping into the man's power in one of his visions.

Watching the strange clouds around them, he wondered if he had been.

He and Makoto checked on everything, searching for something they could squeeze out of the pod: a communication signal, a little more juice for the engines, even just a map to tell them where they were, but everything was either dead or blocked by the Rift's powerful forces. Kano leaned against the viewport, frustrated, and felt a tremor run up through his hand. Had that come from outside? He looked but saw nothing among the clouds. *But that might not be the only way to see out here.* Hauser had said the marauders had navigated this space for a long time. He placed his hand on the glass and let his power trickle there. He felt the Rift again, only there were more pulses this time, each softer, beating at the same general rhythm while adding new notes like instruments in an orchestra. And that orchestra was getting louder.

"Something's coming," he said. He turned around and found his brother had resigned himself to the backseat, lost in thought. Kano claimed the seat in front, set his chin atop the chair, and waited, knowing his brother would eventually speak up.

"I messed up," said Makoto. "I freed Taranis from the cuffs. Our friend could be dead right now because of me."

"Our friends can take care of themselves," said Kano, pushing away the dark thoughts of what Taranis might have done. "Besides, I opened the airlock. It was my fault, not yours."

"But I had my chance to stop him. And I messed it up, like usual. I should've seen it coming. That's my job: to react faster than everyone else. If I can't do that, then what am I doing on this team?" Kano tried to speak but Makoto cut him off. "And *don't* say that I still belong or that I'll figure out my place, because I don't and I haven't. I'm the whole reason we're stuck here."

Kano thought for a moment. "You're right, Makoto. You're the reason I'm in this mess." His brother blinked. "And I wouldn't be in it if you hadn't gotten me out of the last mess, or the one before that, or the one before that. You protected me on Famora, on the *Dormarch*, on Darraden...hell, I would be floating dead out there if you hadn't taken this pod to find me."

"I couldn't even get my suit on in time to save you," said Makoto.

"You didn't have to. You just had to try."

A smile crossed Makoto's face, only to evaporate as his eyes fell on the viewport. "They're here."

Kano turned. Silhouettes of ships floated toward them through the clouds, the spikes on them erasing any shred of hope that they were friendly. Power flowed into Kano's fists, and with it came hundreds of pulses.

Hundreds of heartbeats, he realized.

"We're gonna be outnumbered," he said.

"You don't say."

Something thudded against the airlock door. The marauders had latched onto it. They must have come from behind, too. Kano and Makoto steadied themselves, knowing their enemies would burst through at any moment.

"Charge on my signal," said Kano. "It's the only thing they won't expect."

Makoto drew his batons.

The door whooshed open. Kano signaled, and they charged

through into the certain death of...an abandoned ramp.

They stopped. A dozen marauders waited on the bridge that now connected their two ships, but not one was standing.

They were bowing.

Chapter 19

The Translator

It took a moment for Makoto to realize that his mouth was hanging open in front of all these marauders. *"A fast way to make your first impression your* only *impression,"* his mother's voice echoed in his head. Weird that her voice was the first thing he thought of in the face of killers from the other side of the galaxy.

"Kio a'fazi!" a marauder shouted. They rose at her command, their gruff movements echoing through the connector bridge.

Makoto spotted the one who gave the order: she stood at the front of the formation, her black armor distinguished by lines of blue that the others did not share. When she removed her helmet, the others did as well, and Makoto's jaw fell once again. The marauders were not one species but multiple – Human, Gorv, even a damn Poterian stood in the mix. The leader was the only one who matched the physique of the marauders that Makoto had fought aboard the *Onstappen*. Her face was broader than it was high, orange and scaly with four red eyes across its width. Makoto's hands drifted toward his batons as she approached, though she didn't seem to notice him. All four eyes were focused on Kano.

A wave of her hand summoned the Poterian forward from the rest of the squad. Makoto felt himself shrinking as the Poterian drew closer, broad shoulders looming almost twice Makoto's height. When it opened its mouth to speak, Makoto fixated on the lines of razor-sharp teeth inside; the same teeth said to have torn through the flesh of his people during the war.

"Our commandant bids you welcome," said the Poterian with a short bow. Makoto blinked. He'd expected a harsh accent like Sterling's, not something that sounded like it came straight out of finishing school. "You may call me Varlam. I shall serve as your translator."

"We...appreciate your services," said Kano cautiously.

The commandant waved her hand again. The other marauders turned and left. Makoto assumed they were translators of other languages. *Lucky us: we got the fun one.*

"Do you normally bow to your prisoners, Varlam?" asked Kano.

"We would prefer if you considered yourself a guest aboard this vessel." Varlam shot a quick glance at the commandant beside him before continuing. "All who display the Power are guests of the Abari."

"Then can we choose to leave this vessel when we wish?"

"That would be unwise."

Kano frowned. "Sidebar," he whispered to Makoto. They turned their backs on the marauder delegation and huddled together. "What the hell is going on here? Why are they suddenly so polite?"

Makoto shrugged. "It doesn't make any sense after what you did to their ships. And did you notice that neither of them will even look at me?"

"I might've picked up on that." Kano checked over his shoulder before continuing. "Let me do the talking. Maybe they can tell us what happened to our friends." They returned to the marauders (or "Abari", as Varlam had referred to them). "We thank you for rescuing us. But if we're to be your guests here, then we ask you to extend the same courtesy to our friends – assuming you've taken them prisoner."

Varlam translated for the commandant while Makoto and Kano braced for whatever news they would receive.

"I'm afraid that will not be possible," replied Varlam, a hint of pity in his voice.

Makoto felt a knot form in the pit of his stomach. *They're dead*. "How dare you!" he exclaimed, but the marauders continued to ignore him.

Kano waved at his brother to be silent. "Your attack left our friends in bad shape. Could you at least tell us if they're ok?"

"I cannot speak to the condition of every member of your team, but by our last checks they are continuing along their journey," said Varlam. "That should give you some peace of mind as you prepare for the Trials."

"Trials?!" blurted Makoto.

Once again, the delegation ignored him.

"What trials?" asked Kano, annoyed that he had to repeat his brother.

Varlam whispered to the commandant. There was a great deal of hissing from his superior before he finally returned to a language that Makoto and Kano understood. "The Abari believe you are unique, so we are going to…test that uniqueness."

"So we *are* prisoners," said Makoto. He might as well have been speaking into a vacuum, for all the effect his words were having.

Kano cleared his throat. Makoto knew that meant the diplomat was coming out. "What are the Trials? And how soon can we be finished with them and return to our team?"

Varlam shuffled uncomfortably. "I cannot speak to what the Trials entail. All I can tell you is that it will take several days to reach them. Since I am your translator, I have been tasked with seeing to your accommodations during that time."

How thoughtful. Makoto would have said it out loud if he didn't already know he'd be ignored.

"Why choose me?" asked Kano. "I'm not the only Zoboros with this power. Do you test everyone who attacks your ships?"

Varlam paused for another sidebar with the commandant. The discussion wasn't heated like the last, but it was clear the commandant was being careful with her words, whatever they were. "It was not your Power which impressed the Abari, but your connection to the Homeland," Varlam translated. "A connection such as yours has not been seen in quite a long time. Perhaps ever."

Homeland? Makoto assumed Varlam meant the Rift, though he didn't know how anyone could call this violent place a home. And it also raised the question: why were the marauders able to fly through it so easily when their previous ship could not?

Kano stewed a while before responding. "You're putting a

lot of trust in something that I don't even understand. And I'm putting a lot of trust in you by leaving my friends behind. If I agree to this, I'll need a guarantee that your people will let mine pass safely through the Rift and beyond."

"I give you my word on that point, though I know it would mean little to you," said Varlam. Makoto noted how Varlam didn't need to translate for the commandant in order to make that promise. "What might be more meaningful is knowing that this is our primary vessel. As long as we are traveling toward the Trials, our forces are traveling away from your friends."

Kano nodded. "And you would return us to them after your Trials?"

"Contingent on your survival, yes." Varlam struggled to make eye contact with Kano.

Seven feet tall, and even he's afraid, thought Makoto. How dangerous were these Trials?

"There is another matter. Your friend is not welcome in the Homeland." His eyes fell on Makoto, and for the first time Makoto wished he was being ignored.

"Where my brother goes, I go," said Kano.

Makoto puffed his chest in defiance of Varlam, who glanced back and forth between them, probably puzzled how these two species could consider each other brothers. He spoke to the commandant, who hissed at him again, enough to make the Poterian pale – a strange sight on a face that was such a deep shade of red. Varlam considered his next words carefully, obviously trying to rephrase whatever the commandant had just said.

"Your request may prove complicated. The Homeland does not recognize those without the Power. It will respond to him the way a body responds to a virus. His presence endangers us all."

Makoto shook within his tattered spacesuit. He wanted to speak on his own behalf, to give them a piece of his mind, but knew he'd be ignored, or else dig a deeper hole for himself. He swallowed his pride and deferred to his big brother for a response.

"He won't be a danger while I'm here," assured Kano. "I was able to calm the Rift before. I'll make sure it doesn't harm us on our journey."

"Be that as it may, the Abari rarely accept anyone who does not possess the Power." Varlam leaned in and lowered his voice. "I speak to you as an outsider as well. His presence does not bode well for you."

"None of this bodes well for me, regardless of the company," said Kano. "And the Abari saw firsthand the danger that I can bring to their ships. I would advise *them* to stay in my good graces, or else we might have another…misunderstanding." Kano let his power tremor in his palm for effect. It brought a smile to Makoto's face.

Varlam gulped. Makoto wasn't sure if it was because the Poterian feared Kano's threat, or because he feared what the commandant's response would be during the translation. It didn't seem that he needed to translate, though. The commandant watched Kano's hand, clearly fluent in the language of violence, and whispered to Varlam, a smirk twisting across her face.

"The commandant has agreed that your connection is worth the risk of transporting your…brother. However, the Abari do not inherit the risk for free. If he remains, he will be expected to work."

"I'll work!" exclaimed Makoto, relief spilling out with every syllable. "Whatever you have in mind, I can handle."

Still, no one looked his direction.

"We agree to your terms," said Kano.

Varlam translated for the commandant. She pounded her fist to her chest, then turned and marched off the bridge, leaving them alone with the Poterian.

"You have both entered a dangerous game," said Varlam, finally addressing Makoto directly.

"Nothing we're not used to," said Makoto.

Varlam frowned. "This way. I shall show you to your quarters."

And make sure we stay out of trouble. Makoto glanced at Kano, who raised an eyebrow. As usual, they were on the same page.

"How did you learn to speak our language?" asked Kano as they followed Varlam across the bridge to the marauder ship.

Varlam beamed. Evidently, they'd found a topic on which he could speak freely. "I was a linguistics expert on Poteria, specializing in languages from the other side of what you call 'the Rift'. Of course, books could only get me so far. When I became part of the peace talks between our realms, I learned a great deal about your dialects."

Makoto deflated at the mention of "peace talks". That was how it all started, before the Poterian Emperor decided to place Makoto's homeworld on his hitlist.

"And what happened when those ended?" asked Makoto tersely.

Varlam gulped. "I was made an interpreter between my

people and those we…" Varlam trailed as he stared at them.

"Took prisoner?" suggested Kano. The Poterian neither confirmed nor denied it.

"Looks like your occupation hasn't changed much," muttered Makoto.

Varlam hung his head solemnly. None of them spoke as they entered the marauder vessel, whose interior Makoto could best describe as "industrial". Exposed pipes and wiring were flushed along the gray walls of tall but narrow hallways — Varlam could barely walk through them without his shoulders brushing against the sides. Any marauders they encountered were quick to step out of their way and into other passageways where they could whisper to one another. Most were Abari, with a few more Humans and Gorvs thrown in the mix. Makoto had yet to see any more Poterians.

"Where do the marauders come from?" he asked.

"Be careful not to refer to anyone by that," said Varlam. "They are the Abari, and those who are connected to the Homeland, whom they also name as Abari."

"Does that mean they're all Zoboros?" asked Kano.

Varlam nodded. "Though the Abari do not possess the Power in the way you are accustomed to. It does not thunder from their hands in mighty displays of strength. Rather, it enhances them in…other aspects."

"Like helping them sense their way through the Homeland?" asked Kano.

Varlam nodded. Makoto shot his brother a quick glance. *How did he know that?*

"When my people — my former people — drove them from Poterian space, the Abari found they could survive here where no one would pursue them," continued Varlam. "And so they have remained for over a millennium. But they believe their time here is coming to an end. They speak of signs."

"Signs?" asked Makoto. This was sounding like something out of a bedtime story.

"It is forbidden to speak of Abari scripture to an uninitiated," said Varlam. He checked over his shoulder; they had ventured deep enough that no others were nearby. "Perhaps after the Trials we may discuss this again, though I imagine those higher up than me will take it upon themselves to answer anything and everything you wish to know…should you succeed." He stopped. "Your room is here."

He motioned toward a small door at the end of the hall. Makoto entered first, and found the room about as compact as his bunk aboard the *Shirlena* – though that bunk never had a humming noise coming from the neighboring room. Makoto banged on the wall to see if it would go away.

"Reactor coolant system," said Varlam, anticipating the unasked question. "So best not strike it again."

Wonderful. If there's a reactor leak, my second mouth will be the first to tell them. Even on Makoto's side of the Rift, where technology was not nearly as advanced as it was in Poteria, nuclear energy had been largely phased out. But these marauders existed in a world entirely their own.

As Makoto settled onto one of the two beds (which constituted most of the room), he found himself staring out a small, round window. He figured they were near the lowest level of the ship; the rest of it climbed high and out of sight. He could just make out one of the ship's bulking wings before its end disappeared among the clouds.

"The mess hall sits between the wings," said Varlam. "If you need anything, I—"

"I want to know what *really* happened to our friends," Kano cut in. "On your honor, were any of them hurt? And will the mar— Abari attack them again?"

"What I told you was true: your friends remain on course, though we don't know the extent of their injuries. As to another attack, we have been told that their vessel is now cleared for passage through the Homeland. They will not be interfered with."

"Who cleared them?" asked Makoto.

"Or better yet, why were we targeted to begin with?" asked Kano. "According to our smuggler escort, they'd never seen an attack of that scale."

"It is not my place to know why these orders came down. I am simply tasked with assisting you during your journey."

"Then how do we know they won't change their minds and attack again?" asked Makoto. "How do we know *your* orders won't change?"

"An Abari decision is stronger than calladium. They will not go back on it."

"Like they went back on their original decision to attack?" said Kano.

Varlam stiffened. "There is much you have to learn about the Abari. Just know your friends will make the pass should their pilots continue to prove as capable as they have thus far." He turned to Makoto. "Work will be assigned to you soon. Until then, rest."

"But what about you?" asked Makoto. "You said the Abari only accept other Zoboros. So what are your powers?"

Varlam looked away. "With any luck, you'll never have to find out." He started out the door. "I'm just down the hall if you need me."

"Wait," said Kano. "We never gave you our names."

Varlam stopped in the doorway. "If you complete the Trials, you will have a new name, at least among our people."

"And if he doesn't?" asked Makoto.

"Then his name won't matter much anyway."

Chapter 20

The Exchange

"Brace."

Jaden secured his seat restraint at Hauser's command, his gaze fixed on the fading swirl of hyperspace in the viewport. The bluish glow of the Rift had vanished (thank goodness), replaced by starry blackness. *One problem behind us*. He tightened his grip on his restraints as a planet came into view. *Now onto the next one.*

Guilt stabbed at him. He glanced over his shoulder at Hauser, who sat at the controls among his few remaining crewmembers. They had already been through hell, and yet they had no idea what was coming.

If he was being honest with himself, neither did he.

The planet began to take shape in the viewport, its surface black like Cloraxia's — only the color didn't come from rotted earth. According to Hauser, those were mountains. Lots and lots of mountains.

The *Onstappen* shook as it pressed into the atmosphere. Jaden tried to spot their landing zone, but he couldn't find a single flat feature in the rugged terrain. Not unless he counted the lakes that sat in the pockets between mountains.

"Weather check?" called Hauser, who sounded unfazed about landing.

"Clear as we're gonna get," answered one of his crew. "Rain should hold for another hour or so." Jaden spotted the clouds in the distance, dark and thick, the mountain peaks stabbing right through them.

"Things are looking up already," said Hauser, only half-sarcastically. The marauder attack had delayed their arrival by about two days, and from what Jaden had gathered, their contacts awaiting the levithium were not happy about it.

Soon that'll be the least of their worries.

Jaden finally spotted their destination, being it was the only thing they could possibly land on within a hundred miles: a plateau. It jutted from a mountainside; its half-moon shape sculpted so perfectly that it stuck out like a sore thumb. As they lowered, Jaden noticed a spiked freighter on the opposite side of the plateau, its black exterior blending into the surface. He had been warned about the Poterian terrorists inside it, though the term "Poterian terrorist" seemed redundant. He'd been raised to think that all Poterians were terrorists, so for their empire to label them as such must have made them an especially rowdy bunch. Thankfully, he and the team would be safely here on the bridge while the plan commenced.

"You with the shields," said Hauser, pointing to Cera. "I want you with me, in case things get dicey."

And there goes the plan. Cera exchanged a look with Carmichael. The captain nodded, so she marched toward Hauser, the whole team tensing as she passed.

"If you're going to send one of mine into danger, I'd like another to go in as backup," said Carmichael.

Hauser nodded. "Name your man."

Jaden looked around, having no idea who Carmichael would choose. Of the remaining team members, Li couldn't make anything grow on this terrain, Chenji's powers were still unpredictable, Warp was unlikely to be put into play by Carmichael, and Sterling couldn't be sighted by any Poterians yet, else his return could be broadcast across the empire. Same could be said if T8 was taken and analyzed by the Poterians. Ristin was a potential candidate, but his powers made him more of an escape artist than actual combatant. That left only one eligible member.

"I will go," said Akio. He stood up on his chair, still shorter than everyone else.

Hauser shook his half-burned head. "You forget which side of the Rift we're on, Jakari. If these Poterians see one of your lot walking about, they'll turn tail no matter what excuse we give em."

"I do not wish to be seen unless needed," replied Akio. "I will hide in the Lady Cera's pack. With luck, I will remain there."

Luck had nothing to do with it; both Jaden and Akio knew that. There *would* be trouble, and Akio would most certainly be needed once it came.

Hauser nodded his approval. Akio hopped off his chair, his scaly little feet plopping against the cold tile, yet in that moment he looked as tall as the surrounding mountains, even when he wriggled himself into Cera's backpack full of gear.

"I'll want one more, for insurance purposes," said Hauser.

"Cera and Akio are the best fit given the circumstances,"

said Carmichael, rising from his chair. "If you send someone else, make it me."

"I'm not lookin' for the best fit." Hauser stalked behind the team's chairs like a wolf on the prowl. Jaden felt the hairs on his neck prickle up. "Who's to say that when I leave this ship you won't try and take it for yourselves? We're past the Rift now, so what use is little old me?"

"I've already given you two of my—"

"I have no doubt the *Lady* Cera and your slippery lil' Jakari will fight their way back on board easily enough," Hauser cut in. "I'd like some collateral so we can keep the pleasantries alive." His massive palms clamped down on Jaden's shoulders.

Dammit. Jaden tried to control his shaking legs as he rose. Stepping out there would be dangerous enough for the other two; for him, it might as well be a death sentence. The frightened looks the others gave him did nothing to ease his anxiety.

"Come along, Jaden," said Hauser, his golden teeth twinkling in his stupid smile. "Let's go make your mum and dad proud."

Jaden failed to see how getting himself killed in his parents' smuggling business would make them proud, but he followed Hauser all the same, only stopping when Carmichael caught him by the shoulder.

"Keep as close as you can to Cera," the captain whispered. "I'll do whatever it takes to make sure you get back on this ship."

"Alive, I would hope," said Jaden, the sarcasm helping to calm his relentless nerves. He joined Cera, Hauser, and two of Hauser's crew at the bridge's exit. The rest of the smugglers would remain on board to ensure the ship didn't take off without Hauser's orders. And they would certainly report any funny business to Hauser in the field. Checkmate. It was a clever move, Jaden had to admit. But there was another element in play that Hauser didn't know about; one that would make or break everything, including Jaden.

He maneuvered behind Cera as they marched through the hall and whispered into her backpack.

"Any advice?"

Akio poked his head out. "If anything happens, stay down. Do not draw attention to yourself."

I could've come up with that. He also knew that when Akio said "if" he meant "when". And when it did happen, the smugglers would turn on them quickly. He only hoped whoever Akio had contacted was quicker.

He really wished Kano and Makoto were here right now.

"We've got each other's backs," said Cera. "Remember that."

Hauser chuckled. It didn't surprise Jaden; all the smuggler had ever known was lying and backstabbing. He'd never had a team like theirs. Not that Carmichael didn't do his fair share of lying too, but Jaden still knew that if the chips were down, Carmichael would take a bullet for him. He couldn't say the same for Hauser, though it didn't make him feel any less guilty to see his old mentor walking into a trap.

The smuggler stopped them at the liftgate. "These Poterians have strict customs. Let me do the talkin'. And whatever you do, *don't* look em in the eye."

No problem there. Jaden had spent most of the walk staring at the floor anyway.

The liftgate opened and cold air swept in, carrying a strong, metallic odor. *Sulfuric acid*, Jaden realized. No wonder they ran a rain check; the planet was poisoned. He tried slipping to the back of the formation when Hauser caught him in a bearlike grip.

"Ah-ah-ah. You get a front row seat with me, lil' Upton."

"Lucky me." Hauser led him down the ramp and onto the rocky surface. A dozen Poterians emerged from the freighter across the plateau and approached, each one big and brutish and grumbling in Poterian.

"It's customary for the whole crew to be present for a negotiation, even though only the captains are allowed to speak," explained Hauser. "We'll catch some flak for not bringin' everyone, so just keep quiet till I smooth things over."

He didn't have to tell Jaden twice. But when Jaden looked at the smooth, crystalline floor of the plateau, he found his own frightened reflection staring back at him. In fact, every rock jutting out along the mountainside carried a reflection, like it was some twisted hall of mirrors. One that made it impossible to spot Akio's contacts, wherever they were hiding. But he felt their presence; it resonated with each violent beat of his heart.

"Wasn't always this eerie, they say," said Hauser as they walked along, though whether he was talking to the group or just himself, Jaden wasn't sure. "They say this was once a paradise. Until the eruptions started."

"Are these volcanoes?" asked Jaden, praying they didn't have something else to contend with.

Hauser laughed. "These are the leftovers. Wherever the magma came got buried long ago."

Jaden took a whiff of the putrid air. "Sure smells fresh."

"Still thinkin' with your gut, aye? Good. Glad something I taught you stuck."

More than you know. The thought made him sad.

They met the Poterian crew at the center of the plateau. Jaden found it hard to keep his eyes on the ground when he felt so many hostile stares boring down on him. He tried distracting himself with his reflection, with his blond hair that had almost reached its former length. Be a shame to die when he was so close.

"We detected more crew on your ship," said the Poterian leader, hitting each syllable so hard they were liable to break. "Why do they presume to hide from us?"

"Our ship came under a marauder attack, as you can see from the damage," came Hauser's scripted response. Jaden dared a glance back. He hadn't yet seen the extent of the damage from the outside. It looked like the *Onstappen* had been pounded by a sledgehammer and then singed with flamethrowers.

"Eyes forward!" snapped Hauser. Jaden spun around. That shout had sent him twelve cycles back, back to the child who was scolded for messing up while shoplifting or taking too long to hotwire a hovercar. Wholesome things only Hauser could teach.

The smuggler cleared his throat. "My crew is tendin' to the damage and ensuring none of it affects your cargo. Otherwise, they'd be here to honor you and your crew."

The Poterian leader snorted. "Typical outlander. Showing up late *and* treating tradition like a convenience. You're lucky I don't take your ship for the insult."

"A fair judgment that would be, Zakhar," replied Hauser,

bowing his head. "But few ships and crews could escape the marauders like mine could."

"Do you presume to have me in a bind?!" Zakhar took a thundering step forward that shook the ground beneath their feet.

Hauser didn't flinch. "I *presume* to help you to the best of my ability. If you'd like a replacement, be my guest."

Zakhar spat on the ground. "And here I thought it bad enough you added a woman to your delegation." His crew erupted in laughter. Jaden glanced over at Cera, whose knuckles were whitening over clenched fists. He was thankful it was her accompanying them and not Li, who might have had a few choice comments. Cera knew to keep her cool for the sake of the mission, a quality he was trying his best to emulate given the nasty company.

"Hey!" barked Zakhar, squatting so his face was level with Jaden's, his breath hot and reeking of blood. "I thought he told you to keep your eyes front, *Human*." Jaden brought his gaze back to the floor, where he found each of Zakhar's boots bigger than his own head. He searched for something to say, but all he could think of was that boot popping his skull like a grape.

"Let's keep the conversation between captains, shall we?" said Hauser. "I'd like to avoid breaking any more traditions."

Zakhar sneered and turned away, sparing Jaden his rancid breath. He didn't dare let his eyes wander again, though he was desperate to know where and when Akio's contact would make their move. The sooner the better.

"I presume my cargo remained intact during your…delay?" said Zakhar, cracking the knuckles of his sausage-like fingers.

"Only lost two vials in the attack," said Hauser. "For which I am happy to renegotiate the deal."

"Oh, you better be," said Zakhar, his voice filled with even more malice than before. "Your track record is the only reason I accept the company of your filthy breed. Bringing women and children to a negotiation. Disgraceful. Next you'll tell me you've got Nurranos on board. Imagine, bringing those inbreds here to flood our cities like the roaches they—"

"I sacrificed your vials!" blurted Jaden. He paled as a dozen Poterians glowered at him with death in their eyes. He wasn't sure if it was the insults against Nurranos, women, or Humans that provoked him, but he found he couldn't stop himself from speaking up. "I used the levithium to save your shipment from an army of marauders...so you're welcome, asshole."

Hauser clamped Jaden by the shoulders. A few inches over and he'd have the chokehold Jaden knew he wanted. "This one's new and has yet to learn the rules," assured Hauser. "I'll deal with him in a fashion appropriate, don't you worry."

"The crew reflects the captain," hissed Zakhar. He grabbed Jaden by the collar and wrenched him out of Hauser's grip. *Not good.* Zakhar hoisted him into the air and carried him to the edge of the plateau. *Definitely not good!* Jaden stared at the sharp drop (and even sharper rocks) beneath his feet. Unlike Famora, there'd be no tractor beam to save him from being splattered or skewered, whichever came first.

"Give me one reason not to cast you over right now," hissed Zakhar.

Jaden racked his brain for a response that wouldn't lead to instant death. "Because you have a leak!" he blurted.

Zakhar's eyes narrowed. He pulled Jaden in, close enough for Jaden to spot the bits of meat caught in his jagged teeth.

"What leak?"

"Zakhar, don't do it!" hollered Hauser.

"Shut it!" Zakhar turned back to Jaden, intent on his every word.

"The marauders knew we were coming. They were ready at the entrance and at each of the first three jump points. They wanted your levithium." The last part was a lie, but Zakhar wouldn't know that. "You have enemies conspiring on either side of the Rift."

"The whole damned empire is conspiring against me!" said Zakhar, shaking Jaden in his massive arms. "The empire *I* fought for. Who's to say you're not working for them too? Who's to say you're not the leak?"

Jaden felt the Poterian's grip starting to slip. "Would the enemy only waste two vials?" he said quickly. "I protected as much of your shipment as possible and lost two of my closest friends in the process. I want revenge on the people responsible even more than you do. And you *should* want revenge too, and swiftly, because from what Hauser told me, a marauder attack of that scale has never happened before."

Zakhar stood there, thinking. Jaden wished he would think faster as he stared longingly at solid ground.

"You best have some good information for me, Human, or I'll have your—"

A shot rang across the plateau, like a crack of thunder. One of Zakhar's crew slammed onto the rocky floor.

"*Sniper!*" screamed Zakhar. His crew scattered like flies as more shots rang out. He barreled toward his ship, Jaden bouncing in his grip, probably a forgotten paperweight in the Poterian's mind as fight or flight took over. All Jaden could make out among the shaking chaos around him was the green glow of Cera's shields and the Poterian bodies hitting the floor. But where were the attackers?

A flash of blue whirred by. Hot liquid splashed in Jaden's face. Zakhar cried out, lost his grip, and Jaden hit the hard, glistening ground shoulder-first. He tried to get up, clutching his shoulder, when something small pounced on his back.

"Like I told you, *stay down,*" said Akio in his ear.

"Jakari bastard!" bellowed Zakhar. Jaden saw the massive boots marching toward him, the blood dripping from a cut in the Poterian's hand. "You've sold us out to *her!*"

Jaden didn't have time to consider who "she" was. He was too busy rolling away from the boot as it cracked the crystal rock he'd just been lying on. Akio rolled the other way and brandished his bloodied knife at the Poterian.

"This blade carries the blood of your forefathers."

"All the more reason to make your kind extinct." Zakhar had a pistol holstered at his side, but instead drew a scimitar from his belt. Bullets flashed across the field, reflecting off the curved blade, but did nothing to frighten the Poterian. If he would die, he would die fighting.

He lunged and Akio pivoted out of the way. Jaden crawled as far as he could from their duel, the rings of steel-on-steel echoing across the plateau. All around, Poterians were collapsing. Crying out. Dying. He spotted Hauser's two smugglers lying dead on the rocks. But where was Hauser? He searched, fearing he'd find another body, when he heard the battle cries of that distinct accent.

"Show yourselves you ruddy cowards!" Jaden spotted the smuggler firing his pistol off into the distance; probably at nothing, but who could say for sure? Something came over Jaden. He couldn't explain what, but for some stupid reason he found himself back on his feet and charging at Hauser.

"Stop!" screamed Akio, diving away from another stroke of the scimitar.

But Jaden didn't stop. And Hauser didn't stop firing, either. Not until something burst from the rocks at his feet. Small and covered in soot, it vaulted over Hauser. There was a flash of glinting steel and Hauser cried out. His pistol fell from his bleeding hand and landed beside the creature.

It can't be. Jaden stopped and stared in disbelief. Despite the soot that covered it, there was no mistaking that small frame or those bulbous eyes. All this time, Jaden had assumed Akio had contacted the Poterians. He was wrong.

"You are in the custody of the Poterian Empire," the Jakari hissed, wiping the soot from her purplish scales. "Stand down."

"*Jaden!*" Akio screamed.

A crack echoed across the plateau. Jaden felt a force throw him forward, followed by the heat of the bullet in his back as he struck the ground. He screamed, the heat burning his insides.

"Upton!" Hauser dove on top of him, and he screamed as the weight of the large man came down upon the wound.

"Fool boy," said the Jakari attacker as it wiped Hauser's blood from its blade.

"Where is he hit?!" cried Cera, sweeping in beside them.

"The back," said Hauser, daring to sit up, much to Jaden's temporary relief. Judging by the silence, the firefight seemed over, but the pain shooting through Jaden's upper body had only begun. He writhed on the floor as it blazed there, his mind a whirl of confusion and panic.

Cera drew her communicator. "We need Li, *now!*"

"Jaden, talk to me." Jaden saw Hauser prodding his leg for a pulse. "Jaden, are you alright?"

The pain evaporated from Jaden's mind. As did the noise, the confusion, the questions. Every part of his being focused on one thing and one thing only.

"Hauser…" he whispered. "I can't feel my legs."

Chapter 21

Troops on the Ground

The roar of engines filled the desert air. Junior approached the open side of the chopper, wind and sand bristling through his buzzed down hair as a sea of red dunes rolled by. *Dunes I nearly died on*, he thought. *Let's see how I fare the second time.*

"Junior, come back here," said Angeline, waving her cuffs toward the relative safety of the seat beside her, "relative" being the key word on a chopper built by Del Clorans. Safety wasn't a factor those creatures prioritized when scrapping together their vehicles; if the thing flew, that was good enough.

Besides, if his mother wanted him safe, then she shouldn't have insisted on staying prisoners. She kept saying "patience", yet somewhere between being swept up in a Del Cloran war and being puked on by a Cloraxian queen, Junior's patience had run out. And the fact that they made him wear heavy, stuffy Del Cloran armor was salt in the wound.

The chopper vibrated with every rotation of the propeller blade, shaking the sweat right off his face. He knew any sudden turbulence would be enough to throw him out the door and into the sand (if the chopper didn't shake itself apart first), but to back away from the door now would be to submit to his mother's orders, so he remained planted where he was, watching the distant tree line where life and color burst from the monotony of the sands. An oasis among the dunes.

The River Niscelles.

He clenched his fists, images of the violent current flashing through his mind. That was the place he'd nearly drowned; the place he'd witnessed Del Clorans shooting Zoboros left and right. He glanced back at the creatures assembled within the chopper, all armed and ready to do it all again. If it wasn't for these cuffs, he'd make sure they never got the chance.

"Weapons ready," said Taranis, hand clenched around the hilt of his sheathed sword. The Del Cloran officer beside him gave the same order via clicks. Two dozen insects rose in unison and loaded their rifles.

Junior had to give credit where it was due: Taranis had picked an effective military to enlist. These creatures, in their unquenchable desire to expand across the cosmos, had gained plenty of combat experience. *And* plenty of enemies. He wondered where his old Zoboros friends were hiding now. Judging by the plume of smoke rising from the trees, not far.

"Stick with me."

Junior hadn't noticed Taranis creep up beside him. "Afraid I'll run off without supervision?" he asked.

"If you do something stupid, so will she," said Taranis, quiet enough so Angeline wouldn't hear. "That's how mothers work."

Junior had a hard time imagining Taranis with a mother of

his own. As far as he knew, the maniac had been raised in a government facility by scientists who experimented on him. If Taranis knew anything about family, it came from the ones he'd torn apart. It was, after all, the only reason he'd dragged Junior along: to keep Angeline in line.

They swept through the smoke and over the wreckage of a Del Cloran chopper, which lay dredged in the rich, dark soil, fire burning out its failed engine. Its pilot had managed to land it in a clearing, though Junior figured that might have been pure luck given the propeller was nowhere to be seen. By the break in the mast, it looked like something had sliced the propeller clean off.

"Looks like a trap," said Junior.

"All the more reason to stay with me."

The choppers began touching down in the clearing. Taranis waited for the Del Clorans to pour out and form a perimeter before his boots crunched down onto the dead leaves and twigs.

"Think our old friends were behind it?" asked Junior, following Taranis toward the wreckage. He wasn't sure how to feel about that prospect. Plenty of memories had been swirling through his mind during their journey here – memories of Nera, Brivek, Zivo, and Yui together in the Champion's Club, enjoying an endless supply of food and laughs. He dared to consider those happy memories despite being forced into the fight ring by Clemens. They were certainly happier than how it ended, with Junior lying in the ring, having been thrashed to within an inch of his life, while the others joined Taranis on a killing spree through the arena.

"Let's hope it's them," said Taranis, observing the broken

mast. "Because if someone else did this, we won't want to be on their bad side." He knelt and searched in front of the chopper for tracks – a skill Junior didn't know the formerly masked man had, though he assumed it came from cycles of hunting Zoboros.

Junior spotted a squad of Del Clorans kneeling in the nearby brush and hurried over. They had found the bodies of the advance team and surrounded them, clicking softly in unison and tilting their heads side to side. A prayer, Junior realized. Not something he expected from a people who liked to throw their numbers so expendably at their enemies. He waited until the squad quieted to inspect the bodies.

Blade wounds, Junior noted. Each had cauterized at the point of impact, leaving harsh burns across the torsos of the Del Clorans. But what blade could do that? Even stranger was that the attacker had chosen to take on the advanced team at close quarters rather than shoot at them from the cover of trees.

"Notice anything familiar?"

Junior jumped at the latest unexpected Taranis appearance. He had a feeling he knew what Taranis was referring to, though. When he glanced back at the broken mast of the chopper, he noticed scorch marks there too.

"Same weapon," said Junior. "Or the same Zoboros."

"And a Human Zoboros at that." Taranis traipsed over the bodies and patted a nearby tree where drops of red blood had splattered against the bark. The blood seemed obvious now, though Junior doubted he would have noticed it on his own.

Taranis followed the attacker's tracks, but Junior hesitated as he stared into the overwhelming canvas of trees and brush.

"Shouldn't we have the Del Clorans follow the trail instead?" he asked.

"They'd only meet the same fate," said Taranis, marching toward another patch of blood in the fallen leaves. "And we'd be fools to give up a trail this fresh."

Junior froze as he realized Taranis wanted him to follow. It was disturbing enough being prisoner to his father's murderer, but to take a stroll through the woods with the maniac just felt wrong. He glanced back at the Del Clorans surrounding the wreckage. Would it really kill Taranis to bring a few extra guns? Then again, those same guns could be used to shoot Junior in the back. Or ruin any chance of negotiating with the Zoboros, which he assumed was what Taranis was bringing him along to do.

That gave Junior an idea. Some of the Zoboros out there were his friends (*if* they were still alive). That meant there was a chance Junior could swing them to his side instead of Taranis's. He was sure the power dampener on his hands would win some sympathy among the Zoboros, too, and that they'd be more than happy to take it off.

"Wait!" he called out to Taranis. "We should bring my mother. Better to keep her with us than the Del Clorans."

"I agree," said Taranis, though he eyed Junior carefully. "Be quick."

Junior hustled back to his mother, who was still waiting beside their chopper, and led her away from the thunder of the propellers.

"What's going on?" she asked.

"An opportunity," he said. "Taranis needs our help negotiating with the Zoboros. If we find them, we can turn them to our side."

Angeline stared at the crashed chopper. "We may not want them on our side."

Junior rolled his eyes. "What would you prefer, then? To sit here and let Taranis make all our decisions for us?"

"We have no way to defend ourselves, Aaron. At least Taranis and these Del Clorans intend to keep us intact. Another party may not be so friendly."

"That's a risk we have to take. If we turn our noses up at every chance we get, we'll spend the next fifteen cycles in these cuffs!" He paused. He hadn't meant to say the last part; it just slipped out. He saw the wound in his mother's orange eyes again, though her expression remained unchanged.

"Better fifteen cycles in these than something worse."

"Maybe for you," said Junior, unsure if 'something worse' meant death or using her powers, though he assumed it was the latter. "A life in cuffs isn't worth living. But if that's what you want then you don't have to come." He crunched through the leaves toward Taranis, so frustrated he almost didn't care if he left his mother with an army of Del Clorans. Eventually, though, he heard her footfalls trailing behind him, and a small part of him felt relieved.

Taranis had tracked a decent way into the trees by the time they reached him. He searched in silence while Junior did his best to keep out of the way.

"Where did you learn to track?" asked Angeline.

"Jaculus," said Taranis, more focused on the trail than his answer. Junior had a feeling the Jaculus had taught Taranis how to hunt Zoboros, too. And probably many more dark things that he had trouble imagining.

"What happened between you two?" asked Junior. "Why did you steal his sword?"

"I stole nothing," said Taranis, taking his eyes off the trail for the first time. "I earned it in combat. By then there was no more to learn from him, so I moved on."

"Then there's no bad blood?"

Taranis crunched a fistful of leaves in his fist. "You fish in dangerous waters, Hendricks Junior. Rest assured our partnership should hold as long as required."

Required for who: him or the Jaculus? Junior wasn't sure which one he trusted less. Clearly each had their own agenda on Mogaddu. Junior would have pressed the subject further had his mother not given him a warning look.

"And what happens to our 'partnership' once this is finished?" he asked. A vine snagged his leg and threw him forward, and Taranis caught him from his fall.

"I have no desire to shed Zoboros blood unnecessarily," said Taranis. "For you and your mother to survive all this would be a victory for our people."

Junior frowned. He could fill a book with the things Taranis deemed "necessary" to his cause. Hell, he'd make the first chapter about bombing a major city.

Taranis snapped his head around and drew his blade. "Show yourself!" he shouted into the forest.

Something whizzed past Junior's face and clunked into a nearby tree. He raised his cuffed hands out of instinct, forgetting he could no longer summon fire, and saw that it had been a knife, its blade and hilt made entirely of bone.

"Zivo!" Junior shouted. "It's us!"

Brambles cracked and crunched across the way. A Talak

emerged, a smile on his thin face, his six arms spread in greeting as they dropped whatever bone-made weapons they still retained. "That you, Hellfire? And Big T?! What a surprise!" Zivo's gaze shifted from Taranis to Junior's cuffs, though he didn't address them. "You better be careful out here. The Del Clorans—"

"Await my signal," Taranis cut in. Zivo paled, probably wishing he hadn't given away his position. "I've brokered a chance for peace between our two sides. One that helps our cause."

"You sure about that?" said Zivo as he scanned the jungle. "Del Clorans aren't known to negotiate much." The skin parted at each of his wrists, and through the openings emerged more knives of bone that slid into his hands.

Taranis sheathed his sword. "They are willing to come to the table. I suggest we discuss the rest with your leadership directly. Preferably behind closed doors."

"That'll sure be a sight," said Zivo. He waved them on through the forest, where Junior was able to do some catching up with him. Nera and Brivek were both safe, he was thankful to learn, and many more Zoboros had joined their cause.

"Too many if you ask me," said Zivo, juggling his knives while they walked. "Ever since we took the land, it's been a hell of a time trying to keep it."

"Who's trying to take it now?" asked Junior.

"No one. We just don't know what to do with it. We have so many mouths to feed, and each one has a different opinion of how to manage things. I hate to say it, but it was a lot easier when we were fighting the Del Clorans. At least then we had an enemy to focus on. Now we're too focused on arguing with each other."

"At least you're still good at taking down Del Cloran choppers," probed Junior, hoping for a clue as to who was behind the attack, but Zivo only grunted.

"Zivo, you mentioned some growing pains," said Angeline. "Has anyone stepped up to manage things?"

"That would be Douglas," answered Zivo, his voice sounding strikingly indifferent for one usually bursting with enthusiasm. "He's got some good ideas, just...well, you'll meet him soon."

Junior blinked. *How did she do that?* No one ever wanted to speak their mind when Junior asked questions, yet in a few words she had gotten useful information that he could not. He watched her navigate the brambles without losing an ounce of the regality in her step, her mystery growing all the greater.

They crested a hill. The trees had been cleared from the top all the way down the slope to the river's edge, and in their place stood raised wooden homes, many still under construction. A hundred pairs of feet crisscrossed the flattened grass, carrying lumber or buckets of river water, while others hammered, sawed, or otherwise supervised the development of the new village.

The new *Zoboros* village. Junior found some satisfaction in that.

"We tried settling upriver, but the flooding was too intense," said Zivo as he led them through the winding streets (which were just paths of dead grass) to what was easily the largest building in the village. It only stood one story tall, but was wide enough to swallow four wooden homes, and raised a bit higher than the rest, enough to warrant a short flight of stairs to the entrance.

"As you can see, we've gotten a bit better at this building business." Zivo hesitated at the door as muffled shouts leaked through. "They were discussing sanitation guidelines when I left. Pray they've found something new to shout about."

He opened the door and there was Brivek on the opposite side of a round table. The Vosni looked like he'd lost some weight, though he was still large enough to take up double the space of anyone else. Ten others were seated there, but Brivek was the only one standing, his normally pale face turning bright red as he shouted.

"If that's what you want to do with *your* shit, then you can do your business—!" His beady black eyes fell on Junior. "Hellfire? Big T?!"

"That's not my name," muttered Taranis.

The big guy waddled around the table and scooped them up in a hug so tight Junior thought his insides might come out his mouth.

"Nice to see you too, Brivek," he groaned. Taranis looked ready to send a jolt of lightning through the lumbering Vosni.

"Junior!" exclaimed Nera. The red crown of cartilage above her Norphimian head jiggled as she swept in for a hug, her scaly arms and webbed fingers thankfully much gentler than Brivek.

The other faces around the room were all unfamiliar to Junior, and all looked unsure what to do about the unexpected company. All except a Human who sat with his muddy boots propped on the table. He wasn't particularly large, though his chair was twice the size of anyone else's (including Brivek's). The sly look on his face was one Junior had seen a hundred times while policing Famora on the night shift. This was someone looking for a fight.

"We were starting to think you both would never come back," said the smug Zoboros. He stood up, a full head shorter than Junior, yet he marched over like Junior was an ant in the way of his muddy boots. "Last I recall, you and 'Big T' were at war. Glad to see things have mended." The Zoboros reached out for a handshake, then pretended it was the first time he'd noticed Junior's cuffs. "Or perhaps not."

A real performer, this one. Junior always believed people who made politics into theater deserved a swift kick, and he wanted to be the one who delivered it.

"Junior, this is Douglas," said Zivo, his voice remaining neutral, though the sour look on Nera's face was much more telling.

"I came to help prevent any more bloodshed," Junior said to Douglas.

"By bringing an army to our doorstep?" asked Douglas, more to the village leadership than to Junior. "Why don't you tell us why you're really here?" His suspicious gaze shifted toward Angeline.

"We come to you with a common cause," said Taranis. "One rewarding enough to overlook past differences, just as young Hendricks and I have managed to do."

I wouldn't call it that. The way Douglas raised an eyebrow, Junior could tell the Zoboros leader had a similar thought. He would be a hard one to win over. In fact, a part of Junior didn't want to win Douglas over at all; not if he couldn't be trusted. Suddenly, his mother's advice was sounding much sager.

"No doubt your 'common cause' involves the lost city, Taranis," said Douglas, pacing around the table. Junior looked to the other leaders, including his old allies. Why wasn't anyone else saying anything? "Many come looking, but as I understand it, the door to it cannot be opened. So why bring a hostile army just to disappoint them?"

"Because we know how to open it," said Taranis.

Douglas stopped his pacing. "And what of your Del Cloran escort?"

Taranis smiled. "We have something in our possession that will ensure the Del Clorans fall in line."

The leadership stirred. Many glanced at Angeline with uncertain looks, yet no one spoke loud enough for the whole table to hear. They all waited for Douglas.

"And I suppose you expect *us* to fall in line too," he said. "We who fought for this land long after you abandoned us. We who lost friends and loved ones for it." Many heads nodded around the table. Junior shifted as cold stares came in his direction. "Your reputation precedes you Taranis, as one who cuts a thing off as soon as you no longer need it. You needed us once to start your revolution. Can we expect to become your foot soldiers again?"

"What we find in Iramwerta belongs to no one person," said Junior, drawing surprised looks from Taranis and his mother. He was surprised himself. He'd come here to out Taranis, not defend him, yet he couldn't stomach siding with this smooth-talking Zoboros. Not if he would be trading one captor for another. "It would benefit all of us if we…cooperated."

Douglas gave a cold smile. "That's what we're all here for, isn't it? Cooperation."

"Iramwerta is easily defensible," said Taranis. "And hard for our enemies to reach in large numbers. If you took it, you would be nearly invincible." Heads turned around the table.

Taranis had their attention. "Most importantly, taking back the Zoboros birthplace would solidify your position as a nation rather than a fledgling colony which your enemies are eager to squash. It would attract more Zoboros to your cause. Not just fighters, but builders and planners. People who could contribute to your vision."

"You'd have us cast away the vision we've created already for this...fairytale?" said Douglas. He paced again, slow and deliberate, so that each member heard him clearly as he passed them. "We worked hard to build what we have here, haven't we?" Some heads nodded.

"And you will work hard again when the floodwaters wash away your latest attempt," said Taranis. Any heads that were nodding froze. "This village is a blip in the history of the Zoboros. But to take back Iramwerta...that *is* history."

The village leadership began to stir.

"I for one would like to see this city!" exclaimed Brivek.

"Me as well!"

"Agreed!"

Nera raised a confident hand.

The only thing Junior enjoyed more than the camaraderie was seeing the frown on Douglas's face. The angry leader cleared his throat as the crowd calmed down. "I think I speak for everyone when I say we'd be interested to see you get us inside the lost city...but I wonder, what do you want in return, Taranis?"

Taranis bowed his head. "Merely to see my people thrive."

Bullshit, thought Junior, though he figured he'd leave it to Douglas to call it out loud.

"With you sitting at the top, no doubt," said Douglas on cue.

"And what's to stop us from taking it from you once we've found it?"

The lights flickered. Junior saw sparks jump between Taranis's fingers. "The Del Clorans," said the half-Poterian.

"I can cut through Del Clorans like paper," said Douglas.

He's the one. Junior had assumed so, but now it was clear. A quick scan was all he needed to spot the puff of a bandage beneath one of Douglas's sleeves. That was why everyone let him run his mouth; they were afraid of a guy who could slice through an entire chopper full of enemies. But Junior had learned from Clemens that fear only worked as long as the illusion of power remained.

"I don't doubt you could take them on," said Junior. He leaned close to whisper to Douglas, making sure his arm pressed against the bandage. Douglas winced but didn't dare cry out in front of his peers. Instead, he cast a vengeful gaze on Junior. "But if you choose war, this village will know it. Win or lose, the blood is on your hands. And they won't forget that."

Taranis smiled as Douglas drew back. "Do we have a deal?" he asked, loud enough for the whole room to hear it.

Douglas tapped his foot angrily while he thought. "I will not bet my people on your claim to open Iramwerta," he finally said. "But you will get us inside, and then we'll decide how to split the rewards."

"It is enough reward to serve the Zoboros cause," said Taranis with a bow that made Junior shiver. The maniac had managed to string along the Zoboros *and* the Del Clorans, but how did he plan to cut them loose once he got what he wanted. Somehow, he had a feeling his mother fit into that part of the equation.

"You did well," she whispered, startling him. "But now we will have to tread even more carefully."

Douglas cleared his throat. "So Taranis, ready to show us the city that can't be found?"

"Sadly, I do not know the way myself. I lost consciousness and was brought there by sheer fortune."

What?! This whole time, Junior had been banking on Taranis knowing the way. Junior sure as hell didn't know; the spear had guided him through some sort of magic, and he'd lost consciousness for most of the journey.

"I can lead you there," announced Angeline. Everyone turned toward her, shocked, Junior most of all. He knew she'd sought Iramwerta long ago, but he never knew if she'd found it.

Douglas smiled. "By your lead, then."

Chapter 22

With Great Power...

The Rift swam around Kano, pulsing with its strange power but never touching him. When he stepped forward, it reeled back. When he reached out, it hurried away. Yet like a curious animal, it would creep closer anytime he stood still.

The energy bridge twinkled beneath his feet, the path ahead shrouded in the fog of the Rift. But Kano knew the man was out there.

"I'm here!" he called. His voice echoed along; what it bounced off, he couldn't say. He searched the surrounding stars, expecting them to coalesce into the man's cloaked face again. Instead, he heard footsteps. His heart began to pound. Could it really be him? He straightened his back as a silhouette approached through the fog, his mind whirring with questions: who was he? Where did he come from? Why had he chosen Kano? The closer the man came, the clearer his figure – the clearest it had ever been in Kano's dreams – yet beneath the blood-red cloak was something totally different, and it sent all Kano's questions sailing out the window.

"You're…Poterian?"

"I told you not everything would be as it seemed," the figure replied, its tusks rising and falling beneath its hood with each syllable.

"But you always came to me as a Human." Kano noted the broad shoulders beneath the cloak. "A *skinny* Human."

"If I had revealed my true form to you, would you have sought me out?"

Kano's instinct was to say "yes". But he had to think about the old Kano, the one on Famora who had started having these strange dreams. The one who had never seen a Poterian before or experienced many of the incredible and frightening things he'd found throughout the galaxy. That Kano would have stayed awake just to avoid nightmares of a tusked, man-eating beast. That Kano would never have trusted anything this Poterian offered.

"If you continue, everything you believe shall be tested." The Poterian waved at the path ahead, shrouded in fog. Lightning flashed, revealing the shape of a mountain at the bridge's end. Kano started toward it, yet no matter how much he walked, neither the mountain nor the Poterian got any closer.

"What's happening?"

"I told you to let go, Kano. Only then may you find what you seek."

"I don't even know what I'm looking for!" Kano started running, though he might as well have been on a treadmill for all the progress he made. "What does it all mean? The mountain. This path. *You.*"

"You will understand when you are ready."

The bridge trembled. *No.* Kano hadn't come this far just to be turned away. But he also wasn't prepared to pay the toll. The image of his brother floating helplessly over the bridge played through his mind as the Rift tightened around him.

"Don't forget, you called to me," said Kano as the Poterian disappeared behind the fog. Light blazed from the clouds, threatening to wake him. He shielded his eyes. "You'd really bring me all this way just to shut the door in my face?"

"There are other prospects to answer my call," said the Poterian. "Others who will follow the path I set."

So black and white. Why did it have to be a one-way ticket? He stared over the edge into the great, infinite cosmos. And why did he have to go one direction?

"I'd not advise that," said the Poterian.

Kano smiled. "It's just a dream, isn't it?" He leaped before the Poterian could stop him.

Makoto trudged down the corridor, argyle skin drenched in sweat. Those marauders sure knew how to keep busy. He'd thought engine duty would be like it was on Sterling's ship: occasional checks mixed with gratuitous naps, but marauders hardly left time to breathe. Every waking moment was filled with loud voices barking orders and machines that groaned and churned even louder. His ears still rang, and probably would until his next shift.

His eyelids felt heavy as he navigated the snaking hallways. It didn't help that his call time went against his circadian rhythm; normally he'd be sleeping at this hour, something he was convinced the marauders never did. They were up and about all hours of the day, always moving, always hustling. Makoto supposed when trying to survive the most dangerous space in the galaxy, it was best to keep at full staff.

Everywhere he turned, he found more marauders giving him sideways glances. He tried to hold his drooping head high, but a day filled with people who considered him "unworthy" had taken its toll. They'd given him the hardest tasks just to yell at him in a language that he didn't understand. *A whole new ship, and I still feel worthless.*

A clank echoed down the hall, followed by a scream. Trouble. Makoto rushed in its direction. Could it have been an accident? A fight? Something told him he probably shouldn't get involved, but that only made him run faster.

More shouts echoed through an open door. He found a group of marauders inside, but it was neither an accident nor a fight – at least, not the kind he expected. The marauders stood beneath a raised platform where two Abari squared off with clubs, each dressed in full armor, striking and blocking in a dance as seamless as it was quick, its symphony of thumps and crashes awakening Makoto's tired mind.

"I take it you finished your first shift." Varlam removed himself from the group of spectators and approached, his helmet in his hands, the rest of him armored up and covered in sweat.

Makoto nodded, though his eyes were glued to the blistering action in the ring. "I wanna try," he said.

"This is no place for a newcomer like yourself. You should be resting. You'll find sleep is your most precious commodity aboard—"

"Is there a rule that says I can't fight?"

"None." Several indignant stares came their way from the small crowd. Varlam knelt to Makoto's level. "But there is also no rule that says they cannot break you to pieces in the ring."

"I'd like to see them try."

"If young warrior wishes fight, *lest* him!" came a drawling accent. They turned. The match was over, and one of the fighters was approaching them.

"*Let* him," corrected Varlam. "And you'll learn his language better if you left his jaw intact, Gorrus."

"I learn his language better if he speak for himself." Gorrus tossed a club to Makoto, who caught the fifty-pound weapon with ease. The surprised look on Gorrus's face told him the Abari had never dealt with a Nurrano before.

Makoto followed Gorrus toward the ring when Varlam caught him by the shoulder. "Do you realize if you injure yourself to the point of being unable to work, they will kick you off the ship?" whispered the Poterian.

"Sure do."

Varlam sighed. He motioned for someone to bring Makoto a set of armor.

Space and time blurred into one mind-bending tunnel as Kano plummeted. Civilizations receded. Forests sprang forth. Planets spun backward...*time* spun backward. Deeper and deeper he went, closing in on a particular spot, a particular moment.

He blinked and he was standing in a village, among a crowd.

Humans and Poterians, together in the town square on this sunny day. Such a strange sight, yet he almost overlooked it as his mind struggled to get its bearings. Judging from the small size of the surrounding wooden homes, this crowd must have constituted the whole village, or at least most of it. They were silent, the nearby merchant carts stripped and tarped. Villagers had packed into the windows of the few two-story buildings in the square. Everyone seemed to be craning for a look.

At what? He spotted a Poterian standing on a stage at the center of the square. No wait, not a stage...

Gallows.

He hurried through the crowd, careful not to bump any of the villagers. He was a stranger here, wherever he was...*whenever* he was. Best to keep a good rapport, especially if hanging was a viable punishment here. He stopped at the edge of the crowd, where a line of soldiers with spears held everyone back. Not that they seemed too eager to come to the Poterian's rescue. They all watched with interest as the Human hangman drew the noose around the Poterian's neck.

"Any last requests, thief?!" someone shouted.

"A weak rope," said the Poterian.

Kano froze. He knew that voice, had heard it on the bridge just minutes ago. He'd not gotten a good look at the face beneath the blood-red cloak, but this face up on the gallows was much younger. And cockier.

"Who is that?" he whispered to the stranger beside him, but she didn't answer. In fact, she didn't even look his direction. Something was off. He tried tapping her shoulder, but his hand phased right through her.

I'm not really here. They can't see me.

"It's time, Niscelles. I'll be havin' your final words," said the hangman.

Niscelles?! Kano stepped back, phasing through the villagers behind him. This whole time, the figure who had haunted his dreams was *the* Niscelles? One of the first Zoboros of all time? One of the kings from the old legend?

So why was this "king" standing in a noose in a ragtag village?

The hangman reached for the lever. Kano felt something whiz overhead. An arrow. It snapped the rope as the trapdoor opened. Niscelles fell through it and disappeared beneath the gallows, the severed rope swinging uselessly in the breeze.

"Guards!" shouted the hangman. "He's—!" An arrow caught him in the leg. He cried out and toppled through the trapdoor while the crowd screamed and panicked.

"He's trying to escape!"

"Where are those bastard friends of his?!"

People phased through Kano left and right: guards running to catch the bowman, villagers scrambling to get out of the way. And Kano just stood there in the middle of it all, wondering why he had been brought to this moment.

"You're not supposed to be here." A massive paw clamped around his arm. A Poterian paw. Niscelles stood beside him, shrouded in his cloak, the marks of age much more apparent up close – leathery skin and deep bags beneath the shrouded eyes.

"How did...but you're...?" He pointed dumbly toward the underside of the gallows where the guards were still searching for the missing prisoner. But the younger Niscelles emerged on top of the platform, the severed noose still hanging around his neck. The crowd met him with boos and assorted vegetables.

"What is this?" asked Kano.

"The beginning," said the older Niscelles beside him.

The other Niscelles, beaming and sprightly, gave a bow to the angry crowd while the guards started to climb back onto the platform. "The Three Kings of Mogaddu bid you farewell, good people!" he exclaimed.

A trio of horses trotted toward him, one of them riderless, wedged between one ridden by a Human and one ridden by an Abari. He leaped onto the available horse and together they rode off, while the guards scrambled to hail their own horses and make pursuit.

Niscelles, the older one, pulled a dumbfounded Kano from the crowd and led him toward a tavern.

"You-you're the first Zoboros." No response came from the old Poterian. "But you were just a petty thief!"

"This is Mogaddu. Did you really expect knights and chivalry here?"

Niscelles pushed through the door to the tavern. Men were gathered around the tables, all too drunk to stand. Some laughed themselves out of their chairs, others barked at each other in heated, nonsensical debates. The only one who seemed remotely pleasant was the old bartender limping around the counter as he washed it with a rag. It was only when they got closer that Kano realized he was cleaning off a bloodstain.

I guess some places never change. All Kano needed to really complete the picture was an illegal fight ring in the backroom. But he had to remind himself that Zoboros didn't exist yet.

Niscelles led him to a booth in the back corner, out of all the racket.

"Why didn't you tell me who you were?" asked Kano. "You're kind of a big deal, you know? They named a river after you."

"You haven't listened to anything I've told you so far. Why start sharing now?"

"I'm here, aren't I? Has any other Zoboros gotten this far?" Kano hadn't forgotten Niscelles's threat to find another.

The Poterian leaned back in his chair. His sleeve rolled back, and Kano noticed a brand there: the symbol of the Zoboros, the edges of the triangle seared into the leathery Poterian skin, the arrows pointing from the corners toward the center.

"Let's see just how far you're willing to go, then," said Niscelles

The tavern door burst open. Niscelles stood there, rain dripping off his cloak as it gusted in behind him. *When did it start raining?* Kano realized this version of Niscelles was older than the one who paraded around the gallows, though not so old as the one sitting across from him in the booth. The whole tavern went silent, the patrons sobering as the newcomer marched toward the bar, the spurs of his boots jingling with each slow step.

"Your kind ain't welcome here," said the bartender.

"So I've heard." The younger Niscelles drew back his hood and scanned over all the patrons. That was when Kano realized that everyone except Niscelles was Human, and they all looked ready to make a move if the Poterian did. Gone were the days of an integrated village. But Niscelles just leaned there against the bar, one hand rested on the hilt of his sword.

"I suppose you know how this ends," the younger Niscelles

whispered to the bartender.

"It ended when your side lost," the bartender spat back. Several men rose, armed with knives and bottles.

"How much did we skip over?" Kano whispered to the older Niscelles across from him, forgetting that the angry patrons couldn't hear him.

"To every beginning there is an end," said the older Niscelles, closing his eyes. Kano tensed. If Niscelles didn't want to relive this memory, then Kano didn't want to experience it either.

"But it didn't end, did it?" the younger Niscelles asked the bartender as the angry patrons drew closer to him. "Your king still wants my people dead. He still wants to erase them from the stars. But he and I once shared this village. I'm sure when he sees what's become of it, he'll know I mean business."

The bartender's eyes widened. "You-you're supposed to be dead."

"Wouldn't be the first time I cheated death, hangman."

In that moment, Kano recognized the old bartender from the gallows. And in the next moment, the patrons lunged. Niscelles tore the sword from its sheath. Black fire blazed up and down the steel blade – a blade that Taranis would one day use on his enemies – and startled the attackers. Kano watched the ancient Mogaddan etchings in the blade glow with the fire's strange light, yet he felt no heat. Niscelles swung it in a wide arc and the fire leaped from its tip.

But it didn't burn anyone. Instead, everyone it touched burst into clouds of ash before they had a chance to scream.

"What is this power?" asked Kano, horrified. He turned to the older Niscelles, who kept his eyes closed.

"One I did not deserve."

More fire leaped from the blade, consuming everything in its path. People, tables, bottles, support beams. The bartender limped desperately for the door but only his ashes reached it. Kano braced as the horrible fire surged toward him...and then phased right through him. It continued eating its way through the once full tavern. Now the only sounds were the groans of the failing structure and the jingles of Niscelles's spurs as he marched outside.

"Why are you showing me this?!" Kano demanded of the older Niscelles. Outside, he heard the screams of the younger Niscelles's next victims.

"I simply bridged our minds. You took the leap. You chose to go digging."

"This is your mind?" Kano spun around, shocked, confused, and just starting to realize all the possibilities. The mind of the galaxy's oldest Zoboros, one who had seen so much, had connected with so many, and had somehow survived all this time. So many secrets right at Kano's fingertips.

"Does it make you feel powerful?" asked Niscelles. "It's an intoxicating thing, to hold the advantage over someone else. A feeling our kind can get dangerously used to." The screams outside only accentuated his point. "How would you feel to carry even more power than you already do?"

Kano took a step back. The tavern groaned around him, its broken beams sliding and snapping apart. "I'm not a killer."

"Funny, the boy in the noose would have said the same thing."

Kano ran out the door, but what he found outside froze him in the doorway. Clouds of ash – clouds of *people* – covered the village in a gray fog. Or what was left of the village. Everywhere he looked, homes and shops lay collapsed. The few survivors screamed and ran as fingers of black fire chased them. Consumed them. Erased them.

A crack echoed above his head. The tavern crashed down around him.

"Gah!" He snapped upright in his bed. It was dark in their small room, the only light coming from the glowing clouds of the Rift in the window.

The hell was that? He rubbed his aching head, wondering if that black fire he saw was the power that awaited him in Iramwerta. Or in the mountain. He wasn't sure which at this point. In fact, he wasn't sure about anything anymore.

He climbed out of bed, quiet so as not to wake Makoto, only to realize his brother wasn't there. He checked the time — Makoto's shift should have been over by now. He searched the halls but found them oddly quiet. Had the marauders miraculously stopped their constant duties?

Shouts echoed down the hall. He hurried toward them. *Makoto, if you got yourself in trouble, I swear I'll—*

He turned a corner and crashed into the backs of marauders, all packed into a relatively small room. He sidled his way between them, unable to see over their tall heads, but hearing all the crashes and clanks of what was clearly a fight. And he had a feeling he knew one of the combatants.

Kano squeezed his way to the front and, sure enough, his brother was in the sparring ring, though he was almost unrecognizable in his oversized and mismatched marauder armor. Makoto blocked a blistering wave of attacks from an Abari twice his size. Even the club his opponent wielded was almost as big as he was, yet he deflected the strikes with ease. At least until the Abari's fist landed in his chest.

"Makoto!" Kano climbed inside the ring, to the ire of the crowd.

"Does baby warrior need help?" jeered the Abari opponent.

"I'm fine, Gorrus." Makoto shoved Kano away and rose, using his club for support.

"Are you crazy, Makoto? You're no match for him."

"Says you." Makoto steadied himself for another bout.

"Does brother want to fight too?" asked Gorrus. He tossed a club to Kano like it was a paperweight. But when Kano tried catching it, he collapsed underneath its weight, delighting the crowd.

Makoto scooped the club off Kano's chest. "This is my fight," he said, balancing both clubs in his hands. How Makoto managed to lift even one of those so easily was beyond Kano, but Makoto seemed set on keeping two as he aimed them at Gorrus.

"Think more clubs will save you?" asked Gorrus, his smile showing off his many missing teeth.

Makoto kept a fighting stance. Kano stood awkwardly beside him, brotherly instinct telling him to break up the fight, to defend Makoto from this much larger opponent. He could do it easily with his…powers. His ears went hot, and not because the crowd was shouting at him to get out of the way. In his mind, he saw black fire erupting from his hands to wipe away all the Abari before him. How unfair that would be…how unfair it must feel for Makoto to always be in the shadow of so many Zoboros. Kano climbed out of the ring and returned to the crowd, much to their satisfaction.

Gorrus swung with enough speed and strength to send power rushing instinctively to Kano's palms. But Kano held it back, watching instead as Makoto dipped beneath the attack, then jabbed Gorrus's shoulder. The Abari grunted and stumbled back. The crowd laughed, and Gorrus tightened his grip on his club.

"That all you got?" Makoto taunted.

Gorrus surged forward and their clubs met in a whirl of motion. Swings, jabs, uppercuts, every strike from Gorrus as quick as it was deadly. Makoto deflected them all, the massive clubs in his hands looking like extensions of his own body. The only beat of stillness came when Gorrus swung low. Makoto jammed the opponent's club between his own two, and, despite the Abari's superior size, Gorrus couldn't seem to unjam it.

"Feeling a little stuck?" chided someone from the crowd. More laughter followed.

Gorrus muttered something in his own language, his orange face reddening. He tried swinging a fist at Makoto, but Kano knew that was exactly what his brother wanted. Makoto dropped onto his back, pressed his feet against Gorrus's chest plate, and heaved the Abari over his head and onto its back. The next moment, Makoto was atop Gorrus, his dual clubs pinning the Abari.

"Yield!" demanded Makoto. A silent crowd listened.

Gorrus wriggled beneath Makoto's pin, gargling and grunting to no avail. Finally, he ceased his struggling and nodded.

Makoto rose, ripped off his helmet, and wiped the sweat from his face. He turned to the shocked crowd.

"Who's next?"

Chapter 23

Arrival

Her hands wouldn't stop shaking. Li tried to focus on her breathing, but it didn't help. Not when the hole in Jaden's back was staring at her. Taunting her.

"Anything yet, doc?" asked the hacker. His chin rested against the edge of the table, his exposed back shivering. *At least the part he can feel.* The glow from her hands flickered at the thought. Hauser must have noticed because he offered her a glass of water. The smuggler had refused to leave Jaden's side, much like he had with his last crewmember to end up on the operating table, so Li figured she'd make use of him.

"Try not to speak," she said to Jaden, "however hard that might be for you."

"Like asking a Braiman not to build..." he muttered. Despite the chatter, he'd been uncharacteristically cooperative during the procedure; he even avoided making any snarky comments about her failed attempts to heal his back (of which there had been many). She assumed at first that he was simply in shock, but as the hours wore on, she began to suspect that his shock had turned to acceptance.

But I won't accept it. She brought her glowing hands over the lower part of Jaden's spine, sensed the dead spots and tried to coax them with a hard release of her power, but nothing happened. Not like with tissue or muscle. Those regenerated, albeit slowly depending on the severity of the wound. But nerves...those weren't coded to come back. And no matter how hard she tried, she couldn't recode them.

"Wait a sec...something's happening!" exclaimed Jaden.

"What? Really?!" she said, straining as she focused her power on the spot she'd found. Hauser leaned up beside her excitedly.

Light had returned to Jaden's tired eyes. "Whatever you're doing, it's working! I feel...I feel..." Jaden paused. A sly smile stretched across his face as a foul odor filled the room. "Oh, it was just gas."

"Dammit Jaden!" Li threw herself into a chair and shook out her aching wrists.

"Really had you going there, didn't I?" he said, his laughter fading as he stared at the floor. "You've done all you can, Li. I think it's time we faced facts."

Hauser swore under his breath.

Li was up on her feet again, hands glowing. "I don't give up on my patients."

"I'm tired," said Jaden. "And I think we could both use some rest. Besides, there's more important things happening outside that door."

Li swore too. She didn't want to think about what was happening outside their little operating room, almost as much as she didn't want to think about Jaden being bound to a wheelchair for the rest of his life. She reached down to help him sit upright when Hauser placed the water in her hand.

"I'll get him to bed," he insisted. "You've earned a rest."

Normally, Li would have insisted back, but something in Hauser's eyes told her to let him have this. The poor smuggler didn't have much left. Not since the Jakari had taken over his ship and killed the rest of his crew.

The hallway was quiet despite having Jakari everywhere. They didn't speak, didn't look her way, yet she knew they all sensed her. They were intent on her every move, even if they didn't show it. They had to be when power dampeners were apparently illegal in the Poterian Empire. Instead, the Jakari went the much more civilized route of threatening to slit throats if anyone tried any funny business.

She scraped at the blood beneath her fingernails. Jaden's blood. In that moment, it all hit her: Jaden injured, half the team missing, the other half of the prisoners with no idea where they were going. Their plan to cross the Rift couldn't have gone any worse.

"How's he doing?"

Li snapped out of her spiral as Chenji approached. "The bullet unfortunately missed his sarcasm...but it got everything from the waist down."

It took a while for Chenji to absorb the news. "His sarcasm kept me laughing after I took that hit from Taranis," he said. "With Kano and Makoto gone, who's gonna keep him laughing?"

Li turned away, the tears welling up. She felt Chenji's hand on her shoulder. "Don't beat yourself up over it," he said. "He might not have survived if it wasn't for you. A lot of us wouldn't have."

She sniffled, not daring to look in Chenji's direction. She had to stay strong. This team was lost and she was their rock. They needed her to fix them. Needed her to—

Something brushed against her leg. Something fluffy. She looked down and found a puppy staring at her with its big, sad eyes.

The tears spilled down her cheeks. "Dammit Chenji."

She cradled him in her arms and wept. Wept until her tear ducts ached and her body had sapped its last shreds of strength. All the frustration and confusion burned out with it, replaced by an empty numbness that left her sitting on the floor of the hallway in a daze. Chenji remained there as a puppy beneath her palm, enjoying the scratches behind his ears. It reminded her of the first time they'd met, when he'd pretended to be Carmichael's dog only to transform into a naked creep. How repulsed she'd been, and still would be if Chenji had not opened his gentler side to the team.

Jakari skulked past them occasionally in the narrow hall, each pretending like they weren't there, and each drawing Li's hopeful gaze that this time it would be Akio. Odd, considering Akio was probably the one she knew the least, but at this point any familiar company was comforting. She wondered how that little assassin had ended up in their lives. She knew he'd taken up the cause with Junior's father because of some sort of life debt – a life debt that had been transferred to Kano after Hendricks's death – but had little idea about how their partnership had come about. All she knew for certain was that Akio had turned traitor to his own people, and that these Jakari had not forgotten.

One of their captors stopped in front of them, almost an equal height with her while she was sitting on the floor. She waited for it to say something, but it just hissed and waved for them to follow. That made her nervous. Did the Jakari just want to meet with them, or were they looking to make good on their promise of cutting throats?

Assuming they'd have sent more Jakari if they wanted to subdue her, she followed it down the hall, Chenji scampering at her heels. Despite his small form, she felt safer with him — his hearing would be fine-tuned in case they were walking into a trap.

Like we did on Okeanos. Their hope had been that the Jakari would ally themselves with the team and lead them to Poteria in exchange for catching the terrorists.

At least they had gotten half that deal.

Their escort led them into the *Onstappen's* bridge. The Jakari worked the controls — a strange sight in place of Hauser's former crew — all needing raised chairs just to reach them. The team was assembled in the viewing area, except for Jaden, who Li assumed was still resting.

"What's this all about?" asked Chenji, finally back in his Human form, his specially made combat suit thankfully growing with him.

"Don't bother," said Sterling. He sat on the floor, his bionic arm and leg both confiscated. "They don't answer questions."

Chenji gave the Jakari a curious look. "Do they speak?"

"The Emperor's Shadow answers only to the emperor," said Akio solemnly. He trudged over to Li and climbed onto her shoulder. That made her sad; he usually climbed on either Kano or Jaden's shoulders.

"The *Empress's* Shadow," corrected one of the Jakari, her scales a light shade of purple. Li recognized her from the battlefield on Okeanos. She'd been closest to Jaden when he'd been shot. According to Jaden, she hadn't been particularly broken up about his injury. "Akio son of Ephos and Dorimas would know this if he was not *iznazi*."

Akio tensed upon Li's shoulder. Whatever that meant had cut right through the hardened assassin.

"You would not understand, Mizuki," he muttered.

Mizuki sneered. She turned back to her squad and announced something in their native tongue. They began pulling levers.

"We approach Poteria," Akio whispered in her ear.

Hyperspace vanished and a new planet consumed the viewport, its land barren and gray, its oceans a brackish blue, and its clouds stained a hideous yellow.

"That's impossible," she said without thinking. A dozen pairs of black eyes zeroed in on her. She held her tongue, but her question remained. How could a civilization as vast as Poteria exist in a wasteland?

"It's even more of an armpit than I thought!" came Jaden's voice.

Everyone turned, the stares of the Jakari particularly venomous. Hauser was setting him down in a chair, and he winced as the tender part of his back brushed against the fabric.

"He needs to lay flat," said Li, to which Jaden held up a hand.

"I wanted to see this," he said with a grimace. "It would make me feel better."

Li knew from the look in his eyes not to question him. She

could force him to rest after.

The ship shook as they pressed into the atmosphere. The system's star shone to the right, carving Poteria into a distinct light side and dark side…though the dark side seemed somehow larger. Was it the angle? She noticed Cera staring curiously too. Something was off, they both knew it. Cera was the first to gasp, and as the ship arced around the dark side, Li gasped too.

Another planet emerged just behind this one, its light side lush with green forest and vast oceans of crystal blue, its dark side dotted with millions upon millions of lights, many of them combining into blazing beacons of cities.

Now that's Poteria.

The twin planets revolved slowly around each other in an angelic waltz, each roughly the same size, neither giving any indication as to which dominated the space's gravitational pull. She could only gawk and wonder how these two bodies hadn't collided.

"I never knew there were *two* planets," said Ristin, mesmerized.

"You know," began Jaden, "since they share the same orbit and the same space, you could argue that neither is a planet." That earned him dangerous looks from their Jakari captors.

"Too bad bullet did not take off his mouth," muttered Akio so only Li could hear. Of all people, Li couldn't believe it was Akio who made her finally crack a smile.

Their ship slid into the space between the two planets (or whatever Jaden thought they should be called) and the rumbling ceased. They had achieved an equilibrium, wedged between two opposing atmospheres, two opposing gravities.

She felt oddly at peace. At least until she saw the lights shining on Poteria's surface again. *So many Poterians.* She hoped they'd gotten nicer in the last twenty cycles.

Mizuki, who Li assumed was the Jakari's captain, gave another order in their language. Thrusters engaged, tipping Li off balance as they pushed the ship away from the barren world and toward the lush one. She spotted the city they were angling toward, seated right at the border between day and night. Despite all her fears and all the pressure of atmospheric entry, there was something beautiful about watching daylight creep across the landscape.

The sky around them shifted from black to blue. Clouds parted, pinkish ones that reminded her of home – an odd feeling in a place so far away. Yet the cityscape that emerged robbed her of any nostalgia. It wasn't the compact, gridded layout she was used to on Famora; this city rolled along the hills like it was part of them, its buildings separated by expanses of green grass or long fingers of woods. A city literally built into the land, with the wildlife able to interact with it. Li flexed her fingers, tingling with the pulses of even more life than she had ever felt in a city before.

Their ship swept over the hills and drew out a herd of galloping creatures. Six legs, each hooved, with long snouts and shaggy brown fur. Chenji fixated on them, but Li found herself more drawn to the vegetation. The trees bent at awkward angles, their leaves some of the largest she'd ever seen (given she could see them from way up here). Their vines intwined with the architecture: ancient yet pristine stonework that gave the whole city a regal feel, as though time could not erode its beauty. Bridges rose and fell between the buildings, leaving passageways underneath for the herd of unknown creatures to gallop through while the Poterian citizens marched above.

Li pressed against the glass. Thousands of Poterians, all going about their business no differently than the crowds on Famora. The sight gave her some hope, but she had to remind herself that they were not about to meet the common people.

Their destination dominated the horizon. A palace, one that put even the mighty Orlov palace to shame. Its blood-red walls loomed over even the city's tallest spires, its domes looked fit to house entire arenas, and its watchtowers ended in fine black points that pierced the rising sun behind it.

"The sun rises with the empire," she heard Akio whisper upon her shoulder. Li shuddered. This was an empire vast enough to probably cover *many* suns.

A moat divided the palace from the rest of the city, its water crystal blue. *In the middle of a city?* A civilization built on violence didn't strike Li as the kind that would keep its city water so pristine. Or give animals safe passageways away from traffic. Or let wildlife grow on what was no doubt valuable land. There was a lot she wanted to learn about Poterian culture, far more than she'd anticipated. Hopefully, the Jakari would let them live long enough to ask about it.

They passed the outer gate. Li found the inside to be a dizzying network of walls, bridges, balustrades, gardens, and courtyards, one so vast that an army could easily fit inside it all, maybe even a whole city. But what drew her eye was a stadium at the center of it, taller and wider than everything else. Row after row of stone risers wrapped around the curved wall, and at the bottom sat a massive sandpit. Her powers sensed a darkness around this place, and as they drew closer, she realized why. *Gladiators.* The weapons left in the sand told her so. Centuries of death haunted this place.

Their ship stopped above a courtyard outside the stadium. Nothing about its stonework stood out much from the rest of the palace, at least until the stone began to part.

They lowered through the new opening and underneath the palace grounds, passing stalactites on their descent. Li found herself gravitating closer to the other team members. No one spoke, but they all sensed the danger. A secret catacomb was an easy place for a secret execution.

"Follow me," hissed Mizuki as the ship touched down on the rocky floor. She started toward the door.

"Two of my team require wheelchairs," said Carmichael.

"Accommodations will be made." Mizuki paused to cast her spiteful gaze on Sterling. "Those who can walk should not keep the empress waiting."

The empress? *Here?!* Li froze. She thought they would be faced with a representative at best, if not the execution squad itself. Many worried stares found their way to the captain.

"Do what she says," ordered Carmichael. He led the way, side by side with a Jakari commander a fraction of his size, while the others filed sheepishly behind. But Li hesitated as she realized Jaden would be left behind in his chair.

"Go ahead, love," said Hauser with a wink. "I'll see about them accommodations."

Li managed to smile. Despite his faults, the smuggler was starting to grow on her. He'd proven helpful so far. And given everything that had happened the past few days, she knew they needed all the help they could get.

The ramp lowered, its edge kicking up dust as it struck the

floor. Li trailed behind the team, a squadron of Jakari waddling after her, but her focus shifted to the wide-open catacombs. Towering red arches, some unfinished, climbed up the rocky walls and supported the vast structures high above their heads. The chamber itself had little inside it except for a sandstone temple across the way, one with no windows and only one door. Li needed only to connect to her powers to sense something from it, though she couldn't quite place it. There was a feeling of death like she'd sensed near the stadium, but there was life too. In conflict with each other. And a voice whispering…

"Find us."

She jumped, forcing Akio to grip her shoulder tight.

"Poterians are savage negotiators," he whispered. "Betray no emotion."

She drew a deep breath, trying to bar the strange temple from her mind as she rejoined the team. They had gathered at a seemingly random spot in the middle of the empty catacomb.

"Is this everyone?" boomed a woman's voice through loudspeakers that Li hadn't even noticed. It made her almost jump out of her skin. Who was that? She checked behind her but saw only Zakhar and the other Poterian prisoners marching down the ship's ramp in chains, their heads down. She tried to sense the speaker using her powers, but all she felt was the overwhelming presence of that temple.

Akio pointed toward a pulpit overlooking the catacombs. A figure was seated there, hard to make out from this far below, but the throne she sat in wasn't. Tall and black, with ornate red draperies running down it like blood.

"This is everyone, Your Majesty," answered Mizuki with a

bow so low her face was practically on the rocky floor. The other Jakari did the same. So did Carmichael, and the rest of the team followed his lead. Even with her head down, though, Li could feel the empress's stare boring upon her.

"Your Majesty, the former general requires wheelchair, as does one of the other prisoners," said Mizuki.

Prisoners. Li knew Mizuki had wanted them to hear that.

"Those have been sent for," said the empress. "Though you would not need the second one if you had stayed your hand as requested."

"Forgive my transgression, Your Majesty." This time, Mizuki really did press her face into the rock. "I will accept any punishment Your Highness chooses."

"Be still, Mizuki. You have proven a more faithful servant than most."

Akio muttered something to himself, but Li was more focused on the pulpit as it lifted from the wall and floated toward them upon hoverpads so gentle they hardly disturbed the dust beneath them.

Carmichael turned toward the team. "Let me—"

"Do the talking," Chenji and Ristin finished in unison.

"Which of you has called on Poteria for aid?" asked the empress, her voice no longer booming through the loudspeakers, yet it resonated all the same. Li gasped as the pulpit touched down before them. Up close, the empress was the spitting image of Sterling: the curve of her red face, the angle of her thin tusks, the confident slouch within her throne. Yet there was a fire in her eyes that she'd never seen in Sterling's.

"I have called, Your Majesty." Carmichael stepped forward.

"My team and I have journeyed far to—"

"To bring your war to us," the empress cut in. "That should be cause enough for my Shadow to execute you, but since my family once brought war to your doorstep, I would not see myself called a hypocrite."

"They had many names for you, Typhera, but hypocrite was not one of them," Sterling called out. A Poterian servant brought him down the ramp in a wheelchair. When the servant and wheelchair had entered the *Onstappen*, Li had no idea.

The empress frowned. "And is this the noble army you've brought to reclaim your empire?" Some of her Jakari snickered.

"We come to prevent war," said Sterling. "One that would harm our people as much as theirs."

"So you say." Typhera rose from her throne and climbed down the steps from her pulpit. Her sandaled feet settled against the rocks with such regality Li would've thought she was standing on clouds. "I've heard similar warnings from another, though I'm told it is *your* band of rebels which threatens Poteria."

"From who?" asked Carmichael.

The answer to his question came in the form of a door opening from the side of the pulpit. Gasps rippled through the team as the old man hobbled out on his jeweled cane.

Chapter 24

Tense Negotiations

Jaden's eyes bugged out of their sockets as he stared through the viewport. *Not him. Not here.*

"Is that Danadas ruddy Orlov?!" blurted Hauser.

"We need to find out what's going on down there," said Jaden. As if on cue, a second Poterian servant appeared in the doorway with a wheelchair. Hauser stepped between Jaden and the servant and checked the newcomer for weapons.

"I mean no harm," assured the servant. "I am Radimir, of Her Majesty's personal cadre. My orders are to serve at your pleasure."

Or until he slips a knife into our backs. Despite his reservations, Jaden knew he was missing a juicy conversation in the catacombs. He waved Radimir over and, swallowing the pain in his back, hoisted himself out of his own chair using just his arms.

"Allow me—"

"No." Jaden shooed Radimir away. Hauser looked ready to help too but held back, recognizing how important it was for

Jaden that he make the transfer alone.

Jaden's arms shook as they bore all his weight. Tears filled his eyes while his legs hung limp in the space between the two chairs. With a final push, he launched himself clumsily into the wheelchair, sending another stab of searing pain up his back. But just as quickly, the pain evaporated, replaced by a coolness in his back that eased his mind.

"Numbing agent," said Radimir, patting the wheelchair. "In the fabric."

"Uh huh," said Jaden, in such a lucid state of bliss that he'd forgotten why he was in such a rush to begin with. At least until Radimir wheeled him through the elevator and down the ramp.

"...but you cannot deny that we fight for the same cause, Carmichael," came Danadas's raspy voice, the sound of it pushing Jaden's mind through the fog and back into the present. The old man stood between the empress and her lead assassin, Mizuki, wrinkled hands clasped over the fruit-sized jewel atop his cane. Carmichael and company stood opposite them, and off to the side were the Poterian prisoners, kneeling in a straight line with their heads down, surrounded by Jakari.

"I fundamentally disagree, Danadas," said Carmichael.

"Mr. Orlov has been a loyal friend of the empire for many cycles," said Typhera. "Unlike the Carmichaels."

Jaden felt his attention piqued. He'd heard plenty of conspiracy theories at his family table about powerful people allegedly backing the Poterians, and at the top of that list was always the Orlovs. *So my parents* were *right.* First time for everything.

"I do not come here on behalf of my family," said the captain. "I come because a Zoboros revolution has begun on our side of the Rift. Danadas wishes it to continue, and for you to help make it a full-scale war."

"What I wish is for the Zoboros to be free and the IDF destroyed," said Danadas. "My family spent cycles carefully setting the pieces to make this moment a reality. A moment that will not come again."

The empress pondered that. But Jaden, in all his wisdom, didn't need to. In fact, he felt pretty vocal with the numbing agent clearing his head.

"Danadas's 'wish' is for everyone else to be under his boot," he said. Cera flashed him a warning look, but he pressed on. "He's even killed his own family members to wipe out the competition. If you help him, empress, you may wake up one day and find that you're his secretary...if you're lucky."

"You will address her as 'Your Majesty'," hissed Mizuki.

Typhera waved for her assassin to be still. "My predecessor had an...interesting taste in allies," she said. "I have worked hard to steer as far from Palorex's radical ideologies as possible, but there is one point on which we agreed: your abuse, imprisonment, and enslavement of Zoboros must come to an end. Here in the empire, these acts are crimes of the greatest offense, and if I should miss an opportunity to put an end to them, it would be the greatest failure of my reign."

Carmichael folded his arms. "I may not be too knowledgeable on Poterian politics, but I have a feeling I know what you consider your predecessor's greatest failure to be." Typhera's look hardened, but she betrayed no emotion. "I know what war does to people. I know that twenty cycles ago, millions of Poterians learned their loved ones would not be returning through the Rift. And that has left you with two loud factions that are impossible to please: one that begs you not to send their children into a new war, and one that demands retribution."

"Noble words for a Carmichael," spat Zakhar. His fellow prisoners lifted their heads as he spoke. "It was *his* father who slaughtered our people and left this slut to take the throne."

"You've no right to speak here."

Jaden blinked; he'd expected that comment to come from the empress or her Shadow, but it was Sterling who'd spoken. He was up out of his wheelchair, balancing on his only foot.

Zakhar laughed. "I suppose this bitch is better than a fucking vegetable like you."

Jaden barely knew Sterling, yet even he wanted to smack Zakhar around for that insult. The empress seemed unfazed though. She gave just the slightest nod to Mizuki, who marched toward the bruised prisoner for another lesson in manners. Jaden smiled. He liked a leader who didn't take anyone's—

"Shit," said Ristin. Jaden noticed it too: the steel glinting in Mizuki's hand. She slashed it across Zakhar's throat and blood sprayed across the rocks. Li screamed, Chenji looked away, Ristin almost gagged, but the empress just stood there, her lips twisted into a smile as the prisoner choked on his own blood. Jaden regretted wanting to see him punished. This was the type of punishment he would read in an old history book, the kind of butchery that shouldn't exist anymore. The kind that belonged in...well, an ancient catacomb like this.

Zakhar spasmed on the floor, slower and slower, until finally he gargled his last breath. The other prisoners now looked the empress in the eye, daring her to do the same to them.

"The Red Sabre is as crude an implement as it is annoying,"

said the empress, checking her long red nails. "One that threatens the stability of my empire, just as you claim the Orlovs threaten the stability of your lands." The way she said it, Jaden sensed she wasn't too convinced on that point. "Since you both petition my support, I propose a contest."

Carmichael bowed his head. "We'd be honored by whatever Your Majesty has in mind," he said.

Speak for yourself, thought Jaden as he stared at the Poterian corpse.

"Each of you, as I understand it, has a team of Zoboros," said Typhera. "Whoever can extradite the Red Sabre's leader into my jurisdiction shall prove their loyalty to my empire and have their request considered."

"Considered?!" spat Jaden, earning himself another scolding look from Cera, though even she seemed unenthusiastic about this deal. They weren't guns for hire, nor did the prospect of a competition with a cheating scumbag like Danadas Orlov much appeal to Jaden. His only satisfaction came from the displeasure on the old Orlov's face. *Looks like we're in this together, you old crook.*

"Your Majesty, I must protest," said Danadas, "my team remains on the other side of the Rift and—"

"Then I'm sure you'll have little difficulty getting them across," the empress cut in. "Saving any inconveniences posed by marauders."

Her dig did not go unnoticed by the team, least of all by Jaden. Of course, Danadas would likely have a hand in any "inconvenience" they experienced in the Rift. It made sense then why the old man had arrived here unscathed. And it added the marauders to countless other factions across the galaxy that Danadas had dealings with.

There was another detail, however, that also concerned Jaden. "Your Majesty," he said, the words feeling strange coming out of his mouth, "why would your enemies need extradition? I thought an empress would have no borders to her jurisdiction."

"As rightly they oughtn't," said the empress, smiling. "Jaden, is it? I understand you to be quite a fan of history, though I will spare your friends a lengthy lesson. Suffice it to say that the political situation between New Poteria and Poteria Prime is…tense." Jaden assumed she was referring to the two planets that made up Poteria, though he was more concerned about where she'd gotten this information about him. "Poteria Prime despises the changes I made since assuming the throne, so much so that their governor has granted the Red Sabre all the protections of any other political party despite evidence of their treasonous dealings. And he will keep protecting them as long as they undermine me. If I send my forces in any capacity, it could spark civil war."

Yet another place on the brink of war. Boy did Danadas know how to pick them. But Jaden understood where the empress was getting at. "Sending us keeps you in a safe gray area where you can deny involvement."

"You catch on quickly."

"If I risk my agents in this game of yours, I want guarantees," said Danadas.

"I want guarantees too, Mr. Orlov," said the empress. "Your success will mean you are serious about making a deal."

Carmichael stepped forward. "If you can provide us everything you know on the Red Sabre and anything else we might be up against, then we have a deal." Li and Chenji began whispering amongst themselves, neither sounding too pleased at being volunteered. Jaden knew he sure as hell wasn't.

The empress spread her hands. "Then let the games begin."

Chapter 25

The Temple

Just when Junior thought he had seen everything on Mogaddu, he found himself at the bottom of a river.

Nera led the way, holding her hands up to maintain the bubble that surrounded their party. Junior struggled to keep up, his feet constantly sinking in the wet sand, though he supposed it was better than getting dragged unconscious through the current like last time.

Besides, he couldn't deny the brilliance of the view. The crystal blue water revealed everything from the turbulent rapids above to the serene, sanded floor. Schools of fish zipped past them, occasionally bumping against their bubble before skating a path around. Bottom feeders skirted along the ground, dredging sand and snails in their wake, the latter of which they slurped up in their wide mouths. Junior glanced at his power dampener, its little lights twinkling. He couldn't help but relate to the snails.

"Be prepared," Taranis whispered in his ear, the villain's breath hot upon his neck. Be prepared for what? He still hadn't figured out what Taranis had planned for their Zoboros escorts.

Junior clung to the hope that they could still resolve this without violence, but violence couldn't be ruled out wherever Taranis was involved.

Douglas gave Junior equal cause for doubt. The Zoboros "commander" was out in front beside Nera, pretending to lead the way. This was someone who would do anything to maintain power (or else acquire more of it), so when the time came for Taranis to play his hand, Junior wondered whether Douglas would side with Taranis or turn his forces against them. Neither option boded well for him.

Just like his mother had predicted.

She was in the back, wedged between Brivek and Zivo – who were probably under Douglas's orders to keep an eye on her – marching through the gooey sand in her dignified way. Her escorts, however, were claustrophobic, constantly looking at the water outside their bubble like it would come crashing through at any moment. Junior didn't mind the confined bubble so much (he'd once spent two weeks cramped in an escape pod); he just minded the company...and the destination.

Fallen ships cropped up in their path. Ugly machines caked with rust and algae, probably Del Cloran based on the way the parts had been scrapped together.

"Left a damn mess behind them," muttered Douglas. "And now you two went and brought them back."

"Entertain our bargain, commander, and the Del Clorans will no longer be a concern of yours," assured Taranis.

Junior caught a confident smile cross Douglas's face. He'd enjoyed being called commander, just like Taranis knew he would. But Junior knew the path ahead held far greater dangers than Del Clorans. The entrance alone could kill them if they weren't careful. And he had a feeling some members of their party wouldn't like paying the toll.

But would they have to pay it this time? In the stories, Iramwerta behaved in strange ways, and not always the same way. Would having his mother here change anything? She had told the Del Clorans that she was the "key", whatever that meant. He didn't dare ask in front of such dangerous company.

They angled toward the opposite bank of the river. Holes pocketed its rocky face, giving Junior a spark of recognition. These were the last things he'd seen before blacking out on the way to Iramwerta. But which hole would lead them to it?

Angeline maneuvered to the front of their formation and directed Nera to a hole positioned along the river floor. Sterling had told him once that his mother had led a group of Zoboros into Iramwerta, but the Lusitani had tracked them and trapped them there. Junior still wasn't sure how she'd survived.

Just like he had no idea how they would survive this trip.

Darkness swallowed them as they entered the cavern. Douglas waved back at Brivek, who lit a lantern in his big, pale hand, revealing the few snarling fish who called these rocky walls home. Much less friendly than the fish outside, Junior noted, a trait that seemed appropriate for Iramwerta. He desperately wanted to speak with his mother, to come up with an escape plan, but the small bubble left little room for discretion. He would have to wait.

The path snaked along, darker and deeper, until they came to an opening in the ceiling that led far beyond the reach of the lantern's light.

"We swim from here," said Angeline.

Nera nodded. "I will need to focus, then." She drew the bubble in even tighter around them, forcing them to crowd together. "This is more weight than I'm used to carrying."

"No offense taken," said Brivek with a wink. Nera smiled. Some of the tension lifted from their tight space, but it was quickly restored as the bubble rose through the water. It had some give, bending like rubber beneath their feet. Junior remained still, afraid any movement might cause it to pop, while Nera waved her arms, lifting them higher through the dark tunnel. Her scaly face strained, the bubble slowing as her arms began to tremble.

"Faster!" barked Douglas. "Push, dammit!"

Nera tried, to her credit, but her burst of speed was temporary. And the way her eyes were bugging out of her head, Junior didn't think she could last much longer.

"You're doing wonderful, Nera," said Angeline. "Just a little farther." Suddenly, their pace quickened. Nera pressed harder, yet her trembling decreased. Junior couldn't believe it. Mere words had produced enough power to save them from drowning.

Nera gasped as the bubble surfaced. Her arms gave out and she collapsed in Brivek's arms. A moment later, the bubble burst around them.

Shit. Junior hit the water and flailed, unable to swim with the cuffs binding his hands. Worse, the weight of them combined with his heavy Del Cloran armor was pulling him down. He spotted Brivek swimming across the surface with one arm, Nera cradled in the other, and two companions swimming alongside him. *No, no, no*. His mother was sinking beside him, a stream of bubbles issuing from her mouth. He wanted to cry for help, but that would just suck water into his straining lungs. Only when the others got to the shore would they realize—

An arm wrapped around his waist and pulled him toward the surface, the half-Poterian face beside him determined to reach it. Angeline was caught in the other arm, while Taranis kicked his feet furiously. Junior started kicking too, as did his mother, and their speed began increasing. Light trickled through the water above, drawing closer, calling Junior toward sweet oxygen. They burst through and Junior gasped in as much as he could, relieved despite what loomed ahead.

The Gate of Iramwerta. Fifty feet of stone, etched with a thousand markings of a dead language, standing upon an otherwise barren shore within a cavern of wet stone. Fragments of sunlight peeked through cracks in the rocky ceiling high above, the only hint that anything existed beyond this secret shore.

Taranis pulled them onto that shore and they collapsed in the sand, chests heaving. A strange sight, the three of them beside each other, made stranger by the fact that Taranis had been the one to rescue them. The maniac needed Angeline for his plans, of course, but Junior was expendable. He'd never imagined his sworn enemy *saving* him. Not after what Taranis had done to his father.

Junior was still catching his breath when Taranis rose, already looking recovered. *His Poterian half is showing.* The unlikely rescuer joined the others at the mysterious gate, leaving Junior alone with his mother.

"I hope...you're not waiting...for a miracle," he rasped between ragged breaths. "We need...an escape plan."

"I told you before...best not to tempt fate..." She drew a

deep breath and composed herself. "Taranis and the Jaculus still need us alive."

"They need *you* alive." Junior still didn't know exactly what they wanted with her, but the possibilities frightened him.

Angeline shook her head, the back of it rubbing against the sand. "If they control you, they control me."

So much for Taranis's heroics. "And when they play their hand, there won't be any controlling the situation. Either the Zoboros, the Del Clorans, or both are going to get betrayed and we're going to be caught in the middle. We should break away as soon as we have the chance."

"And go where?"

"Whichever way you escaped the last time you came here."

Angeline paused. "If we're lucky, we'll never have to go that way." She rose, brushed the sand off her Del Cloran uniform, and marched smoothly across the uneven sand. Junior stared at the massive gate looming over them, finding it filled with even more mystery than before.

When he finally shook the sand off his uniform and joined the others, he found Zivo rubbing the back of his neck with one of his six arms. "Sorry Hellfire," he said. "Forgot you were back there." Brivek looked similarly ashamed, though Junior cut the Vosni some slack considering he was still cradling Nera in his arms, her eyes closed and her chest rising and falling ever so gently.

"Don't sweat it," said Junior quickly. "The hardest part is still ahead."

Douglas cleared his throat. "If we're done with the sentiment, can we get this gate open already?"

Junior had a few choice things he'd like to say to that, but it was Taranis who spoke first.

"The gate requires as much from you as it will from the rest of us. As their commander, I hope you are prepared for it."

Douglas puffed his chest as he stared into Taranis's cold eyes. "I'll do whatever's necessary."

"Music to my ears," said Taranis, approaching the gate. The inscriptions in the stone were ancient Mogaddan, a script that looked closer to musical notes than an actual alphabet. Junior's father had taught him to read it, so he was surprised to discover that the words had changed since last time.

"It's a new riddle," he said, puzzled. Those etchings looked permanent. So who changed them, and how? "It says 'Day or night, I stand tall. Over many a place where man can fall.'"

"We're not here for riddles," said Douglas, brushing past them. "We're here to see the lost city." He pushed against the gate, but it didn't budge.

"This city has rules, Douglas," said Angeline. "I suggest you play by them."

Douglas muttered something to himself before addressing the group. "So I just shout an answer and it opens?"

"That is more or less the first step," answered Taranis.

"Alright then, how about a king?" said Douglas, in response to which he got some confused stares. "Because a king stands tall. And it was three kings that found this place, right?"

"It's definitely not a person," said Junior, thinking. "The riddle went out of its way to suggest that."

"Maybe a kingdom?" suggested Zivo. "If it stands day and night?"

"But a kingdom could fall," said Brivek. "Just like a king."

"Bridge," rasped Nera, eyes barely open. "The answer is

bridge."

Junior nodded to Taranis. They had found an answer.

"Gefya," said Taranis in the old tongue. The inscriptions began to glow white, leaving the newcomers to gawk and stare. But the magic was lost on Junior, for he knew what came next.

Douglas reached for the glowing gate, but Taranis held him back. "There is one more step that must be taken," he said, placing his half-Poterian hand on it. A thunderous crack echoed through the stone. The newcomers jumped as Taranis slumped back in a daze, and Angeline used her dampener to keep him upright. Why she chose to help their captor, Junior didn't understand.

"It is done," said Taranis, regaining his balance. He drew his sword and drove it into the sand.

"What's done?" demanded Douglas, fear in his eyes.

You already know the answer, thought Junior. *You just don't want to accept it.*

Taranis snapped his fingers: no electricity jumped between them, nor would it for the duration of their stay in Iramwerta.

Zivo gasped. "Do we all have to...?" he trailed. Taranis nodded.

"Shit on a stick," muttered Brivek.

"It's alright," said Junior, approaching the gate. "We get them back when we leave. But just like in the story of the Three Kings, we can't take weapons into the city. And that includes our powers." He placed his dampener against the stone. Another crack echoed, this one fainter, more like a tap. Was that it? Junior felt no different. There was no dizziness like last time. Maybe because the dampener had already drained him? Had the gate missed his powers completely because of it? The tap that echoed when his mother offered her powers only increased his suspicion.

Brivek and Zivo exchanged nervous glances as Junior and Angeline stepped away. Together, they placed their hands on the gate. Another crack boomed from within its stone. Zivo slumped and Brivek teetered. *The reaction I should be having.*

Douglas watched the duo try and fail to summon their powers. Color drained from his face. He took Nera's limp hand and placed it on the gate in a desperate attempt. There was another crack, but the gate did not open. Not without his input.

"This was not part of the deal," he hissed, pointing a finger at Taranis. "I will not be left defenseless!"

The etchings in the gate began to glow red.

"Then you doom us all," said Taranis.

Heat emanated from the gate, enough to make the water steam from the sand, enough to make Junior drip sweat beneath his heavy uniform. *Don't be a fool, Douglas.* He could tell the Zoboros leader wanted to summon his powers, whatever they were. Junior wanted to summon his own, too, and snuff out the idiot for endangering them. In fact, he felt it, a faint tickle rising through his arms toward his chest. *Did the gate weaken my dampener?*

"Douglas, please…" murmured Nera from within Brivek's arms, her scales drying and cracking.

"Fine!" Douglas placed his hand on the gate. There was a crack, and the red glow faded, as did the heat. Douglas backed away from it, trying to maintain his composure in front of his subordinates, but Junior could tell he was rattled, especially when no power came to his hands.

"This had better be worth it," the Zoboros muttered.

"It will be," assured Taranis.

A groan echoed through the cavern. The ground shook. A seam appeared down the middle of the stone door, and air hissed out as it pushed apart across the sand.

Here we go again.

The newcomers gaped as they stepped through the gate and onto the ledge that overlooked Iramwerta. It was a city built from the stone that surrounded it, so ancient that nothing stood more than one or two stories tall, except for the temple at its center, which almost touched the rocky ceiling. A sphere of light glowed dimly at the temple's peak, enough to give the city some sliver of illumination. It should have been enchanting, but Junior remembered what else sat at the top of that temple. He shuddered, knowing it would be their destination. It was the only logical place to look for the power of Iramwerta, even if he'd not seen an ounce of it last time.

"Come on, then," said Douglas, starting down the path that snaked toward the city. "Let's see what this place has to offer."

Death, Junior thought spontaneously, but kept it to himself, though he had a feeling Taranis was thinking something similar. The half-Poterian trailed Douglas like a shadow, doing nothing to hide his eagerness. Taranis always had a fascination with the mystic — the ancient Mogaddan markings in his old mask had been Junior's first indication of that. Junior would never have believed any of it, but that all changed the first time they came to Iramwerta. Now he didn't know what to believe anymore.

His mother caught up with him as they followed the others down the trail. "How do you feel?" she asked.

"Like something isn't working right," he whispered, nodding toward his cuffs.

"Agreed." She glanced back at the gate. "Taranis would not be such a fool to leave himself powerless among enemies. We should assume the Jaculus will not be far behind."

"Then let's make our move now."

"No. There is a cost to using violence in this city. Let our enemies be the ones to learn that lesson."

So she does *have a plan.* Junior glanced at the gate. "Will it—?"

She cut him off with a wave of her hand. "Just be ready," she said.

Junior could only nod. He didn't like trusting some mystical force with their rescue, but he knew his mother understood this place far better than he did. For now, he would follow her lead.

"Who's that down there?" asked Brivek as they drew closer to the city, Nera still in his arms. "I see something moving in the streets."

"A lot of somethings," added Zivo.

"Those aren't people," said Junior. "Not anymore." He explained the time projections to them as best he could. He didn't fully understand them himself, but from what Taranis had told him last time (if that source could be trusted), the "people" walking the streets of Iramwerta were projections of those who had walked these streets at different points in history. As their party entered the city, that explanation seemed to hold some ground. Each projection they passed came from different species and wore different clothing, some primitive as loincloth, some as advanced as combat suits.

"How is it possible?" asked Zivo, shivering as a Nurrano projection phased right through him.

Junior shrugged. Their source remained a mystery to him. He noticed his mother keeping her distance. He'd heard from Kano, who had heard from Danadas (if *that* source could be trusted) that it could have been caused by an incredibly powerful energy source. The easy answer being Iramwerta, but he couldn't help but wonder if it was something else.

"I don't like this," said Brivek. The projections had taken on panicked looks, many of them running toward the temple. "Did these people die here?"

"Perhaps," said Taranis. "Or perhaps they discovered something in the temple. Something which saved them."

Based on the expressions of the people running, Junior wasn't so sure about that.

Steps ran up the face of the temple. The group climbed them slowly, carefully, dodging the skeletons they found along the way.

"There's IDF on these steps," noted Zivo, nodding toward a few fallen helmets, their signature blue faded almost to gray.

Douglas remained quiet. Junior could tell by the way he was rubbing his fingers that he wished he had his powers now. Junior tried readying his own. The lights on the dampener flashed faster. He felt his power collect in his hands, but it dissipated. The dampener was still too strong. *Patience*, he reminded himself. He had to be careful what he did here.

"What is this horrible place?" whispered Nera. She glanced around within Brivek's arms, alert again, and at the worst possible time.

They climbed over the final steps and a gasp ran through the newcomers. Even knowing what was here, Junior still felt sick to his stomach at the sight. Skulls, Zoboros skulls, hundreds of them piled beneath the pillar where the orb of light rotated. All murdered by the IDF. By the Lusitani. Junior remembered thinking, the first time he'd been here, that one of those skulls had belonged to his mother. How thankful he'd felt to be proven wrong, and how strange to be standing here with her now.

"This is why we fight," said Taranis. He said it to everyone, though Junior sensed he was singling out Angeline.

"It is indeed," said Douglas. He lifted an IDF helmet off the ground and heaved it over the side of the temple, then froze as he gazed over the cityscape. One by one, the others turned and gaped. Junior tensed. He had a feeling he knew what they were staring at.

Del Cloran choppers. Five of them, all rushing through the open gate. River water poured from their uneven sides. Junior hadn't realized they doubled as submersibles – he had to give the Del Clorans some unexpected credit for that.

"You betrayed us!" shouted Douglas. He drew a knife from his sleeve and lunged at Taranis, who ripped the knife away and kicked Douglas to the ground in one move.

"You betray Iramwerta," said Taranis, sticking the knife in his belt. "Blood is not meant to be spilled here. I intend to honor that code...if everyone cooperates."

Junior exchanged a look with his mother. She would want to wait and see if these people cooperated, but he knew they needed a better plan than that. His heart raced as the choppers thundered closer, calling power to his hands only to have them sucked away by the dampener. *Come on, give me something.*

The choppers circled the top of the temple. Del Clorans descended from ropes; Junior counted over a hundred crowding the temple's top. The Jaculus descended with them, the ancient sword in his scaly hand still sandy from where Taranis had left it.

"It has been a long time," said the Jaculus, though Junior wasn't sure if he was referring to the sword or Iramwerta. The assassin padded by on bare feet that seemed to relish the sensation against the cold stones. He stopped, yellow eyes set on a circle of stone at the bottom of the pillar, its center hollow. Junior had noted that odd feature on his last visit but thought little of it then. The way the Jaculus stared at it, though, made him afraid to discover its purpose.

The Jaculus waved his hand. Two Del Clorans grabbed Angeline by her arms and pulled her toward the circle.

"Hey!" barked Junior, to which his mother gave him a warning look.

"She will not be harmed, Hendricks Junior," said the Jaculus. "Though I cannot say the same for you."

A hand caught Junior by the throat. Taranis! The maniac aimed Douglas's knife at his throat.

"Stop!" shouted Angeline.

"You can save him, Angeline," said the Jaculus. "You know what to do."

Angeline stared at that circle of stone. Junior watched, afraid of the cold steel against his flesh yet wanting to charge forward all the same. How *dare* they use her like some puppet! Rage filled his belly. Rage and...power.

"What's going on?!" demanded Douglas. A dozen Del Cloran rifles aimed his way, but Taranis waved them off.

"She is the key," said Taranis. "The key to Iramwerta's power."

Junior stared at that circle of stone again, at the ancient Mogaddan inscribed into it. It was the same riddle that had been inscribed in the Gate.

It's a bridge.

"Mom, don't do it. Whatever they want you to open, don't—"

"I can't help them even if I tried," she said. "The gate took my powers."

The Jaculus turned to Taranis, who shook his half-Poterian head.

"Oh Angeline, you were always a terrible liar." The Jaculus nodded to the Del Cloran escorts, who ripped off her dampener. "Any funny business and the boy suffers."

Junior braced, thinking Taranis was about to use the knife on him, but his old enemy stayed his hand. The Jaculus glanced back and, frowning at Taranis's hesitation, tipped his sword back, nicking Junior's arm with it. Junior gritted his teeth as blood trickled down his arm. He met the Jaculus's twisted gaze, felt the heat rise from his chest and settle just below his neck.

"Leave him alone!" shouted Angeline. The orb of light flickered above them. "Or none of you will leave this place alive." Whether she meant by Iramwerta's power or her own, Junior wasn't sure. He just knew that, right now, he wanted to melt that smug assassin where he stood.

"Do it, Angeline," said Taranis softly, though without his customary air of command. "You've done it before. You can again."

"And this time your efforts will not be cut short," added the Jaculus. He scooped an IDF helmet with the tip of his blade and placed it in his hand. One squeeze and it crunched into pieces.

Angeline turned. A hundred Del Cloran weapons aimed at her, but she saw only her son.

"Don't do it, Mom. Please."

"I'm sorry," she said, tears welling in her eyes.

"Wait, stop!" shouted Junior. Taranis tugged him back, and he felt the heat rise through his throat.

Angeline aimed her palms at the stone circle. Black, staticky energy formed around her hands, pulsing unevenly like it wanted to burst free in every direction.

"*Don't!*" Junior broke from Taranis's grip and dove underneath the blade. Taranis made no move to pursue him, but the Jaculus was quick to kick him in the belly and bring him to his knees in a blitz of pain; pain that made the fire in his throat grow hotter. Stronger.

Angeline launched her power from her fingertips in a straight beam. It struck the stone circle, not breaking it or eating away at it like Junior had seen her powers do on the *Dormarch*, but collected there, making the inscriptions glow black while it stretched across the circle's hollow center.

"Finally," said the Jaculus.

The energy swallowed in on itself at the circle's center. Junior held his breath, his throat cooking with fire. *Was that it?*

A gale of wind exploded out of the circle, whipping Junior's face and stinging his eyes. White light blazed from the circle's center, emanating from a hazy energy that swirled inside it now.

A bridge, Junior realized. A portal.

"She's done it!" exclaimed the Jaculus. Angeline fell to her knees in a daze. The Jaculus marched straight for her, sword in hand. "Thank you for your services, my dear."

"NO!" Junior screamed. The heat flowed up through his cheeks and settled in his eyes. His vision turned orange as he watched the Jaculus draw the sword back. The assassin chanced a glance Junior's way and froze.

"Impossible…" the Jaculus muttered. "Taranis! Taranis you fool, stop the boy!"

Junior sensed Taranis coming up behind him, but all he could see was the assassin, all he could feel was the power of that orange light wanting to release.

"Let it go, Aaron," he heard Taranis whisper. "Be free."

Junior screamed. Twin beams of light jetted from his eyes and sliced clean through the Jaculus's abdomen. The assassin fell in two halves as the beams carved through the Del Clorans unfortunate enough to be standing in their path. Junior kept screaming, and the power kept surging through him. The Del Clorans ran, and still he kept cutting with every turn of his head, kept chopping down every enemy caught in his vision. One Del Cloran in his periphery tried to get a shot at him but a knife lodged itself in the insect's throat. Junior cast his deadly gaze upward, caught the choppers in his twin beams and brought them down in fiery balls of rubble. Finally, he raised the cuffs and cut them clean down the middle as the energy began to fade away.

He gasped, drained and dizzy, his vision returning to normal, his power settling back in his hands where it belonged. Or did it? He couldn't explain what had just happened, but when he looked around, the results were clear. Dozens of Del Cloran bodies surrounded him, all sliced at vicious angles.

"What did you do?" said Douglas. He and the other Zoboros rose cautiously from the floor, afraid what Junior might do next.

"I-I don't know…" he trailed. He found the sword lying beside the Jaculus's severed body and picked it up, barely feeling its weight in his numb hands.

"The portal!" shouted Taranis, rising. Junior cast a dangerous look at the half-Poterian, who froze, raising his hands in surrender. "We must go through it. *Now.*"

"Junior!" shouted Nera, pointing at the distant gate. Its inscriptions glowed bright red, as did the sphere above the portal, casting its color over the entire lost city.

It's going to kill us, a vague part of Junior's mind warned him, but all he could register were the bodies…the bodies and the skulls piled near them. Below, Junior knew the time projections were still running their way, still repeating themselves as they ran toward their fate atop this temple.

A crack echoed from the gate. Junior looked. A wall of red, fiery heat surged from it, washing over the entire city but not damaging anything it touched. Yet as Junior stumbled back into the pile of skulls, he knew that heatwave would have a very different effect on everyone standing here.

Douglas was the first to rush through the portal, not bothering to check that those under his command did the same.

"Go through now or you're dead!" barked Taranis.

"What's on the other side?!" demanded Zivo.

"GO!" Taranis shouted as he leaped through.

Junior saw the others all running ahead of him. He stumbled, his knees weak and his head spinning, watching as Brivek, Nera, and Zivo all dove through.

"Hurry!" His mother pushed him along. Junior picked up the

pace, her touch against his back giving him a sense of balance amid the chaos. They were almost there, but so was the heat, baking them like they were in a furnace, choking the air from his lungs. The wall of fire was almost here.

"We're not gonna make it," he gasped, the sword shaking in his limp hand.

"Yes you are!" She shoved him hard and he stumbled into the white unknown.

"MOM!" He spun around as he fell into nothingness. The heat was gone. Iramwerta was gone.

And so was his mother.

Chapter 26

Needed Practice

One week on the ship, and no one had told Kano a damn thing about the Trials.

Most of the Abari didn't speak his language (or else pretended they couldn't). Anyone who did directed him to Varlam, who was an expert at dodging questions. Even Makoto with all his newfound friends in the sparring ring hadn't been able to get a peep out of them on the subject.

Kano paced their tiny room. He'd been doing that a lot lately. More and more as they drifted closer to these Trials.

And farther and farther away from their friends.

Every minute of every day he wondered if he'd made the right choice – if allowing the Abari to take him had really done anything to protect his friends. Sometimes, he wondered if it had been his choice at all; the Abari had seemed pretty set on taking him to the Trials regardless of his demands. He could only hope his friends were alright, though something told him they weren't. A lot could happen in a week (especially to their team), and he'd left them in probably the most dangerous place in the galaxy.

Power swelled in his fist. He wanted to unleash it, to blast the room apart in his rage. But then he noticed the nearby bluish clouds of the Rift had pressed up against his window. It wanted to get inside; to connect with his powers. It gave him an idea, one that made his frustrations fade into the background.

He placed his hand against the window and let his powers trickle into his palm, making the reinforced glass vibrate ever so slightly. He sensed the clouds on the other side of it carrying the faint heartbeats of the many nearby marauders, but not the heartbeat he was searching for. *Where are you?* He pressed harder. The heartbeats faded, overwhelmed by a stronger rhythm. One he hadn't felt before; one that resonated from somewhere deep within the void.

"Come on, talk to me," said Kano to himself.

"Sure, but I'd like a shower first."

Kano jumped. Makoto stood in the doorway, covered in sparring pads and sweat.

"Didn't you have an eight-hour shift today? How do you still have energy for that?"

His brother shrugged. "Nurranos have a better battery life than you, I guess. You should've seen it, though. Gorrus had this new tuck and roll technique. Took the legs out from under me. I found a weakness though. Next time he tried it, I leaped over him and clopped him on the head. That got a laugh even out of Varlam."

Kano nodded, only half listening. He was more interested in the clouds outside, and wherever that pulse had been coming from.

His brother shuffled uncomfortably in the silence. "You know, you should really join me in the ring. It would be good conditioning for the Trials."

"We don't even know if the Trials are physical. And if they are, I don't want to be too tired for them. We have no idea when we'll arrive or when the Abari'll decide to throw me into it."

"Excuses, excuses," said Makoto. He tossed a club into Kano's lap. Much lighter than the fifty-pound item Kano had been hit with last time, it was still heavy enough to knock the wind out of him. He didn't have much time to catch his breath, though, as Makoto had already pulled him to his feet and started out the door.

"Come on, the others all cleared out. The ring's ours!"

"Oh joy…" Kano struggled to keep up with the heavy club in his hand, slowly realizing that this past week of worrying and vegetating might not have been the best thing for him.

True to Makoto's word, the sparring room was empty. Plenty of padding was left hanging on racks to the side of the ring, all of it oversized and reeking of use. Kano tried grabbing a breastplate, the pressure from his fingers enough to squeeze out a sickening waterfall of sweat. He shuddered.

"We can just practice forms until we find you a set of your own," suggested Makoto, much to Kano's relief. They entered the ring, and Kano immediately felt awkward trying to balance the club in his stance. He wasn't used to weapons beyond his own two hands.

"Do you have anything smaller?" he asked, checking if any marauders were peeking through the doorway. He wanted to keep any impending embarrassment as quiet as possible.

"That's the smallest one," said Makoto, twirling his dual clubs like a majorette.

Kano sighed. Might as well get it over with quick. If he was lucky, Makoto would get bored of his bad forms and end the practice early, leaving Kano to send more pulses through the Rift. There at least he felt like he had something going for him.

"Keep your weapon upright," said Makoto. "You're letting it lean. That leaves you vulnerable."

"Keep my tip up. Got it. Any other pointers?"

"Yeah, don't make it weird." Makoto went for a high jab. Kano blocked it, only for Makoto's second club to smack him in the belly.

"I thought you said we were doing forms!" shouted Kano, clutching the fresh welt on his chest.

"We are, you just suck at them." Makoto kept swinging, left and right, high and low. Kano knew his brother was only going at a fraction of his normal pace, yet it took all Kano's strength to try and keep up.

"That's it, Kano. Watch my arms, not my weapons. That'll tell you where I'm really going." Kano watched one arm arc and then stop suddenly. He knew then the attack was coming from the other side and blocked it in the nick of time. "Very good! Now we speed things up a bit."

Fun, fun, fun. The strikes came faster. Kano inched back, keeping his weapon as centered as possible so that nothing broke through.

"Use your backfoot! Push forward!"

Kano pushed, the extra press of strength driving Makoto back. "Keep pressing, Kano!" He did, his attacks coming faster and faster, adrenaline fueling him forward as his brother backpedaled. Each strike felt more natural, more confident. His chest was heaving but he barely noticed, too focused on landing a hit on his brother.

"You're coming on a little strong now," said Makoto, but Kano didn't hear him, barely recognized the power behind his own swings as he got swept up in the dance. Then he saw it, his brother's club dipping low. *Watch me take a note out of your book*. Kano leaped over the attack and went for the head. His brother's other club came around and smacked him in the temple. The floor came up fast. Kano flopped there, head spinning and throbbing at the same time.

"I bet you're pretty proud of yourself," he groaned. He lifted his head, but his brother wasn't there. Instead, a cloaked Poterian stood upon a bridge of transparent energy.

"Am I unconscious?"

"I was going to say 'overambitious.' But yes, you're unconscious too."

Kano rose, no longer feeling pain in his head or chest. He had no complaints on that front. But he had plenty for Niscelles.

"Where did you go? You haven't spoken to me all week, so why are you here now?"

"Because you rang loud enough to alert half the Abari in the Rift. If they didn't think you were their *Ay Nyid* before, they will now."

"Their who?"

"Their 'chosen one'," said Niscelles with enough emphasis for Kano to sense the eyeroll happening beneath the hood. "These are a superstitious people, Kano. They believe someone will lead them back to their planet."

"And would someone who completes their Trials qualify as this Ay Nyid?"

"Now you're catching on."

"Then you know what the Trials hold for me?"

"Even if I shared, the answers would help you little. Everything you need to complete them I've already told you."

Kano racked his brain. He couldn't recall much that Niscelles had shared with him in their brief conversations, but one thing did stand out.

"To complete the Trials, I have to give up everything, don't I?"

Niscelles nodded. "And in doing so, you will gain something more, if you are prepared to take it."

All Kano could think of was the black fire coming from Niscelles's sword. The power to erase life with a flick of his finger.

"That's what you've been leading me to all this time then," said Kano, stepping back. "You wanted me to come to the Rift. You wanted me to be captured by the Abari."

"I want you to save the galaxy, Kano." Niscelles marched forward, the bridge trembling beneath his feet.

"From what? Everything I've ever done has only made the galaxy worse. What would I be saving it from besides what I've already started?"

"War."

That word rang through Kano's mind. He'd seen battle, he'd seen the aftermath of the last great war, but the real thing remained a mystery to him. One he'd very much like to keep that way.

"Who's war? Who starts it?"

"Everyone. The Poterians, the IDF, the Zoboros, the Orlovs, even the Abari…soon all their fates will be tied to you. I have sensed it."

"Sensed it? Then why don't you *do* something about it?!" snapped Kano.

"I am bound to the mountain, just as it is bound to me." Lightning flashed, and through the mist Kano saw it looming in the distance, black and spiked. "But its power connects me to many. I can hear things. Whispers. I know our enemies are closer than ever to what they seek."

"To what? To Angeline?" Kano's gaze had fixed on the mountain, but when he looked back at Niscelles, the Poterian was on fire. Just like he had been in Kano's old dreams, back when all this was new and Kano had yet to discover that his fate would be tied to a pyro living in the same city.

"Junior…" trailed Kano. Again he sensed that powerful heartbeat in the Rift. Not Niscelles, but Junior, somehow more connected to it than anyone else.

"I have watched your progress closely, seen each of you set yourselves apart from the Zoboros around you." Niscelles waved his hand and the clouds of the Rift took the shape of a serpent. *The Jaculus.* "But you have split, and now the two of you stand on opposite sides of the bridge."

"What happened to him?" demanded Kano. "The Jaculus is behind it, isn't he?"

"It is not the Jaculus I fear anymore, but something darker. Something Junior may be powerless to stop."

"But I can help him. If you show me how to—"

"*Walk this path.*" Niscelles's voice boomed across the cosmos. The bridge disappeared and Kano fell, not into visions and memories like before but into the darkness of the universe.

"Everything depends on it," a voice whispered.

Kano opened his eyes and gasped, chest heaving. His vision was blurred, but he could tell his brother was standing over him, as was someone else. *Niscelles?* No, Varlam. Everything was coming back into focus, including the throbbing in the side of his head.

"Good, you're alright," said the Poterian, passing Kano a glass of water. "Drink."

"Varlam, listen to me. Something's gone very wrong. We need to turn the ship—" Kano paused. He hadn't realized so many Abari were standing just outside the ring, all dressed in full armor, fists held against their chests.

"I'm afraid there's no turning back now," Varlam whispered. By the somber look on Makoto's face, Kano knew what Varlam was going to say next.

"We've reached the Trials."

Chapter 27

Extradition

Time seemed to slow as their transport hung in the dead space between two gravities. Two planets. The old and the new.

Li braced. She knew what came next. The thrusters erupted outside the ship. She shook beneath her seat restraint, the pressure nudging her head closer and closer to her lap. She glanced down the aisle at the other seats, the other familiar faces. So few of them left.

"Five minutes till landing," T8 announced over the loudspeakers as the pressure subsided. The bot was their pilot today. Strange having it and not its maker at the helm, but the empress couldn't risk the old Poterian being sighted during their mission. If he was, the royal family would be more than implicated, and the empress would have the war she wanted to avoid.

But if she really wanted to avoid one, she wouldn't be sending us *to do her dirty work.* Li knew the others shared the same sentiment. The only thing motivating them through this mission was the idea of beating Danadas. Whether their success meant the empress would help them defeat the old man, though, remained to be seen.

"You all know your assignments," said Cera beside her.

"Stick to them and this should go smoothly."

"Not with our track record," muttered Li, surprised at herself. She hadn't meant to say that out loud. The others looked equally surprised. It was the kind of comment they'd expect from Jaden.

Li couldn't help but stare at his empty seat. He was recovering at the Poterian palace, though she doubted he was getting any actual rest. Not when his team was on a mission. She wouldn't be surprised if he was trying to hack into their comms right now, just so he could help from a planet away. The thought of it made her smile.

Their transport slowed. They were close to their surveillance altitude. She had no windows through which to survey the planet's surface, but she didn't need them. Her powers could sense—

Nausea overtook her as her hands began to glow. *What is this?* She stifled a gag. She'd meant to connect with life forms, but all she sensed was...sickness. Poison.

Cera touched her shoulder. "What's wrong?"

Li relinquished her powers and the sickness evaporated. "I'm fine. Just a little dizzy from the pressure change." She hoped Cera wouldn't question her further. They had enough to worry about without taking another team member off the roster. Besides, she was on reserve for this mission anyway – a position she'd gotten used to as healer. Whatever was bothering her, she would handle it.

"First team, standby," announced Carmichael. Chenji and Akio approached the liftgate at the back of the transport. Li braced, not for the pressure change, but for what came next. When the liftgate opened and the compressed air cleared, yellow fumes snaked into the ship. Smog. Like a veil over the whole planet. One that made her wonder how anything survived here.

Chenji morphed into a bird. Ristin hurried over to help him into a beak-shaped face mask and a pair of goggles while Carmichael ran a check on Akio's pack.

"Akio will have a new mask for you once you morph on the surface!" the captain called over the rush of the wind, placing a tracker in Akio's pack. "We have your location! If anything goes wrong, Warp will teleport to you back here!"

The Jakari nodded and climbed onto Chenji's feathery back, a pair of oversized goggles covering his bulbous eyes. "This planet always makes me look ridiculous," he muttered. Li smiled. Ridiculous or not, she was thankful Akio would be down there with Chenji. The empress had opposed sending him for fear of implication, but Carmichael argued that Akio's betrayal of the royal family would only strengthen Typhera's alibi. Besides, without Sterling, Akio was the only one familiar with Poteria Prime. Li hoped the planet hadn't changed too much in the last twenty cycles.

Chenji cawed and flapped his wings, fanning more smog in Li's direction. Her eyes stung, and by the time she'd rubbed them out the duo had flown away.

The liftgate closed. Li waited for the smog to filter out before taking another breath, a detail that Cera did not fail to note.

"This air is affecting you, isn't it?"

"I'll handle it."

Carmichael, similarly, did not miss a beat. "Sounds like someone's in tune with the local ecology...or lack thereof.

Fortunately, I have an opening I think you could fill."

Li looked from Carmichael to Cera, puzzled. "What did you have in mind?"

◁◆▷

"A lot of people assume Poterians settled on Poteria Prime first, but technically it was New Poteria," said T8, its wiry fingers tapping the transport's controls faster than Li's eyes could follow.

"You don't say," she muttered. Carmichael had made coming to the cockpit sound like a good way to ease the headache all this pollution was causing her. Unfortunately, T8 proved to be as big a history buff as Jaden, and with a larger catalog of data to pull from.

"It's true. But when the Poterians first tried to settle, Evernight proved too long for them to sustain any crops."

"Sure, sure." Li was focused on the datapad Carmichael had given her. Jaden's datapad, where multi-dimensional models flashed across the many windows on the screen, each model blipping with Chenji and Akio's location. She pulled up another tab and the feeds from hundreds of security cameras appeared, all hacked by Jaden prior to their departure. Sorting through them could wait, though. For now, she just needed to figure out how to connect her new headset to the datapad.

"Button on the back," said T8.

Li pressed it and the headset connected with a ping. Noise filled her ears: a dozen conversations from strangers in the embassy, footsteps echoing down hallways, the howling wind feeding in from Akio's comms. It was too much at once.

T8 reached over and tapped a few audio wavelengths in the corner of her screen, dimming the noise to a few mercifully quiet conversations. "You won't need all that feed," the bot explained, the red dot on its visor pinging faster than usual. "I'm processing it. Checking for keywords that might mean the embassy is alerted to us."

Li nodded dumbly. T8 had such an unassuming personality that she often forgot it was a computing machine. That explained why the bot was able to keep their transport on course – all Li could see through the viewport was smog, but T8's scanners did the work that her eyes could not. *Meanwhile, I can't even figure out how to adjust the volume on this thing.*

"If you're doing all that, then what exactly is Jaden's— my job?" she asked.

"Moral support," said T8. "I can feed you most of what the team needs to hear. You just focus on where your teammates are. Be the voice that keeps them moving forward."

"Are...are you saying that's what Jaden's been doing this whole time?"

T8 shrugged. "He laces it with strategy and does much of the hacking, but essentially yes. He likes to make sure no one on the ground feels alone."

"That's...thoughtful of him." Words she never thought she'd say about Jaden.

"Thoughtful? The boy just loves having a captive audience for his history lessons. A trait he and I share, I'm afraid."

Li smiled. "Tell me about Evernight."

"That's when Poteria Prime eclipses New Poteria. Happens multiple times a cycle and lasts for weeks. Life on New Poteria is adapted to it: animals hibernate, plants slow down their organic processes. Unfortunately, it makes for an agricultural nightmare. That drove everyone to Poteria Prime, where Poterians built most of their infrastructure and pumped out their pollution. The worse the air became, the more motivated scientists were to solve the Evernight problem. They engineered crops that could continue producing under limited sunlight, and now New Poteria is responsible for most of Poteria Prime's food supply."

"So if the empress controls their food supply, why is she worried about retaliation?" asked Li. "I'd imagine a food shortage would take civil war off the table."

"Possibly, which is why Poteria Prime uses shadow groups like the Red Sabre to do its dirty work while denying involvement. They want to undermine her in the hopes they can install someone more akin to Emperor Palorex, but all it's become is an annoying game of poke the bear, and personally I'm excited to see who gets mauled."

Well hopefully it's not us. But T8's comment did make her wonder just how the Red Sabre *could* hurt the empress.

"Where does the levithium come into the picture?" she asked.

T8 raised a mechanical eyebrow. "You saw what it did to the marauders. What do you think?"

Li pondered it as she stared through the yellow haze toward the shadow of New Poteria, looming in the atmosphere like a great weight about to drop.

"Could enough levithium push the two planets apart?" she asked.

"Theoretically yes, and with a frightening number of potential side effects. The Red Sabre would never need to find out what those side effects are, though. Just the threat of using so much levithium would be enough leverage over the empress."

Li found this political game of chess as exhausting as it was disturbing. The leaders of both planets could be having a profound impact on their citizens, but instead they endangered those very citizens just to score points against each other. It gave her almost as bad a taste in her mouth as the pollution.

"We are in position," hissed Akio's voice through the headset.

Li snapped to attention, having absolutely no idea where on the datapad to look.

"They're at the rooftop entrance on the northwest platform," whispered T8. "Check the security feed."

She searched the screen. A hundred feeds, each labeled, with northwest cameras in the top left and northeast in the top right. A method to the madness.

"No guards," she said into the headset. "You're clear to enter." It felt strange saying what Jaden usually said in her ear. She was just glad she didn't follow it up with a bad joke.

The creak of a door sounded through her headset, as did the footsteps in the hallway. Her friends didn't appear on the hallway's camera, though.

"It's recycled footage now," said T8, anticipating her question. "Every time they enter a room, I set the cameras to play on a loop. The guards may catch on to my trick, but as long as we're quick, we have a chance of going unnoticed."

A chance. Li didn't want to know the actual probability (which she was sure T8 had already calculated). It wasn't like their missions normally had a good chance of success, anyway.

Though she couldn't help but think they'd have a better chance if Jaden was sitting in her place.

She pulled up a three-dimensional map of the embassy on the right side of her screen. The building looked more like a labyrinth in this view, with branching hallways and staircases all interwoven across seven vast floors. *An awful nice embassy for a terrorist organization*. Li understood why the empress didn't trust Poteria Prime. They'd pulled all the stops on the Red Sabre's accommodations. No subtlety required.

Akio's tracker blipped through the maze, a little red dot against seven floors of enemies. She followed the sequence of security cameras on the left side of the screen. The nearest Poterians were a whole floor below, and only a few were guards. Most were employees in suits not so different from the ones she would see in Downtown Famora; the key difference being the Red Sabre members made sure their suits had at least a hint of red, if not the whole thing. Well, that and the fact that each Poterian was large enough to crush Chenji and Akio, regardless of job title.

"I'm getting a partial facial match on our target," said T8. "Check camera 618. One floor down."

Li pulled up the correct footage, feeling pretty good about herself while she did it. A Poterian sat behind a desk on the screen, scratching his large chin as he read his datapad. His face was tilted toward his reading, keeping most of it in shadow. Li pulled up a picture of their target on the screen and compared. It certainly *could* be him, but the shadows on the face gave her doubt.

Movement. She leaned closer to the screen. The Poterian was speaking. She tapped the video window and the audio channel opened.

"...and I'll need those reports before tomorrow's meeting please," he said, a surprising amount of charm in his deep Poterian voice. *The charm of a politician*, Li told herself. *He still leads a murdering, racist, sexist terror cell.*

"Yes, Senator Ivanov," answered the voice on the other line.

Gotcha. "Location confirmed," she said into her headset. "Room 618."

"Check on room 718, please," requested Chenji, back in his Human form.

"Room clear," she said. This was becoming easy.

T8 went to cue up the recycled footage for that room when the red dot on its visor froze.

"What's wrong?" asked Li. She could hear the door to room 718 opening.

"The footage in there is already being recycled," said T8. "It's a trap!"

"Abort, abort!" cried Li. She heard Chenji gasp, tried to pull up something on the screen that could help, but all she found was more useless security footage.

"Hello boys," said a familiar voice over the comms.

Chenji stood his ground, Akio on his shoulder. Neither of them dared to make a move. No sense accidentally starting the fight, though they knew the Nurrano standing across from them would welcome it.

"Funny," said Yui. "Halfway across the galaxy, yet we end up in the same room." A dangerous smile crossed her argyle face of blue and black.

From his shoulder, Chenji sensed Akio drawing a knife. Slowly, subtly, but if Yui noticed, the ice would be coming their way. He tried to think up a creature who could withstand that amount of cold, but he had none in his catalog. Worse, he was still standing exposed in the hallway should any Poterian enter. He started into the room when Akio gripped the doorframe and tugged him back.

"Careful, boy of many faces," hissed Akio. He pointed his knife down. The floor had been iced over. A defensive strategy, or did Yui plan on smashing through and landing in the senator's office? He assumed both.

"Got nothing, changeling?" said Yui, an icy mist swirling around her hand. "I'd like to see you give it a try as a penguin."

"I'd have turned into a snake, but the guards might mistake me for you."

Yui bristled. The mist in her hand solidified into a spear.

"Behind you!" shouted Li. The duo dove inside the room, one going left and one going right. Chenji turned, expecting Kazan or Mila to be standing there, but instead he found a skull-shaped mask staring at him.

"There's a face I didn't miss," he said. He morphed into a Kimikan hog, the Lusitani shrinking beneath him and his new tusks. But he knew better than to present such a large target to the hunter. Already it was reaching for the device on its wrist, programmed with a countermeasure for his new form.

Chenji lunged. The Lusitani fired a net from its wrist, which pulsed with electricity as it sailed toward him. Chenji's heart raced at the sight of it. *Focus.* He tuned out the electric crackle and morphed into a zeefly that sailed clean through the netting, his compound eyes nearly blinded by the electric charges that jumped between the fibers, each one large enough to fry him whole, yet his mind didn't retreat into animal instinct. Instead, the two became one, instinct guiding him through the danger, while his mind kept his plan in motion. He came out the other side and snapped back to his hog form, the Lusitani now pinned under his massive paw.

"Duck!" Akio heaved his knife over Chenji's head. Another Lusitani appeared in the doorway, but the knife stuck into its wrist weapon, jamming it. Chenji scooped up the one beneath his paw and heaved it into the other, sending both enemies tumbling down the hallway.

He turned toward Yui, who had her spear raised over the icy floor.

"Wait—!"

She drove it straight down. The floor crunched and gave beneath them. Chenji's hooved feet crashed down upon a desk, pulverizing it to splinters. He found the Poterian senator to whom it belonged sitting there, pen shaking in his hand where he'd just been signing.

"Th-that desk was a gift from the governor," stammered Ivanov as he stared up at the monstrous hog.

"I'm sure he'll be devastated," said Yui. She swept in behind Ivanov and aimed the tip of her spear at his neck. "He leaves with me, or he leaves with no one."

"Or *you* can leave with something generous," suggested Ivanov as she ripped him from his chair. "More generous than whatever they're paying you to—" Yui edged the freezing spear tip along his neck and he clammed up.

Footsteps echoed from the other side of the door. Chenji

locked it with his paw just before hands began rattling the knob.

"Senator, are you alright?!" someone shouted from the other side. Others in the hallway were having panicked side conversations, indistinguishable to Chenji's weak hog ears.

Yui nudged Ivanov with her spear. "I-I'm fine!" he called. "My shelf just fell. Cleaning up a bit of a mess."

"Unlock the door," commanded a voice in the hallway.

"I'm afraid it's quite embarrassing. I'd rather not."

"Someone get a key," Chenji heard someone say. They were running out of time.

"No one has to die," he said, shrinking down to his Human form. He scanned the floor quickly, hoping to find Akio hidden among the icy wreckage, but the Jakari was either buried or too well hidden. "We can leave here together."

"Not a chance." Yui tugged Ivanov toward the window. That was when the senator noticed Chenji's Human form for the first time.

"You..." he said, his eyes lighting up. "You're one of the Liberators. Chenji the Changeling, correct?"

"The what?"

"The Liberators. You, Hellfire, Makoto the Bold...the heroes that destroyed the *Dormarch*."

"Heroes?" Chenji stared at the senator, dumbfounded. Where had he gotten all this information? Or these nicknames?

The senator blinked. "Do you not know?" He turned to Yui. "Does he—?"

"Enough!" Yui smashed the window behind her and pulled Ivanov toward it. "I have a ride to catch."

Akio scrabbled across the ceiling, outside Yui's line of sight, but well within Chenji's.

The changeling smiled. "So do we." He feinted toward Yui, then dove to the side as icicles shot from her hand and stabbed into the door behind him. Akio leapt onto her and knocked the spear from her other hand, then sliced at her face, nicking her cheek. She screamed and let go of Ivanov, using her hands to instead launch an icy blast that sent Akio hurdling toward Chenji, who caught him.

"Are you alright?" he asked as the Jakari shivered violently in his arms, nursing scales on his chest that had been scalded black with freezer burn.

"I have had b-breakups with w-worse wounds than these, boy of many f-faces."

Chenji laughed, curious what the Jakari dating scene looked like. The senator had made it over to their side of the room, leaving Yui with nothing but a cut on her cheek.

"If they take us prisoner, we'll *all* be denied help from the outside," said Chenji, nodding toward the door on which the staff continued to bang. "We can escape together and deal with the delivery of the senator later."

"When you say delivery—" started Ivanov, but panicked shouts from the hallway cut him off. Orange light emanated from the seam of the door.

"I suggest you move," said Yui, smiling.

Chenji pulled the senator away from the door as a fireball blasted it off its hinges. Kazan marched inside on bare feet, a fireball levitating over each of his open palms. "I'd love to stay and play," he said, the firelight making the blue scars on his face glisten, "but we're on a tight schedule."

"So are we," said Cera. Everyone turned. She stood at the

edge of the room amid a cloud of smoke, Warp standing behind her, one hand on her back, the other on an also newly arrived Ristin.

Kazan shrieked his war cry at Cera, one that he'd no doubt perfected in the fight rings, but before his flames could blast her way, she snapped a hand of green energy around his torso and pinned his burning hands to his sides.

"Lusitani incoming!" came Li's voice through their earpieces. The assassins leaped down from the crater in the ceiling, but Ristin caught them in a bubble of antigravity that kept them hovering in midair.

"Freeze!" shouted the guards. They appeared in the doorway, finally regrouped after Kazan's fireball had dispersed them, pistols raised. Cera blockaded the door with another field of energy, leaving herself exposed with both arms occupied. Chenji saw Yui winding up to strike her, but he was too far away to do anything. He was about to shout when Warp appeared next to Yui, grabbed her, and teleported her away.

If only we could fix all our problems so easily.

"Get the senator out!" ordered Cera. The Lusitani activated weights on their boots that pulled them through Ristin's gravity bubble and onto the floor. Ristin kept his powers focused on them as they marched forward with heavy footsteps, aiming their wrists at Ivanov.

Chenji morphed into a giant bird and snatched the senator in his talons. With a flap of his wings, he was sailing out the broken window and into the smoggy air.

The city lay before him in the haze. No one was outside this sunny afternoon, and that was when Chenji realized that there was nowhere for them to go. Everything in the city was built indoors, interconnected through covered tunnels and passageways. He began to understand why, as the smog burned his eyes and throat.

"That rooftop has a filter!" Ivanov called up, pointing. "Land us there."

Chenji had no idea what the senator meant about a filter, but everything hurt so much it didn't matter. He swooped onto the prescribed rooftop and the air suddenly cleared. A large electrical box hummed nearby; Chenji assumed it to be the filter. He morphed back into his Human form (a form that required considerably less oxygen) and gasped in the clean air.

"Thank you for saving my life," said Ivanov. "Though I'm not sure how long your plans are meant to keep me alive."

"Neither do I," rasped Chenji. "But I promise you our team will do more to protect you than theirs."

"Based on your resumés, I'm inclined to agree."

Chenji's eyes narrowed. "How do you know so much about us?"

"Why, here in Poteria, people tune in every night to hear about your latest adventures."

"That's impossible." Chenji rose. He was a full head shorter than the looming Poterian, yet he approached with such intensity that the senator started to back away. "We don't know the first thing about your side of the galaxy, so how could you know so much about ours?"

Ivanov hesitated. "Our empire made a mess of many aspects of the war, but they were good at leaving surveillance equipment on your side. At first for spying, but it turns out your side had a real flair for dramatic storytelling. We started relaying your news and other media to our stations. It was free entertainment for us, and our people gobbled it up."

"So...we're just an evening news special for you?"

Ivanov tutted. "My dear Chenji, you are so much more than that! Your team is now the face of your side of the Rift. The face of a new age. One where your people can gain the equality we failed to win for them."

"Equality?" Chenji felt a rage bubbling inside him. "You murdered billions of people in the name of *equality*?"

Ivanov shrugged. "Well, yes."

Chenji took a step back. He couldn't believe what he was hearing. "You used the Zoboros to justify *your* war."

"As I understand it, you are no stranger to being used, Chenji the Changeling."

Chenji froze. How dare this man...this *Poterian* pretend to know him. How dare he go digging into his past. Did all Poteria know? He stared out at the vast, indoor cityscape and felt sick to his stomach. "Don't try to get into my head, senator."

"And you think the empress isn't doing the same thing?" Chenji scrambled to come up with a lie to cover for her, but Ivanov laughed. "There's only one person who would go through all this trouble to capture little old me."

"Maybe I just wanted to hurt you myself." The way Chenji was feeling, that wasn't too far from the truth.

"No, but I'm sure you want to hurt the one who sent the marauders after you."

"We already know it was Danadas."

"Danadas has nothing to offer the marauders. They can't be bought with money. Only promises. *A* promise to be precise, and it's a promise only one person can fulfill."

Chenji took a step forward. "What are you talking about?"

"The marauders hate the empire for driving them from their homeland, and they hated Palorex most of all for clearing them out of the way to wage his war. There is only one Poterian in generations who has been able to turn things around. Only one who has been able to bring them to the table and grant them concessions in exchange for certain…favors." Chenji paled, and Ivanov smiled. "You know of whom I speak."

Chenji shook his head. "Why?" he demanded. "Why try to kill us only to use us instead?"

"Because you've entered a larger game. One that—"

Ivanov gasped. Chenji tensed, his animal instincts recognizing a predator. He spotted the Lusitani leaping through the shadows, its red bandana trailing behind it as it fled. When he turned back to Ivanov, the senator lay motionless on the ground, a knife protruding from his back.

A larger game indeed.

Chapter 28

Shadows of the Past

A horn blared through the open window. Junior grumbled to himself and hugged the pillow tighter over his head, a futile effort during rush hour.

Why did Famora have to stay busy on his day off?

He climbed out of the safety of his sheets and crossed the frigid room toward the open window.

"Is letting in the cold worth the early wake up?"

His mother stood in the doorway with a smirk on her face while the greasy aroma of sizzling bacon wafted in behind her. His stomach growled.

"Keeps me from getting lazy like the rest of them," he said. They were somewhere out there, his fellow cadets, monitoring the distant lines of hovercars that flowed between the floating buildings. Or more realistically, they were nursing hangovers at their stations and mouthing off about whatever they had done at the Sphere last night. Something stupid, he was sure.

"There's nothing wrong with having a little fun from time to time." She hugged him from behind and kissed the back of his head. He felt a strange warmth, one he'd not felt since…for a moment, he swore the traffic outside his window had disappeared. He blinked and it was back, silhouetted by the sun rising through the pinkish clouds.

"Come on," she said. "You know what happens if we leave him in charge of breakfast."

There'll be none left. They hurried down the stairs and, sure enough, the bacon was already charring in the pan, a haze of smoke filling the kitchen. The sous chef stood at the crime scene, face buried in his datapad as he scrolled through the morning news.

"At least pretend to be helping!" exclaimed Angeline, pushing past her husband and salvaging the bacon with a few abrasive jabs of the spatula.

"I was!" he replied, still reading. "Tastes better a little burnt."

"A little?" Junior glanced from the blackened strips to his mother's disappointed face. They shook their heads in defeat.

Hendricks chuckled. "More for me then." He kissed Angeline on the cheek. Junior noticed something strange about his long, clean-shaven face. Not just that it was smiling, but something else. An image flashed before him: his father's face oozing blood from a gash that ran down his cheek to his lip. Junior stumbled back.

"You alright, Junior?" His father caught him by the shoulder. Junior looked up and saw no blood. No cut. No scar.

"Yeah…just a long day yesterday." He sat down at the table, struggling to remember what had happened the day before.

"Some eggs and juice will have you feeling better," said his mother, busying herself at the stove.

Junior nodded, rubbing his forehead. He couldn't explain what he was feeling. Everything felt so right, so normal, yet completely off at the same time.

Hendricks sat beside him with his datapad and cleared his throat. That was the signal that he was about to spark casual conversation. "How long you think before Marcus botches traffic control?"

Junior cracked a smile. His second in command could barely be trusted to put on his own uniform correctly. "I give it an hour before Novak calls cursing up a storm."

"We can always trust Novak to interrupt a day off."

Trust. Suddenly, Novak was sitting across from him, aiming his pistol. Junior leaped from the table and backed into his mother.

"Junior, what's gotten into you?" She abandoned the stove and Hendricks abandoned the datapad, just like the image of Novak had abandoned the table.

"I-I'm not sure. I—"

"*Wake up!*"

Who said that? Junior spun around, but there was no one else here, nor was there a wall anymore. Just smoke billowing from a burning Famora in the distance.

Hendricks coughed. Junior turned and found his father stumbling toward him, a sword protruding from his chest.

"Dad!" Junior caught the big man as he keeled forward, easing him to the floor while hot blood stuck to his hands. "Mom, call the hospital!" But when he looked, she had disappeared, and her breakfast was burning on the stovetop.

His father cackled. Junior looked down and found the Jaculus in his arms instead, green face contorted into a sickening grin. He slapped Junior in the face.

"Ah!" Junior sat up and rubbed his cheek as dead leaves fell from his back. A dream? The lump on his cheek certainly felt real. But he didn't remember falling asleep, nor did he recognize the forest around him, its towering trees concealing any trace of sky above. The last thing he remembered was his mother pushing him through a portal.

Mom! He spun around. Instead of her warm smile, he found the cold scowl of his sworn enemy. Junior was about to summon fire when he noticed the sword in Taranis's hand; the sword Taranis had used to kill his father; the sword Junior had carried through the portal after killing the Jaculus. *After killing a lot of people.* Junior knew Taranis had every reason to use that sword on him if he'd wanted to. So why hadn't he?

"Where are the—?" Taranis clamped a hand over Junior's mouth before he could finish.

"The others were taken," whispered Taranis, motioning past the bushes they were tucked behind. Hooves clopped slowly on the other side of it, crunching through leaves. Junior peered between the brambles and followed the four legs up, expecting them to be attached to a horse, but what he found instead made him want to gag. It was a monster with no skin or fur, just glistening, exposed muscle. Everything from its torso up was humanoid in shape, with gaunt arms that hung lazily at its sides and a long jaw ready to snap its prey beneath razor-sharp teeth. There were no eyes on the creature; instead, it felt around with its hands, the leaves and vines wilting at its touch.

"What is that?" he whispered.

Taranis shushed him, but it was too late. The creature's

savage head twisted their direction. Junior felt the whole world turn cold. It clopped toward them, listening, its jaw coming unhinged. Taranis grabbed a rock and heaved it over their heads. It cracked against the bark of a distant tree and rustled the leaves as it fell, more than enough noise to send the creature galloping after it.

"That was a Nuvanok," said Taranis, once the beast was well out of sight, the air warming back up in its absence. "And they do not like visitors. We're lucky it was alone. The pack was much harder to elude."

Shame it didn't take you. "Did they get the others?" He took Taranis's silence for a yes. "My mother?"

"I don't know."

"You'll have to do better than that. This entire mess is your fault. You dragged us here. You forced her to open the portal. And now she's…" He didn't dare let himself think it. If anyone could survive Iramwerta, it was her. "Now we're being hunted," he finished.

Taranis glanced at Junior's warming palms. "As amusing as it is to stoke your anger, Hendricks Junior, I would advise against using your powers here. The Nuvanoks are attracted to them, as I learned the hard way."

Junior's eyes narrowed. As he recalled, Taranis had given up his powers in Iramwerta. Did he really have them back, or was he bluffing? The Nuvanok thing seemed a convenient excuse to avoid proving whether he had them.

"Believe me or don't, but blasting fire in this forest presents an easy target regardless," said Taranis flatly.

You've got me there. Junior looked around. Trees and bushes flourished out of almost every inch of soil, yet the whole place felt...empty. No buzzing of insects or chirping of birds, nor rustling of leaves since the Nuvanok departed. Just eerie silence.

"Where are we?" he asked.

Taranis marched a few paces ahead. "A realm beyond our own," he answered, pulling back a veil of vines.

Junior gaped. Massive rocks floated in the distance, dozens of them, like Famoran platforms only home to lush forests instead of buildings, each rock progressively lower until they came to a central platform where a single tree dominated it; a tree that made even the tallest ones on the surrounding platforms look like twigs by comparison. It must have been miles away, yet its silvery branches reached far enough that they concealed the sky above their heads.

Only there was no sky, Junior realized. In the expanses between the floating rocks, he found nothing but starry cosmos. The whole place was surrounded not by atmosphere but by space itself. So where was the gravity coming from? How were they breathing? Was he still dreaming? Everything here felt real, even—

"You slapped me in the face," he said, rubbing his cheek.

Taranis shrugged. "You were making too much noise in your sleep. I had to keep you from attracting the creature." He marched along the edge of their rocky platform and Junior followed, trying to ignore the wisps of cosmos flowing lightyears beneath his feet, ready to swallow him up should he slip.

"Why didn't you just leave me behind?"

"This realm is dangerous. Better to have backup." Taranis stopped and glanced over his shoulder. "Backup that stays quiet."

Junior bristled but heeded the warning nonetheless. This forest was as vast as it was dark, and his footfalls alone were enough to attract a predator amid the silence. He treaded lightly despite not knowing where Taranis was leading him, sticking to rocks rather than leaf-covered earth whenever possible. He wanted to know more about this place; he wanted to know how Taranis knew about it. And most importantly, he wanted to know where his mother was within it.

He saw their destination just ahead – a long root that bridged the gap between the rocky platform on which they stood and the next. A root that came, he assumed by its silvery glow, from the massive tree. He noticed more roots bridging the various platforms, connecting the entire floating forest like a single, mighty organism.

The root proved much thinner than Junior had anticipated. His foot covered almost the entire width of it, and the cosmos swirling beneath his feet did nothing for his confidence.

"These paths will get thicker the farther we go," said Taranis, already making headway on the root with his methodic steps. "Until then, take it slow."

Junior willed himself forward, one step at a time, while the root sagged beneath his weight. He dared not go too slowly though, else Taranis could get to the end and chop the bridge if he so pleased. Not to mention Junior would be out of range to ask questions.

"How do you know about this place?" Junior whispered.

"The Jaculus spoke of it often," answered Taranis. "As do the ancient texts."

The image of the Jaculus severed in two flashed through

Junior's mind. "Why did you help me kill him?"

"We had reached the end of our agreement. We each wanted to open the portal, and we had."

"And why did *you* want to open the portal?" Junior's foot slipped. His weight shifted against him, the infinite cosmos hungry to snatch him up. *Shit!* A hand clamped around his arm and righted him.

"I came seeking answers," said Taranis, nodding toward the big tree. "The Jaculus sought something…darker. But what is it you want, Hendricks Junior?"

"I just want to find my mother," he said, heart racing from his near fall. That now made two saves from Taranis today. He would have felt indebted, had it not been the maniac who had put him in danger both times.

"You may find your answers on the path ahead, too."

They continued in silence for a while. What answers *did* this place hold? Junior assumed it to be the place of Zoboros power, the place the Three Kings of Mogaddu discovered long ago. And if it was, they would need to be careful. In the story, the powers they found were deceptive, corruptible, destroying each king in his turn. Junior had always treated the story as fiction, but now he wondered how much truth was behind it.

"You mentioned a darkness here," he said. "Did you mean the Nuvanoks?"

Taranis shook his head. "Something the Nuvanoks locked away long ago."

"A power?"

"A person." Taranis nodded toward a blackened patch beneath the great tree. A patch where nothing grew. "A thief who once tried to rob this land."

Chapter 29

A True Warrior

The shuttle rocked like someone had thrown it into a blender. Kano had endured enough atmospheric entries over the months to know this wasn't normal. Or rather, the Abari shuttle wasn't normal. From the way the bolts squeaked and the engines coughed, he would have preferred landing in a Del Cloran scrapper than this Poterian junker.

Some way to treat your future Ay Nyid. Not that he thought of himself as a prophesized hero; it was said that the Ay Nyid would survive the Trials, and Kano really didn't want to die.

"Five minutes," announced Varlam. He sat across from Kano beneath the dim lights, empty seats lining the aisle to either side of him. The transport bay had no windows, for which Kano was thankful given the chaotic entry, though he couldn't help feeling a little déjà vu. He'd been in this exact same position on his very first shuttle ride, except instead of a Poterian, it was Novak leading him to an unknown fate against his will. And he hadn't been allowed a guest last time.

"All this shaking's making me nauseous."

"Please don't throw up on my shoes, Makoto."

Kano tried to find comfort in his brother's company, but he knew the only reason the Abari had let him tag along was because they wanted to be rid of the non-Zoboros on their ship. Odd how contrary their prejudices were to the ones Kano was used to, though he found them just as unsavory.

The shuttle did what felt like a somersault. Kano clutched the armrests, feeling as sick as he was frustrated. All that time with the Abari, time he could have spent helping his friends, and instead he was stuck here knowing that he'd have to give up those same friends to complete the Trials. It went against the very reason he'd set off on this whole adventure. If he gave them up, what would he have to fight for?

Every reason. Black fire flashed through his mind. War was coming, at least according to Niscelles. But why, and how? And what impact could his completing the Trials possibly have on something as massive as a galactic war? Apparently, Junior was tied to it too, though he didn't understand how. Niscelles had claimed that Junior was poised to fail at something important, but the dodgy old Poterian had left him with more questions than answers regarding the details.

He worried the Trials would do the same.

The rumbling ceased and the rickety shuttle smoothed into its final descent. Varlam rose, head almost brushing the ceiling. He looked like a statue looming over Kano, a statue with deep, penetrating eyes that spoke of judgment to come.

"It is time," said Varlam. "Once you step off this ship, I cannot allow you back on until the Trials are complete. I will wait here three days for your triumphant return."

Kano didn't have to ask what happened after three days. He

picked up his pack, an extra sense of urgency behind his movements, while his nauseous brother managed to stand up beside him.

"I'd like to go, too," he said. Kano tensed. He knew this would come, just like he knew Makoto's life could come between him and completing the Trials. That was what Niscelles had warned him about. He just hoped Varlam was prepared to handle it.

The Poterian hesitated before speaking. "My task now is to keep you bound here until your brother's return." Kano sighed with relief, but then Varlam did something strange. He knelt so his eyes were level with Makoto's. "However, should I return claiming I was overpowered by a mighty Nurrano who snuck his batons onto the shuttle, I don't think anyone would bat an eye. Not given your record in the ring." Varlam drew the batons from under his seat and winked.

Makoto beamed as he scooped up his weapons. A happy moment, but not for Kano.

"Is…is that allowed?" asked Kano.

Varlam shrugged. "There are no referees in the Trials. No witnesses. Just one rule: survive." The ship shuddered as it touched down on the surface. "So what do you choose, Makoto?"

Kano turned to his brother. That was the first time Varlam had referred to either of them by name. Makoto stood up straight, for once taller than the kneeling Poterian. "I'm going."

"Good luck, then." Varlam nodded toward the exit. "It has been a pleasure to serve you both."

The brothers marched toward the liftgate, one glowing with pride, the other filled with doubt. Kano couldn't help seeing the image of Makoto floating helplessly through the Rift.

"What if you're not allowed to enter the Trials?" asked Kano. "This whole thing is shrouded in so much tradition. We wouldn't want to upset...whatever we find there."

Makoto shrugged. "Doesn't sound like there's anyone around to get upset about it, but I guess we'll find out...wherever it is that we're going."

Kano sighed. Danger never deterred his brother. If anything, it was Makoto's muse. He could only hope that something forced Makoto to turn back without killing him in the process.

Rain sloshed into the transport as the liftgate opened. Cold and heavy, it acted as a veil for the black mountain behind it.

No. Sharp rocks jutted like blades from its surface, climbing all the way to its spiky peak that hid within a sea of dark, swirling storm clouds. Kano shook himself. Was this a vision? No, he had a clear memory of everything that had brought him here: Varlam, the Abari, the shuttle. This was real.

Makoto waved a hand in his face, severing him from the image of his nightmares, and offered him a raincoat. Kano realized it was the only one the Abari had left for them.

"You take it," he said, but Makoto forced it into his hand and marched down the ramp, spreading his arms as he basked in the downpour.

"My people were built for this kind of weather!" exclaimed Makoto.

Kano shook his head and wrapped himself in the coat's warm embrace. Even with it, though, the rain still lashed at his face and leaked down his chest, helping the gusting wind to chill him further. It made him wonder what Nurranos could possibly be made of, to deal with this.

They followed a trail that snaked from their landing zone. Kano assumed it was the right path, else they wouldn't have landed in front of it – unless that was a trick of the Trials. Kano shook the thought away; he didn't need mind games plaguing him now. Not when Makoto was getting so far ahead without a soaking raincoat to weigh him down.

"Watch the rocks!" he called after Makoto. Even here at the mountain's base they encroached on the path, some of their points angled toward it. "They can slice your arm open if you're not careful."

"How would you know that?"

"I just do."

The higher they climbed, the slower they went. Their path wasn't particularly steep, not yet, but Kano felt the altitude changing. The air grew colder, thinner, grinding his windpipe as his lungs worked harder. And all the while the rocks kept pressing tighter upon them. Soon they had to go single file just to avoid being cut, and still they had to stop periodically to inch their way around the more intrusive ones. Such a slow process, and they had no way of knowing if they were on the right path. They could hit a dead end, and then what? Three days seemed like hardly enough time to even reach the peak, let alone make the return trip.

"How many trials do you think there are?" asked Makoto, crawling beneath an outlying rock.

Kano frowned, the subject alone making him even more stressed. "Three. That's how stories with trials usually go."

"Just three? I feel like there's gotta be more. I mean, it would be sad if no one in history has completed *three* stinking challenges. Unless they're really hard, then—"

"Enough!" snapped Kano. His brother lowered his head like a scolded child and plodded on in silence. They stayed quiet, and the only thing Kano heard for a while beside the patter of the rain was a single word in his mind.

"Unworthy."

He wanted to feel guilty for yelling at his brother, but all he felt was frustration. Frustration that Makoto had tagged along; frustration that he might have little say in Makoto's fate. And still the rain came harder, rushing down the path and threatening to drag them with it. Every icy step stung Kano's feet, shriveled like prunes in the damp. Even Makoto struggled to maintain his footing, finally starting to shiver as his breath rasped in the increasingly frigid air. *Now you wish you took the raincoat, don't you?* There was still so much more to climb, and already the temperature was too much for them to handle with what little the Abari had provided them. This climb was impossible.

At least, it was impossible alone.

Kano grabbed onto Makoto's side, matching him step for step, using each other's weight to keep balanced against the slippery rocks, and using each other's warmth to ward off the bitter cold. Their synchronized steps became stronger, wider, bounding up the mountainside faster than either could do alone. Kano chanced a glance over his shoulder, spotted their shuttle far below beneath sheets of rain, tucked in a pit amid a sea of jagged rocks.

But the peak was still so much farther.

"Cave," rasped Makoto, pointing. Kano spotted it: an alcove just off the path, not a single jagged rock standing between them and it. Easy shelter. Too easy. But against the freezing rain, he'd take anything.

They flung themselves into the cave, Makoto sprawling himself against the dry ground while Kano wrang out his soaking coat, relieved to be out of the deluge. Makoto shivered there on the floor, coughing deeply and violently. Kano threw the semi-dry raincoat around him and hugged him for warmth until the shaking ceased and the coughing calmed.

"I'm ok," said Makoto, sitting upright. His voice was hoarse, but the color was returning to his face. "How much farther to the top?"

"A long way." Kano didn't find himself in much better shape. Every muscle shivered, yet felt frozen stiff at the same time. He had no desire to move, not even to warm himself further. He just wanted to sit.

"We can try waiting till the rain stops," suggested Makoto.

Kano shook his head. "I don't think it will." It certainly never stopped raining here in his visions...

He snapped back onto his feet. That was it.

"What's up?"

"I had a vision of a cave once, back when we still lived in Famora. It was inside a mountain like this one. There was a strange light inside it, and a pool."

"And you think it has something to do with the Trials?"

Kano shrugged. "Only one way to find out."

Darkness consumed them quickly as they inched along. The rocks along the walls were smooth, though, unlike the outside. *Just like they were in the dream.* They used them to feel their way along, at least until Makoto had a sudden epiphany.

"Wait, I've got just what we need!" He sparked one of his stun batons, and just in time too, for his next step would have been into a pool of water. "Oh."

They each took a baton and searched for a way around, but the pool ran the breadth of the cave, and stretched on for as far as their minimal light could show them. Kano tried to remember how he'd crossed it in the dream, only to realize that he hadn't. In the dream, Niscelles had appeared here and presented him with incredible power that woke him before he could get any answers.

"That's weird," said Makoto.

"What?"

"Look."

Makoto pointed at their reflections in the water. Or rather, Kano's reflection. Makoto didn't have one...and Kano's didn't match. It was older, broader at the shoulders, bearded with specks of gray, and a hardness in the stare that frightened Kano of the future.

"Guess you won't always be a skinny shit."

"Shut up, Makoto."

Kano knelt toward the water and reached for it.

"*Find us!*"

He spun around. "Did you hear that?"

"Hear what?"

A screech echoed through the chamber.

"I heard *that*," said Makoto, snatching his baton back so quickly that Kano slipped and his hand brushed the water.

The wind sucked out of him. Glowing wisps flowed from his fingertips into the dark water, forming a beacon of light that swam across the pool.

"What is that?!" blurted Makoto.

Kano picked himself up, catching his breath from the

sudden rush. He had a feeling he knew exactly what was swimming toward the opposite bank. He tried summoning his powers, but they wouldn't come. He turned to his brother, the horrible realization hitting him.

"I think the Trials have begun."

Light exploded from the opposite bank. His power had connected with it, and now the black rocks around them glowed with a mysterious aura. Another shriek echoed from the stalactites that dotted the ceiling, this one louder than the first. Angrier. A creature the size of a man swooped out on two great wings. Its black fur rustled through the cold air and its red eyes squinted against the harsh light, its talons like great hooks out to carve through whomever had disturbed its slumber.

"Let's go!" shouted Makoto, grabbing Kano.

"Wait, I can't—" Makoto pulled him into the pool before he could finish. He flailed there, the cold water sinking its needlelike teeth into him, and managed to take a deep breath before Makoto tugged him underwater. He watched those long talons graze the water's surface as Makoto pulled him deeper. His ears began to hurt. His lungs begged for oxygen. But above, he saw more of those creatures flying through the chamber, ready to pounce should the intruders surface.

Bubbles spouted from his mouth involuntarily. His lungs demanded air but he fought the urge, even as his vision began to fade, while Makoto sped them toward a bright tunnel at the opposite bank.

Chapter 30

Beginnings and Endings

Follow the bubbles.

Makoto resurfaced, oxygen filling his screaming lungs.

"Kano!" His brother dangled limply in his arms. Makoto barely had the strength to keep going himself, but he pushed anyway. There was a shore nearby. He just needed to get there.

The current washed him onto the sand. Relief swept over his aching muscles, but he didn't have time to savor it. He laid Kano on his back and pumped his chest. *Come on, come on.*

Water spouted from Kano's mouth. Kano sat up and coughed the rest out, drenching the sand beneath him. Makoto patted his back and waited for him to catch his breath, noticing for the first time that the cavern around them had changed, its polished black rocks now gray.

"Thanks," rasped Kano, head lolling. His gaze then rolled up the shore and his whole body snapped into motion, awake with horror.

"Impossible...we...*how?*"

"What?" Makoto spun around, expecting those creatures to come swooping down on the attack again. But there was no sign of them. No sign of anyone. Just a massive door looming over the shore, strange symbols etched in its stone.

Then it clicked. Iramwerta. The door matched Kano and Junior's description, but that door was supposed to be on Mogaddu. Could this be a copy? Something about the change in scenery told him otherwise. *When we passed through the light, did we somehow…magically…?*

"We need to turn back," said Kano.

Makoto found his brother had already backed halfway into the surf. "Are you kidding?" he said. "If this is one of the Trials then we hit the jackpot. You've already opened the door before. You can do it again."

"That was with my powers. Without them, I don't know how it will react."

"React? It's a door."

Makoto started toward it. His brother splashed after him, calling out with weak lungs, too slow to catch up. Makoto tried pushing the massive door to see if there was any give, a hinge somewhere, but it didn't budge. Instead, he felt a strange tickling sensation in his hand. Then the symbols began to glow white. There was a groan, and the stone door opened, dredging sand.

Kano arrived beside him, speechless.

"How…the riddle?" stammered Kano.

"What are you talking about?"

"There was supposed to be a riddle. Last time there was a riddle. And your weapons…" Kano pointed at the batons strapped to Makoto's belt. "You shouldn't be able to enter with those."

Makoto shrugged. "Maybe it just likes me." He stepped through and gaped. The cavern around them was gone. He stood atop a hill beneath a hot sun, overlooking a city of stone.

The buildings were all small except for a temple at the center, where a great orb of white light blazed for the whole city to see.

"I'll bet that's where the next trial is. Come on!" He scampered down the hill, Kano trailing far behind. Weak as Kano was, Makoto sensed something else…something holding his brother back.

Merchants lined the outskirts of the village, calling to him in languages that he didn't recognize, each showing off their spices and silks. It reminded him of Famora, only this city lacked the familiar hustle and bustle. The townsfolk here strolled about their business, none in any rush, many waving greetings despite never having seen him before.

Awfully easy if this is a Trial. The only challenge seemed to be climbing those temple stairs, though Makoto knew better than to underestimate his surroundings.

Like he had in the cavern.

He started up the stairs, his brother lagging. Makoto stopped halfway, letting Kano catch up while he massaged his tired legs. He noticed Kano kept glancing at the villagers below, confused.

"Were they here the last time?" asked Makoto.

Kano scratched his head. "Not quite. It's hard to explain."

"Well we've got a long climb ahead of us."

Makoto did his best to follow along as Kano explained. He liked to imagine the time projections as haunted, ghostly figures roaming the streets. He knew it wasn't entirely accurate to Kano's description, but he found the image oddly amusing. And puzzling. Why had everything changed since Kano's last visit. Had that underwater light transported them through space *and* time? And if it had, why did it bring them here, to this moment?

"Kano, what's at the top of this temple?"

His brother paused. "A graveyard. But I don't think that's what we'll find this time. At least I hope not."

A shadow fell over them. Great storm clouds rolled in without warning. A wind swept through and chilled Makoto to his bones. The streets below had cleared, the last of the townsfolk sealing their doors and windows.

"Hurry," said Kano, despite being in no state to do so. They climbed faster, Kano's breath rasping the whole way. Makoto let his grip fall to his batons. If something waited for them at the top, it was up to him to handle it.

They scaled the final step. Makoto whipped out his batons, expecting danger, but found none. Just a circle of stone with a hazy, white energy glowing at its center and an old Poterian lying with his back against it.

"We meet at last," said the Poterian. Makoto blinked. That had been the first person here to speak in their own language. But where did he come from? And how did he know them? He looked worn and weary, a white beard hanging from his sagging red skin, his tusks grown out well in front of his tired face.

"Niscelles?" said Kano. "But...but we've already met."

What?! *The* Niscelles from the old stories? Tales of the kings of Mogaddu were legends among the Nurranos. Tales of heroics and greatness that turned to bitterness and betrayal. But how could this legend be sitting right here, in front of them? And how the hell did Kano *meet* him?

"In another time, perhaps," answered Niscelles. "But my

time is near its end."

Thunder cracked behind them. Makoto spun around to find the sound hadn't come from the storm clouds, but from the cannons of hundreds of warships descending toward the city. Makoto shrank back, his batons feeling puny, useless in his little hands. The cannon fire exploded high above, striking a translucent dome that enveloped the city. Had that been there the whole time? Makoto could only see the dome in the places where it was struck, of which there were many. Could it be Niscelles's power? The old stories never made it clear what the ancient kings could actually do, only that they were incredibly strong. Yet even this power flickered against the barrage of artillery.

"What's happening, Niscelles?" asked Kano. "Why are we here?" Makoto wondered the same things, but the shock and awe had rendered him speechless.

"Help me up so I may show you."

Kano and Makoto each grabbed an arm and hoisted him onto his feet. He felt light for such a tall Poterian, but that may have been because he was mostly skin and bone. *And tusk.*

Niscelles drew a sword from his belt and Makoto gasped. He knew that blade, had fought it many times in the hands of Taranis. The old king's knees trembled against the weight of the blade. Makoto was about to reach over and help when Niscelles grabbed hold of the stone circle. All at once, the trembling ceased. Niscelles stood himself upright, looking regal despite his unkempt face, like he'd been born to command armies. Yet there was no army here for him. None that Makoto could see. Just the three of them standing beneath a crumbling dome.

Soldiers in gray armor crested the hilltop from where Makoto and Kano had just come, thousands strong, swords drawn and ready to savage the city below. From the stone homes emerged Niscelles's warriors, no more than a few dozen, each armed with clubs and axes. These were farmers, not soldiers; Makoto could see as much from high atop the temple. Yet when the enemy force charged over the hill, Niscelles's small force exploded with the power of a hundred warships. Jets of fire, columns of stone, rushing walls of water all converged upon the invaders – yet with each one burned, crushed, or drowned, ten more came charging over to take their place.

"Etorea was always stubborn," muttered Niscelles, his eyes glowing as white as the energy within the stone circle.

Etorea. Makoto recalled that name from the stories. Another of the three kings. They had turned against each other at the story's end, though he couldn't remember why.

Cracks tore across the dome. Enemy shuttles swarmed through them and zeroed in on the temple.

"Help me defend this place!" said Niscelles, such command in his voice it made those little batons feel somehow larger in Makoto's hands. Black fire shot from Niscelles's sword. Makoto felt no heat from it, yet when it struck the shuttles they turned to ash. Now *that* was more like the power from the stories. Yet its strength waned, retreating toward the sword while the swarm closed in. Niscelles drove his sword into the strange white energy, drawing from it, useless for the time being.

"Looks like it's up to us, Kano," said Makoto, gripping his weapons tighter.

"But I don't have my powers," said Kano, drawing back.

"And if you want them back, you'll fight!" said Niscelles.

A shuttle lowered before them, cables dropping from it. Armored soldiers slid down the cables and onto the temple's top, the enemy faces clear beneath their metal helms. Abari, each so much larger than himself.

But Makoto was used to that.

He charged into the fray. His opponents swung too high, as expected, leaving him room to slide low and catch them by their legs. They dropped to one knee with zap after zap until one got wise and went for a downward cut. Familiar. He rolled out of the way and struck the Abari's exposed chest. Too easy. They all came on with the traditional fighting stances (the tradition had to have started somewhere) and soon a tangle of cables swung above his downed opponents. More came in, though. Shiploads more. The ships didn't use their cannons — Abari would not dispatch a worthy opponent so crudely — and still Niscelles's sword charged in the circle's energy. Kano had picked up a fallen sword and used it to fight off what few Abari managed to slip past Makoto, but as more ships swept in, Makoto doubted their defenses could hold.

"They're veering off!" exclaimed Kano.

Makoto looked to the skies. He couldn't believe it. Just when the enemy was about to overrun them, the ships had drawn back. But why?

The ground shook so hard Makoto almost spilled down the temple's steps. He turned, expecting to find an enemy Zoboros had joined the battle, but what he saw instead was far worse. A ganomorph, a beast of ancient lore, tall enough to reach the giant orb atop the pillar if it tried and large enough to catch Makoto in its fist and squeeze him into juice. It had no armor, only rags stitched together over its bulking body, its thick gray scales constituting all the armor it would likely ever need.

"Now this is a trial!" Makoto called over to a catatonic Kano, his own voice cracking as even he recognized the magnitude of the challenge.

"Reminds me of a Gorv," was all Kano managed to get out.

"An ancestor," said Niscelles, drawing his sword out of the hazy energy ever so slowly. "Keep him busy, please."

How would he know that? Makoto didn't have time to question it. The brute marched forward with thunderous steps, squinting its beady black eyes as it sized up its three targets. But why did it hesitate? Makoto glanced at the battle below, realized the creature probably thought they were Zoboros. *It wants to see what we can do.*

Makoto thrust his hands toward the creature in the manner Kano would summon a shockwave. The creature took a mighty step back, arms instinctively guarding its face. *So that's where it's weakest.* Judging by the rocklike scales that made up its face, he couldn't imagine where that weakness would be. And reaching its face was another matter entirely.

The Gorv lowered its arms and huffed, its breath slapping Makoto like a gale-force wind, one that reeked of blood. The ganomorph didn't like being tricked. Makoto took a step back. That was all the invitation the creature needed to barrel toward him.

"Look out!" Makoto rolled out of the way, the creature's foot crunching the stone just inches from him, and watched the ancient creature skid to a stop, its scaly feet grinding across the stone like nails on a chalkboard. Makoto wanted to cover his ears but didn't have time. The creature was on him, swinging those massive fists, each near miss a killing blow.

"HEY!" Kano shouted. He heaved a fallen spear at the monster, a clean shot right to the neck. The weapon pinged off it and spun away over the edge of the temple, entirely ineffective except for the fact that the creature now turned toward Kano, murder in its eyes.

"Sorry!" The creature barreled toward him. Niscelles wasn't far behind him, the sword only half drawn from the stone circle. *Slow old man.* Makoto chased after the ganomorph and noticed a long ponytail hanging down almost to the beast's knees. He'd never known Gorvs to have hair, but he could worry about when they'd gone bald later. Right now, he had an opportunity.

"Kano, grab one of the Abari's cables!"

"I'm a little busy!" Kano was dodging the clobbering fists as they pounded the stones around him.

Makoto caught onto the ponytail and swung off the ground, clinging to the thick braids as he rotated around the monster, who stopped its charge on Kano, aware of the attacker in its hair. It whipped its head around, swinging Makoto in a wide arc. He clung for dear life, the orb of light flashing past him.

"I've got the cable!" exclaimed Kano.

"Great!" shouted Makoto, the surrounding battle becoming a nauseating whirl as he spun round and round the creature. Eventually, mercifully, the spinning stopped, though the world still spun in Makoto's vision. The same must have been true for the beast, who teetered, dizzied from its own stubborn maneuver.

Just like Makoto hoped it would be.

Kano seemed to have caught onto the plan, because he was

running the cable around the creature's tree-trunk-sized legs.

The creature shook its head, coming too. It snarled, its beady eyes falling on Niscelles, who was just within its reach, too focused on drawing power to turn and check the status of the fight.

"Not so fast." Makoto ran with the ponytail in hand and swung off the ground, while the beast tripped on the cabling around its legs and fell forward. Makoto pulled with all his strength, yanking the beast's face toward the orb of light. Sparks exploded from it on impact. The monster roared as the heat melted through its hardened scales, then screamed as the orb reached the softer stuff beneath, charring it. Makoto leaped from the ponytail and staggered back, watching the beast's final thrashes as it slumped away from the sphere and crashed down beside Niscelles, its face a blackened, unrecognizable ruin.

Niscelles looked from the fallen beast to Makoto, a strange twinkle in his eyes, the sword finally free of the stone circle and infused with glowing energy.

"It is time to seal this place from Etorea's grip once and for all." Niscelles raised his sword toward the heavens, where a thousand ships descended toward him. "Thank you both for giving me this last bit of time."

Power burst from Niscelles's sword in great wisps of blue. It pulsed with an energy that climbed high into the sky, piercing the ships above, piercing the clouds, piercing the very atmosphere itself. Energy that Makoto knew all too well.

The Rift.

"Etorea and his kin will not reach this place for a very long time," said Niscelles, his eyes glowing white. "And when they do, they will not be the ones you need fear.”

Rocks rose from the surrounding hills and magnetized to the cracked dome of energy. Makoto felt the ground tremble. The whole city began to sink, the rocks that had once been beneath it stacking themselves above.

“You must go. Now!” Niscelles pointed to the stone circle, the hazy energy within it fading.

“What’s through there?!” demanded Kano.

Niscelles fell to his knees, his thin arms straining beneath the sword and its power. “Your final test,” he rasped. “Find the power that was taken from you, Kano. There you will find me again.”

“But what about you *now*?” Kano grabbed Niscelles by the arm, but the Poterian shook him away.

“No, no! My time has come. But yours has just begun.” His eyes fell again on Makoto. “Both of yours…should you succeed.”

The energy retreated from the stone circle’s edge, shrinking in on itself.

“Go now!”

Makoto grabbed his brother and together they ran from Niscelles, ran as sunlight and sky vanished from the city, ran as the battle disappeared around them, and together they leaped into the unknown.

Chapter 31

The Land Beyond

The great tree only got bigger with each platform they crossed. Junior stayed silent, his head filled with questions but his heart filled with fear. Every rustle of the leaves forced him and Taranis to duck low in case of another Nuvanok. They'd not seen one since he'd first awakened in this mysterious forest, but he felt their cold presence growing sharper. The chill sunk into his very bones, telling him to turn back. But one thought kept him marching on.

I need to find my mother.

They started across the final root bridge, this one by far the widest and sturdiest. It fed into a tangle of roots at the base of the main platform, each belonging to the one, central tree. The place of answers, or so Taranis claimed. Junior wondered what questions kept his father's murderer marching through the cold.

The black patch drew his gaze. Shriveled, rotted plants caked the floor, feeding into a tunnel that dipped beneath the tree's roots. The place where the Nuvanoks had allegedly locked away a thief. But who? And what had he tried to steal? Taranis claimed to have no interest in it, which seemed odd considering it was the perfect place for one as evil as him. But

Junior was certainly interested. If the Nuvanoks had taken one prisoner down there, who was to say they hadn't taken others?

"Do not risk it," said Taranis, noticing his gaze. "Down there is something only the Jaculus would tamper with."

A great shriek echoed from the tunnel. The ground shook. Junior and Taranis dropped flat on their bellies, hoping the root bridge would keep them concealed at this angle, and that whatever was coming chose a different bridge to cross.

A herd of Nuvanoks, a dozen strong, stampeded out the tunnel and dispersed across the many bridges. None came their way, thankfully, and Junior let out the breath he hadn't realized he was holding.

"Come on," said Taranis, rising. "The Nuvanoks must have sensed a disturbance. This is our best chance to climb past their outpost."

They crossed the rest of the bridge and found the path ahead ran around the edge of the great tree, spiraling round and round toward the top. Clear and simple. But Junior looked to the tunnel again. And this time, someone was standing at its entrance.

"Mom!" He sprinted over the roots as she retreated into the cave. "Wait!" His feet crunched into the funk of the dying patch. He stumbled along, expecting Taranis to come running after him, but the half-Poterian made no such move.

And so Junior entered the cold alone.

One moment, Kano was running for his life atop the temple of Iramwerta; the next, he lay in a bush. And not a particularly comfortable one at that. Brambles snapped as he struggled to pry himself free from the tangle.

A red-black hand clenched around his shirt and hoisted him out. He landed on his feet in front of Makoto, only it wasn't the spry Makoto who had rushed into the Trials. This one was ragged, his combat nylons stained and slashed, his shoulders slumped forward and his eyes barely open. Kano supposed he'd look the same if he'd just fought off an army of Abari.

"Thanks for the lift," said Kano, though he knew he owed his brother so much more. He just didn't know what to say. And Makoto didn't seem to hear him, anyway; he just stared into the distance with his jaw hanging open. It didn't take Kano long to realize why.

Now that's *a tree*. The silvery behemoth encompassed everything, so grand and enchanting that Kano didn't even care that they were floating upon a rock in space (he'd already abandoned all logic in these Trials anyway). It reminded him of the Orlov Mansion back on Famora – the first place he'd ever seen a live tree. How big it had seemed back then, yet it was a seedling compared to what stood before them now.

"I guess we make for the tree," suggested Makoto, pointing to a root that stretched over a chasm of starry cosmos and onto the rock holding the great tree afloat.

Kano nodded. Like the temple in Iramwerta, the tree seemed the most likely place to house one of the Trials. He kept craning his neck to try and see the top. Were they supposed to climb it? And what would they find if they did? He really wished these Trials came with an instruction manual.

"Do you think this is the last one?" asked Makoto as they started across the bridge. "The pool, the temple, and now this?"

"I certainly hope so." The way Makoto trudged along, Kano worried his brother couldn't handle another climb, much less another confrontation with anything hostile. They needed a place to rest.

Makoto stopped. "Something's coming."

So much for rest. Kano tried summoning his powers only to be reminded that they had been taken away. Now he and Makoto were already halfway across the bridge, sitting ducks for whatever was coming. He could only hope it was friendly.

An earsplitting shriek rang out, shattering his hopes. A nightmarish monster burst through the trees, its lanky arms trailing behind it as its hooves clopped against the bark. Its exposed jaw muscle came unhinged, revealing rows of razor-sharp teeth. Kano and Makoto exchanged a look, then sprinted back the way they came.

The clopping grew louder as the monster pursued them. Kano felt a cold wash over him, an emptiness that wrapped its fingers around his very soul.

"We'll never outpace him," said Makoto. He skidded to a stop and tore a vine from the bark with a great snapping of roots. "Hold on."

Kano grabbed onto his brother's back and gazed at the cosmic oblivion beneath their feet. So far to fall. And yet the monster's shrieks frightened him even more.

Makoto leaped. Kano held his breath. The wind whipped his face, the air warming around him as the clopping sound fell away. Then he felt a mind-numbing rush as they arced back toward the root, his trembling hands clenched tight to his brother.

"Let go…*now!*" said Makoto right as they swung over the bridge. Kano obeyed. His momentum carried him through the air before he connected with the silvery bark, too fast for his feet to keep up. He tumbled across while his brother jogged out of a perfect landing. *Show off.* Kano's momentum slowed and he picked himself up, his arms and legs bruised and bloodied but his adrenaline dulling the pain. He raced after his brother to the end of the bridge, the monster somewhere behind them, coming closer as the clopping resumed.

"Follow me!" Makoto sprinted toward a tangle of tree roots, each at least three times as tall as the Nurrano, but that didn't slow him down. Makoto planted his feet against the wall of bark and kicked up, launching himself to a handhold from which he vaulted the rest of the way over the root.

"Some of us can't do that!" Kano called up. He managed to snag onto the handhold and Makoto pulled him the rest of the way up. They watched as the creature skidded to a stop below, jaw snapping in their direction, trotting back and forth as it searched for a way up. It was then that Kano realized the creature had no eyes. *So how did it know to stop?*

"Come on, before he figures out a way to reach us," said Makoto. Kano followed him up the path that spiraled around the tree, thankful to escape the tickle of cold the monster had brought with it. That was when he realized something: Makoto was calling the shots now. And he deserved to be. Kano may have been the one the Abari had selected for the Trials, but Makoto was the one beating them all.

He just hoped Makoto's streak of luck didn't run out.

"Think we'll have to fight one of those monsters at the top?" asked Makoto, twirling his batons. It seemed the last encounter had reinvigorated him. How long that would last, Kano wasn't sure, but he'd do what he could to keep Makoto motivated.

"I was actually hoping there'd be a nice lodge up there," said Kano.

Makoto cracked a smile. "Oh of course. Complimentary drinks?"

"All-you-can-eat buffet."

"Spoil me."

They laughed as they climbed. It helped Kano ignore the stinging, aching pain in his legs. At least for a little while.

◄♦►

No Nuvanoks came for him in the darkness. Not yet. Junior felt his way along the slimy, rot-covered walls, afraid to attract anything by sparking a flame.

His hand slid underneath a layer of dead vines and struck the sturdy tree root hidden underneath. Suddenly, the cavern came alive with light and color at his touch. The vines regrew along the tunnel walls, gaining a bioluminescent glow that twinkled in a spectrum of colors. But Junior hardly noticed all the newfound beauty; he was too focused on his mother standing across from him.

"You're alive." He stepped forward and she stepped back. What was wrong with her?

"This way," she said, nodding toward the path behind her. "He needs you."

"Who?"

His mother turned and ran. He chased after her, the glow of

the vines disappearing once he let go of the tree root. He grazed his hand along the wall, occasionally dredging it deep enough to reach the root, giving him flickers of light that brought his mother in and out of view.

"Why are you running?!" he called after her. He rounded a corner and she was gone.

But someone else was there. A Human, huddled against the wall, rocking himself back and forth.

"Douglas?" Junior crept toward him, keeping one hand on the root to maintain the light. He wasn't sure if Douglas had his powers back, and didn't want to learn the hard way. But Douglas just sat there and muttered to himself.

"I don't want to kill him, I don't want to kill him, I don't—"

"What are you talking about?"

Douglas leaped to his feet and Junior stumbled back, the light vanishing as his hand left the wall, replaced by two glowing blades of energy that emerged from Douglas's hands. *Blades that chopped the Del Clorans to bits*, Junior noted. He kept his distance.

"I-I didn't want to do it," said Douglas, his eyes wide and bloodshot. "I didn't want to kill him."

"Kill who?"

Shrieks echoed through the tunnel. Nuvanok shrieks. Junior looked again at Douglas's blades. *So they can detect powers.* Taranis had been telling the truth.

"Not them…" said Douglas, curling back into the fetal position, his powers retreating into his hands. "Please not them."

Junior slipped around Douglas in the dark – easy to do, when the Zoboros kept muttering to himself – then broke into a run, keeping his hand against the roots to light the way. He didn't get far before he found Nera kneeling in his path. Zivo lay with his head in her lap, eyes closed.

"Is he alright?" Junior knelt beside them, checking Zivo's wrist. He was thankful to find a pulse, however faint.

"He won't wake up," said Nera, her voice sounding distant, empty.

"What happened?"

"Those things…" Nera paused and began to tremble. "He tried to fight them off. All they did was touch him and he…fell asleep. They brought us here."

"Did they hurt my mother too?" It would explain her strange behavior. "Did you see her come through here?"

"I'm so cold, Junior. So cold." Nera curled up around Zivo and fell silent.

Junior heard sobs coming from up ahead, deep and rumbling. *Brivek*. He hurried along and found the big guy bent over with his head in his massive hands.

"Brivek, it's me. You're gonna be alright. Have you seen—?"

"Alright? Alright?!" Brivek bellowed through the hollow tunnel. "How can I be alright? They took everybody!"

"I know, I saw the others right over—"

"I heard they experiment on them. Torture them."

"Torture? Where would you hear—?"

Brivek grabbed him by the collar and hoisted him up. "I watched them all get dragged away in bags. Bags! Mom, Dad, even little Lenny." He sniffled. "You have to find them, Junior. You have to…" Brivek broke into unintelligible sobs.

Another shriek echoed through the tunnel. This one louder, closer. Brivek's sausage-like fingers loosed and Junior slipped out of his grip and hurried deeper into the tunnel. This place was making them crazy. He had to get his mother out before it did the same to her.

Or to him.

"Mom!" he called, no longer worried about attracting the Nuvanoks with noise anymore; Brivek was making plenty with his sobs already. "Are you here?!"

He turned a corner and discovered a faint red light glowing in the distance. His hand was off the root – this was glowing on its own. He approached it, the walls becoming blacker and slimier with every step. Drapes of rot hung down and coated the floor, squelching under his shoes. He shivered. The temperature was dropping with every step. He readied his powers, expecting to find a Nuvanok up ahead.

But the light led him to a dead end. Bioluminescent fungus glowed along the walls, each burrowed into the rot, casting their blood-red glow upon it.

Something moved against the back wall. Fire ignited on Junior's palms. "Mom...is that you?"

The fire revealed a Poterian face standing against the back wall. No, not standing. *Attached* to the wall. Tree roots had wrapped themselves around the big creature, binding him in place. The only part of him visible was his saggy red face with long, untrimmed tusks that stuck out at odd angles.

"We finally meet, spawn of Hendricks."

"And you are?" asked Junior, keeping his flaming palms aimed.

"One who sees all who are connected to the tree." The Poterian's eyes began to glow white. "A blessing and a curse, to see yet be severed from such great gifts." His eyes lost their glow as they fell on Junior's hands. Tired eyes weighed down by bags.

"Where's my mother?"

The Poterian turned his head away. "Angeline has returned to the tree."

"I know. She was in this tunnel. Where did she go?"

"She is a part of the tree, young Hendricks, as we are all destined to become someday."

No. Junior stared at the death-covered walls with newfound horror. "You're lying. I *saw* her."

"You saw what the tree wanted you to see."

Junior ripped a patch of slimy rot from the wall and placed his hand on the root, but no light came. No vision of his mother.

"What is this place?!" he demanded. "A dream? An illusion? What happened to us in Iramwerta?"

"You came to a place beyond space and time. Beyond life and death." The Poterian paused. Angeline's face emerged through the rot in the wall, eyes closed. Junior started toward her, only to have her face cruelly sink back.

"No. *No!*" Junior tore at the place where her face had been, but there was nothing beneath the rot. "Get out of my head!"

"I am not the one twisting your thoughts, young Hendricks. You need not look far to see the architects of your suffering."

Faces flashed through Junior's mind. His father. General Mezo. Captain Carmichael.

"Enough!" Junior rounded on the Poterian, flames bursting from his hands and catching onto the rot on the walls. "Give me one reason not to kill you."

"Because I can help you free our people," said the Poterian, unfazed by the flames as they spread nearby. "Many times I have watched you try and fail to be their champion." Pain flared from the scar in Junior's back, so intense it brought him to his knees. "You are strong, young Hendricks. Together we can change everything."

Junior stared at the roots binding the Poterian to the tree. "You want me to free you, but I don't even know who you are."

The Poterian smiled. "You do. You just haven't said my name yet."

What is he talking about? Shrieks echoed through the tunnel, matched only by the clopping of hooves. The Nuvanoks were close. Junior shivered as the temperature plummeted in their little chamber, the flames not enough to stop it.

"You are no match for them. Free me and we can escape this wretched place." The Poterian leaned forward, the roots crackling, crunching, stiffening as the red face came within inches of Junior's. "We can avenge your mother and father. Together, we can accomplish what they could not."

Junior held up a flaming hand, unsure whether to strike the face before him or the roots holding it hostage. *He's a liar.* Junior knew that much. *Just like everyone else.* The Nuvanoks were thundering ever closer. He'd seen what they had done to the others. He needed help.

"Stop!" Junior turned. Taranis stood there, sword in hand. "Do not let him loose."

"Who is he?!" Junior demanded.

Taranis froze, lowering his sword as he stared into the Poterian's black eyes. "The Jaculus said you would be—"

"The Jaculus lied, Renat, as he always does. A skill he has perfected over the millennia."

"That is not my name," said Taranis. "Not anymore."

"Shame," said the Poterian. "It comes from your people. Our people. Before you were taken by our enemies and made to taint my sword with their foolish plans."

Is he *Niscelles?* Junior wondered. Had the original owner of the sword been locked here all this time? How had Taranis recognized him? And who did Taranis think was supposed to be down here?

"I want answers," said Junior, one palm aimed at each of them. "Now!"

"You are not the only one who came here seeking answers." The Poterian leaned back against the wall, gaze still fixed upon Taranis. "You came here wanting to know who you are, Renat. Why you are cursed to be an abomination in the eyes of both sides of the galaxy. But you are so much more. The galaxy just can't see it yet."

The Poterian's eyes began to glow again. Taranis cried out, clutching his head as he fell to his knees.

"What are you doing to him?" demanded Junior, unsure why he felt pity for his enemy.

"Showing him truth."

Taranis's eyes widened in bewilderment. Exhilaration. Fear. A hundred emotions flashed across his twisted face, until finally he calmed into a state of acceptance.

Junior knelt beside him. "What did he show you?"

"Destiny." Taranis rose and aimed his sword toward the Poterian, its metal glowing with the surrounding firelight. The Poterian smiled as the shrieks of the Nuvanoks filled the smoky chamber.

"Free me or you die."

Taranis raised the sword, whether to cut Poterian's head or

the roots holding him, Junior wasn't sure. But before Taranis could strike, a slick, muscly hand reached out from the smoke and caught Taranis around the neck. The half-Poterian collapsed, the sword falling from his hand.

"No!" Junior reached out, hand aflame. The sword sailed to him and caught fire in his hand as the Nuvanoks surged into the chamber, their cold penetrating the warmth of the flames. Junior didn't have time to think. He swung the sword and hacked through the roots like butter, freeing the Poterian to fall to his knees.

"Thank you, young Hendricks."

The Poterian grabbed his leg. Junior gasped. The flames snuffed from the sword, from his palms, from himself. He collapsed, the rotted floor crunching beneath him. He felt...empty. Emptier than even a power dampener could make him feel. He stared up at the Poterian, the thief, in horror.

"What are you?" he whispered.

"Annihilation." The Poterian's eyes glowed blue. Twin beams shot from them, cleaving the Nuvanoks in half. The creatures screamed, their legs and torsos still galloping around while their bottom halves clawed against the ground. The Poterian stepped past Junior and Taranis, palm raised, and launched a jet of flames that consumed the breadth of the tunnel, silencing the Nuvanoks' pained shrieks. The cold they had brought became a distant memory. Now all Junior felt was the searing heat.

What have I done?

Chapter 32

Royal Secrets

Hauser snatched the knife off his dinner tray and stuffed it into a pouch beneath his sleeve. Jaden knew it was no substitute for Hauser's real knife – which the Poterians had confiscated – but it would have to do.

"Take no more than you can carry," said the smuggler.

Jaden bent over the arm of his wheelchair, the small of his back screaming where he still had feeling in it, adding to the constant throb that pulsated from the edges of his wound. He scooped his satchel off the floor and sat himself upright, gasping as the pain subsided, replaced by the numbing agent in his seat.

His satchel felt light in his lap – donating his datapad to the team had seemed the right thing to do. But that was before he overheard a certain conversation on the comms, where a certain now-deceased senator told Chenji that they were basically screwed.

"Should've guessed Typhera would be behind the whole ruddy thing," said Hauser. He started to pull the curtains shut, severing Jaden's view of the commotion in the courtyard. All afternoon, the servants had busied themselves, raising tents and decorating long tables for what would no doubt be an extravagant evening in the Poterian palace. Jaden laughed to himself.

"What's so funny?"

"The last time I went to a palace for a party, I got betrayed there too."

"Well thanks for roping me into your good luck streak." Hauser grew quiet as Radimir entered with his usual syringe.

"Your evening medicine as requested," said the Poterian servant. "Though I must say it is a bit early for it, Master Upton."

"Just do it." Jaden leaned forward, the motion sending a stab of pain up his back. He couldn't risk that happening during their escape. He needed something more than fancy fabric to get him through.

Radimir positioned himself behind the wheelchair. "Deep breath."

Jaden tensed as the needle slid into the small of his back; a moment of eyewatering pain that the medicine erased like a cool breeze.

"More," he said.

"That would be unwise, Master Jaden."

"I won't get another chance to explore the grounds in the daylight. I don't want the pain creeping back in the middle of my stroll."

Radimir sighed and reloaded the syringe. "A stroll during Evernight can also be quite pleasant, Master Upton."

Too bad I won't be here to experience it. "So is all that setup outside gonna last the whole Evernight? Like an all-night party that never ends?" He gasped as the syringe slid back in and a fresh dose of drugs swam into his brain.

"Tis more than just a party, Master Upton. Tis a mark of great change. Of new beginnings."

"Uh huh." The room had started to spin. Good. He was ready.

"But this'll be his last chance to see sunlight for a while, isn't it?" asked Hauser.

Radimir looked up, the surprise on his face quickly replaced with his usual smile, but not quick enough for Jaden. "Indeed, Master Hauser. Shall I wheel him down?"

"No thank you," said Jaden. He knew now that Radimir expected him to be out of the sunlight for a while, and he doubted it was because of an eclipse.

"Ania will be expecting you," said Radimir as Jaden rolled out, Hauser right behind. Ania was the servant who usually attended to him downstairs while Radimir tidied the room. Unfortunately, Ania wouldn't be seeing him anytime soon.

Hauser hurried ahead as soon as they were out of Radimir's sight, checking corners as they crossed the lavish hallways. All were empty, the usual staff too busy with the preparations outside, but Jaden kept his ears perked. The empress had far sneakier agents than smiling servants.

His arms kept spinning against the wheels, so numb from the drugs that he felt no soreness. Good. He couldn't afford to let that slow him down. The speed of his wheelchair was his only defense, which he assumed was why they'd never given him an automatic one. They certainly had the technology for it.

Hauser stopped at Sterling's door. He was about to knock when the Poterian's gruff voice leaked through.

"...he's no threat to you," said Sterling. "He doesn't even know what he is."

And who might be visiting the heir apparent this evening? Jaden took the microphone chip out of his mouth – the one that let him communicate with the team – and placed it in the seam under the door. Pain should have stabbed at his back from the bending motion, but the extra dosage was working wonders.

He tuned his earpiece to the channel of his own microphone and the empress's voice chimed through. "As long as he breathes, someone could tell him what he is. And the galaxy too. Then we'd both be doomed."

Jaden turned up the volume, hoping to hear the name of whoever they were talking about. He noticed Hauser doing the same with his own earpiece.

"I think you have more pressing matters on your doorstep," said Sterling. "The Red Sabre is but the spear tip of a much larger force. One that will be emboldened by this operation of yours."

"What choice do I have? They become bolder regardless of what I do. To do nothing would be to allow this cancer to grow until it can't be stopped."

"There are alternatives."

"Like what? *Running away?*" The silence that followed was palpable. Even Jaden felt the dagger she'd just hurled at Sterling. "I will not allow my people to spiral into another war."

"Then don't let the Orlov whisper in your ear, Typhera. He has spent his life playing the galaxy like an instrument. However good you think you are at this game, he is better."

"What would you do in my position?" she asked, soft yet firm.

Sterling drew a long breath. "Call off the attack. Bring the

Red Sabre to the table. They are being played too. Danadas would not have risked the trip across the Rift, nor his alliance with you, on the gamble of a single operation. He only agreed to it because both sides are in his pocket."

"Then he would know neither side truly has the strength to give him the war he wants," said the empress, her heels clicking as she paced the floor. "Danadas must have recovered Angeline. That was always meant to be his ace."

"I do not think they are in the picture now. Your marauders saw to that."

He knew. Jaden's head spun, and not just from the drugs. Hauser grabbed the wheelchair and raced him away from Sterling's room. *Always a betrayal at a party*, he thought lucidly, the hallway rotating in his vision. Without Sterling, they had no ship, no escape route, and no friends in a palace full of enemies. Not until their team returned from their mission.

If the empress allowed them to return at all.

He needed to get a message to them. He tapped his earpiece only to realize that he'd left his microphone behind. Hauser still had his, though. He tugged on the smuggler's sleeve as his jaw began to numb.

"Caw de uvers," he slurred.

"I am calling the ruddy elevator!" shouted Hauser as he jammed the button.

"No, de…" Jaden trailed as he heard the creak of a door through his earpiece.

"Your Majesty," hissed a Jakari voice, pausing for what Jaden assumed to be the usual bow. "We received word: Ivanov is dead." A glass broke. *Probably the empress throwing a tantrum.* "W-worse, Your Majesty. He was killed on a rooftop.

Many witnesses. Word spreads quickly. Talk of war.”

The elevator dinged, but Jaden hesitated, waiting to hear what the empress said next.

“Tell me, Chuyi, why is it not Mizuki delivering this news to me?” she asked.

Hauser grunted behind him. Jaden felt the blade against his neck before he could react.

“Not so fast, boy of the computer.”

⊲♦⊳

“Jaden…Jaden, do you copy?”

The line remained silent. The others hovered around Li, waiting for a voice to come through her communicator.

“Sterling? Hauser?” she pressed. “Does anyone copy?”

Still nothing. She wanted to punch a hole through Jaden’s datapad — the datapad she knew he needed more than they did right now. Their mission had failed, and Typhera would be quick to eliminate any ties to their team.

“I had him!” blurted Chenji. He threw his equipment pack down the aisle of the transport bay. “If I’d seen that Lusitani coming, Ivanov would be alive and we wouldn’t be in this mess.”

“I doubt it would have mattered,” said Carmichael. “Danadas seemed more intent on sabotaging us than completing the mission for Typhera.”

“But why risk losing Typhera’s favor?” asked Ristin.

“Because he doesn’t need it,” said Cera. “He just wants us out of the way.”

“Then why am I still alive?” asked Chenji. “His Lusitani had the drop on me. And not just any Lusitani, but the one with the bandana. The one who killed Eines on the *Dormarch* and beat Kano in a one-on-one fight. He could've killed me, but he ran away instead."

"Maybe Danadas still needs us alive," said Carmichael. "A scapegoat to pin the senator's murder on."

"You fleshlings nailed it," came T8's voice over the loudspeakers. The bot was in the cockpit, keeping them idle in the space between two atmospheres while they figured out their next move. "Poteria Prime is mobilizing its forces to retaliate, and I guarantee Danadas hedged his bets with them."

"I thought the Poterians couldn't risk open war with each other?" said Li.

"At the rate they're mobilizing, they might just snuff Typhera out before they could face any repercussions," said T8. "They've clearly been planning this for months. Maybe longer."

"So they *wanted* their own senator killed?" asked Ristin.

"Sometimes dead politician is more useful than living one," muttered Akio. Warp nodded her agreement.

"What Akio means is Poteria Prime wanted a good pretext to make its move," explained Carmichael. "Avenging Ivanov is something their people can get behind."

Li tightened her grip on the datapad. Were there any depths too low for their enemies to sink to? She remembered the horror of watching half the Orlov family slaughtered under Danadas's orders. His own family, in his own home! And now the old man and his allies could bring their destruction and death on an even larger scale.

"That's it then," said Ristin, plopping into a chair and tugging back his thick, uncomely hair. "We came all this way just to be surrounded by people who hate us even more than they do back home."

Chenji raised his head. "Maybe not..." he whispered.

"What is it?" asked Li. The others all looked to the changeling.

"Ivanov told me something crazy," said Chenji. "He said we're popular here. That they get our news feed or something. They think we're heroes."

"Well then, at least our funerals will be well attended," said T8. "Your funerals, I should say. I'll get reuploaded into—"

"Shut up," said Li. "We could be on to something."

Carmichael scratched his chin. "If you're looking to the people for support, they might be a little too preoccupied with a looming civil war."

"We wouldn't need that many people," said Ristin. All eyes turned to him. He gulped. It wasn't until Li gave him an encouraging nod that he continued. "When you perform for big crowds, you get rushed through a lot of backdoors, most of which the crowd doesn't even know about. If they did, they'd be all over them. I'll bet Typhera has backdoors. And if we can find a fan who knows them, we can slip in and rescue our friends."

"So you're saying we go in *while* the palace is under attack?" asked Cera.

"It would be dangerous, but it would be the best distraction we could ask for," said Ristin.

Chenji cracked a smile. "That might just be crazy enough to work."

"You're both crazy," said Cera. "Li, back me up here."

Li looked from Ristin to Cera. Under normal circumstances,

she'd agree that this was too crazy, but these weren't normal circumstances. In fact, this was a strong contender for the worst situation they'd ever faced.

And she was tired of making excuses.

"We chose to sail on when Junior and Angeline were taken," she said. "When Kano and Makoto...disappeared. If there's even the slightest chance that we can get Jaden and Sterling back, I say we take it."

"And Hauser too," added Ristin. "I think he's more loyal than he lets on."

"Hauser too, then," said Li, managing a smile.

Carmichael paced the floor, soaking in everyone's words. "T8, how long until the enemy ships begin their attack?" he asked.

"The optimist in me says about one hour," came T8's voice. "But given how much they've prepared, I'd say they could be ready much sooner."

Carmichael looked upon his weary yet determined team and flashed his trademark smile. "Well, that gives us less than an hour to make a plan. Any questions?"

Warp signed to him, a phrase Li had seen often enough to understand by sight.

Let's do this.

Chapter 33

The Tree

Kano's legs felt about ready to fall off, and still the path looped round and round the great tree; a gentle incline at best, yet after so many hours it took its toll.

But had it really been hours? There was no sun or sky here to mark the passage of time, and the clock on his communicator had frozen the moment they'd entered. That made him nervous. His first trip to Iramwerta, which had lasted mere hours at most, had been two weeks in the outside world. Did time work similarly here? Were they even *in* their own time? These trials made him question everything he thought he knew.

Just like Niscelles said they would.

Makoto kept marching ahead, never stopping to catch his breath. Kano wondered where his brother found the strength – even for a Nurrano, this was unprecedented. Kano suspected that Makoto, after waiting so long to prove himself, was pouring every ounce of that desire into these Trials. And he wouldn't rest until either they finished the Trials or the Trials finished them.

That being said, Kano didn't have quite such lofty aspirations for himself. "I need to sit," he called ahead, plopping onto a sturdy branch that hung above the cosmos. Instead of relief, his legs stiffened against the sizzle of lactic acid. He patted them out, the fantastical floating forest below doing little to make him feel better. As far as he could tell, the view looked no different than it had hours ago.

"Come on, just a little further," said Makoto.

Kano shook his head. "You've been saying that the whole damn time."

Makoto sighed and joined him on the branch, stretching his legs like he'd just finished a morning warm up. "Am I going crazy, or have we been in the same spot for a while now?"

"I thought I was going crazy too, but now I'm pretty sure we're going in circles, literally *and* figuratively."

"Caught in a loop," said Makoto. He squinted at the tree like he'd find its secrets written somewhere in the bark. "It's a puzzle. And I don't think we're supposed to solve it by going forward." He started heading back down the way they came. A logical move, but too easy. Too black and white.

"Wait!" Kano jumped up, legs cramping from the sudden motion. He winced and swallowed the pain. "Maybe our path is something less obvious." He pointed up. Dozens of branches hung there at varying heights. A much harder climb, but it was possible.

Makoto smiled at the challenge. He vaulted onto the nearest branch and swung to the next. *This boy's gonna give himself a heart attack.* Kano did his best to follow, but his stiff muscles and general lack of climbing experience had him playing a game of inches with each slow, overcalculated step. Thankfully, Makoto stopped on a nearby branch, giving Kano time to catch up.

"I take it back," he said, breathing hard. "I'd rather go around the tree for eternity than keep doing this."

Makoto didn't answer. He just kept staring at the branch...at a fruit on the branch. Red and ripe, it just sat there for the taking. Kano's stomach growled. He oddly hadn't felt hungry the entire time here, yet now he was suddenly starving.

"I think it's a test," said Makoto.

"Of what? How fast we can eat it?"

"No, it might have another—" Makoto paused. His ears perked. Kano heard it too: clopping. Only it was coming on slow and uneven now. He spotted the monster on the path below. One of its muscly legs was seared black, the burns fresh and glistening. *Junior?* Kano had sensed his friend's presence in his visions; could he have been the one to fight off the creature?

It limped along, careful not to put too much pressure on the bad leg. Kano felt the familiar chill of its presence, but somehow it no longer struck fear in him. In fact, as Kano listened to the creature whimper, he found himself feeling a sliver of pity.

"I think we should help it," said Makoto.

"What are you—?"

Makoto snapped the fruit off the branch and hopped down before Kano could finish.

"*Come back!*" Kano hissed as loud as he dared. But his brother ignored him as he landed just behind their foe.

The eyeless beast snapped around at the sound. Kano expected that long jaw to snap his brother up that instant, but the monster hesitated. Makoto drew a deep breath and held out the fruit in his open palm. The monster sniffed at it. The jaw opened. Kano gripped the branch tight, ready to leap down to the rescue.

But the monster only took the gentlest bite of the fruit.

"Good boy," said Makoto.

Kano couldn't believe what he was seeing. And that wasn't even the strangest part. The blackened leg began to *heal* to its normal, muscly color. The creature straightened, its strength returning. Kano's heart jolted as it took a hard step toward Makoto, but his brother held his ground. The creature loomed over the little Nurrano and gave him a sniff with that long, deadly snout.

Then it bowed its head.

No way. Kano slid down from the branch as his brother scratched the beast behind the ear. Its head snapped up when he landed, ready to either pounce or flee. Kano froze in place.

"It's okay, he's a friend," said Makoto, stroking the creature. It relaxed at his touch. "Come on, pet him."

"I'd rather not."

The creature bristled. Kano took a step back. Had it just understood him? Would it understand an apology? He watched it carefully and realized its attention had strayed elsewhere. It began walking up the path, slow and purposeful.

"I think we should follow Reggie," said Makoto.

"Please don't name him."

"Too late."

They followed...*Reggie,* and the path began to change. The branches sagged lower, more leaves blooming off them, and more fruits ripe for the picking. Kano still didn't dare take any for himself, though he was tempted. If these things could heal, they'd be a blessing for his aching legs.

He noticed the air had warmed around the creature too. It

felt nothing like the monster that had chased them earlier on the bridge.

"How did you know to give it the fruit?" asked Kano.

Makoto shrugged. "They're a part of this ecosystem, right? Figured it couldn't hurt."

"But it could've. It *definitely* could've. These things look like the embodiment of evil."

"If these creatures were evil, they would have destroyed this tree a long time ago. But the tree is thriving, and I think they have something to do with that."

Kano found that to be a bit of a stretch, but he wasn't going to argue with Makoto's instincts. Not when they had gotten him this far.

The creature stopped and stared at the trunk of the great tree. Kano noticed etchings in the bark: Ancient Mogaddan — he recognized some of the letters from the Gate of Iramwerta. The creature touched the bark and the letters began to glow in a tall arc. *A door*, Kano realized. The creature pushed. The bark opened along the glowing seam and white light poured out of the tree, inviting them to the unknown.

Kano waited for the creature to enter, but it only stepped aside. Slowly, he and Makoto entered, shielding their eyes from the bright light. When it subsided, Kano was shocked to find the tree hollow, all the way from root to the canopy some miles above their head, all lit up by bioluminescent vines that twinkled along vast walls, creating the illusion of a starry night. Only a single path ran through the whole interior: a bridge leading from their door to a platform in the middle of the tree. A pool of water shimmered within that platform. Just like the pool inside the mountain.

It ends where it began. At least, Kano hoped it did.

"That can't be the end, can it?" he asked. He turned to Reggie, who stood guard at the entrance like a sentinel, offering no indication that he had even understood what Makoto said.

"Like everything else here, I think there could be more to it than meets the eye," said Makoto. He turned to Reggie and bowed in thanks.

Kano gave an awkward bow as well and together they marched toward the glowing water. It churned several feet below the pool's edge, pushing and pulling in unnatural directions. Even an experienced swimmer would struggle against such force. For someone like Kano, it was a death sentence.

"We have to jump," said Makoto.

"But we don't know how deep it goes."

"It's a trust fall."

"You think I trust this place?!"

Makoto shrugged. "Trust me."

Kano gulped. He would have argued the point if he didn't notice something in his brother's eyes, something that hadn't been there before. *He's not that kid on Famora anymore*. This was someone ready to take a leap into the deadly abyss.

"On three," said Kano, taking an anxious step toward the edge of the pool. "One..."

A shriek echoed through the hollow tree. They spun around. The door was halfway shut, orange light blazing behind it. Even from here, Kano could feel its heat. *Junior?!* Another wretched shriek, and then the creature went silent.

"*Reggie!*" Makoto grabbed for his batons.

Junior wouldn't have killed that creature, Kano told himself. Something else was about to enter.

It burst open and a massive being marched through, body ablaze from head to toe. *The Man on Fire*. The one from his visions, here before his eyes, on fire yet showing no sign of pain. And too large to be a man.

"That's not Niscelles, is it?" asked Makoto, fuming.

"I don't think so," said Kano, glancing back at the pool "Two…"

The Poterian reached a fiery hand toward them, hot enough to sting Kano's skin just by being raised in his direction.

"Three!" shouted Makoto. He pulled Kano over the edge and together they splashed into the churning waters. Kano flailed and kicked, barely able to keep himself afloat. "Stop resisting," said Makoto. "I'll see you on the other side."

"Other side of what?" Kano watched as his brother relaxed and sank beneath the violent water. "Makoto!" He looked up and saw the blazing body standing over the pool. With a final gasp, he let his body go limp.

The water was quick to swallow him up. He held his breath as the light faded and darkness surrounded him, the Poterian's fire and the water's glow a distant memory. But something did glow; something far beneath him. He dove, doing his best to flail his body toward it as his lungs began to cry out.

A red-black hand reached down and pulled him the rest of the way. Kano burst through the water's surface, gasping for breath as Makoto heaved him onto the rocky shore. Familiar black rocks, with familiar stalactites hanging above.

"We're back," said Kano as water poured off him and streamed into the pool they had started from. Familiar energy thrummed into his hands once again. *It's over.*

His relief was short-lived. A pair of large feet stood in front of him. Poterian feet. Had the Man on Fire followed them *here*? He looked up and found a familiar old face frowning at him atop a paper-thin body.

"Your friend has failed," said Niscelles. "He's coming."

Chapter 34

Master and Apprentice

Junior stepped over the charred remains of the Nuvanok, sword held limp in his fingers. The stench of burnt hair and flesh hung over the entrance to the tree, but he was numb to it now. Numb after all the corpses he'd passed on the way here. Numb to the violence he had unleashed. Numb to what the Poterian had told him in the cave.

She's gone. He didn't know how the Poterian knew, nor whether he could trust the thief's words, yet somehow he knew in his heart it was true. She had perished at the hands of Iramwerta. And now his only hope to escape lay in the hands of the one who had stolen his powers.

But who was this Poterian? And how was he unlocking abilities that Junior never thought possible? It had taken Junior this long just to figure out he could channel through his eyes, but the Poterian was already doing it through his entire body. Junior wanted to know his secrets. It was the only thing that kept him moving forward.

"Junior."

He turned. Nera was struggling to catch up on the path up the tree, still exhausted from her efforts to guide them through the river. Brivek lumbered alongside her, carrying Zivo over one shoulder and Taranis over the other, both unconscious. Douglas trailed behind them, eyes darting every direction like another Nuvanok was coming for him. Though Junior had led them out of that evil cave, the cave remained with them.

"We shouldn't go in there," Nera continued. "Not with *him* inside."

Junior needed only to look at the Nuvanok corpse to feel her same reservations. Her same fears. But those same fears compelled him toward the tree. Toward the Poterian who could show him how to harness such power.

"Stay here then. I'll let you know when it's safe." He started inside when Douglas grabbed his arm.

"You're lying to us," said Douglas, his shifty eyes widening, making Junior tighten his grip on the sword. "You'll have that maniac kill us all."

"Don't accuse me of something you would do." Junior tore his arm away and marched into the tree, leaving a speechless Douglas behind. The others didn't follow either, afraid of the Poterian.

Fire flickered along the walls of the hollow tree. His fire. It singed away the last brambles that hung blackened against the scorched bark. The flames faded from the Poterian's body as well, leaving him naked, a state that made him even more terrifying, like there was nothing to mask the raging animal inside.

"You have accepted it, then," said the Poterian. "Her passing."

"Yes," he muttered, doing little to mask the knife lodged in his heart.

The Poterian turned toward the glowing pool. "Some things cannot be changed. But others can."

"Is that our way home?"

The Poterian spread his hands wide toward the surrounding tree. "*This* is our home. We are but visitors in the world you know. Always to be feared. Always to be controlled."

"So you want to stay?"

"I *could* stay. I could wipe away the Nuvanoks and take this world." He stared longingly at the hollow tree. "But it would be empty. Nothing but a reminder of my people on the other side, waiting to be brought out of the shadows."

The Poterian's words sounded familiar. His father had often spoken of someone who wanted to "bring the Zoboros out of the shadows." Someone who had once tried to unite the Zoboros in blood and glory.

"Palorex!" He raised the sword, heart pounding as a small smile crept across the Poterian Emperor's face.

"Not many know that name anymore. Not after they redacted me from the history books." He took a step forward and Junior took one back. "They wanted to erase my work. My purpose."

"You slaughtered billions."

"Freedom has a price." Junior smelled the Nuvanok corpse outside, suddenly fresh and frightening. "I was so close to wiping out the pretenders. The slave masters. I would have made the next generation flourish in a way their ancestors couldn't dream of. Instead, the weak held onto their power and robbed you of a future where your powers are accepted.

Celebrated. The future you deserved."

"That future doesn't exist."

"It can. All over the galaxy, we could have freedom. And with that freedom comes peace, because there would be Zoboros to protect it."

"And you're supposed to lead us to it?"

Junior turned. It was Douglas who had spoken, stumbling his way along the narrow path, close to falling through the smoky haze to an oblivion far below. "My family served you twenty cycles ago. And now look at me." He slipped, and Junior caught him before he tipped over the edge. "An orphan with nothing!" Douglas ripped free of Junior's grip and pointed a finger at his enemy.

"Moraine and Lyle," said Palorex. Douglas froze, mouth agape. "They were faithful to the end. And they would be proud of what you have built, Douglas. As am I."

"You don't know what—"

"An entire Zoboros village," Palorex cut in, marching toward them. "In a time when such a thing should be impossible, you of all people organized them. Protected them. Imagine doing that on a larger scale."

Junior saw the confusion in Douglas's eyes. Was it just the delirium from the cave, or was Douglas warring with his own hatred of Palorex?

"I-I can barely protect the ones I have," Douglas stammered.

"I will help you," assured the emperor. "We will organize them into something that can't be stopped. I have seen it. And soon the galaxy will too."

Douglas sat upon the walkway, mind grappling with the

vision laid before him. Junior couldn't believe it: Douglas, the one who had pressed an entire Zoboros village into submission, quelled by mere *words*. Palorex's words. Junior had tried and failed to do the same with the people around him, yet the Poterian Emperor made it look easy. How many others could Palorex topple without firing a shot?

"The Zoboros are scattered," said Junior. "How would you unite them?"

"I have done it before. The pieces are already in place." Palorex glanced back at the glowing pool. "Only this time, I will have the one piece I was missing."

The power of Iramwerta. There was a reason Palorex had once made Mogaddu his base of operation; a reason that people believed he had perished there. Junior's father had told him stories of Palorex's obsession. He'd claimed it was the emperor's undoing. But what if Palorex *had* succeeded all those cycles ago? Would the galaxy be different? Would his life be different? Would his mother have been able to be a part of it?

And would she still be here now?

"Junior!" Nera called from the entrance to the tree, not daring to come closer.

He barely looked at her, too consumed by the pool at their feet. "My mother once chased Iramwerta," he said to Palorex. "It killed her."

"Because the power is protected. But we can change that. We can set it free."

Junior turned to Palorex, frightened and awed at the same time. "Are you saying we can create more Zoboros?"

"We can create a whole new age." Palorex stepped toward

the pool. "What do you say, Aaron Hendricks Junior?"

What do *I say?* Palorex was the greatest evil the galaxy had ever seen, or so he had been told. Yet Palorex's goal wasn't to destroy; it was to create. Create something that Junior's enemies despised. That the people who branded Palorex a villain despised.

"What happens if the Zoboros we create don't side with you?" asked Junior, lowering the sword.

Palorex shrugged. "Do they really have a choice?"

Junior stared into the pool, the faces of all those who had used and suppressed him swirling in its strange glow.

"No. They don't."

Niscelles ripped open a vaulted door and shoved them through it, surprisingly strong for one so frail. As frail as he was in Kano's old visions, before he'd begun appearing as a Poterian. So was the real Niscelles a cross between the two versions? Skinny and Poterian? It was worth noting, but Kano's mind quickly moved on to more pressing matters.

The Poterian Emperor is back. But how? Had that been Palorex approaching them in the tree, all engulfed in fire just like in his old visions? Why couldn't those visions have been more specific? Hell, Kano was struggling to get answers even now, with the ancient king standing right before him.

"We must protect it," said Niscelles, barring the door and hurrying past them. Kano looked around, but all he saw was an empty room, most of it hidden in shadows.

"Protect what?"

Makoto tapped his arm and pointed. Kano had to squint to see it: a root protruding from the rocky floor at the room's center. It was only a few feet tall, yet so thin he would have missed it if not for the faint white glow at its tip, one that made its silvery bark glisten.

"Is that…?" Kano approached it. "How is the tree all the way over here?"

"The pool turned us upside down," said Makoto. "The tree is right below us."

"In a manner of speaking, yes," said Niscelles quickly. "The tree and the mountain exist parallel to each other. Connected yet apart."

Something clattered on the other side of the door.

"He is here." Niscelles steadied himself in front of the feeble root, his robes hanging loose off his shriveled body. "Hide. Do not put yourselves in danger unless you have no choice."

"Why is he after this…root?" demanded Kano. "Why have you brought us here now?"

"The tree brought you here. At the moment it needed you most."

Time dilation, Kano realized. Only now it had been controlled. Manipulated for Niscelles's benefit. Or the tree's. It was all very confusing.

A long, blue finger of flame melted through the door and blazed along it in a wide arc. Even from way back, Kano felt its heat. He drew up his fists, trembling without any powers to fight back. Could it be Junior? He'd never seen Junior do anything like what this burning figure was capable of.

"Move," said Niscelles flatly. He stood hunched over the root like it was his walking stick. Kano wanted to help, but something told him to trust Niscelles, that the old Poterian knew much more than he did, so he ran to the shadows, his brother following. They would wait – at least for as long as they could stand to.

The fire completed its arc and a chunk of the door collapsed. A towering Poterian lumbered through the new opening, fire in his hands and no clothes to cover him. His red face reminded Kano of Sterling, though Sterling's scowl had been replaced by a look so arrogant it made Kano feel insignificant in its presence.

"Time has not been kind to you, my old master," said Palorex.

Chapter 35

The Champion

The two Poterians stared each other down. One powerful, one old...so old, Junior wondered how long he'd lived here among the shiny black rocks. Yet Palorex regarded the Poterian with caution, so Junior did too, keeping the sword leveled against their elderly adversary.

"Once again, you hoard the power to yourself," said Palorex.

What power? Junior noticed the old Poterian holding onto a thin root that stuck a few feet out of the ground. A *silvery* root. He felt the sword trembling in his hand, drawn to it. Douglas seemed drawn to it too, his eyes fixated.

"I keep it not for me," said the old Poterian, "but for those who deserve it."

"As I did," said Palorex. He raised his hand and, nonchalantly, launched a jet of flame. The old Poterian waved his wrinkled hand and water rushed out of thin air, snuffing the fiery blast in a burst of steam. The whole exchange was merely a feint and parry. A probe. They had done this dance before.

"You chose *me*, Niscelles," said Palorex, stepping forward.

"And I was wrong."

Niscelles! Before Junior could process that the ancient king was standing in front of them, twin beams launched from Palorex's eyes. Niscelles's skin turned glassy, and the beams reflected off him and sliced into the floor. Junior took a step back. He'd never seen a Zoboros with multiple powers before. Unless...maybe there was a reason Niscelles was holding onto that root.

"You were wrong not to kill me when you had the chance," said Palorex.

"You were wrong to think mercy is a weakness," replied Niscelles, looking away.

"And yet you will get none." Palorex engulfed his body in flames. "You made a mistake when you left me for the Nuvanoks. I heard your whispers through the tree, your call for a new champion. And I learned to make calls of my own. You tried to suppress them...and look what that's done to you."

Niscelles remained hunched against the root, protecting it as much as it was protecting him from falling. "I have changed since our last meeting, that is true. I had hoped imprisonment would do the same for you, yet I see the same foolish boy who stumbled in here all those cycles ago. The same wasted potential."

Palorex frowned. "The only thing wasted was time. Time you stole from me." He launched an inferno that shook the very ground they stood on. Even Junior felt its fiery sting while standing behind it. Surely there was no power to stop such a blast.

Yet new flames appeared, not orange or blue but black as night. They consumed Palorex's attack, erased it. When all had settled, Niscelles still stood fixed to the root, his old body trembling.

"That was mine," muttered Palorex.

Niscelles shook his head. "I thought you'd have learned by now," he rasped. "These powers belong only to the tree. To the gods. Consider yourself lucky to have tasted them in your short life."

All Junior could think about was that black fire. So much more powerful than his own. So much more dangerous. If Palorex could do all this with Junior's fire, what could he do with that?

Wage war.

"And here you stand playing a god," said Palorex, smiling in a way that frightened even Junior. "You summoned a champion to stop me. I sense him here." Palorex aimed his palms away from Niscelles and toward the surrounding shadows. "One of you will die today. Who will that be?"

Niscelles looked ready to spring into action, if that was even possible in his fragile state. But something flashed past Junior, so quick he'd not even seen it emerge from the shadows. It was only when the figure's sticks struck Palorex at the back of the knees and made them buckle that he realized who it was.

"Makoto!" shouted Junior.

Palorex launched fire at his assailant, but the Nurrano dipped out of the way, a blur of red and black.

"A Nurrano?" said Palorex. He laughed, a deep, harsh laugh that echoed off the rocky walls. "You spent all this time, all this *power*, searching the cosmos for an insect."

Yet when Junior looked at Makoto standing there with his weapons drawn, he didn't see an insect. He didn't even see the little boy who always botched the missions.

He saw a warrior.

"You'd be wise not to underestimate me," said Makoto.

"Really?" said Palorex. "And what power did this old cheater grant you?"

Makoto smiled. "Deception."

A shockwave roared from the shadows. It caught Palorex from behind and threw him across the rocky floor, snuffing his flames as he tumbled away into darkness.

Kano emerged, palms aimed, eyes not leaving the spot where Palorex had disappeared as he addressed Junior. "How did he get your powers?"

"Something to do with the tree," answered Junior, not daring to say more, else they might realize that he agreed with some of Palorex's ideas.

"You *dare*!" shouted Douglas. He marched toward Kano, energy blades extending from his fists. "He can change everything." Makoto dove between them, his batons looking puny next to blades that could cut through them like butter.

"Wait!" said Junior. "No one has to die here."

"You're wrong, Aaron Hendricks Junior," came Palorex's voice from the shadows. "Someone does." Twin beams launched out of the darkness and sliced through Niscelles's arm, the one holding the root. The ancient king cried out as he collapsed, his severed limb landing beside him. Junior watched with what should have been horror, yet instead he felt a pull. The power was there for the taking. His power. Other powers. Enough to ensure that no one challenged the Zoboros again.

"Niscelles!" shouted Kano. Makoto ducked, and Kano launched a shockwave over his head that threw Douglas across the room. Palorex emerged into the light and he and Kano took aim at each other.

Stalemate.

"You're outnumbered," said Makoto, pacing around Palorex, searching for an angle to strike.

Junior realized Makoto was including him in that count.

"Junior, take him from the left," said Kano.

But Junior stayed planted where he was. This was it. His moment to choose: run away with the team and be forced to run forever, or open the door to something new.

A new era.

Palorex smiled. "Go ahead. Choose."

Something came over Junior. He dropped the sword and rushed Makoto, tackling him from behind and pinning him to the ground.

"What the hell?!" cried the Nurrano.

"Stay down!" said Junior, struggling to keep Makoto's small yet strong arms pinned. "This is our chance."

"Our chance for what, Junior?" demanded Kano, keeping his palms aimed at the Poterian Emperor. "Palorex is evil, don't you see that?"

Junior hesitated. "You're wrong," he said. The words felt strange to him. Strange yet right. "This galaxy is evil. And we can fix it."

Kano froze. "Junior, what happened to you in there?" he asked. His answer came in the form of a bolt of lightning. It threw him against the rocks, where he convulsed in the aftershock.

"Stop!" Junior held up his hand as Taranis stumbled into the room, dazed after awakening from the Nuvanok's spell. Junior prayed the crazed half-Poterian wouldn't finish the job.

"Well done," said Palorex. "You will make a most faithful heir."

Taranis bowed his head. "Thank you, Father."

Junior's whole world flipped on itself. *Father?!* Was that what Palorex had shown Taranis in the cave? Whatever he had done to Taranis's mind had shocked him, changed him. Was this truly where Taranis's Poterian half came from, or was Palorex just messing with his warped mind? The more he thought about it, the more plausible it became. It would explain why the IDF wanted to study him as a child, why Carmichael wanted to keep him hostage. The heir to the throne was the perfect bargaining chip against the might of the Poterian Empire, the perfect tool to sabotage the Poterian leadership from the inside.

Junior grunted as Makoto drove an elbow into his gut. He rolled over, gasping for breath, frustrated that he'd let himself get distracted. The Nurrano scooped up its batons and took aim at Taranis, then at Palorex, then at Douglas, who was emerged from the shadows, looking bruised from his tumble.

"You all think you're so mighty?!" shouted Makoto. "Then fight me without your powers!"

Douglas laughed, but Palorex silenced him with a wave of his hand. "You are stronger than I gave you credit for, Nurrano," said the emperor. "If also more foolish." Palorex held out his hand; the sword sailed into it.

Makoto gulped, standing his ground. Junior's heart raced. He tried to intervene, but Taranis held him back.

The Nurrano swung at the Poterian in a whir of motion. Palorex blocked and parried as he retreated, an odd sight given their size difference. The rapid clangs of metal on metal filled the room. *Someone's been practicing.* Every strike Palorex attempted was deflected and answered with a welt against his bare flesh. He had no armor, no clothing, yet the emperor seemed willing to take it. Eager, in fact. The smile on his face told Junior that he relished this moment, the like of which he'd not experienced since Niscelles had trapped him within the tree however many cycles ago. Junior knew then that Makoto was in trouble. He turned to Kano, hoping for help. But Kano still spasmed on the floor, arms outstretched toward Palorex, trying to summon power but finding none with his body so out of control.

Palorex went low and swept the sword toward Makoto's legs. Makoto vaulted over the attack, over Palorex himself, and swung his baton down at the emperor's head.

Palorex caught it deftly.

He threw Makoto aside with all his might. The little Nurrano's belly slammed into an outlying rock with a crunch. Junior froze, heart pounding as Makoto collapsed on the hard ground, gasping, blood trickling from his mouth.

"Well fought, Nurrano," said Palorex, stepping over him and toward the root.

"NO!" screamed Kano. He stumbled forward on shaking legs, palm aimed for a shot that Junior knew he couldn't make. And Kano didn't get the chance to. Taranis knocked him back with another volley of electricity; enough to hurt, but not enough to kill. Like with Junior in the temple, the maniac seemed willing to keep Kano alive. For now.

Junior rushed to Makoto's side. The Nurrano grabbed his hand and opened his mouth, but his labored breath couldn't summon any words.

"He needs help," said Junior.

Palorex shook his head as he approached the root. "He will only try to stop us."

Niscelles reached his remaining hand toward the root, but Palorex kicked it away. Junior noticed a brand there on Niscelles's wrist. The same symbol his father had given him before he died – the symbol of the Zoboros.

"Enough hoarding, old man." Palorex touched the root and his eyes glowed white. He smiled as its power surged through him, but it didn't take long for that smile to fade.

"Where is it?" he demanded.

Niscelles stared in defiance as he lay on the floor. "Out of your reach," he rasped.

Palorex snarled. He drove the sword through Niscelles's chest, skewering him against the rocks. The old Poterian gasped, his blood leaking onto the floor.

"The merciful man would end it quickly," said Palorex, smiling down as Niscelles clutched at the blade protruding from his chest. "Come here, Aaron."

Junior paled as the emperor waved him over. He approached, careful to avoid the expanding pool of Poterian blood.

Palorex held out his hand, the other clenched around the root. Junior took it and felt a familiar rush shoot through him. He stumbled back, fire returning to his hands.

"Th-thank you," he stammered.

"It served me well," said Palorex, black fire emerging from his own large hand. *Upgraded fire.* "As have you, young Hendricks. I have a task for you now." He pried the sword from Niscelles's chest and placed the bloodied thing in Junior's hand.

Junior stared at the old Poterian dying at his feet. "I...I don't want to kill him."

"I wouldn't ask you to. I want you to do the honors." He waved his hand at the root, so thin, its light so faint.

"Why?"

"Because it killed your mother."

What? Junior stared at the puny root, confused.

"The tree is part of a higher power," explained Palorex. "A power that reaches into our world. It grants us a fraction of that power, yes, but it also tries to impose its will upon us. At least in the places where its connection is strongest: the tree, this mountain..."

"Iramwerta," finished Junior. Its gate had been the thing that killed her, that wiped her from existence without a trace.

"This root is the filter. Destroy it, young Hendricks, and we may free its power for our *people* to decide how it is used."

Junior tightened his grip on the hilt as he stared at that root, so small that he had trouble believing it could be so powerful. Or at least, a major part of something so powerful. And yet everything had led them to it. To this moment. It had been what Taranis attacked Famora for, what Danadas had betrayed them for. *What my mother had died for.* He screamed and swung, cleaving the withered bark in two. The top half fell. Its light faded, yet more burst from the root, wisps of it launching across the chamber and phasing through the rocks toward the world beyond. The galaxy beyond. Hundreds of wisps...thousands. The flashes lasted just moments, and then all went dark.

Junior sparked a flame, illuminating the Poterian face hovering above him.

"Well done," said Palorex. "Now comes the fun part."

Junior glanced at Makoto, a pang of guilt as he watched his old ally's labored breaths. "And what would that be?" he asked.

"Revolution."

Chapter 36

Brothers

"No no no!" Kano clung to his brother's broken body, tears streaming from his face. Makoto opened his mouth but only air rasped out, the words trapped in his crushed abdomen. Their enemies had long abandoned them in the dark – *Junior* abandoned them in the dark – and now the only light in the chamber was that which glowed faintly from the severed root. Kano trembled there, both from the pain of watching his brother die and from the aftershock of Taranis's electricity. If only he'd been stronger. If only—

That's it. "Stay with me, Makoto." He raced to the root, or what remained of it, and grabbed hold.

But he felt nothing.

"No…please!" He fell to his knees, feeling foolish and desperate for begging a plant for help.

"It won't work," rasped Niscelles, clutching his wounded chest, blood dripping down the triangle brand on his hand. "But I know something that might. Help me up."

"But you're—"

"Help me, or have you forgotten to listen to your elders?"

Kano hoisted Niscelles to his feet. *So light for a Poterian.* Together they hobbled toward Makoto, blood trailing behind them, every step feeling like it might be Niscelles's last. But the ancient king managed to reach Makoto and knelt beside him.

"I once championed this place," said Niscelles, his face somehow regaining its color. *But after all that exertion? After being stabbed*? Kano gave the Poterian's wound another look. The place where the blade had exited through Niscelles's back had healed over, leaving nothing more than a welt.

Niscelles glanced at the severed root. "I failed my charge to protect it. It is time someone new stepped in." He took Makoto's hand in his own. Makoto winced, back arching. Kano rushed forward, but Niscelles waved him back. "It will only last a moment."

Kano smelled smoke. It came from Makoto's wrist. A triangle brand was etching itself into his skin, the same as Niscelles's was — or at least as it had been: Niscelles's brand was fading. Blood trickled down the Poterian's back, the wound reopened.

Niscelles turned to him, his face once again pale. "Just remember: this power comes at a price." The Poterian slumped beside Makoto.

"Niscelles...Makoto!" His brother's breathing ceased, eyes staring blank toward the ceiling. "Come back. Please." Kano curled up beside his brother and wept.

Makoto gasped, air flowing into his chest as it reinflated. He shot upright, his bruises and cuts all fading from his body. "What the hell just happened?!" He turned to Niscelles beside him. The Poterian lay unmoving. Dead. Makoto scrambled back. A rock scratched his wrist and he clutched it, noticing the brand for the first time.

Kano watched in shock, elation. He grabbed his brother and

hugged him tight.

"Admit it, you cried a little," said Makoto.

"Come off it."

Makoto spasmed in Kano's arms. *What could possibly be wrong* now? Makoto's eyes glowed white, as did the new brand on his wrist. It only lasted a few moments before the glow faded and Makoto snapped back to the present.

"How long was I out?" Something in Makoto's voice sounded different.

"How long do you think you were out?"

Makoto rubbed his head. "A long time…" He wandered over to the broken root and touched it. His brand glowed, and the root began to straighten. "It will take time to heal," he said.

Kano stared at him, unsure if he was even looking at his brother anymore. "How would you know that? Who told you how to fix it?"

"A new friend," said Makoto, glancing at the Poterian body on the floor. "He showed me many things, including our friends."

"Did they make it across the Rift? Are they alright?"

Makoto nodded. "For now. They're in Poteria, and Palorex is eager to join them."

"But Palorex didn't come here in a ship. How does he plan to leave?"

"There are other ways," said Makoto, pointing to the triangle now burned into his skin. It didn't seem to hurt as he traced each of the arrows running from the edges toward its center. "Three, in fact. Three bridges to the tree: Iramwerta, this mountain, and a third that was kept secret by the Poterians. Niscelles broke it many ages ago so his people couldn't cross it, but it can still be opened from the other side. And it will bring Palorex dangerously close to our friends."

"We should follow him then," said Kano, but Makoto shook his head.

"He and his new allies are too powerful. And that's without counting the Poterian army assembling as we speak."

"Well what would you suggest, Mr. Suddenly All-Seeing?"

Makoto smiled. "Come with me." He walked out the door that Palorex had melted through and down the dark path toward the cave entrance. Kano noticed something different in Makoto's step as he followed along. A confidence, a strength, like Makoto had traveled this dark and rocky path his entire life.

They reached the glowing pool that spanned the breadth of the cave. Kano checked above to make sure those flying creatures weren't coming.

"The Gal'nathi won't disturb us," said Makoto. Before Kano could ask how Makoto knew their name, his brother reached down and touched the water, turning its surface to ice.

Kano threw his hands into the air. He was beginning to resign himself to asking questions. "Do you have any other new powers I should know about?"

Makoto shrugged as he crossed the ice. "I'm not Zoboros. I just carry the power which the mountain grants me."

Kano scratched his beard. Makoto could heal himself, turn water into ice, revive the root...not to mention all his newfound knowledge. If he wasn't Zoboros, then that brand had made him something more.

Perhaps something that could connect to other Zoboros?

Sunlight blazed from the cave entrance. The storm had

passed. The ground rumbled as they approached. There was something outside. Many somethings. Kano slowed, drawing power into his fists.

"Don't be alarmed," said Makoto. "I told you our enemies were gathering an army. So I called up one of our own. One that was *very* close by."

They stepped into the sunlight upon a rocky ledge, where Kano spotted hundreds of silhouettes spanning across the sky.

Marauders.

Kano never thought he'd be so happy to see them. "You can speak to them through the Rift, can't you?" he asked. Makoto gave no reply. Kano took that for a yes.

One transport lowered toward them, and a familiar voice boomed through its loudspeakers. "We heard you needed a ride, young champions!" announced Varlam. Kano smiled, basking in the warm blast of the ship's many thrusters. *Let's see Palorex take us on now.*

"I told them to follow your orders," said Makoto. "They will serve you well."

Kano spun around. "But what about you? Aren't you—?" He stopped himself, recalling something Niscelles had once said in a vision.

"I am bound to the mountain, just as it is bound to me."

Makoto nodded. "Like he said, this power comes at a price."

Kano felt like a hot knife was sinking into his heart. Never again would Makoto join him on his journey across the stars. Never would he rejoin the team. Never would he return to Famora, or to his own mother.

"This is my fault," said Kano.

Makoto gripped his shoulder tight. "It is...because you

helped me survive this far." Kano smiled at his own words being used against him. "Plus, I'm kinda the most powerful being in the galaxy, so...swings and roundabouts."

Kano laughed even though he felt ready to cry again. He embraced his brother as the transport touched down before them.

"Will I be able to reach you?" asked Kano, tapping his head.

"Through the Rift, yes," said Makoto. "Beyond that it's a little hazy, but with practice we might just make it work."

"I hope so."

The liftgate lowered and Varlam stood there with a squad of marauders. They all bowed to Makoto. "By your blessing, Ay Nyid," said the Poterian.

"To the Homeland, take you," said Makoto.

Kano looked to the transport, then to his brother, the idea of leaving him behind seeming unthinkable.

"Go," insisted Makoto. "But first, there's something you should know about our enemy."

"About Palorex?"

"No. About Junior."

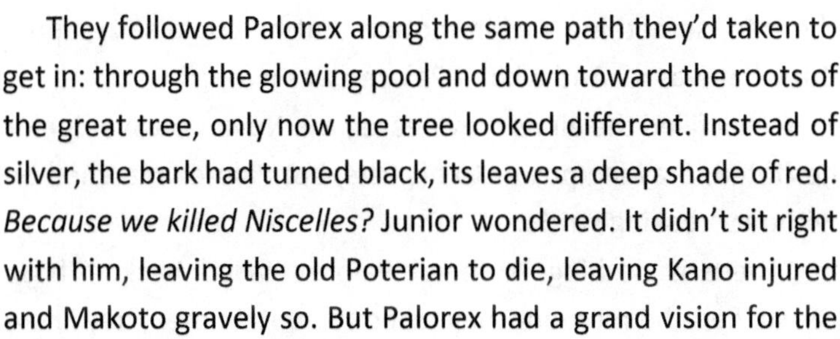

They followed Palorex along the same path they'd taken to get in: through the glowing pool and down toward the roots of the great tree, only now the tree looked different. Instead of silver, the bark had turned black, its leaves a deep shade of red. *Because we killed Niscelles?* Junior wondered. It didn't sit right with him, leaving the old Poterian to die, leaving Kano injured and Makoto gravely so. But Palorex had a grand vision for the

Zoboros, and they had gotten in the way of it.

Junior searched along the path, hopeful that Nera, Brivek, and Zivo would soon turn up. They hadn't followed him through the pool, and he had yet to find a trace of them along the path. He hoped the Nuvanoks hadn't found them again.

"Your friends chose not to follow," said Taranis suddenly. Junior jumped. The walk so far had been in silence, and he hadn't realized the maniac had crept so close to his ear. "Their fates may have been decided already."

"I thought we were here to save all Zoboros," said Junior.

"We are here to give them all a choice."

Junior picked up the pace, leaving Taranis to saunter well behind him. Junior may have agreed with Palorex's ideas, but that didn't mean he had to be friendly to Palorex's allies. *Or children*. It disturbed Junior to know that his father's murderer was also heir to the Poterian throne. But would Palorex truly name him heir? For what little he knew about Poterians, he knew a half-Human ruler would not go over well. Yet Palorex marched with such conviction that Junior had a hard time imagining anyone going against *any* of the emperor's decisions.

But Junior also had no idea what modern Poteria looked like. Would the people there still love Palorex? Despise him? The emperor seemed confident in what he had seen through the tree; something was in motion that he could seize upon. But what was it? And what if Palorex was wrong?

A chill filled the air as they neared the Nuvanok cave. Junior hesitated, drawing power to his fists, but Palorex marched on without breaking stride.

"There is nothing to fear," Palorex called back. "Those beasts fled the moment they failed to contain me. They know they cannot challenge me any longer."

Junior nodded, though Palorex's assurances made him feel little better as he stepped into the cold cave of death. Even the flame he sparked in his hand seemed insignificant against the darkness, like its light was being choked down, but it was strong enough to reveal branching paths in the cave that he'd not seen before. New paths. He'd resigned himself to trying to understand the magic of this place, though he wondered what had prompted the change. Was it the freeing of Palorex, or the killing of Niscelles, or perhaps scaring off the Nuvanoks? Whatever it was, it had left them with a maze to navigate, one through which Palorex led them deftly, never hesitating as he weaved through passageways caked with rot.

Junior's shoes squished into something wet. Something fresh. He looked down, holding his nose against the stench of decay, and he found the juicy, pinkish remains of what he assumed to be the fruit from the tree. Only, there was so much. It trailed along the floor and up the wall, where it appeared to have come from a single, massive fruit that had exploded. But how had it grown down here? And why had it burst?

"Keep your guard up," said Palorex. "Dangerous things still walk here."

Douglas stared at the pinkish slop in disgust. "Like what?"

Palorex didn't answer. He kept weaving through the various paths, a black flame in his hand now. It provided no light, but certainly protection. *He must know how this place works, considering how long he's been trapped here.* It gave Junior hope that they would find their way out of this chilling maze, even if he had no idea where they would end up next.

Something crunched through the dead brambles along a

neighboring path. Junior stopped. "That could be them," he said to Douglas. "Nera!"

Silence. Douglas cleared his throat. "Well then they can come to us," he said, hurrying closer to Palorex and away from the crazy pyro whose shouts could attract an unknown threat.

Some leader he is, thought Junior. He started down the opposite path alone. Taranis lingered at the entrance to it and watched him curiously, but eventually ventured off with the others.

He crept along slowly, the path shrouded in shadow, every crunch of his step making his heart quicken. "Nera, Zivo," he whispered. Something crunched up ahead, far louder than his own footfalls. "Brivek, if that's you, say—"

Junior leaped back as his fire illuminated a scaly face.

"Miss me?"

Junior set both hands ablaze and aimed them at the yellow-eyed assassin. "You're dead! I-I *killed* you."

"You wouldn't be the first," said the Jaculus, looking bored as he picked his nails. "But it appears the tree is still not done with me yet."

"It...brought you back?"

The Jaculus glanced at the bits of slop stuck to Junior's shoes. "It always does. So I suggest you don't bother trying to kill me again."

Junior let the fire in his hands reduce to a simmer, though he kept them aimed. "Where are my friends?"

"Friends? What a curious term for you right now. I wonder what the others will think when they learn you've expanded your social circle."

"As I recall, you worked for Palorex once."

The Jaculus tutted. "We've been over this. I don't work for anyone. And as soon as Palorex figured that out, he lopped my head off." He turned toward the rot in the wall. "That's curious..." He ripped the rot away and found a small black branch pushing through, its red leaves young and tender. "Is there new management in the tree?" he asked. "Has someone been playing a game of gods?"

"Palorex killed Niscelles," said Junior.

"Niscelles cannot die so long as he's connected to the mountain. I never shared that detail with Palorex; I was curious if he'd learn it on his own. I was curious what all of you would do once I opened this door." He touched the budding branch and his eyes glowed white. His smile widened. "And you didn't disappoint."

"This was all an experiment?!" blurted Junior, his fire flaring. "My mother died because of what you did."

"No, she died because of what *you* did," said the Jaculus. "You who drew the fury of the gods and now walk with Palorex onto the precipice of war."

"Why would you bring us here if you didn't want Palorex back in our world?"

The Jaculus shrugged. "I wanted change. The galaxy gets boring after so long. But I can't just do it myself. That wouldn't be fun." A thud echoed down the passageway. "It seems your new 'friends' have found their way out. I'd hurry along if I were you."

"What aren't you telling me?" said Junior. "What change are you trying to bring about?"

The Jaculus didn't seem to notice his question. "Don't worry about your friends getting lost in this tree," he said, backing into the shadows. "I'll make sure they find their way home."

"Wait!" Junior raced into the shadows, but the Jaculus was gone.

If he'd ever even been there at all.

Chapter 37

Beneath the Palace

Water dripped onto Jaden's head. Again. He tried nudging his wheelchair forward, but it wouldn't budge with the brake activated. Having his wrists bound to the armrests didn't help the situation either, nor did the fact that the numbing agent on his back was starting to wear off. But what did it matter? He was dead anyway.

Thunder shook the stalactites along the high ceiling, freeing more water to rain upon the catacombs. *Couldn't the Poterians pick a different day to firebomb their own city?*

"Real pickle we're in," muttered Hauser. The smuggler sat strapped to a wooden chair, his large frame seeming puny beneath the towering arches that supported the weight of the vast palace grounds.

"I've been in a 'pickle' ever since you showed up," said Jaden, turning away. He found himself facing a strange sandstone temple that sat wholly out of place in the otherwise empty chamber. He'd noticed it when they'd first come here to meet the empress, but thought little of it then, having been both lucid and freshly paralyzed. The more he stared at it, though, the more he felt it pulling him into its secrets. No doubt it was a place of ancient rituals, of ancient religion. Something the Poterians held sufficiently dear not only to preserve but around which to construct their glorious palace. A place that time couldn't touch.

If only I could've been tucked away like that. Instead, the past few days had brought Jaden all manner of hell. He'd lost everything, even his best friends, and was left with nothing but one of the least trustworthy people in the galaxy.

"If we're lucky, them Poterians'll wipe each other out by the day's end," said Hauser as another distant impact drizzled more water on their heads.

"Did you know the Poterians were going to do this?" asked Jaden.

Hauser raised his half-burned face solemnly. "No."

"So you smuggled weapons to the most war-hungry civilization in history thinking they would just sit on them?"

"I *thought* keeping the Poterians preoccupied with each other would keep our side of the Rift safer."

"And is that what my parents thought too?"

Hauser huffed. "I don't think your parents saw far past the ruddy dollar sign. Few do, in my line of work."

Jaden wasn't so sure. Money was merely a tool for the Upton family. Whatever this plan was, it meant better positioning for them. But how?

"I see that brain of yours workin'. Don't think for a second that your parents are like them ruddy Orlovs. If anything, they were hoping to drive a wedge in the old man's plans."

"Well, Danadas got what he wanted anyway," said Jaden, embracing the falling water as distant bombs shook it down. "Poteria's under his thumb. If you decide to take employment with him, I won't hold it against you."

"Listen here you lil' pup!" boomed Hauser, his voice making Jaden feel like the frightened little boy in one of Hauser's lessons. "If you haven't figured out that each side of the coin in this galaxy is a rusted piece of shit, then you haven't learned a damn thing. The Red Sabre, a backstabbing empress, an IDF that kidnaps children – it's all different shades of shit, and I'll happily take their dollar and spend it somewhere better. But if you believe for a minute that I'm gonna let the brightest little boy ever to crawl out of Vasilian high society give up and let the Orlovs stamp their shiny shoes all over him, then you've got another thing comin'."

Jaden sat frozen in place. Did Hauser really think that of him? Most others just labeled him a spoiled, sarcastic brat. And they weren't wrong. But take away his parents' money, his friends, his legs, his damned datapad, and what did he have left?

A ding echoed across the catacombs. A rock façade in the wall split open, revealing the elevator hidden behind. Jaden expected a Jakari to come waddling through, possibly with its knife already drawn. But it was Sterling who emerged, and in a wheelchair that drove automatically. *Guess they save the best ones for royalty.*

Jaden steadied himself as Sterling approached. He wanted to believe that the traitor was here to explain his sudden betrayal, but he knew that wasn't Sterling's style. It was hard enough to get a word out of the brooding Poterian on a good day, much less an apology. No, the Poterian prince was only here because he needed something.

The familiar gears began to turn in Jaden's brain. Desperate people could be useful, he reasoned, if steered correctly. And as the ideas of how to manipulate Sterling took form, he smiled.

Take everything else away, I've still got my mind.

"You kept the empress's secrets this long, Sterling, and she still won't give you back your limbs," he said, the sarcasm rejuvenating him. "What's a Poterian to do?"

"They would have executed you if not for me, boy," said Sterling with what Jaden assumed was a scowl, though it could still have qualified as Sterling's resting face.

"Forgive me for not kissing your feet…or foot, I should say."

Sterling huffed, and Jaden could feel the hot air coming from his big Poterian nostrils. "There's no reason for her to cut ties with Carmichael now that Poteria Prime is here. We still have use of you, Jaden."

"I wouldn't consider myself combat ready," he replied, patting his legs.

"There won't be any combat. Not after the Orlovs sabotaged palace security systems. Even T8 can't handle the virus they planted. If you can't get the cannons back online, we may lose any chance of saving the empress."

"I thought you wanted to stay out of Poterian politics, Sterling. Why such an investment now?"

Sterling pounded his only fist against his armrest. "This is my family we're talking about, damn you!"

Jaden watched the Poterian's angry, frightened face. His loyalty ran awful deep despite being away from his niece so long, unless…

"Typhera isn't your niece. She's your daughter."

Sterling stiffened. "Save her, and I will make sure she spares you.”

Jaden turned to Hauser, who shook his burned head.

“What’s to keep you from leaving me here for dead?” asked Jaden.

“No ship is getting out of this palace in one piece if our cannons can’t protect it. You fail, we all die. You succeed, I’ll protect you. You have my word.”

“Surprisingly, your word isn’t as valuable as it used to be,” said Jaden. The ceiling shook, and more water cascaded onto them. “In fact, I feel inclined to take my chances with Poteria Prime.”

“You’d be letting the Orlovs win,” grumbled Sterling through gritted teeth.

“Your daughter let them win when she sent my team away.” Jaden got a satisfied nod from Hauser for that one. “I would’ve thought you taught her better.”

Sterling leaned back. “So that’s what this is about. You won’t do it unless we protect your team, too.”

“A team you were once a member of,” said Jaden. “Where are they?”

“Coming here for you. And they won’t make it in time if you don’t get the damned cannons up.”

Jaden gulped. His back-and-forth with Sterling had just wasted valuable time, and he still had no guarantee that his friends would be safe from Typhera once he brought their defenses up.

“I need your answer,” said Sterling. “Are you going to help, or are you going to let this place come down on top of you?”

“I—”

The ground shook. Not from distant bombs, but from

something closer. Something powerful. It rocked Jaden's wheelchair so hard he had to press his weight from side to side to keep from falling. Light blazed inside the temple, shining through the seam of its single door.

"What Poterian witchery is this?!" blurted Hauser.

Sterling grabbed his communicator. "Typhera! It's—"

The temple door burst open. Wind gusted out, sending Sterling's wheelchair rolling backward. He tumbled out of it and over the rocks, his communicator clattering across the floor to Jaden's feet. *So close.* Jaden tried to reach for it, to lean down against the piercing pain in his broken back, but neither his bound arms nor his useless legs brought him any closer.

Figures stepped through the temple door, silhouettes against the light blazing behind them. Four total, all of them big and menacing. Whoever they were, Jaden knew they weren't friendly.

"Galorin, is that you?" asked a voice both cool and commanding. It belonged to the tallest silhouette, its large footsteps echoing off the rocky walls like thunder. *Another Poterian.*

"Impossible…" said Sterling, mouth agape as new arrival's shadow fell over him.

"You watched my army perish, but not I," said the Poterian. He lifted Sterling back into the wheelchair, his red face finally coming into view. The same face as Sterling's, but younger and more arrogant.

The face of a dead emperor. An unaged dead emperor. Now Jaden really wanted to get those cannons back online.

"All this time, I thought you were dead," said Palorex. "I could see so many in my exile, brother, but not you."

How Palorex was able to see people during his exile wasn't of much concern to Jaden right now; he was too busy figuring out a way to reach the communicator at his feet. He kept checking to make sure Palorex's goons didn't notice it. The light from the temple was fading, and their faces became clear to him. There was Taranis (no surprise there) and a young man he'd never seen before, but it was the third that shocked him.

"I see you've found a new apprentice, brother," grumbled Sterling.

Taranis stepped forward. "You taught me everything you dared to, old man," he said. "But the rightful emperor will teach me so much—"

"I wasn't talking about you," interrupted Sterling, his gaze shifting to Junior. Jaden sat on the edge of his seat, waiting for the explanation, but Junior stayed silent, either too arrogant or too afraid to answer. Sterling nodded toward his missing leg and continued. "I followed my brother once, and I lost much more than this."

Jaden expected the Poterian Emperor to frown at that. To lash out in anger. But Palorex stewed on Sterling's words, everyone hinging so tightly upon what he was about to say that Jaden saw his opening and began rocking himself as quietly as he could in his wheelchair, his feet loosening from their footrests.

"The cycles have not been kind to you since our defeat, Galorin," said Palorex finally. "Few sacrificed as much as you did. And if I had made it through the battle unscathed, I would have taken us the rest of the way. I would have finished what we started."

"There is no 'finishing' it," said Sterling. "You will scour the stars for your cause, and yet all that will change are the number of weeping mothers."

Jaden managed to free one of his feet from the footrest. It landed limply on the communicator, the toe of his shoe jammed into the dial button. Perfect. It would connect him to whatever channel Sterling had it set to. *Likely Typhera's channel*. Ironic how his captor had just become his only lifeline.

"Mothers cry now, don't you see it?" pressed Palorex, his face growing somehow redder. "As they did before we set out to do our work. If we finally unite this broken galaxy, we will ensure generations of peace and prosperity."

"At what cost?" asked Sterling.

Disappointment filled Palorex's cold, black eyes. "Your mind is an asset to me, Galorin. But if you will not lend it to me willingly, then do it for the one who sits my throne." Black fire sparked in his hand. Jaden had never seen anything like it before. Instead of creating light, it sucked light away.

Sterling paled at the sight of it. "I will...convince her to cede her claim."

"It will require all your faculties, brother. She's a stubborn one, I have seen it. How very familiar." Palorex patted Sterling on the cheek, then turned to Jaden and Hauser. "What are these?" he asked coldly.

"Your Majesty," said Hauser, bowing his burned face until it was practically in his lap. "I'm a key supplier to your most loyal servants. Even now they're using what I've provided to—"

"A smuggler," Palorex cut in. "And I assume your allegiance lies with the highest bidder?"

"What's your offer?" asked Hauser.

"Your life."

"Then we have a deal."

Palorex smiled, but it faded as his gaze fell over Jaden like a dark cloud. "This one is strange. I sense a…thread upon him." He stepped closer, drawing a sword. *The* sword. "One that connects him to the mountain."

"Mountain?" said Jaden, faking a laugh. "I-I'm not much of an outdoors guy. More of a soak up the view from a five-star hotel, if you know what I mean."

Palorex knelt in front of him, his hot breath making Jaden sweat even more. "You're not a Zoboros. Yet somehow the mountain can see you. Can see us through you."

"Maybe Niscelles still lives," said the guy Jaden had never seen before.

Niscelles? Like from the stories?

"No," said Taranis. "This one, Jaden, shares a connection with Niscelles's champions."

"Then they will be devastated when I sever it," said Palorex, raising his sword.

Jaden braced. He heard Hauser protesting in the background, but it did nothing to stop the blade from swinging toward his neck.

"Unless that connection could be useful!" blurted Junior. The blade stopped a hair's breadth from flesh. Jaden looked to his old ally, as surprised as he was terrified. Junior seemed surprised by his own outburst, too, but he continued. "We have leverage over them and their team if we keep him hostage. It would be a mistake to waste him while they're still a threat."

Hostage. Thanks Junior. Real hero.

Palorex and Taranis exchanged a look. "You know, Aaron, you are absolutely right," said the emperor, placing the sword in Junior's hand. "It would be a mistake to waste this opportunity."

Jaden's heart began thumping out of his chest. He saw the fear in Junior's eyes, the disbelief, but he also saw a scenario where the crazy pyro went through with it.

"I-I shouldn't," said Junior. "Like I said, he could be useful."

"He could be dangerous," said Palorex. "Show your enemies mercy and you will come to regret it. We can have no regrets on this path."

Junior looked down at Jaden with those orange eyes, his mother's eyes. *Where is Angeline in all of this?* Jaden wondered. She was always the voice of reason amid the madness. But Junior looked lost. He had to be, to be among these monsters.

"I...I understand," said Junior, raising the blade. Jaden saw his reflection in it, saw his crippled body strapped to a wheelchair in the underbelly of a doomed Poterian palace. He'd never imagined dying in a place like this, yet somehow it felt fitting.

"Don't do it, Junior," he said. "Don't be on the wrong side of history like Palorex was." Junior drew back the sword to strike. "For goodness's sake, Junior, one of them killed your father!"

Junior froze. "It was...necessary," he said.

Jaden's heart sank. There was no convincing him now. No fighting the inevitable. He closed his eyes and braced for the sting of the blade, the quiet dark at the end of all things.

Instead, he heard the ding of the elevator.

"Traitors!"

Jaden opened his eyes. A dozen Poterian guards poured

from the elevator, rifles raised, and charged right at them.

Lightning sparked between Taranis's fingers. Blades of energy emerged from the other Zoboros's hands – much like Cera's power, but pink and far less stable. They started toward the attackers, but Palorex waved them back.

"You dare strike your one, true emperor?!" Palorex bellowed, his voice resounding off the distant walls, so powerful the guards stuttered to a halt. They turned to one who Jaden assumed to be their captain, and he stepped forward.

"We serve the one true empress," he said.

Palorex shook his head as rifles aimed at it. "So be it."

Black flames erupted from his palm. Jaden watched in disbelief, in horror, as the guards were engulfed by it. Their screams lasted only a second before they were silenced. And when the flames cleared, only ashes remained.

"Ruddy hell," muttered Hauser.

Palorex turned proudly toward Jaden as if he should feel blessed by his royal gaze. *The gaze of a mass murderer.* "Who is on the right side of history now, boy?"

Jaden saw only madness in those eyes. But he noticed something else, something behind the emperor, rocketing toward him out of the elevator.

An arm?

It caught Palorex in its metal fingers. He shouted as it carried him across the catacombs. Taranis and the Zoboros with blades on his hands spun around, expecting the next attack to come from the elevator, but it came instead from above, flashes of blue and purple that leaped down from the stalactites to slash at them.

"Get Sterling!" shouted Taranis to Junior as he zapped a Jakari away.

Junior was frozen in place, face filled with regret. That same face ducked away a moment later as Mizuki slashed a knife at it. She landed in Jaden's lap with a thump. Though his legs didn't feel it, the wound in his back certainly did.

"Leave now, boy of the computer!" she shouted. She slashed his hand restraints before leaping back into the battle.

"Easier said than done," he said, disengaging the brake of his wheelchair with his freed hands. His back throbbed and his free foot dragged on the floor.

"Wait for me!" shouted Hauser. He threw his chair against the ground, smashing it into splinters. His arms were still bound to broken beams, but he just carried them with him as he raced over.

"You could've done that the *whole time*?!" said Junior.

"Didn't have a reason to leave this dungeon before," he said, pointing at the ashes that were once guards. "But I'll take bombs over that shit any day!"

Sterling caught up with them, running on his own legs, the bionic one reattached. The bionic arm was still missing though, likely occupied with Palorex.

"*Now* will you help Typhera?" demanded Sterling.

"If it gets us out this madhouse, then yes!" said Jaden.

The three of them piled into the elevator. Hauser jammed on the close button, and Jaden watched between the sliding doors as black fire erupted within the catacombs.

Chapter 38

Evernight

Thunder roared miles beneath their little transport, powerful and constant, enough to make Li's soul shake.

The sound of war.

She dared not use her powers. To activate them would be to connect with the pain and screams and death spreading across the capital city. Across the planet. For once, she was thankful the transport didn't have windows. She couldn't bear to see what horrors their missions had accidentally sparked.

Chenji was huddled across the aisle, hands clenched within his shaggy hair, arms covering his ears as he rocked himself. Li knew he was reliving that moment on the rooftop; the moment Senator Ivanov died under his watch. The moment Poteria Prime had used to justify this attack.

She crossed the aisle and embraced him, not saying a word. Not needing to. Nor did she need to tap into her powers to feel his pain.

"I should've saved him," said Chenji, tucking his head into Li's shoulder.

"It's not your fault."

"Yes it is!" he blurted. "I was distracted. I've been distracted ever since Taranis zapped me with his stupid lightning."

"You've been healing. There's a difference."

"You can't heal this." Chenji tore from her embrace and climbed out of his chair, standing almost twice her height. She felt afraid; afraid of whatever wound had just opened inside him. "Not unless you have a time machine to bring that little boy back to his parents. But don't bother, they didn't want him anyway. No one wanted him. So he went to the only place that would take a freak like him."

He sprouted fur along his arm. "'Chenji the Changeling' they called me. The best act in Manoran's Intergalactic Circus...but that didn't mean I got any special treatment. It just meant they were afraid to lose me, so they kept a collar around my neck. If I tried to change form outside of my act, *zap*. Leave my cage, *zap*. Say anything they didn't like, *double zap*."

Li clutched his shaking arm. "I'm sorry, Chenji."

"I didn't know when I faced Taranis that it still affected me. But after feeling that pain again in the middle of a transformation, I...I..."

"You turn into that child again every time you transform," said Li, not with judgment but with understanding.

Chenji put his head back in his hands. "And according to Ivanov, the whole empire knows it."

"We'll work through this together, Chenji," she promised. It was all she could do for him now. "Bit by bit."

The door opened between the transport bay and the cockpit, and Carmichael stepped through. "We're almost above the target. Strap in."

Li was quick to claim the seat beside Chenji. The last thing the changeling needed was to dive into a warzone alone.

And a warzone it was. Even from what little she could see through the windscreen — which was all the way down the narrow aisle — she could tell the city had gone dark to hide its buildings from the bombers, but enough fires raged to light the city up anyway, more blazing to life every second as bombs and artillery pounded the once tranquil capital. She snapped on her seat restraint and grabbed Chenji's hand. He squeezed hers back, too horrified to look up at the slaughter.

Li noticed something else outside. It should have been evening, yet the sky was dark, with only a sliver of orange peeking beneath the edges of a great black orb on the horizon.

Evernight. Poteria Prime had blocked the sun just in time for the attack.

"Any word from Jaden or Sterling?" she asked.

Carmichael shook his head. "The whole palace went dark. Even their defenses are down."

"Then it's as good a time as any to make our approach, considering only *one* side will be shooting at us," said Ristin. He'd been sitting farther down the aisle with Warp, learning to sign from her. A good way to distract himself from the explosions.

"I wouldn't be so sure," said Cera from the copilot's seat. "Most of the city's remaining cannons and fighters are focused on protecting the palace, and you can bet Poteria Prime is pumping every missile it can at it."

"That doesn't give our friends much time," muttered Chenji. "Should I even ask what our chances are of making it to the surface?"

"Not good, fleshling," said T8 from the pilot's seat. "Not good."

Li rubbed her temples. It seemed everything was going terribly wrong for them, and terribly right for Poteria Prime. There was, however, one contingency plan they had come up with should they fail to get support from Typhera and her regime.

"Is the message ready?" she asked.

Carmichael nodded. "Cera recorded it herself. It's quite compelling."

"Once we send it, our fate is in the hands of the Poterians," said Cera. "*All* the Poterians."

Li tensed. Both sides of the conflict would be alerted to their arrival. Had they been flying in Sterling's ship, they could have opted for a stealth approach, but in a transport commissioned by Typhera, they would be easy to spot at a low altitude. She could only pray that the most war-hungry species in history would listen to their plea.

"Maybe we shouldn't send it," said Ristin, despite being the one who had first suggested this whole rescue idea. "Maybe we take our chances."

"Do you really want me to calculate them for you?" asked T8.

"What other choice do we—?" started Chenji, but Carmichael held up a hand that silenced the frightened team before they could start spiraling.

"My father took his chances once," said Carmichael. "You may have heard the story: attacked a much larger force, destroyed the Poterian fleet, ended a war and saved our side of the galaxy from certain defeat. They've hailed him as a hero for it. But people tend to overlook the fact that everyone under his command died that day. 'Small price,' he would have said. Well, I'm not my father. If there's a better chance of ensuring every member of this team makes it through the day, then I will take it. But I need to know that everyone here is ready to take it too."

Slowly, Li raised her hand. Warp raised hers too, followed by Ristin. Akio raised his from the back corner, where he had been sharpening his knife, silent as a ghost. Cera raised hers, and T8's shot up after his eyes pinged with the calculation.

That left Chenji.

All eyes turned to him. "Why the change of heart, Chenji?" asked Carmichael. "You said in the beginning this plan might be crazy enough to work."

Chenji cleared his throat. "Because I was still in shock at what Ivanov told me. That the people here *loved* us. It made me think I could be loved by people outside of this team. But then I remembered how ordinary people 'loved' me before: as a spectacle. They didn't care if I was hurt, if I was tortured...just as long as I entertained them. And I think we're all here for that reason, in one way or another, so why should we leave our fate up to them?"

Li didn't know what to say. All she could think about was the moment on Famora when Kano and Junior's powers were revealed to a crowd of thousands. Thousands of neighbors, thousands of friends, yet those powers changed everything. They were booed. Hated. Rejected. And though Poteria was supposedly different, she couldn't help but fear that same rejection here. That same betrayal.

Carmichael approached Chenji, his trademark smile erased.

In fact, Li'd never seen him more serious. "You're right to be afraid," he said, kneeling beside Chenji. "It's all any of you have been conditioned to know. And so I ask you: would you want your children and your children's children to live with that same fear, one that's been passed down since the Zoboros first came into existence? My father had that fear, and he passed it on to me. I grew up believing the Zoboros should be eliminated. They were part of the reason my father never returned from that battle, after all. But one day, despite my own hatred, a Zoboros saved my life. I never learned her name. Never learned why she did it. But she saved me. And they shot her for it."

The room was silent save for the bombs bursting far below. "But she taught me something that day. That just one person could have an extraordinary impact on another. I assembled this team because I believed a group of extraordinary people could change even more minds. You didn't need to have powers to join," he paused, glancing at Akio. "But you had to believe in something greater. And that would make others believe in something greater. It sounds like that's exactly what we've accomplished here on Poteria. But there's only one way to prove that theory, if you'll allow me."

The whole room leaned toward Chenji, bracing for the answer. He sat there staring at the floor, arms pulled inward. Finally, he raised his head.

"I'm in," he said.

Carmichael rose, the smile back on his face, a smile Li had seen a thousand times, yet this time it gave her goosebumps.

"T8!" he called down the aisle. "Punch it!"

"Message sent," said T8. "Might want to hold onto

something, Captain."

Li perked. That was the first time the bot had referred to anyone besides Sterling as 'captain.'

Carmichael claimed the seat beside Li as the ship dipped toward the surface. The thunder of artillery grew louder and louder until it made Li's ears ring. She didn't dare cover them, though; her hands were gripped too firmly against her restraints, the nearby explosions rocking them in every direction.

"Li," began Chenji, "thank you for—"

T8 banked the ship hard as a missile exploded beside them, the force of it making Li's teeth chatter. It stunned Chenji into silence.

"Don't mention it!" she shouted, jaw hurting from the explosion.

"I probably don't need to tell you this," said T8, "but Poteria Prime is decidedly against us."

Go figure. Their ship pivoted left and right, up and down, the motion making Li sick, but the thought of getting blasted out of the atmosphere making her even sicker.

"Picked up a bandit," announced Cera as the ship banked hard again.

"Relax, fleshlings. This is what I was programmed for!"

The ship spun in a barrel roll, the blood rushing back and forth through Li's head. Ristin vomited as T8 plunged toward the surface, his bile floating in the air. They leveled out and it splattered at Warp's feet, who was too unconscious from the spinning to react.

"Please tell me this ship has some defensive weapons," said Chenji.

Carmichael shook his head. "Just T8's flying."

"Robot, get us low enough to use buildings for cover!" called Akio from the back.

"You want to get up here and do the flying then?!" shouted T8.

"NO!" the team shouted in unison, recalling the Jakari's disastrous piloting when he brought them to Mogaddu. That had been months ago, and the team was still traumatized by it. Almost as traumatized as they were right now.

"Warp's coming to," said Ristin, patting her face. Her eyes opened and she jerked her feet away from Ristin's mess on the floor.

"I'd stay asleep if I were her," muttered Chenji. Li patted his hand, happy at least that his humor was coming back.

"Oh boy…" trailed T8.

Li gasped. Through the windscreen, she could see fighters coming straight for them, dozens of them. And with a bandit on their tail too, they were trapped.

"Any more tricks up your sleeve, T8?" asked Ristin.

"Hope and prayer."

Li closed her eyes and braced as the enemies closed in around them. Then she heard something crackle. She jumped, expecting an explosion, but it was coming from the ship's comms.

"Liberators, come in," came a deep voice that Li assumed to be Poterian.

Cera glanced back at Carmichael, who nodded. She hesitantly tapped the microphone. "We're here. Who is this?"

"Salvation."

The incoming ships fired their missiles high and wide,

overshooting their transport and exploding not too far behind.

"Your tail is clear," came the Poterian's voice over the comms. "We'll get you down to the palace."

Collective shock and excitement filled the aisle as the Poterian ships turned around and formed up alongside their transport.

Li turned to Carmichael. "What was in Cera's message?"

"Oh, you know, a little apologizing, a little Orlov blaming, but mostly she told them who each of us are. Where we come from. Why we ran and what we fight for. Don't forget, these people lost a lot not too long ago. And they might lose everything again if we can't help them now."

Li nodded, a nervous excitement rising inside her. It wasn't just their teammates' lives at stake anymore. It was an entire empire hanging in the balance. An entire people.

Suddenly she felt like maybe, just maybe, they could stop this war.

T8 steered them into their landing vector, bringing them lower and lower until they were level with some of Poteria's tallest buildings, many of them burning from the onslaught. The palace began to take shape on the horizon, once-glorious red domes and towers now alive with firelight. A swarm of what appeared to be flies hovered above it, but Li knew what they really were.

"More fighters incoming," announced T8.

"All fighters open fire," ordered the Poterian pilot over the comms. Tracers pounded into the oncoming swarm, sending a few enemies plummeting toward the palace in little infernos. The rest formed into wedges and steered straight for them.

"Get ready for the drop," said T8.

Li tightened her grip on the restraints, palms sweating, heart pounding. Tracers flashed at them from the enemy fighters, thundering against the reinforced hull above her head. T8 pulled a lever and Li felt weightless as the engines died. Missiles exploded up ahead where their ship should have been, but they stalled and dipped lifeless toward the palace grounds, which grew wider and wider in the viewport. Closer and closer. Too close.

T8 punched the lever again and the transport roared back to life. He swerved them away from the stony ground and up over the inner walls toward a tarmac within the palace, lit only by the burning structures surrounding it. It was enough for Li to see the row of tanks assembled on the paving.

"Whelp, looks like Poteria Prime got here first," said T8, banking left as the tank barrels flashed and thundered, their projectiles bursting near the windscreen.

"Where else can we land?!" called Carmichael.

"No options look good, with all the damage the palace has taken," said T8. "We need—"

Lights sparked to life across the runway, nearly blinding everyone inside the little transport.

"Someone call for help?" came a nasally voice over the comms.

"Jaden!" exclaimed Li. The others all beamed in their seats.

"Don't mind me, just got the defense systems back online," their friend chided over the loudspeakers. "Just hold your applause until the…" he paused as a barrage of rockets pounded across the row of tanks, pulverizing them in a wicked display of fire and smoke.

"I-I think we're clear to land," said Cera. No sooner had the message come than T8 looped them around and put the wheels to the tarmac with a jerk. It wasn't until they finally came to a stop that Li exhaled.

Everyone unstrapped their restraints and immediately opened their overhead compartments. Warp grabbed a pair of stun batons, Ristin a pair of pistols, Carmichael his trusty shotgun. Li latched medpacks to her belt, praying she wouldn't have to use them, and loaded seedling pods into the slots beneath her wrists. That's when she noticed Chenji was the only one not in motion.

"I should transform into something useful," he said. "But I'm afraid I won't be able to do it."

"We're all afraid," she replied. "It's ok to embrace that."

Chenji nodded. He drew a deep breath and morphed into his six-legged lizard form, his echolocation reverberating almost unnoticed through the ship. He nodded his big lizard head toward the liftgate.

"There's someone outside, isn't there?" said Li.

The lizard nodded.

T8 checked the outside camera. "Oh thank goodness!" It punched a button and the liftgate opened with a blast of compressed air.

"Sterling!" exclaimed Ristin. For once, everyone was thrilled to see the grumpy Poterian as he sauntered in on his bionic leg. He had a rifle slung over one arm, his bionic arm missing.

"Heard you all were coming," he said, his gruff voice music to Li's ears.

"What's the situation on the ground?" asked Carmichael.

"About as shitty as you'd expect," said Sterling. "Palace defenses can buy us some time, but the city will be lost within the hour, and the palace won't last much longer than that."

"How many civilians are still inside the palace?" asked Cera.

"Many, including the emp—" he paused, exchanging a look with his bot. "Including my daughter."

Gasps filled the transport, but Li just folded her arms in satisfaction. She'd thought the resemblance was pretty obvious.

"Then we rescue her and as many as we can," said Carmichael. "Are there any ships still intact?"

"The only hangar still intact is hidden beneath the keep, but that keep is surrounded by enemies," said Jaden over the comms.

"Not for long," said Carmichael, pumping his shotgun. "I expect they'll try to kill anyone still loyal to the empress. We clear a path to that hangar and get as many people out as we can. Any questions?"

No one raised a hand. Li only toyed with the seedling pods beneath her wrist, eager to do some rescuing.

"Good," said Carmichael. "Now let's go save an empire."

Chapter 39

Besieged

Jaden wheeled away from the console, eyes locked on the security feed playing on its monitor. *They made it.* The team was crossing the palace grounds on a straight shot to the keep. Now the real trouble began.

He passed other stations like his own, each staffed by Poterian servants who he'd chanced upon in the hallways. They'd been eager to lend a hand in getting the palace defenses online (no surprise, considering they were being bombed) but Jaden did hear whispers about a video. Something to do with Cera. Whatever the case, this group was proving capable of maintaining the defenses on their own.

"Hauser, time to go."

"I was just gettin' comfortable," said the smuggler, rising from his cushy seat. He grabbed Jaden's wheelchair and led him out the door, where a familiar face was approaching them.

"Master Jaden!" exclaimed Radimir, bowing low. "Word among the servants is you've restored our defenses. You have my gratitude."

"You're welcome..." said Jaden, still suspicious of the servant whom the empress had tasked with watching him. "I-I left an open station you could take."

"I thought I would assist you here. These halls can be difficult to navigate."

"That's alright, we know the way," said Hauser, wheeling Jaden around Radimir.

"Yes, the direct path to the keep, where your enemies will no doubt be waiting for you," said the servant.

Hauser stopped. He and Jaden exchanged a look. Neither liked that Radimir already knew where they were heading; it meant he probably also knew the best way to get there. Jaden hesitated as he weighed their pitiful options: risk fighting through a hundred enemies, or trust the servant of a traitor?

"I do not mean to rush, but I do have a rendezvous to make," said Radimir.

Jaden sighed, ignoring Hauser's warning look. "Lead on, then," he said.

Radimir hurried out in front, but not before Hauser caught him by the arm. "I'll be watching you closely, Poterian." The smuggler twirled a knife in his hand, one he'd picked off a dead Poterian.

"You are right to be wary," sighed Radimir, waiting until Hauser released him before continuing down the hall. "I told you that Evernight is a time of great change, but even Her Majesty did not anticipate the circumstances we find ourselves in. She deemed it necessary to…reevaluate her alliances."

"Desperate times…" muttered Jaden.

A door creaked open as Radimir rounded a corner. "Get back," he hissed, standing in plain view of whoever this newcomer was. Hauser wheeled Jaden back into a nearby room, where they could just see their guide through the crack of an open door.

"You, *Poterian!*" barked a harsh voice. Radimir raised his hands as four soldiers in red armor surrounded him, their spears aimed. *Orlovs. Why did it have to be Orlovs?*

"Which way is the control room?" one of them demanded.

"Down there," said Radimir, pointing the opposite direction of their target. "I'm happy to show you to—"

"He lies," snapped one of the guards, bringing his spear just inches from Radimir's neck. "How many are holed up in there? Tell us now!"

"It is not them you should be concerned about," replied Radimir.

Flashes of blue and purple rained from the ceiling. A string of choked gags escaped the guards as they collapsed, blood leaking from their throats.

Hauser carefully wheeled Jaden back into the open, dodging the fresh corpses. Mizuki stood waiting for them, clutching a wound on her left arm. Based on the dried blood caked around it, Jaden assumed she'd earned it in the catacombs.

"Thank you for the save…again," said Jaden, nodding to the assassins who had once put a bullet in his back. Strange, that he didn't feel fear around them anymore. Instead, he felt guilt. Of the many who had come to his rescue in the catacombs, he only counted seven remaining.

"The empress's defenses hold by thread," said Mizuki. "We are all that remains to reinforce her. Will you help us rescue her?"

Jaden nodded.

Hauser shrugged. "As long as it gets us off this ruddy rock." His eyes shifted, and he started with alarm. "Jaden!"

He shoved the wheelchair aside just as Jaden spotted the bleeding Orlov on the floor, its pistol raised.

"Hauser!"

"No!" shouted Radimir, raising his hand. The gun fired. Jaden braced, but no bullet came. He noticed it hovering just outside the gun barrel. The Orlov who fired it was unmoving…frozen, the drops of blood from his neck suspended mid-fall.

Jaden turned to Radimir. "Did you just…you were a Zoboros this whole time?"

"I…no…" Radimir stared at his hand. "This has never happened before."

"Well whatever it is it's ruddy useful," said Hauser, stepping out of the path of the frozen bullet. "I suggest we get movin'."

"You're right." Radimir placed a shaky hand against the wall. A pressure plate slid back. "Be warned, your enemies are not only outside the keep. If they were, Her Majesty would already have reached the hangar through a secret passage. Something impedes her."

"Danadas," said Jaden.

"I do not like to make assumptions, but I believe you've 'hit the nail on the head', as you say," said Radimir. He pushed open a hidden door in the wall, revealing a tunnel that sloped through the innards of the palace. "Mizuki shall lead you from here."

"You're not coming?" asked Jaden, surprised by his own disappointment. Two minutes ago, he hadn't trusted the servant at all. Now he was scared to go anywhere without him.

"I will assist the others here, as you recommended. Especially if these newfound abilities can keep them safe. What waits ahead requires a…unique skillset." His eyes shifted to the Jakaris' bloodied knives.

Jaden wheeled closer to Radimir. "Promise me you'll lead the other servants out before the Orlovs storm your position."

"It is my duty to maintain these defenses as long as—"

"*Promise* me," insisted Jaden. He'd never felt more serious in his life.

The servant bowed his head. "I will do my best."

Jaden nodded. Hauser wheeled him into the passageway, but Jaden waved for him to stop. "You know, Radimir, I used to think no Poterian could be good."

The servant smiled amid the thunder that shook the palace. "I'm glad we're living up to our reputation, Master Jaden." With that, he hurried down the hall.

I'm Chenji the Changeling. I'm Chenji the Changeling.

Chenji ducked as blaster fire pinged off the disabled hovertruck he was using for cover. The others were similarly pinned nearby, outgunned by an impenetrable wall of Poterians and Orlovs around the keep. Hundreds of them, plus a host of armored vehicles. Yet none were trying to get inside — they seemed more concerned with keeping everyone else out.

And away from the only ships out of here.

He knew he needed to change form, but would he be able to keep control? He wasn't so sure after what Sterling had told him on the way here: Palorex had returned, and he'd brought Taranis with him.

Lightning flashed through his mind. *Keep it together*. The team needed him. The *galaxy* needed him. Somehow, that didn't help his anxiety.

"Are you gonna just sit there or are you gonna do something?" barked Sterling beside him, firing a rifle with his only hand.

I don't know. Blaster fire whizzed overhead. Bombs burst in the distance. Fires raged everywhere. This was a nightmare; one with no escape.

"Team, come in," came a nasally voice through his communicator. "This is the handsome one."

"Jaden! I thought you lost your communicator."

"Sterling gave me a new one."

"Already regretting it," grumbled the Poterian.

"Where are you, Jaden?"

"Taking a secret tunnel to the keep. Are you there yet?"

"Nope," said Chenji, peeking over the tank. The keep towered just ahead, a massive stone cylinder stuck right in the middle of the main courtyard with a moat surrounding it. "There's only one bridge across the moat, and a lot of enemies between us and it. More than we can handle."

"Who says you have to handle them alone?"

Footsteps echoed in the distance. Lots of them. Chenji turned around. A mass of Poterians was marching toward them, dressed not in armor but in servants' uniforms, or suits, or just about anything in between. They could have been teachers, construction workers, politicians...yet they had all come to defend the palace, armed with nothing but bats, pipes, knives, and occasionally a pistol.

"Radimir opened the main gates," said Jaden. "Whatever

Cera did really worked some magic."

"Radi-who?"

Carmichael hustled out from cover and toward the newly arrived army, Cera right behind, blocking enemy fire with her shields until they were out of range. The Poterian civilians cheered at their arrival. Chenji could only scratch his head. Carmichael, the man whose father wiped out so many Poterians, was being celebrated by them. Chenji supposed this crowd saw things differently. Perhaps they, like the empress, believed in peace. A peace they were ironically willing to fight for.

"Team, we're mounting a charge," announced Carmichael over the comms. Chenji paled as he stared at the mass of soldiers and vehicles ahead. *So many guns.* "Wait for Cera to pass you with her shields, then charge in behind her as fast as you can. These people are scared. They don't think they can win. Let's give them something to believe in."

Chenji shook like a leaf. There was no way they could charge against that.

The private line on his comms switched on. "I believe in you," said Li.

"But what if I hurt one of those innocent people?" he whispered, hoping Sterling wouldn't hear him. "What if I can't tell friends from enemies?"

"Do what I do in a battle," said Sterling, apparently in possession of ears like an aivin's. "Keep pushing forward. Your enemies are guaranteed to be ahead of you."

Chenji nodded. The simple directive gave him some small sense of control amid the chaos. Never had he imagined fighting an army like this, let alone an army of Poterians. He prayed they weren't as brutal as they were in the stories.

"Here we come!" announced Carmichael. The ground shook as thousands of feet stampeded toward them. Chenji saw the shields closing in, sensed Sterling readying next to him to charge, yet he couldn't get himself to move. All he could do was shake as he crouched beneath the gunfire.

Carmichael and Cera drew closer, the crowd beginning to fall behind them. *The people aren't charging*, he realized. They were jogging at best, afraid to meet the enemy line. Afraid to lose. Afraid to die.

They need a hero.

Something came over Chenji as the shields swept past him. He sprang from behind cover, bullets and blaster bolts striking the shields in front of him from all directions. Li caught up with him, vines rising from beneath her wrists, Akio perched upon her shoulder with his knife drawn. Sterling thundered along not far behind, his bionic leg driving his old bones forward. Ristin and Warp caught up too, and T8, despite all the guns strapped to his wiry frame, managed to keep pace close behind. *Bots don't tire*, Chenji supposed. He needed a beast that wouldn't tire either.

Cera slowed as the enemy gunfire intensified against her shields, forcing the rest of the team to slow down too. Soon the nervous crowd would press up behind them, then break at the sight of all the gunfire. Chenji spotted where the heaviest firepower was coming from: a massive rotating machine gun set upon an armored transport. It needed to go. And he had an idea.

He jogged over to Warp's side and whispered in her ear. Her eyes widened.

"It's our best option," he insisted.

She didn't look like she agreed, but she nodded all the same.

Chenji pointed ahead to where he wanted her to stand. Then he fell a good distance back and took a deep breath. *Keep pushing forward*, he reminded himself. *Chenji the Changeling always pushes forward.*

Li glanced back as he set up for the sprint. "Chenji, what are you doing?!"

He charged for Warp. *I'm Chenji the Changeling.* His heart raced as the machine gun pounded against the shields, slowing Cera to a crawl. *I'm Chenji the Changeling.* His feet turned to hooves and tusks sprouted from his face.

I'm a hero.

Warp touched his arm as he morphed. One moment he was a small man behind the shields, the next he was a 600-pound Kimikan hog smashing his massive shoulder into the face of an armored transport. The armor caved and the vehicle wheeled back at a high angle, its machine gun spraying bullets harmlessly into the night sky, unable to tip low enough to reach its attacker. The Poterians shouted in panic, unsure why their vehicle was plowing straight through their defenses. *Keep pushing forward.* Other vehicles were crunched out of his way, his hooves stamping forward with all their might, his back bracing for gunfire that would no doubt pound it. But as he drove the wretched transport all the way into the moat, no shots came.

Instead, the enemy Poterians and Orlovs were too busy tumbling into the moat themselves. He turned around. The frontline had disappeared, broken by the civilian mob that now stampeded over the soldiers in a hellbent fury. And there was little the enemy could do to stop them: their vehicles were being levitated by Ristin, their guns were being teleported out of their hands and into civilian ones by Warp, and any of them resilient enough to hold the line were being picked off by T8's precise shooting, convincing more of them to break.

"Chenji!" Li ran up to him. He braced for a lecture over his foolish maneuver, his massive form looking silly as it whimpered, but Li only pointed to the bridge where the enemy was still holding. "Ready for some crowd control?"

He smiled. Crowd control remained his specialty. He morphed into his aivin form and she hopped onto his feathery back, threading her vines through his beak as reins. He swooped over the edge of the moat, caught the wind and careened toward the bridge, gaining enough momentum so that when he landed, he was already back in his Kimikan hog form.

Not a bullet was fired. His roar alone was enough to send the soldiers racing off the bridge and back across the palace grounds before the incoming mob could box them in. Chenji pounded his chest in victory.

"Look!" said Li. Chenji turned. The gate to the keep was lowering, and sitting behind it in his wheelchair was the hacker. Hauser stood beside him with his jaw hanging open at the sight of the battle.

Warp appeared and disappeared around him, delivering the other members of the team to the bridge in puffs of smoke. Chenji was relieved to see no serious injuries among them, just a few cuts and bruises that Li was quick to work on.

"What's the situation inside?" asked Carmichael.

"The Shadow is clearing us a path to the throne room," said

Jaden, who couldn't help but glance Akio's direction. "They believe the empress is trapped there by an old friend of ours."

"Then we have to move quickly, before my brother arrives," said Sterling. He limped past them, his bionic leg looking crooked after the battle.

"You're in no shape to fight," said Carmichael, stepping in Sterling's path. "But you do know how to reach the secret hangar. There are thousands of your people here who need you to show them the way."

"I'll not leave my daughter in danger," said the Poterian flatly.

"I know how to get to the hangar," said T8. "I can plug into its mainframe and get the ships rolling out of here. Yours will be ready to fly too…just promise me you'll all get out of this scrap alive."

Chenji smiled. The bot really did have a soft spot for them.

"We will," said Carmichael, patting the machine on the back. "Now get going."

"Poterians!" shouted T8, waving the crowd its direction. "Follow me if you're allergic to fascism!" Its visor began flashing brightly. The crowd followed, cheering and hollering as they passed the team. One of them thumped her fist hard against Chenji's chest. The changeling stumbled back, startled.

"A sign of respect, boy," said Sterling. "You fought well."

More fists came their way, as well as cheers and applause. It was invigorating. Even those who were injured perked up at the sight of the team, not to mention Li's healing hands. *The Liberators*, Chenji recalled. That name was starting to grow on him.

Sterling led them away from the crowd as it flooded into the lower levels. Chenji expected the Poterian prince knew the best way to the throne room, so it was no surprise when he opened a secret door behind a bookshelf. There was a second door behind it, which Sterling's biometrics were surprisingly able to open. *The empress must have coded it for him as a contingency.* How right she'd been.

The path curved, circling tightly and steeply toward the top. It would be a hard climb for any of them, but especially Jaden.

"You should get to the ships," Cera told him. "You'd be more help there."

"I'm not missing this," said Jaden. There was a firmness in his voice that Chenji had never heard before. A conviction he wouldn't expect anyone to have after just losing the ability to walk. Jaden stubbornly began wheeling himself up the incline until Ristin had the good sense to levitate him instead.

Sterling climbed quickly, far quicker than his limp should have allowed, forcing the others to hustle after him.

"You're going too fast," said Chenji, struggling to catch his breath.

Sterling shushed him. "These walls are thin," he whispered. "Generations of emperors have used this pass to eavesdrop on the court after making a royal 'exit'."

"Some family he's got," muttered Jaden.

The higher they climbed, the more they began to hear voices through the walls. Voices they knew all too well.

"I do not *need* to keep you alive, Typhera," said Danadas. "I am merely entertaining a courtesy which my master extended to his brother."

"And I'm sure your master will be most entertained when he learns I've not ceded my throne," said the empress. "I wonder which of us will draw his wrath most."

"Toy with me all you wish," said Danadas, the normally composed old man sounding ready to snap. "You cannot stop what has been set in motion. Palorex spent cycles masterminding this day. Calling to his faithful servants from the depths. And now he will take what is rightfully his."

Sterling stopped at a door near the top of the climb, his tired breath rasping. Despite the exhaustion, the Poterian looked ready to barrel through with everything he had left in him.

Carmichael signaled Sterling to wait, then positioned Cera by the door, shield ready for when they breached. He had the others form a chain of arms, Warp at the center of the formation, then telephoned orders down the line. Soon they each knew their tasks. Chenji was eager for his: turn into a lizard and pin the invisible girl if she was inside. Classic.

"Danadas," hissed Kazan on the other side of the wall, "the line is broken. They will be here any moment."

"Silence!" said Danadas. "This is your last chance, Typhera."

"I do what is best for my people," she said, her voice sounding distant. Resigned. "To surrender my throne to my uncle would be to surrender peace."

"Peace is already gone, dear," said Danadas. "But you can have a say in what happens next. The sidelines can be a powerful place...if you make the right alliances."

There was a palpable pause. "To be a player in your game, Danadas, is a fate worse than death. You will have to plot against my uncle without me."

"Don't die for your pride," said Danadas.

"Now!" ordered Carmichael.

Sterling kicked the door open and Cera's shield covered the

opening as they stormed inside.

A puff of smoke surrounded Chenji. Next thing he knew, he was within the throne room. What had likely been a beautiful display of red tapestries and hand-carved furniture was now an overturned mess of tatters, splinters, and dead guards. The throne still stood – the tall windows behind it giving everyone a sickening glimpse at the armada's bombardment of the city – but Typhera sat on the other side of the room, her mouth gagged. *But she was just speaking?*

A shockwave struck them from behind and sent them tumbling toward the middle of the room. Chenji hopped back to his feet and joined a circle formation the others had started. Fire ignited the torn tapestries along the walls, illuminating their enemies in the shadows: Danadas, Kazan, Yui, Mila, a new guy with energy blades extending from his hands, Taranis (of course), and…

"No…" Sterling had told him that Junior had turned, but he hadn't believed it. He had to see the big guy standing among their enemies to know it was true.

"This isn't you, Junior!" exclaimed Li.

"Don't bother," boomed a voice from the shadows, one that resonated off the burning walls with such power that Chenji felt swallowed by it. Its owner emerged from behind the throne, shadows following him as he walked, a black flame sparked in each hand. "He has seen what must be done to save our people. I offer you this chance to see the light, too." He paused. "Even you, Carmichael."

All eyes turned to the captain.

"You and my father fought many times, Palorex," said Carmichael. "And while he got a lot of things wrong, there's one thing he and I could both agree on: you seriously need an ass kicking." He pumped his shotgun, the sound filling Chenji with defiant, perhaps foolish confidence in the face of evil.

"Don't make us destroy you," said Junior, his eyes glowing orange. *When did he learn to do that?!*

"You wouldn't dare," said Cera, readying her shields.

Muffled shouts came from beneath Typhera's gag. Palorex motioned, and Kazan ripped the gag from her face with his slimy, scaly hands.

"I will cede," she said, gasping. "I will cede on one condition: spare their lives and let them leave this place."

Palorex smiled. He approached her, his footsteps echoing like claps of thunder. "Why? So they can gather our enemies and rebel against us? Do you think me a fool?"

Typhera smiled. "Yes."

As Palorex raised his hand to strike her, fire erupted across the Evernight sky. Out the window, Chenji spotted explosions coming from many of Poteria Prime's ships. Other Poterian ships rained down from the atmosphere. Older ships. Ones Chenji had seen before.

"Marauders!" shouted Danadas.

Jakari dropped from the ceiling and began slashing at Palorex's henchmen. Chenji saw his opening. He tried tackling Mila, but she vanished. The others threw their powers at their nearest opponents, the throne room overwhelmed with flashes of color. It was too much motion for his echolocation to pick up anything. He needed a different form.

Black fire swelled around Palorex, eating through the surrounding debris like it was made of paper. It reminded Chenji of Angeline's powers when they had torn apart the

Dormarch, only this was more controlled. Still, he knew then that they were doomed.

"Look out!" cried Li.

Chenji thought she'd been referring to Palorex's attack, but then he sensed something else. Something much bigger. *The window!* A transport ship smashed through it. Everyone ceased their fighting to either watch it go by or else jump out of its way. When it finally ground to a stop, its liftgate opened in a blast of compressed air and an average-sized figure stepped through.

"Miss me?" asked Kano.

Chapter 40

The Battle

He marched past everyone – the friends he'd not seen since the marauder attack, the enemies he'd collected over his adventures, the dead guards strewn across the floor – and approached the one who needed his help most.

"Before we do this, Junior, there's something you should know," said Kano.

"What, are you going to tell me there's another way? That we can keep the momentum going after what we did on Famora? Because if you ask me, it's only caused more suffering. Suffering that Palorex can end."

Kano took a deep breath, knowing what he was about to say would change everything. "You're not the only one who thought Palorex could save us. Someone else sided with him in the beginning, and she came to regret it. Imagine what she would say if she saw you standing here now."

Fire swelled in Junior's palms. Clearly, he knew who Kano was referring to. "She wouldn't understand. And if Palorex had his way back then, she would still be alive!"

Some of the team members gasped. They'd not known of Angeline's fate. But Kano pressed on. "But she *did* understand, Junior. Your mother knew Palorex much better than you do…better than anyone else did." Kano turned to Taranis.

Junior followed his eyeline. "What are you talking about?"

"Makoto saw things when he tapped into the mountain's power," Kano explained. "He saw your brother."

Both Junior and Taranis turned to Palorex.

"Is this true?!" barked the half-Poterian. "Why did you not show me this?"

Palorex stiffened, drawing his seven-foot frame somehow taller. "Angeline and I had the chance to unite the two sides of our galaxy. Not just in treaties and alliances, but in blood." His gaze fell upon Taranis. "But her heart changed after your birth. She stole you from me and ran away with the fool Hendricks. And so I brought my fury to Mogaddu. I knew if I could tap into its power I could find you. But then Admiral Carmichael came and destroyed everything." He turned to the captain with venom in his eyes. "I fled to Okeanos with nothing. Only the knowledge that my old master had secrets which he had blocked me from. But I was more powerful than when I left him. I thought I could take his power and learn how to restore both my bloodline and my army of Zoboros. But his power came at a price I couldn't pay. I was defeated and dragged to the other side, where I waited. And listened. And learned what to do this time so that no enemy could stop me."

Everyone stood there in shock, especially Taranis. "You…lost the war over me?" he asked.

"I merely lost the battle," said Palorex. "Together, we can win the war."

Taranis drew back. "Why did my…why did Angeline leave you?" he asked.

"Because she lacked conviction," said Palorex.

"Why?!" demanded Taranis.

"She didn't want the war, Renat," said Palorex. "She didn't want to bring a child into a galaxy like that."

"But I *was* brought into a galaxy like that," said Taranis, turning toward the windows where battle raged across the landscape. "It was cold, and cruel, and loveless."

"Because I was not able to finish what I started," said Palorex.

"You abandoned me for power!" he screamed. "You were there on Mogaddu. On *my* side of the Rift. You could have found me. Instead, you went for Niscelles."

Kano stepped back. He'd expected his words to affect Junior, but not Taranis. Not the most unstable person in the room.

"This is our chance to right the wrongs of the past," said Palorex. "Do not throw it away."

"You're right," said Taranis. "It is." He threw a bolt of lightning at Palorex. Black fire swept it away, and the room was set into motion. Junior threw a fireball that Kano matched with a shockwave, the blast sending them both skidding back — Kano to one side with Carmichael, Cera, Jaden, Chenji, Li, Ristin, Warp, Akio, Sterling, Hauser, and the Jakari guards; Junior with Danadas, Kazan, Yui, Mila, and Douglas. Powers flashed and fighters dipped and weaved around the room. But Kano stayed fixed on Junior.

"If Palorex takes over, it won't be the paradise you picture in your head," he said.

"It will be whatever we shape it to be," said Junior, launching a jet of flame.

Kano rolled out of the way. "Just because we have these

powers doesn't mean we can fix everything. We're not gods."

"Not all of us." Junior turned to Palorex, who was pressing Taranis away with his blasts of fire and ash. In that moment, a vine snapped around his torso and pinned his arms to his sides.

"I've got him, Kano!" said Li as fire blazed along her vine. "We need you to get Danadas!"

A shockwave sent Ristin and Akio tumbling past him. Kano charged at the old man when he felt a sting at his back. He fell, convulsing, as Mila appeared beside him with a stun baton in hand.

"Well done, granddaughter," said Danadas.

A Kimikan hog landed in front of them, crunching the ground beneath its hooves.

"Stay back!" said Mila, zapping the stun baton's tip for effect.

Chenji started backward, his massive form looking silly against a girl with a single baton. But then his gaze shifted toward Taranis, toward the electricity jolting in all directions in a battle with Palorex. Something came over him, a rage that made even Kano frightened to be near him. The beast grabbed the baton, its tip pulsing against his massive paw. He winced as he wrenched it from her hands and tossed it aside.

"You don't scare me," said Chenji in a deep, booming voice. Mila ran as he pounced. Danadas went to blast Chenji back, but Kano caught him first with a shockwave that threw his old, hunched frame against the wall.

"Great job, Chenji," said Kano. The beast nodded to him and leaped back into the action. Kano quickly assessed the battlefield: Cera was locked in a duel of energy swords with Douglas; Warp had engaged a fleeing Mila, and now they were locked in a duel of their own, stun batons flashing, the two appearing and disappearing around each other. Akio and Ristin tag teamed Yui while Sterling, Carmichael, and the Shadow led Typhera toward the secret passageway. Li was locked with Junior, her vines burning and dying. Kano was about to rush to her aid when Jaden wheeled up beside him.

"Kano, we've got a situation!"

Kano paused, absorbing the sight of his friend in a wheelchair for the first time. "Jaden, I'm so sorry I wasn't—"

"Ah, shove it!" said Jaden. "We've got Lusitani coming in hot!"

The tall windows shattered and armored warriors in skull-shaped masks leaped through.

"Wouldn't be a party without them," said Kano, turning toward his crashed transport. "Varlam, *now*!"

The Poterian emerged from the transport and held out his hands. His eyes rolled back. Kano tensed. He'd never seen Varlam's powers in action, nor had he seen a power have that effect on its user before.

"Holy hell..." whispered Jaden. The power wasn't emanating from Varlam's hands, at least not in a way that Kano could see, but it was here in the throne room with them. It was the only way to explain why the dead guards were rising.

"That's *metal*!" exclaimed Ristin from across the room.

The undead sprinted at the Lusitani, absorbing the attacks from their wrist devices and still pressing forward, not seeming to feel a thing.

"Jaden, in case they can't hold, I need you at the transport's guns," said Kano.

"On it!" exclaimed Jaden. He waved Hauser over, who'd

been tucked comfortably behind cover, and the faithful smuggler wheeled him up the ramp into the ship.

"Team," came Carmichael over the comms, "enemy forces have reorganized and they're marching on the keep. It's time to retreat!"

But what about Poteria? thought Kano. They had control of the battlefield. They could win this and end the civil war on its first night. But when he saw Palorex drive his big fist across Taranis's face, he knew the tide was about to change.

"Those who oppose me will join these dead!" the emperor shouted. He threw black fire behind him, washing away the horde of undead in a cloud of ash and taking some of his Lusitani with them. "Even you, my son." He grabbed Taranis by the throat and held him out one of the broken windows. It was a fifteen-story drop to the bridge across the moat, if Palorex didn't turn him to ash first.

"Just remember, father: it was all your fault." Electricity zapped Palorex. He cried out, lost his grip, and Taranis plunged toward the surface.

"No!" shouted Kano.

Palorex turned toward him, rage and pain written across his red face. "Who's next?!" he demanded.

"That would be me, sir," came Jaden's sheepish voice through the transport's loudspeakers. Its cannons erupted in blaster fire, driving the emperor and his henchmen behind cover.

"Kano!" cried Li. Junior hadn't gone for cover, instead opting to laser through Li's vines. She dove for cover as he marched toward her.

"That's enough, Junior!" shouted Kano. He stepped

between Junior and Li, palms raised. "I don't want to fight you."

"Then stay out of my way." Beams shot from his eyes and sliced just inches from Kano's feet. The floor crumbled and Kano fell through it. *I hate this new power of his!* He threw a shockwave at the ground that launched him back into the throne room, where Junior was blasting the transport with a jet of flame. Its cannons melted, unable to fire, and still Junior pressed his power upon it.

"Stop!" Kano threw Junior back with a shockwave. "Our friends are in there!"

The pyro picked himself off the floor. "Your friends, not mine." He sent a jet of flame roaring at Kano, who ducked underneath it, launching a shockwave meant to take Junior's legs out from under him. But Junior vaulted himself over it with a blast of fire and landed across the way.

"That's more like it," said Junior. He aimed his palms at the floor. Fire flared and lifted him into the air. He flew circles around Kano, eyes aglow, looking for the shot.

Kano hurled shockwave after shockwave at him, but Junior was too fast. And all the while, their enemies were regrouping, pressing upon the team with Palorex's black fire to lead them. Kano knew there was no getting past that power, and no escaping while Junior was hovering over their heads. He needed a way to solve both problems. The thing was, he already had the solution. It was just a really bad one.

"Kano, what are you doing?" demanded Li.

"Help the others escape," he said, drawing back for the charge. "I'll hold them off."

"I'm not leaving you behind again!"

"And I'm not giving you a choice." Kano charged, leaping

over the vine he knew was coming for him. He threw a shockwave at the ground that launched him into the air just as Junior arced in front of the windows. The *broken* windows. Kano realized his miscalculation too late. There would be no landing behind the enemy line. He caught Junior midflight and together they sailed into the Evernight sky.

"You're an idiot!" screamed Junior as they plummeted toward the moat.

"You say that like you're surprised!"

Kano felt the heat as Junior launched jets of flame behind them. He clung to Junior's back as they angled out of their freefall and soared over the palace grounds, where fires raged and rockets exploded left and right. A procession of Poterian troops marched toward the keep, their Red Sabre red a perfect match for the Orlov crimson among their ranks. It wouldn't be long before they reinforced Palorex and wiped out anyone associated with Typhera.

"I'm going to put us down," said Junior. Their momentum slowed. Kano spotted Junior's target: a landing platform beside the arena, one filled with Orlov guards. No good. Kano threw a shockwave sideways that sent them flailing into the arena. They separated in midair, Junior cursing as he fell. Kano used a shockwave to break his own momentum, though he still tumbled through the sand at dizzying speed.

Whoa. He laid there on his back, the sky above alight with battle. Even in his spinning vision, he could tell the secret hangar had opened. Dozens of ships, thousands of Poterians, all sailed out of the palace and into the darkened sky. *We did it*, he realized. The team had saved the civilians. They had saved the empress.

Now could they save themselves?

"Junior!" he called, rising. The world spun around him; he didn't even know where to place his feet. He spilled into the sand again, then stubbornly kept pushing forward. "Junior, are you alright?"

Beams launched his direction, whether two or twenty he couldn't tell. He fell flat on the ground and let them sizzle overhead. "Junior, it's over!"

"I'm just getting started!"

Kano spotted Junior leaping high above him from a fire-enhanced jump, one he came down from with flaming hands. Kano rolled out of the way, the nearby impact enough to throw him into the air amid a wave of sand. He crashed down with it, then scrambled to his feet as fast as he could, sand cascading from him.

"This is where I learned everything!" shouted Junior, waving toward the empty arena stands. "I learned what Zoboros are really worth to the galaxy. We're slaves, Kano. And we always will be if we don't make a stand!"

"Junior, he's evil," said Kano. He could barely stand straight. He felt tired. Dizzy. Drained.

"And the rest of the galaxy isn't? They kidnapped our people, *murdered* them because of what we did on Famora. Carmichael says things will 'get better', but I'm tired of the lies. And I'm tired of running."

"Junior, I'm sorry your mother died." Junior fumed at Kano's words, but he pressed on. "I'm sorry that I wasn't there to help her. To help you. But to go against everything she stood for, against everyone who cares about you...this is a dark path. And a lot of people are going to die if you follow it."

"We'll kill everyone we have to!" shouted Junior as he paced through the sand. "Everyone who stands in our way...even if that means you and your friends."

"You wouldn't dare," said Kano, power rushing to his fists.

Junior turned. A ship was floating away from the keep – the *Onstappen*. T8 had found it!

"Kano, come in," said Jaden over the comms. "We're all aboard and ready to leave this shitshow. Is that you in the arena?"

"They're not going to stop, Kano," said Junior before Kano could hail his friends. "You and I both know it." His eyes glowed with fire as he aimed for the ship.

"NO!" A shockwave roared from Kano's mouth and threw Junior across the sand. Kano hurled shockwave after shockwave after him, kicking up a cloud of sand that hid the ship from Junior's vision. But Kano didn't stop. Couldn't stop. He kept surging forward, throwing shockwaves anywhere his enemy might be.

"Where are you?!" screamed Kano

Junior burst from the sand at Kano's feet and kicked Kano's legs out from under him. Kano brought up his hands to defend himself and Junior clamped his own hands over them. Then Kano felt a searing pain. He screamed. When Junior released, Kano's hands had turned into a red, raw mass of blisters.

"What have you done to me?!" screamed Kano, writhing on the floor as the pain consumed his every thought.

"I can't have you getting in the way, Kano. I'm sorry."

"That's enough, Junior!"

Kano spotted Carmichael floating down through the sand cloud. He landed right behind Junior, keeping his shotgun aimed at the pyro's back.

"Ristin's here too, I take it?" Junior called behind him. "Or did you get levitating powers all on your own?"

"He can lower me from the safety of the ship. It's just us here." Carmichael approached slowly. "Put your hands up, Junior. *Now!*"

Junior's face twisted with rage. He didn't dare summon fire, but he also didn't raise his hands.

"There's no stun option on this one," said Carmichael, pumping the shotgun. "Please Junior, don't make me do it."

Slowly, Junior raised his hands. Kano felt a tinge of relief despite the blistering pain. But then his eyes met Junior's, and he saw they were glowing with fire.

"Junior, *don't!*" Kano tried throwing a shockwave, but the effort only sent a brutal stab of pain through his hands. He cried out and watched as Junior spun around. Twin beams shot out, only for a split second, and Carmichael gasped.

Kano struggled to his feet, heart thumping, scarred hands trembling as he stared at the two holes in Carmichael's abdomen.

"NO!"

The captain still had the shotgun aimed at Junior. Kano braced. Carmichael squeezed the trigger but nothing came out. The empty chamber just clicked.

"Never did teach you how to bluff, Junior." The captain flashed his trademark smile, then collapsed in the sand.

"Captain!" Kano rushed to his side and tried to roll him onto his back, but the mere touch was enough to send Kano into bouts of fiery pain. He turned and, through tears, saw Junior walking away.

"Look what you've done! You've ruined everything! *Everything!*"

Junior never looked back.

Epilogue

She watched him sleep. Watched him thrash. It was almost a relief when she had to wake him up. Almost.

He stirred at her touch, instinctively moving his bandaged hands. He winced, but her glowing hands were already where they needed to be. There wasn't much she could do in the way of healing at this point, but she could alleviate some of the pain. At least enough to get him on his feet.

"It's time," she said.

Kano only nodded. He'd hardly spoken the last three days, not that there was much to say anyway. He climbed out of bed using only his legs and followed her down the hall.

"Find us."

Li turned. "What did you say?"

"Nothing," shrugged Kano.

Li shook her head. She'd been hearing things on this ship. Sometimes the voice sounded like…no, it was impossible.

They found the same uncomfortable silence on the bridge. The team had been assembled, their heads bowed.

"Is this everyone?" asked Cera. She stood beside the empty command chair. Her hand had been hovering over a button on it since Li had left to get Kano.

Warp signed that it was.

Cera drew a deep breath. "Ok." She stared at the button but couldn't seem to push. Sterling lumbered over and placed his big hand, his only hand, over hers.

Together they pushed.

The ship shuddered as the airlock burst open several floors below. Everyone approached the viewport and watched as the little crate floated across the starry void. So small against the rest of the universe, just like the man inside it.

"Would anyone like to say anything for the captain?" asked T8.

Silence. Li felt like there was so much to say, yet she couldn't find the words. Finally, Ristin of all people cleared his throat. "The captain gave me a place to call home. He accepted me when he had every reason not to. He was a good man."

"And a good warrior," added Akio.

"Aye," said Hauser.

"He gave us something to fight for," said Jaden, sitting up straight despite the pain in his back.

"He taught us that we can be better," said Chenji, looking not to the coffin but to the stars.

Warp placed her hand on the glass and bowed her head.

"He should still be here," said Kano, turning away. Li reached for him, but he was already halfway to the door.

"We buried him in his blue suit," said Cera. The odd comment drew everyone's attention, including Kano's. "Cufflinks and all. His 'disguise' on Famora, though I think he really enjoyed that one. It helped him fit in with the biggest names in the city. He was always good at fitting in wherever he needed to, whether he was undercover with the Taipa or surrounded by a team of people more powerful than himself. But I don't know if there's anywhere he'd say that he truly belonged. I like to think it was this team. I like to think that he saw himself in all of us. Misfits. Troublemakers. Fighters. Where others saw nothing, he saw greatness. He saw it in us, and he saw it in the galaxy."

Marauder ships floated in along the coffin's path, dozens of them. They fired off rockets that burst in great displays of light before the vacuum of space snuffed them out. Quick, fleeting, beautiful.

"Thank you, Varlam," whispered Kano. Li turned. She hadn't realized he'd rejoined the group. They stood there and watched for a while, the whole team in silence as the coffin faded into the void. It was only then that Li found the words she needed.

"He was a hero," she whispered.

Kano stared into the abyss, and Li knew he was thinking about more than just Carmichael. He was thinking about his friend, lost to the enemy, about his brother, lost to some ancient power, and about his greatest foe, whose body had never landed at the bottom of the keep.

"We'll find them," she said. "We'll find a way."

"I don't think there is one," said Kano, hugging his bandaged hands to his chest. "Not with both sides of the galaxy out to kill us."

Cera turned to them. "There's always a way. And he would want us to find it." She marched across the bridge, everyone watching her as she planted herself in the command chair.

Li wasn't sure how to feel. It seemed strange not seeing Carmichael there, yet it felt right to see Cera there in his place. The others all seemed to be processing the same emotions. Everyone except Sterling, who stepped up to the controls.

"What's our heading, Captain?" he asked.

Cera gazed upon her team and drew a long, deep breath.

"War."

Michael Ciccarelli-Walsh lives in Tallahassee, Florida, where he attended Florida State University for both his undergraduate and graduate degrees (Go Noles!). He is also the author of *Trouble in the Floating City* and *Project Vortex*, the first two novels in the Zoboros series.

ciccarelliwalsh.com